The Treason of Mary Louvestre

My Haley

NEW YORK

VIRGINIA

The Treason of Mary Louvestre
by My Haley

© Copyright 2012 by My Haley

ISBN 9781938467189

Editing by Joe Coccaro
Cover Design by John Köehler
Line edits by Cheryl Ross

Published by
 köehlerbooks™
an imprint of Morgan James Publishing

5 Penn Plaza, 23rd floor
c/o Morgan James Publishing
New York, NY 10001
212-574-7939
www.koehlerbooks.com

 Habitat for Humanity® Peninsula and Greater Williamsburg Building Partner

In an effort to support local communities, raise awareness and funds, Morgan James Publishing donates a percentage of all book sales for the life of each book to Habitat for Humanity Peninsula and Greater Williamsburg.
Get involved today, visit www.MorganJamesBuilds.com

Author's Note

Mary Louvestre and the other characters in this work are fictional composites based upon real historical events and places. There was a real Mary Louvestre, and her acts of espionage against the Confederacy did occur. *The Treason of Mary Louvestre* is broadly based on Mary's life, the era of slavery and the Civil War, but it is not intended, and should not be viewed, as an exact historical record. The real Mary Louvestre was a seamstress in her mid-fifties when she arrived in Washington in late 1861. She did, as this book portrays, travel more than two hundred miles through a harsh Virginia winter to reach the Secretary of the Navy, who later presented a commendation and cash award to her.

In memory of my grandmother,
Julia Marie Dickerson,
and mother, Lillian Russell Lewis

My Roots

And all who gave their lives for
their beliefs during the Civil War

PROLOGUE

She knew she looked like hell, but she didn't care. She was alive.

Pausing a moment, she dug into her bag. From a small pouch she retrieved the ring with the Louvestre crest and returned it to the middle finger of her right hand. She straightened her clothes, which were mostly rags now. Slipping her gloves back on, she worried over their threadbare condition. They would have to do, as they were her last pair. A lady could not meet an important government official without her hat and gloves. Reaching into her knapsack, she drew out her last remaining kufi. Placing the elegant cap on her head after so long, it punctuated the importance of her mission.

She lifted her shoulders and her chin and took a deep breath. "I'm ready now, sir."

She limped down the long, ornate hallway, following the young assistant. Having lost her walking stick as well as her make-do staff, walking was a painful hobble.

"Ma'am," the young man said, holding out his arm to help her.

"Thank you, but I've made it this far on my own. I can make it the rest of the way." She set out on this incredible journey upright and on her own two feet, and she was bound and determined to finish it that way.

The plaque on the door read: Gideon Welles, Secretary of the Navy. The assistant pushed inside and held the door open for her to enter.

The older man stood up from behind his desk, impressive, stocky. An expansive white beard flowed like a bib from his jaw. He looked at her directly with a curious expression. "I was told you had important information for me." No preliminaries.

"I do," she said, "right here in this gourd." She gestured toward the dried husk slung over her shoulder.

The assistant backed out and closed the door, leaving them alone.

"I'm very busy and some runaway slave or vagabond is always passing information about Southern doings," he said impatiently. "We have specialists in the field for that."

"I see," she said, returning his direct gaze. She waited. If this man was going to be an officious bastard, he could work out this war on his own.

Welles regarded her curiously a long moment. His expression softened. This woman was different somehow. He could feel it. He came from behind the large mahogany desk and extended his hand. "I'm Gideon Welles. Won't you sit?"

The visitor's chair faced another which was where he sat. The room filled with light piling in through paned windows.

"What do you have?" Welles asked, crossing one leg over another comfortably.

"Blueprints for the refurbished CSS *Virginia*."

His eyes opened wide and he scratched his cheek, still assessing her. "The former *Merrimac*? We already know what that ship looks like."

"From the inside? With all of the latest modifications?"

"Where did you acquire such detailed documents?"

"I'm from Norfolk, born and raised. I was a fashion designer there, owned by a very influential family."

"You're a slave?"

"Was a slave. But my life was that of no common slave and because of it, I came into possession of these plans."

Welles's interest was piqued. "I have to admit, you and your story make a striking pair, indeed." He glanced at her hand. "May I comment on the ring you're wearing? It's an elaborate, obviously expensive piece."

"It's the Louvestre family crest set in a stone of carnelian, trimmed in gold. Everyone in the family wears one, me included." She said nothing further.

Welles's eyes twinkled, appreciatively entertaining her features, especially her long auburn hair. "Hmm."

Let him get it all out, she told herself. Men, especially, seemed to need to comment on her looks and, from time to time, her unique ring.

He cleared his throat. "Why do you bring these papers to me?"

"You're the Secretary of the Navy. There's a war going on between the states. Your Northern ship is going to fight that Southern giant very soon and you need to know how to beat it. Isn't that correct?"

"Well put. Go on."

"Your surveillance has probably told you that the ship is huge, thickly iron plated, looking invincible. What you likely don't know is where her weaknesses are—one in particular."

Welles ran his fingers through his hair, thinking.

"You're telling me that inside that gourd are papers that will show me where to hit the *Merrimac* and score a lethal blow?"

"Exactly."

Welles hit a button and the assistant opened the door. "Yes, sir?"

"Please bring us a pot of coffee, lad. We're going to be a while."

"Right away," the assistant said and closed the door.

"You stole these papers?"

"I copied them weeks ago, just before I left Norfolk."

"How did you get here carrying items that could have gotten you hung if you'd been caught?"

"I walked."

Welles's eyebrows arched. "Walked? Two hundred miles? In this weather?"

Her dry lips turned up in a slow smile.

"I'll be damned," he exclaimed. "You're a spy."

"That's not how I thought of myself before," she sighed, "but I suppose I am."

Welles leaned back in his chair. "Well, well," he replied. "I'd like to hear how that came to be. Will you tell me?"

"It will take more than coffee. I need something to eat. But yes, I will tell you everything."

He buzzed his assistant again and ordered food as well.

"I'm sorry, what did you say your name was?"

"Mary. Mary Louvestre."

"Well, Miss Mary, may I see the ship's blueprints?"

Mary's glance swung momentarily out the office window to the bustling landscape below. She took a deep breath to muster strength. "They're in pieces and in code. I'll put them together for you."

More interest bloomed on his face. "I want to know about you too. No one goes from slave to spy just like that." He snapped his fingers.

"It's a long story. Not a pretty one."

"Please."

Mary sighed long and sank deeper into her chair. "It feels like an eternity ago, but it all began ..."

CHAPTER 1

Mary glanced up into an August Virginia sky that was baby eye blue, clear and bright with eager promise, but she was late, again. Punctuality had become difficult. So much to do for what was being proclaimed the biggest social event of the South fast approaching; details added up as did problems. One of the biggest was that her best embroiderer, Cecilia, was sick. Together with that, she'd had to turn away Confederate Army representatives begging her to make uniforms for soldiers or, God willing, men who might be soldiers after a strong, intelligent hand took hold of them.

She sighed and quickened her step as fast as her gimpy left leg would allow with the assist of her ebony walking stick. With a shrug, she adjusted the large shoulder bag. When she had set out from home, she felt sure she could be at Cecilia's in about an hour, see to her, and get back to her duties at the salon. She had taken a short detour to the docks to see what Scoots Dunham had in the way of shells for buttons. He'd had shells all right, baskets of them, but not one was the size or shape she needed. Her new line of unique fashions for the upcoming gala required a precise look. She berated herself for not previously drawing the man a picture or writing a description of precisely what she wanted. But doing so could have placed her or Scoots in peril. Negroes—slave or hire-out—were forbidden to have anything to read or write in their possession. And these days the local sheriff wasn't granting much latitude.

The bell-shaped Sheriff Claude Bridges had been testy lately. Every day, the town was filling with men and boys running to or from the war, others looking for work. An uncouth bunch largely, they spent time getting drunk, spitting on the streets, brawling, and shooting each other, filling up the jail and throwing off the sheriff's regular routine. The word on the street was that anyone who delayed the sheriff from sitting down at Mother Clara-Jean's table "was just itchin' for trouble." Not only did such orneriness clench the sheriff's stomach, but it vexed his mother and the other Presbyterians. Mary recently heard Mother Clara-Jean huff down the street muttering to herself, fit to be tied that, once again, she was inconvenienced to bring Sheriff Claude a plate from her kitchen to the jailhouse. She was his mother, for God's sake, her querulous voice sputtered as she plowed down the street, not his slave. Both of her chins and the hairs sticking out from them quivered with pure upset. She'd for darn sure bring this nettlesome problem up with the town council. They'd herd these varmints under control. They weren't gon' keep tartin' on her nerves, by damn!

Norfolk's citizenry was responding to the attack on Fort Sumter, South Carolina at twenty-seven minutes past four in the morning, April 12, 1861, when Confederate forces fired on Union soldiers in Charleston Harbor. President Lincoln then called for volunteers from each Northern state to form a military contingent to recapture federal property. No way was the South going to stand for any Northern reclamation, so it was assembling its own army. Several slave-owning states, already riled by the North's righteousness, were seceding from the Union. Thorny in the face of Southern stubbornness, the Union established a naval blockade of the South.

Many who had answered the recent call to fight the Yankees were little more than ignorant kids out of back hollows and off dirt-scrabble farms, still so young that facial hair was a distant promise and their high-pitched voices sounded more like women than men. Roughnecks came from all over too, loud and coarse, with nothing but what they had on their backs. What they did possess was moonshine-inflamed bravado displayed with proudly puffed-out chests and muddy mouths. "We gonna show them good-for-nothin' blue bellies what it means to be a Southerner!"

Mary chuckled to herself, remembering a demanding, officious Army officer, Lt. Cyrus Buchanan Lutrell, who recently showed up on the doorstep of her fashion salon. With the air of one sniffing something rank, his superior tone declared, "Don't y'all know there's a war goin' on? Our boys need everything. Now."

Mary smugly nodded, but said nothing.

"You got to make us three dozen shirts, six dozen socks, a score of gray pants all sizes."

Mary shut the door on the lieutenant while he was in mid-sentence.

She had already made several batches of clothes for them and had too much else to do. The men wouldn't go naked, she reasoned. Norfolk boasted at least five other seamstresses capable of meeting their pressing needs.

She, on the other hand, was no ordinary seamstress and there was nothing common about the upcoming high fashion affair. Strained to her limits, Mary was determined to see it come off without a hitch. She had worked diligently to reach what could launch her to a higher pinnacle, one that might provide her the security she so desperately sought. Already celebrated as a fashion designer extraordinaire, this was her time, her event. Everything was on the line for her success.

Prompted toward growth and prosperity for its inhabitants, Norfolk, at the same time, was getting what it wished for but in ways it hadn't counted on.

Bars and boarding houses—in that order—sprang up almost overnight, the wood still raw and unpainted, to accommodate the influx of people arriving every day by horse, wagon, boat, train, and especially straggling in on foot. The advent of the War Between the States, whites' hardening attitudes toward slaves and Negroes in general, a free-floating anxiety, and a kind of desperateness all combined to set a pall over the city.

Alarmed folks were bearing arms, not yet against the Yankees but against each other. The rich blamed the riffraff, the riffraff blamed the rednecks, the rednecks blamed the coons, the coons blamed the ignorant, the ignorant—the whole restless passel of them—blamed everybody and divvied out hell to boot, just because. Overcrowding flourished and rank poverty provided the breeding ground for chaos and violence despite the patriotic boastings. Both the outright dishonest and the stouthearted fell in together, fraternally offering, "Lemme stand you a drink, buddy." Then, red-eyed and swaying unsteadily, they pulled their pistols and drew down on each other over any perceived slight. Leading citizens fled inside their mansions with guns loaded to defend against intruders. Frustrated city officials called for new regulations, for reform, and demanded better law enforcement for Norfolk's refined residents.

Mary had never felt so vulnerable. She already had many influential clients from all over the region that relied on her for their wardrobes, both professional and social. Her popularity mounted as newspapers mentioned her frequently. Yet, Mary wanted more. Now, at age forty-three, she felt stressed by an urgency to vault into a never-before-known position of prestige and protection—that of the untouchable, the one who had the proud eyes of the world upon her.

Regal, with the look of a woman ten, maybe fifteen years younger, Mary was in a word, "striking." Her complexion remained near perfect, with just a couple of shallow crow's feet on the outer edges of thoughtful eyes flecked with gold. The skin beneath her jaw held firm as did her splendid figure. She was a few inches taller than the average woman of her time, at just over five foot five. Even with her cane-assisted gait, men, even white gentlemen, openly admired her. She was dignified, well-spoken with a deep, some would say molten, erotic voice. Her genetic cocktail of European and African traits allowed her to straddle all spheres of society.

Still, she was a second-class citizen by birth, a Negro slave gifted to the Louvestres, who embraced Mary as kin, even bestowing her with the family's surname. Mary enjoyed the reverence of those in the vaunted Louvestre social circle, becoming a celebrity among them, so much so that city leaders were eager to showcase her. Asking her to host her own fashion show and new line would, by extension, make Norfolk feel less backwater. If Mary received national, or even international, recognition for her designs, so would Norfolk. She would be a high-fashion ambassador, proof of Norfolk's sophistication. And she would bring further honor to the Louvestre name. "Set it on its ear!" Mayor William Lamb had urged her after she agreed to do the show. "Maybe that will solve the divisiveness among us, and usher in a new spirit of uplift. We need a revival of unity and purpose to transform bitterness, enmity, and in-fighting into community."

"Give everybody a sense of puttin' on a new suit of clothes," was the way doyenne Tesh-Lucianne Louvestre had put it. "No longer would we be either patriarchs or peckerwoods. We'd strut, one and all, as truly what we are—

Virginians!"

Mary didn't have to be asked twice. She jumped at the chance to make that happen.

It seemed like forever that she had thrown all her creative talent into the challenge of staging the world-class fashion show. She ignored nagging fatigue, sore fingers, and a bad leg, in order to design, sew, and deal with mounting details for preparation. Up before dawn, she went right to work. Only a growling stomach made her stop mid-morning for black coffee and a sweet. Her schedule had grown demanding and feverish, seeing clients during the day, doing fittings for her clothing ensembles into the afternoon, often stopping only when burning, red eyes in the lantern's light made her fall into bed late at night.

She bought lace, tatting, ribbons, wools, cottons, and silks. She searched town shops for just the right buttons of all shapes and sizes. When she couldn't find them, she went to her sources among the fishermen for materials to create them. She knew she would beat the odds and become celebrated beyond Norfolk. Her vision was to be rich and more famous than anyone like her. She would finally have the power to make her own decisions, be her own person, and live the rest of her life in a style that few attain. She really could compete with the fashion centers of the world, especially Paris. Perhaps she would even travel there and win European admirers. Yes, with a little luck she would achieve her destiny. In her quiet moments she even wondered if she would stay in Norfolk. If not, where would she go?

Right now though, she was behind schedule again, and frustrated. Only thirty days to finish! Even getting the right buttons was becoming a major undertaking. It wasn't coming together as quickly as she hoped. Mary had just left Scoots Dunham's shop, a little lean-to with a thatched roof near the docks. Dunham was a fisherman whose physique reminded her of a gnarled tree branch, but no kinder man or steadier worker could be found in all of Norfolk. He and his two sons labored to supply fish and seafood daily to not only the restaurants in town but the growing Army and Navy. And for her, he made buttons. He was used to her exactness and took no offense when she looked and then shook her head disapprovingly at the mussel shells he had brought in this morning. "I swear you got yo' own mind," he said, pushing aside the ever-present chaw of tobacco in his lower lip. "All right, I'll get you more tomorrow."

The sun was already on its way to fierceness this early August morning. The breeze off the water's frothy chop was salty and rich with smells of lichen, seaweed, and dock pilings. The humid air was already warm, just under the brow of heat and sweat that would later torment green flies to swarm both two-legged and four-legged creatures with the ferocity of angry bees. Now, on her mission to get to Cecilia, she strode down the narrow cobblestone streets along the west side of the common, passing the open-lane market sellers setting up for the day's demanding commerce. Goods and wooden crates crowded the walks and passageways.

Lola Burdine was one of the sellers. Black as pitch and skinny as a railroad tie, she boisterously cursed through the only two teeth she had in her head on whoever overturned her bucket of innards. Hers was a sausage stall. She made all the selections herself and was rowdy about her distaste that Norden

Bedalia, another seller, crowded alongside her with his odious cages of birds—chickens, pigeons, quail, turkeys—all clucking and squawking an ear-splitting racket. They saw Mary passing by and both nodded deferentially.

Mary crossed by Fat Johnny Two-Fingers, named that simply because that's what he had—two fingers. A popular fishmonger, he was an affable sort who didn't just stand, his six-foot frame towered over others. With stained apron tugged around his ample middle, Fat Johnny Two-Fingers galumphed around his stall in rubber boots the size of canoes. He trumpeted orders to a younger man who dashed about pouring water over big tin tubs filled with crabs clacking their claws as they tried to escape. To Mary he took a wide stance, swiped off his cap, lowered his head, and bowed with a flourish as she passed.

Mary glanced around. Now where was he? She was supposed to meet up with her assistant for the morning. He was one Devereaux Rainier Leodegrance de Perouse, driver for the Louvestres. She continued through the growing crowd but kept an eye out for him. As a rolling pushcart vendor whose booming baritone hawked oysters and clams cut through the growing crowd, she finally spotted Devereaux.

A mulatto in his late twenties, he strutted along. Erect, carrying himself with pride, his chest was thrown out. He pleated his forehead and with a hand raised to shade his eyes, he scanned the people. Mary watched amused as Devereaux screwed up his full lips and gingerly lifted his Balmoral boots, negotiating smelly brown piles of street debris. When he saw her, he took on a long-suffering expression. He let his body list to the side as he staggered toward her theatrically, carrying a cast-iron pot. His smooth, French-accented voice whined, "So early in the morning we do this. And without the carriage." He sniffed and swatted air. "It is a shame to be here, a shame. The company you keep. My, my. And me, a beast of burden to haul this heavy pot."

"Devereaux!" Mary called.

Ever the dandy, Devereaux wore black trousers fitted to his slim hips; his white shirt with blousy sleeves emphasized broad shoulders, while attention was drawn to his narrow waist by a red and black patterned vest tapered to his figure. Pale-golden sun burnished thick, black hair—his pride. It was pulled back from his buff-colored, aquiline features and tied in a thick ponytail at the nape of his neck.

He was not just handsome, she marveled, he was graced with true beauty. "Onward young soldier!" She marched off ahead of him.

Devereaux harrumphed. "I am no soldier. I do not wish to be soldier. Anyone can be soldier. I, Devereaux Rainier Leodegrance de Perouse, am fine gentleman, expert horseman, and splendid carriage driver."

"Don't say that too loudly now," she said. "Somebody might think you're tooting your own horn."

"Toot! Toot! Toot!" he said.

Leaving the city's small shopping district, their route took them into a rougher, residential part of town. Devereaux darted glances over his shoulder while continuing his tirade. "This place I do not like."

"Really? Who would've guessed," Mary said sarcastically.

His New Orleans inflections were more pronounced under distress. The halting English he now crucified even more. "This is not good place. High-class fine woman like you should never be in hovels like these. Dogs and pigs and children running all about." He made tragic sounds.

"If you spill that soup," Mary said, "you'll have Cook Roguey to answer to and I don't think you want that, surely."

Devereaux sighed dramatically and readjusted the pot he was carrying. "I do not understand," he insisted. "Why do we not use the carriage? Such a fine, nice carriage. Padded seats inside. So comfortable."

"Too dangerous," she said, increasing the pace. "Unusual displays of luxury do not make good sense here."

Suddenly a laughing seagull cawed overhead, startling Devereaux, who screeched, ducked, and jigged. "Sweet Mary and Joseph!" he exclaimed.

She chuckled and watched the bird, with a wingspan of a larded acre, tuck and dive exuberantly from at least twenty-five feet high, beak first, into the cold river water after sighting food. "Patience, Devereaux. That carriage would draw even more attention to us. And, in the time it took us to get upstairs to see about Cecilia and back down again, it would be robbed down to nothing. You wouldn't want me to leave you out front to stand guard, would you?"

His eyes grew wide. He drew himself up and with his free hand gestured as if cracking a whip. "Devereaux Rainier Leodegrance de Perouse is many things. He is man of honor. He is courageous protector of the famous fashion designer who leads him into curious," he darted a look around, "and life-threatening situations." Then he raised his voice playfully. "He is trickster. But crazy person, he is not."

"I've never been to Cecilia's before but I think we're almost there," she said.

"Praise the god of Moses, Abednego, and ...," he thought a second and exclaimed, "Sarah and Martha!" Devereaux quickly made the sign of the cross.

"Devereaux, you're not Catholic," Mary said, watching his antics interestedly.

"I am ...," he made a rude sound, "Presbyterian, Episcopalian, even Baptist if it will see us away from here safely."

"Sounds like you've got a practical fix on religion."

Devereaux nodded absently.

She pressed on. Where Mary was headed sat among a haphazard arrangement of dilapidated three-story tenements. Surely unintended by those who had constructed them, those forced by circumstance to reside in the slum enjoyed a spectacular view of the planked wharf and the Elizabeth River, where boats with sails rode the blue-green horizon.

Devereaux set the heavy pot he was carrying on the ground, stretched his arm, and worked his hand. "I rest a moment."

"No time. If you'd wanted a rest, you should have been here sooner. We're late."

Devereaux sighed mightily, and Mary heard his footsteps lagging behind hers. "Why do we have to come here at all?" he asked almost petulantly.

"You know I've a deadline to meet. Cecilia is my best seamstress. She's sick with I don't know what and I need her well." Mary continued on the way recounting how yesterday Cecilia's young daughter, Pluck, ran all the way across town to let her know, "'Ma's got the consumption! She ain't fit for nothin'!'" Then she dashed off again. Mary said, "There's a lot riding on her skill with the intricate needlework to be done on one of the most important dresses in my collection. Mrs. Lyon-Hall of one of Norfolk's most prominent families will be modeling it in the show."

"Why her? She is whale with monkey face," Devereaux said, swiping at gnats that had begun to swarm. "I have nothing against monkeys. But on her, such face is frightening."

"Devereaux, how can you say things like that? That woman has a lot of influence in Virginia." Indeed, she thought, Mrs. Lyon-Hall was all those things Devereaux said, but she was effusive when touting Mary's designs. Getting the woman's praise was better than a month's worth of newspaper advertisements. And her praise had continued to bring in business among the influential of the Commonwealth and beyond.

"I hope you made something to fit over her face."

Sharing the joke, Mary laughed. "Mind yourself. The saying goes, 'The Lord don't love ugly.'"

"Another saying is, 'Tell the truth and shame the devil,'" Devereaux countered with a scornful wave of his hand. He scowled as they turned into the section where Cecilia lived. It was choked with noisy occupants—domestics, stevedores, ditch-diggers, poor colored, and newly arrived Irish immigrants.

Mary noticed some of them paused in their scurrying to stare at her. A couple of street urchins with rotting teeth stopped chasing each other to gape. They openly admired her small pillbox hat, called a "kufi," which she always wore low on her forehead, made of the same color as her dress with trim in slivers of crimson thread.

She was obviously Negro, but the thick, long hair that cascaded over her shoulders like a rustle of river water in the sunlight was an astonishing shade of auburn, lighter than precious bourbon whiskey, and iridescent in the morning's backdrop.

"Devereaux, put that heavy pot down here. Now I need a minute," she said. Leaning against a tree, she took a deep breath and placed her walking stick next to her. Perspiring, she reached down and massaged her leg, which throbbed even more than usual. I miscalculated the distance to Cecilia's, she thought. I could have let Devereaux drive me part of the way if I weren't so stubborn.

Devereaux set down the pot, still steaming with aromas of a delicious vegetable soup, and propping his hands on his hips, shot her a look of consternation. "What I am to do with you? Uh-uh-uhn!"

She frowned at him but said nothing.

He took from his trouser pocket a red lace handkerchief and mopped his brow. "I pain to see how your sick leg hurts you. Long ago, we could have arrived at Cecilia's but for you, yes?"

"I've already explained that," she said, exasperated.

But he was on a roll. "People will say, 'Who can trust Devereaux Rainier Leodegrance de Perouse? He does not do well his job. He takes no pride in protecting his charge, the most famous fashion designer in the whole of the South.'"

"I can protect myself very well, thank you," Mary retorted.

"Bah!"

The pair had no sooner passed another half-block when a man stepped out from between a tavern and a low wall. Mary quickly took his measure. Tall, about thirty, he had the weather-beaten look of a cowhand who rode horseback across country under scorching sun. High cheekbones limned either side of a pert nose, giving him an almost cute appearance. His fawn-colored hair, more wavy than curly, was parted on the side and left to hang in casual disorder. Taut muscles stressed the seams of the starched white shirt he wore, tucked into fitted, brown canvas pants covered under a light duster. He was a man other men might envy for his shabby elegance; women would dream of his company alone. Two things worked against him in Mary's summing up: glacial eyes so penetrating as to be invasive, and lips thin enough that, when curved up, looked less like a smile than a crescent brand. He turned his intense blue stare on her.

"Y'all in the wrong neck of the woods?" His was a slow, honey drawl—Deep South, Mary guessed—contrived to sound friendly. He grinned, showing dusky teeth.

Devereaux stepped protectively next to Mary and peered down his nose at the intruder. "Who is asking her business?"

The man's shrewd eyes were amused as he studied this new object of interest. His look raked Devereaux up and down. "You squirrely? Swishy? Quare, something like that?"

Devereaux sucked his breath and drew himself up imperiously. "Swishy? I, Devereaux Rainier Leodegrance de Perouse, will show you who is 'quare,' as you say it."

Laughing, the man held up his hands with long, tapered fingers. "Whoa, partner. No need for conniptions. You seem a might ... delicate, is all."

Devereaux growled.

The man pulled back his duster and displayed a shiny lawman's star on his front shirt pocket. "I'm Elam Gates, new deputy working with Sheriff Claude Bridges. Y'all just look out of place up in here."

Mary gazed thoughtfully at Gates. She judged him to be as slick as snake oil, and all her instincts told her to trust him like she would a roused adder. She did not introduce herself.

"The clothes y'all wearin' alone could buy, sell, and feed the folks around here for a month. Ain't got the best element filtering around these parts," Gates said.

Devereaux huffed, "You are filtering around these parts."

Gates snickered. "You're a funny man." He looked at Mary and hooked his thumbs into his belt. "He's a funny man."

"I'm squirrely. I'm swishy. I'm quare. Now I'm funny." Devereaux wrinkled his nose and sniffed indignantly. His eyes raked Gates up and down. "You are ... gauche."

Gates said nothing, then regarded Mary with a leer. "You're a right smart-looking woman. I'd be more careful if I were you." He glanced down at her, shook his head, and spoke as if talking to himself. "Lord, Lord. She's even using a gold-headed walking stick. And I ain't never seen me a nigger wearin' a ring.

How come you got it on your middle finger? What is that?"

Mary thrust her middle finger up to Gates. "It's the Louvestre crest. Carnelian and gold."

"Carnelian," Gates said as if pondering, and missing, the gesture. "That don't sound common."

"It's a gemstone believed to soothe arthritis and other ailments," Mary said informatively. "The gold L's surrounding it symbolize the family name. All Louvestres wear it on the middle finger. Does that answer your questions, Mr. Gates?" she responded curtly.

"You better watch yourself, girl. It's *Deputy* Gates." He narrowed his eyes at her. "I believe you sassed me right then but I can't make it out for sure."

Don't say anything back, Mary told herself, swallowing her rising anger. Give him nothing to work with.

"She is Mary Louvestre, famous fashion designer," Devereaux stated with feeling. "All around here know her, respect her, love her, revere her. She will come to no harm."

Mary was astonished at Devereaux's bravado. She made her face inscrutable as she swung back to Gates. The air lifted the deputy's scent, a mixture of tobacco and bay rum. He waited for her response. She refused to give him one. Rather, she assessed him circumspectly. She hadn't been in business with the public this many years not to know this man for who and what he was.

Strained silence vibrated between them as the deputy cocked his head, examining Mary sideways, then straight on, then, exaggerating, tilting his head in the other direction. He stuck his little finger in his ear and twisted. He arched his eyebrows and opened his mouth in an "Oh." He snapped his fingers. "Louvestre. Right. Mary Louvestre. Why, I hadn't hit town two seconds before I got wind of you. Special nigger. I surely am glad to make your acquaintance. But, Lord God, nobody pulled my coat that you were such a head-turner." His hands made circles in the air. "Enchanting. You are a knockout piece of oak."

Mary's face flushed hot. She heard Devereaux pull a breath loudly. She pursed her lips against the revulsion she felt, constricting her throat.

"I see you know what that means," Gates said, never turning his eyes from her or losing his lopsided smile. "Calm, cool, and collected. Unflappable?"

"Mr. Gates," Mary said, nodding and turning on her walking stick, "we must be going."

"Yes ma'am," Gates said jovially. He tipped his beige, high-crowned hat, shifting it saucily over his forehead. "'Til we meet again. Y'all be careful with Dotey here. Anybody with a brain and two good eyes can see he's not all there."

Devereaux uttered a small snarl. Mary grabbed a firm hold of his arm. Gates let out a guffaw and sauntered on.

"Devereaux," Mary said in a quiet tone, "can't you see he was picking at you?"

Devereaux harrumphed, picked up the soup pot, and stalked onward. "'Funny,' 'swishy,' and the disrespect to you."

"I can handle things. Keep your peace."

"That man is a clod. I hate him."

"Miss Mary."

She heard Gates's molasses tones and looked back. He was standing in the street, arms folded over his chest, a mocking expression on his face. "I was just watching you walk away. You look real good walking away. Just wanted you to know that."

Anger flashed across Mary's face, but as suddenly as it came, it was gone. She could tell Gates was gratified to note he'd gotten a rise from her. She paused, cleared her throat, and then spoke deliberately. "It's hard to run away from who you really are, Mr. Gates—your past, so telling, trailing behind you and all. The very act of trying can be such a burden, can't it?" For a moment, she watched Gates shuffle his features as he tried vainly to hold his smile, his stance, his position of control.

"Some things are a sin and a shame. Others are both, wouldn't you agree?" She paused a long moment. She stared at him genially, head high and dignified. "Deputy Gates." With poise, she turned away. "We're late, Devereaux."

"Yes," he said, glancing back at the deputy who stared at them through narrowed eyes. "We must hurry."

Mary's back-mind told her that she and Gates had just shaken grudging hands over a dark, mysterious precipice. She didn't believe, in the long run, such a portentous welcome bode well for their future.

CHAPTER 2

Ⅰt took several more minutes to wend their way through manure-laden streets and skirt a few seedy sorts pushing out of doorways, who, though upright, were still clearly in a tussle with last night's brews. Mary and Devereaux passed two lively but unsteady comrades weaving along with their arms around each other's shoulders, arguing animatedly. Devereaux glanced at her, rolled his eyes, and crossed himself again. Mary chortled.

Their destination came into sight. It was a gray clapboard building where leggy impatiens made a feeble attempt to add some prettiness. The air stank of privies, hidden in back, which sent trickles of excrement down into the street. Mary's eyes burned and she swallowed hard. Sanitation had always been a troublesome civic problem, but on this hot day the stench of raw sewage was choking. Despite epidemics of smallpox and yellow fever that took the lives of hundreds at a time, even government nurses who tried to educate people threw up their hands. In places, gutters were so filled with reeking offal that fresh air was cheated two streets away.

Scrawny chickens pecked at the ground in search of morsels, pigs squealed from somewhere near, and tenants at windows hollered conversations to each other. From above, remnants of a slop jar soared through the air and, by the grace of God, just missed Devereaux. He stopped—stunned—then hissed and held his nose.

"Pigs!" Devereaux snorted in derision. "Why they do not clean up this place?"

"We can't judge them. Most of the folk who live here feel lucky. They are hod carriers, barrel rollers, store sweeps, plantation workers, laborers of every description, and domestics who work from can to can't. When they get home at night, I imagine cleaning is not high on their list, even if they have the desire."

"P-hew!" Devereaux wasn't willing to give up the point.

"Patrick O'Shaughnessy!" a woman bellowed, interrupting Devereaux's next comment. Her voice could have shattered glass and frightened dogs into hiding. "You get your lard ass back in here. If you don't, so help me God, I'll follow you to that hellhole you call work and tell every mother's son within earshot in great detail your sad performance below my waist the last few nights!"

Patrick, a florid-faced man who had just escaped their sagging front door, skidded to a stop, did a curious pirouette, and lowered his shoulders in defeat. He shuffled his lard ass back inside.

The warped front door on Cecilia's building complained loudly as Devereaux put his shoulder to it and pushed it open. They crossed a small, littered area where paint not so much peeled off the walls as gave up the effort to hold on. Pale light filtered from a scant window high above.

"This way, I think," Mary said, crossing over to the staircase.

Devereaux let out a low whistle as they mounted rickety stairs that creaked and whined as they climbed toward the third floor. Mary had to let go of the banister as it swayed too much to give support. Through thin doors and walls they heard babies crying, shouts and hoots, and children playing, and felt—rather than just smelled—the assault of breakfast foods from cultures other than the South. They halted briefly on the second landing when they heard the sound of tiny skittering feet.

"Rats!" Devereaux shrieked, snatching up his feet, twisting, wildly searching around for them.

"There." Mary spotted three big black ones in a dim corner, their jet eyes glaring at the intrusion. "Those're babies compared to some I've seen in town alleyways—big as small dogs and willing to fight wild pigs for what scraps of food they can find."

Devereaux sucked in breath.

"If you don't bother them," she continued, "they won't bother you."

"Uh-huh. That's why they show me sharp teeth."

Heaving up again, they reached the third landing. A Negro girl of about sixteen, wearing a plain gingham frock, answered their knock. "Miss Mary," she said softly, cheerfully, "and Devereaux, come on in." She stepped aside and held the door open.

"Thank you, Pluck," Mary said. Pretty in a pudgy young girl way, she was shy and faded into the background as fast as politeness would allow.

Once inside the modest but tidy quarters, stale air, closeness, and the stench of sickness blistered Mary's nostrils. She glanced to the only small, dingy window in the room, which was tightly shut and harnessed by heavy curtains partly drawn. Only a sliver of light shimmied its way inside. The heat in the room could have broiled meat.

"Mon Dieu!" cried Devereaux. He used his free hand to fan himself.

"How is she, Fortune?" Mary asked, striding to the window while addressing the older girl standing near the room's sole table. Mary clubbed the window frame with her fist until it popped open. She pushed the curtains back and air poured in, to her audible relief.

"Old folks say to keep the windows closed on the ailin' so's not to let in more sickness," Fortune said.

"Are these old folks still alive? You've got to clear out the bad air."

Fortune was pleasant-faced, dark and thin, older than Pluck by two years. She wrung her hands nervously. "The remedies you give us for Mama helped some, but she ain't riz out of bed. It's been a hard three days."

In the far corner on the floor was a thin corn shuck mattress. Curled on it lay an older woman, skin and bones, moaning. Mary went over to her. "Cecilia, it's Mary and Devereaux. We brought you some of Roguey's vegetable soup. Can you sit up?"

"Eat," Devereaux clucked. "You will feel better soon." He set the pot on the small wooden table.

Cecilia struggled upward with the aid of elbows pressed against the mattress. Angled halfway, she grabbed her head with one hand. "I'm spinnin'," she said and flopped back down on the bed. Sharp-featured, her dark face bore the marks of her illness. Deep circles of purple puffed under her red-rimmed eyes. The skin over her thick lips had the look of torn parchment paper, cracked open and bleeding in places. Sallow cheeks sucked in and out with raspy breathing. Wisps of ragged hair stood out from her head—gray now, as if the sickness had leeched all of its previous brown color.

Mary took a small pouch from her bag and pinched a few large leaves with wavy edges. "This is borage," she said to Cecilia, offering her a little. "I want you to chew it. In a few minutes, you'll feel better and it'll lift your spirits too."

Cecilia took it into her mouth and chewed slowly. She looked surprised. "Tastes like fresh cucumbers," she whispered.

Mary then removed a small copper pot and a large pinecone from her bag. She set these aside. From another small pouch, she fished out tiny leaves of greenish-gray sage and sprinkled the pinecone. Aromatics for healing, Mary also used them to counteract the acrid smell. She lit the pinecone from a match in her sack and, once the smoke was curling up, she took out a candle made of pig fat, lit it, and set it in a small holder. In just minutes, the sick woman roused from the swift effects of the borage.

"Miss Mary." Cecilia stopped and cleared phlegm from her throat. "I'm so worried, so scared. Me an' the girls, we ain't hardly got nothin' but the sewin' work you give me to do."

Fortune brought a straight-back chair and guided it behind Mary. "Rest a spell."

"Thank you," Mary said, sitting.

Pluck appeared near her mother with a Mason jar of water. "Here you go, Mama. Drink this." Cecilia tried to drink. She coughed and dribbled onto the ragged gown she wore.

"Take your time," Mary said gently. "Sip it."

"Miss Mary, I been workin' for you five years and ain't never let you down. This time I gotta. I ain't fit for much right now but I been teachin' the girls the kind of needlework you like. They're good if you give 'em a chance." Cecilia's brown eyes were pleading as she lay back exhausted. "Can't you use 'em?"

"Of course," Mary said. "In fact, I brought a few fabric pieces and some supplies." She indicated the paper-wrapped bundle she'd carried in. "I'm sure they'll do fine. My latest dress design calls for tiny intricate stitches that will take more time than I have, trying to oversee everything."

"I know you got your hands full," Cecilia said.

"Before a show, madness seems to set in. One of my weavers is down, you're not well, two other seamstresses are about to deliver babies, fabrics I was counting on from Europe can't get through the Northern Blockade, and Scoots Dunham hasn't managed to catch enough mussels to get the right buttons done. I could go on."

Cecilia folded her hands over her chest. "This is the biggest thing to hit Norfolk since I don't know when." Then she fell into a wracking fit of coughing. Mary put a comforting hand on Cecilia's shoulder. In a few minutes the woman took a deep breath. "That Slippery Elm syrup you made me before helps."

"Give it awhile longer," Mary said.

"Of all the times for me to be sick, an' it ain't hardly lettin' up on me that much. When's the do now?"

"Three weeks and counting," Mary said. "This is the time I really feel the pinch."

"Folks say, 'cause of you and this show, everybody north and south gonna know about Norfolk," Fortune added.

"Virginia got the finest tobacco, but Norfolk got the only Mary Louvestre," Pluck said with pride. Cecilia started to laugh, but wracking coughs hit her again. Her body bucked and tears flooded her eyes until the fit passed and her breathing quieted.

Mary glanced over her shoulder at Devereaux. "Please dish out the soup. I'm sure Cecilia and the girls could all use some."

Cecilia shivered, pulling a tattered blanket to her chin.

"What you think's done got me down so?"

"Pneumonia, likely. You show all the signs," Mary said.

"Your remedies done helped."

"Not enough."

Pluck cut in. "Talk say Mr. Louvestre got it too?"

"It's possible, though he may just have a bad cold," Mary said. "People who've never been sick a day in their lives are coming down with whatever is going around. He's one of them. Tesh-Lucianne is a doting wife. She frets after him like nobody's business because he won't stop working long enough to get well. He says he can't. The Navy has him under a deadline project and he's going to hold up his end no matter what."

"Stubborn man!" Devereaux put in as he gave Mary a bowl of soup for Cecilia. "Seems to run in the family." He eyed Mary.

As Mary spooned a sip into the woman's mouth, she could smell Cecilia's rank breath. She knew the odor signaled a worsening condition.

"Ahh, bless Jesus, that's good," Cecilia sighed.

"Roguey's a fine cook," Mary commented, "and she made a special effort to make a healing soup for you."

As Devereaux set out bowls for the girls, Pluck said, "Miss Mary, Fortune and me'll be there to help with your party. Won't we, Fortune?"

"Oh, yes, Miss Mary!" Fortune agreed. "Anything you need."

"Good. I'm glad to know I can count on you. Mr. Louvestre's birthday party is about the last thing I need added on my plate right now. But Tesh-Lucianne is on her head to do it."

"I wouldn't miss it," Fortune said. "I can hardly wait to see all those rich ladies' dresses and jewelry and hats."

"What if I told you I'll make pretty party dresses for the two of you?"

The girls gasped, clasping delighted fingers to their mouths. They squealed, linked hands, and bounced with glee.

"When you're going to serve some of the richest white people in the South, then you've got to dress for the part."

The girls hugged each other and chorused, "You ain't nothin' but the bes', Miss Mary!"

"Cecilia, I asked Tesh-Lucianne to send for my teacher, Miss Effie, to come help you," Mary said.

"Who?" Pluck asked.

"Only the greatest medicine woman alive today," Devereaux said. "She teached Miss Mary, who is great too, of course. Miss Effie, she better than any white doctor for colored people. She is most exceedingly excellent."

"You know her?" Pluck asked Devereaux, who was gesturing for the girls to sit at the table. "What's she like?"

"Well," he stammered, "I … I don't exactly know her. But if she is teacher to Mary, she has to be fantastic, no?"

The girls giggled at him.

"Why would Miss Louvestre do that for me?" Cecilia said.

"You know that woman," Mary said. "A truer, kinder heart never beat in a human chest."

"Some white men don't like it when good white people help us," Devereaux grouched. He made a scoffing noise. "They stupid, bad men. No-counts. Acting like they are not housebroken and getting worse now with war."

"Seems like ever since the South fired on Fort Sumter, ain't nobody been like they was before," Fortune said.

"They president, Mr. Lincoln, say he gon' free the slaves," Pluck added.

"White folk 'round here ain't even gonna try to be havin' none of that," Fortune said matter-of-factly. "Too much hard work to do and they ain't gonna break a sweat to do it. When the last you seen some rich white man plowin' his own fields, much less hitchin' up the mule?"

"Well, no sense concerning ourselves with that," Mary said. "What needs your attention is in this package. You girls get onto the needlework." She pointed to the paper bundle next to her, then turned to Cecilia. "Your job is to rest and get well."

Cecilia nodded weakly.

"Thank you for the food, Miss Mary," Pluck said, spooning the soup into her mouth. "Seem like we be's so hongry sometime my stomach think my throat been cut."

Mary took some coins from her purse and laid the money on the table before she left. "Make sure your mother eats now. I'll come again soon and will try to have Miss Effie in tow."

Once back outside, Mary breathed deeply. The weather was sweet. Birds cawed and chirped. Insects chattered drowsily and the slow chugging of a train rumbled in the distance. She felt a frisson of pleasure, then caught sight of Deputy Gates edging along the street, now dense with people. The tiny hairs on the back of her neck stood up. "We'd better hurry home," she said. "I don't want to miss the eleven o'clock ferry to Portsmouth. Tesh-Lucianne wants me to take Simeon his lunch and try to convince him to come home early and rest."

Devereaux placed the back of his hand to his forehead and heaved a melodramatic sigh. "No rest for the wicked, or is it the weary?"

"Speak for yourself about the wicked part," Mary said, amused by her animated assistant.

"This day I have been pegged for squirrely, swishy, quare, delicate, and now wicked. The world has gone out and out crazy if you ask me."

Mary set off not asking him. She could feel Gates watching them. She said nothing to Devereaux. She knew he was prone to making a scene and she didn't need that.

"Miss Mary?" Devereaux hustled to keep up. "When we pack up soup for Mr. Simeon's lunch?"

"Umm." Mary glanced about in a surreptitious attempt to spy Gates, who seemed to have disappeared. She relaxed a bit.

"I will drive the carriage." Devereaux's face was disarming.

Mary laughed, her rich contralto rising on the credit of being on such good terms with a friend.

After a time, she heard a crunch that sounded like footsteps behind them. She tightened and glanced over her shoulder. Nothing. Still, her heart beat faster. She wondered if she should begin carrying Tesh-Lucianne's gift. She remembered how her irrepressible mistress had lately become so concerned about Mary's safety after dark as she went about supervising her weavers, seamstresses, and other workers at the warehouse in town. Over evening drinks, she had surprised Mary with a polished oblong box. When Mary opened it, her jaw dropped. Tucked inside the red velvet cushion was an exquisite pearl-handled Colt.

"You've got to take care. I can't have anything happen to my Mary. Why, you've got a show to deliver and everybody who's anybody's coming to the festivities!"

Mary stared dumbfounded at Tesh-Lucianne, who could not have looked more innocently girlish and pleased with herself. "You like to live dangerously, don't you?" Mary handed the box back to her.

Tesh-Lucianne's face was perplexed. "You don't know how to use it?"

"That's not the point. If I was found out to carry this, the last you'd see of me would be dangling from a tree."

Tesh-Lucianne giggled, then pouted. "So silly, make sure no one does! You have to have an equalizer against the hooligans parading around our streets these days."

Mary held the box on her lap. "Tesh-Lucianne? You're crazy as a betsy bug."

She took Mary's face in her hands. "Isn't this the best fun?"

Mary regarded her mistress, then the magnificent firearm. "Couldn't be better."

CHAPTER 3

"Off the sidewalk, niggers! Let white folks by. Y'all know better." Gates ordered a well-dressed couple of elderly Negroes off the pitted plank walkway by the town shops and onto the dirt road.

Clearly startled by his rudeness, they said nothing and complied. Their flinty eyes weighed him in at "tetched."

"What y'all lookin' at?" he said. "Move along."

They did.

Gates stared at the couple walking down a ways, wagging his head at them in general contempt. Surprisingly, they stepped back onto the sidewalk as if nothing had happened. They turned speculatively and smiled at him. Their expressions leveled into a quick strong stand of defiance before they went on. He wagged his head. Damn these niggers! Who the hell do they think they are! Hellfire!

He had waited by Cecilia's building, surveying for Mary and Devereaux, wondering what they might be up to in there. And why, with all of the derelicts about, did they walk, exposing themselves to possible dangers? Something about that woman intrigued him. Her designation as "special" didn't make him as curious as her physical appeal did. He had to lay it on the line. A woman did it for him or she didn't. In the case of this Louvestre woman, though she had a little age on her, he'd never have to argue the merits of her natural-born favor. Thinking, he propped a cigarette between his lips and lit up. He lowered his head in supplication. Who knew the ways of the Almighty!

Gates watched two boys scamper about the courtyard and then disappear inside. Rat traps, he thought disgustedly. Somebody ought to burn 'em down. Though when you destroyed a rat's nest, where did they run to but somebody else's house? He shrugged. They and the rats deserved each other. He yawned and scratched his chest, reflecting on Mary. Actually, he wasn't thinking, he was feeling. Following her might have some real purpose after all.

He glanced up as the front door opened. There she was. For goodness sake, followed by the twitchy little man, no doubt complaining. Give him two cents and two minutes and he'd damn sure to give that boy something to complain about. He, for one, wasn't about to forget the morning's insults. Humpf! Yes, there'd be a reckoning down the line.

Gates drank deeply of the warm summer air, though the odor irritated his throat. He thrust his head high and his shoulders back. He felt in fine fettle. To his mind, he had already sized up the situation in Norfolk and believed that the heart of the city's problem lay in blacks who had been led to believe they had the right to act like white people. Many of them were tradespeople—wheelwrights, carpenters, cobblers, blacksmiths, barbers, coopers, seamstresses and the like, who had the gall to feel indispensable. Astounding was that so many white folk encouraged such misguided thinking. Why, it was no surprise at all, he thought, that Norfolk was having its share of troubles.

Such wrong-headed idea-bearers had already set good white people in jeopardy. Sixty whites wound up getting killed in the mess caused by Nat Turner and other rebellious slaves not far west of Norfolk. Then there was the raid for arms not too long ago at Harper's Ferry. No way was that going to happen in Norfolk, not in *his* town. He had a patriotic duty to put these uppity niggers in their place, in both mind and deed. He'd had chance to encounter hire-out slaves who had lived too long among permissive whites and had come to regard themselves as equals. He shook his head sadly at the idea. Terrible thing was, he told himself, they were like unruly children and untamed animals. Give them an inch and it was as hard to discipline them as putting a collar on a rabid dog. He concluded it was time to remind these darkies who was top dog and to grind out any notions of a full-scale rebellion. That would be for everybody's good.

———◆◆———

By carriage, the route for Mary and Devereaux eventually took them to the docks where steam-powered paddle boats taxied passengers about a mile over the Elizabeth River between Norfolk and Portsmouth. The ride was a short and convenient one over the usually-still waters of the river. Horns tooted when the boats arrived and departed. The paddle wheels churned up the water behind them, leaving plumes of spray trails for gulls to follow. Lots of folk ferried from Norfolk to their jobs at the Gosport Navy Yard. Businessmen and professionals like Simeon who worked with the Navy, kept offices, shops or warehouses near the shipyard. The fleet of six ferries not only added a charm to the waterfront, they were a vital link for commerce. Just three cents to cross. As one boat pulled in, Gates glanced up and spied just the person he believed to be a main source of Negroes' bad behavior in Norfolk. He hiked up his breeches and scratched his balls. Time for introductions.

A tall man, blond, broad-shouldered, with taut muscles that bulged like small boulders, angled his way out of Gordon's Bait and Tackle Shop hoisting a heavy burlap sack across his wide chest. He made his way pleasantly through the pedestrians to a wagon parked in front of the store. Behind him trudged a

Negro man, two or three times his size, hauling two burlap sacks, one on each shoulder.

Jesus, mused Gates, is that a man or a mass of drifting rock?

"Tall Man" moved aside as "Black Rock" finished loading the wagon, untied the horses' reins and hoisted his bulk to the driver's seat. Tall Man was about to step up when Gates called out.

"Y'all! Hey!" he threw up his hand. "Hol' on a minute."

Both men turned his way and stopped.

Gates casually strolled up to the wagon. He addressed Tall Man. "Say, ain't you the one own that spread of prime land out by the Peak they call Stonehaven?"

"The very one," Tall Man said, extending his hand.

Gates ignored the mannered gesture. "I'm new in town. Introducin' myself around. Name's Gates. Deputy Elam Gates." The grin he flashed was as bright as the badge he flourished.

Black Rock, holding the reins in close, relaxed his hands, kept his eyes straight ahead. Even so, Gates could tell he was alert to everything.

"Pleased to meet you," Tall Man said. "I'm—"

"I know who you are," Gates cut him off. "Heard about you and your sorry ways before my feet touched Virginia soil. You're Thurston Stone. Responsible for a lot of niggers thinkin' they can do as they please, traipsin' 'round actin' like they white, livin' better than most decent citizens of this town. What you thinkin', man?" He drove his fingers through his hair.

Thurston Stone raised an inquiring eyebrow, then smiled, unconcerned. "I can see yo' principles standin' up stiff as a poker. Pleased to make your acquaintance, Deputy Gates."

A small crowd of men hunched nearby, sensing tension. Like schoolboys on a playground, they edged around from seemingly nowhere. All wanted to make sure they got the full details to relate it to others later over cold brews, if they could get them, and definitely hot women.

Thurston Stone drew a large red and white bandana from his back pocket and mopped his forehead. "It's a hot one today," he said. "Could practically drown in your own sweat."

Gates took a wide-legged stance, his duster-hem flapping in an errant breeze. Stone turned soft doe eyes on the dubious threat shifting from foot to foot in the close dust and chuckled.

"You want to say what's so funny?" Gates said, gathering spittle in the corner of his mouth.

"No," Stone replied. A tentative smile played at his lips.

Gates watched him. "Hey. You laughin' at me?"

"In a manner of speaking."

Gates worked his jaw like he was chewing tobacco. "Why?"

Stone glanced up at the blue sky as he tucked the bandana back in his pocket. "This is a perfectly splendid day God has made, and here you're insulting it and me for no reason at all."

"I got my reasons," Gates said sullenly.

After a pause, Stone patiently asked, "And those are?"

Gates canted his head and blew an irked breath. "I done already told you

I don't like you puttin' ideas in niggers' heads. Hear tell out your way they got good houses of their own. Eat offin' from the land they work. You even teachin' 'em readin' and writin.'"

"You've been to Stonehaven?" Stone made his face a question.

"Don't have to. I been done heared 'bout it."

"And they've been to Stonehaven?"

"I s'pose." Gates huffed air through his nose and tried to appear menacing for the growing crowd. He swallowed hard and let the back of his hand swipe at the jewels of sweat lining his forehead. "How else would they know you also got a brick dormitory out there for some of them to live in and all kinds of contraptions you invented. Say you got a way to weed several rows of plantin's at once and a mechanical hoist that'll lift up bales of hay into the barn loft without any of 'em lifting a finger. A hammer don't have to hit me in the head to know yo' niggers got more'n they ought to. The very idea that some even got white-painted picket fences around their places ..."

Gates paused. Smug-faced, he continued showing his teeth. He hitched up his pants and squared his shoulders to demonstrate his undeniable authority.

Stone grinned back casually. "Do tell, Deputy. You sure you're not a mouse? Scurrying like a varmint around my property at night? You sure seem to know a lot."

"True or not?" Gates demanded.

Thurston turned and put a foot on the wagon to climb up. Gates reached out a hand and grabbed his arm. Stone stopped, his smile fading, his eyes turning hard. He took long inventory of the deputy.

Gates slid his duster back to give Stone a glimpse of the sawed-off shotgun holstered at his hip.

"I don't know about you, *friend*," Stone gave the word emphasis, "but I've got work to do. He started to climb up on the wagon again.

Again Gates's hand stayed him back. "Ain't your friend, friend."

Murmurs rounded the crowd.

Stone let his eyes go to Gates's hand on his arm. Gates let go. "Just what is it you want from me this morning, Deputy Gates?"

Gates glanced around, noting the eager eyes of the men egging him on—or so he wanted to believe. But he didn't know how to answer Stone. He wasn't really sure what he wanted from him.

"I ... I want you to think about what you're doin'." Gates's voice broke, betraying weakness behind the words. Then more forcefully, he continued, "I'm here to bring law and order to this town and I can't do it with white folk like you puttin' abolitionist ideas in niggers' heads. Ain't right. Ain't patriotic neither."

Stone made no response.

After a moment, Gates cocked his chin at the big black man. "What *is* that anyway? Can't be human, big as all that."

Stone chuckled wryly. "Bear? He's human all right. Got his name 'cause he's big as a grizzly. A grizzly'll tear your face off when riled. So will Bear. I suggest you treat him decent, Deputy Gates."

"That so?" Gates said, feeling challenged. He turned full attention to Bear, studied him, thinking he might prove to be an easier target than Stone. "Why'n't you get down from that wagon and let me see what you got."

Bear didn't move.

"Listen," Stone said. He pushed his hat back and scratched his forelocks. "Is it me or did you get stuck on the privy this morning? You seem a might locked up. Know what I mean?"

The men around began to snicker. A few boys laughed out loud.

"What?" Gates said.

"A good remedy for that is to take a bar of soap," Stone said as if instructing a child, "cut a triangle from it and shove it up behind where the wool is short. Fix you right up in no time. Put you in a gentler mood to boot."

Gates eyed Stone coldly. He couldn't let this joker humiliate him in front of the townsfolk. Word would spread like smoke that Gates couldn't hold his own. That would sound a death knell over his new career. "I don't think I like your attitude, *friend*. Believe I gotta to do somethin' about it."

Stone returned Gates's direct stare. He paused a long time, his expression unfazed, totally unafraid. "Like what?"

"Well," Gates said, maneuvering himself around the wagon, stalling for time until he could think of something. "Arm wrestle Grizzly here."

Stone outright hooted at that. "Sorry, Deputy Gates. I can't let that happen. I don't want your blood on my hands. Look, if you want to keep your arm in its socket, you'd best be leaving Bear, and me, alone."

Now the men in the crowd laughed too.

"Sounds like you just threw down on me," Gates said, puffing out his chest.

A voice from the crowd called out: "Bear'll snap your whole body like a dry twig!" The crowd laughed louder.

"Whoa! I ain't met a man I couldn't take," Gates bragged. "Lay 'im spang-out before you can bat your eye."

Stone simply turned, stepped up on the wagon, and sat down. "Let's go, Bear."

A slight smile turned on Bear's lips.

Gates caught it and was instantly furious. With one hand he drew his shotgun, and in a flash, light flared. The shot had been aimed at Bear's head, but Stone had shifted in time to intercept the bullet. A unanimous gasp went up from the crowd as blood quickly spilled from the hole in Stone's upper arm. Shock registered on his face, but pain had not yet set in. Bear grabbed him and helped him lean back on the bench.

"Get Doc Sloan! Quick!" somebody yelled from the crowd, and a small boy took off running down the street.

"You're a lawman?" Stone said, staring disbelieving at Gates. "You shoot for no reason?"

Bear's neutral expression had not changed. He calmly removed the bandana from around his neck and wrapped it onto Thurston Stone's arm in a tight tourniquet. Then he stood up, slowly hooked a boot over the wagon side, and hopped down. His fingers opened and closed into hard fists, his knuckles swelling like knots on a log.

"You come any closer and you gon' be next," Gates stated, trying to put some force behind his words.

Bear lumbered toward him until they were inches apart. When he spoke, his voice sounded like gathering thunder. "Which hand you arm-wrestle with?"

"Wouldn't you like to know," Gates said, wanting to back up a step or two. They were so close he could smell sarsaparilla on the big man's breath. Wait a minute, he thought, what real man drank sarsaparilla? But the pressure Bear was exerting over him, just by his huge physical presence, made him reassess that question. Anyway, he knew that if he shifted back, the crowd would see he was trembling. Gates held still as the giant's broad chest loomed before him. "You touch me, I'll arrest you for harassing an officer of the law."

Bear peered down at the deputy. Gates could see his face reflected in the dark eyes shining above him. A huge hand swept out, the size of a paw. Bear snatched the lawman's weapon by the butt. With his other hand he grabbed the barrel and, while holding Gates's eyes, made ready to snap the gun in two with no effort.

Stone's voice shot out, "Bear!"

Bear stopped. Without lowering the gun or looking away, he said, "Boss, you know I hate guns. Don't like the wrong kinda folk misusin' 'em neither."

Gates felt the bile rise in his throat but was prudent enough to stay quiet. The way Bear held his shotgun, one wrong move and he'd have a hole in his gut.

"Give me the gun, Bear," Stone said. "Sheriff for sure will haul you off and I don't need you in jail."

Bear hesitated, then handed the gun up to Stone, who reached his good arm out to grab it. "Deputy Gates, I'll see you get this back when you've cooled off a bit." As he stuffed the gun under the seat, Doc Sloan raced up. Bear climbed back aboard the wagon.

"Not a thing I can do with a wound like this out here," the doctor said. "Get him down to my office. Now!"

Bear was about to swing the wagon around when Gates blocked the way. Glaring at both men, he said, "This ain't over. I want you to know that."

Bear sighed. "You got the right to move—or not."

Gates was still trying to demonstrate some threat as the crowd of men, tired of the scene, began drifting away. Anxiety agitated his chest.

Bear spoke up again. "You got one mo' time to trouble my friend, Mr. Thurston Stone. What I say got promise in it."

"What?" Gates swelled with embarrassment and fury.

Stone moaned. Bear glanced at him and nickered at the horses. He peered at Gates, who rolled off the tips of his boots and side-stepped himself out of the way.

Where do these niggers get off? Gates thought. Back talk! Not just as equal to whites but acting damned superior. First that Louvestre woman and now this freak of nature! He had intended to make a public example out of Bear. In his mind's eye, he saw the big man face-forward in a fresh patch of horse shit, bleeding in a heap from the whipping he put on him. In reality, the goliath, black as a nightmare, had never flinched, never acted as if afraid of a white man, let alone a peace officer, like himself.

"You promise me?" Gates uttered in the direction of the disappearing wagon. He looked around at the last of the dispersing crowd. "You promise me!" He laughed hollowly allowing it to slowly die into nothingness.

The men and boys were gone, leaving the area silent under the late morning sun. Gates stood, blinking. For a heart-crushing moment, he could not casket the feeling that he had the value of a fart.

"A'Lawd! You lookin' plum spiritually afflicted!" he heard a man's voice declare.

———❖———

Gates glanced up to see Meander Gordon Jr. standing in the door of his immense emporium. Gordon favored his daddy with his bright aqua-blue eyes twinkling merriment and stubby blond hair fighting a cowlick. Seemed he'd also been bequeathed the old man's quick smile and gift of gab. Gates thought Gordon Jr. did lay it on a little thick with the molasses corn-pone accent.

"You ol' silly," came the high-pitched voice of a big-haired woman. Gates recognized her from recent gossip. Dame-Gracie's face was impish, which appeared even more so under hair that looked like a dandelion fluff dyed a startling, indisputable shade of henna. Nearby, red-suspendered Jethro Wanzer and his brother Albert, regular checker-playing fixtures stationed at a table in front of Sheriff Claude Bridges's office, tapped their work boots to the lively tunes of Able and Roger-Bob Runyon, two long-bearded brothers, known as the hard-drinkin'est, hard-drivin'est banjo players in the Commonwealth.

These days, Norfolk was steadily filling up with all sorts of characters. Since Virginia seceded, they came like lemmings. From large tobacco plantations, dirt farms, and backwater turns-in-the-road, eager faces popped up in line at the military recruiter's desk. His pine deal table set pitched in front of the courthouse, where he stood behind it erect in full regalia. Faithful souls screwed up their mouths, bit their tongues, eyes intent as they clutched awkward fingers around a pencil and etched in black, for all time, their X on the muster roll.

With the firm belief they'd signed a covenant to defend God and country, they stood ready to commit their all or at least have some fun as long as it lasted. With bright images of themselves in colorful uniform, new rifles over their shoulders, and shiny boots on their feet, they'd be soldiers, by damn! "Gon' whup us up some Yankees!" A jolly crowd, they'd shoot off their mouths and slap one another on the back. Flushed and laughing heartily, one of their number would hold high his jar of moonshine, knock back a belt, and raise a frightfully off-key but hearty chorus of *Dixie*.

"C'mon in here, young sir." Meander gestured to Gates.

"We aim to feed the hungry," added Dame-Gracie, holding up a large mug.

Gates started up to the doorway when he glimpsed a black man angling up near Mary as they left out of the other end of Gordon's. He took her package to carry. Good-looking black buck, Gates thought, not an ounce of fat on his six-foot frame. Gates stepped inside the emporium's coolness, surprised at feeling himself no little jealous.

CHAPTER 4

"I'd sell my mother's cousin to an Irishman if that were only true." Mary heard the man's voice boom from the open shop window. The sign hanging from a high post on the grassy lawn read: S. Louvestre, Ship's Chandlery. "Wonder what price I could get?" he said with a hearty laugh that segued into a phlegmy cough.

The main store, popular to fishermen trolling the mighty Chesapeake, was a sizeable white-frame edifice with a wide-shingled roof and black shutters. It was situated midway among other commercial establishments, set along the plank boardwalk facing the beach, outlined by graceful weeping willows. A covered cobblestone walkway on the right connected this building to the voluminous, white-painted warehouse next door that, for decades, had serviced nautical needs, big and small. Mary could see wagons bustling in and out of the loading area as she neared the red-painted front door of the shop. She smiled at the sight of the bright brass door handle. Simeon had followed her advice to add these two style-enhancing features. Seagulls spread wide wings on air currents, soaring and dipping above. Scents of wisteria and wet humus wafted on briny air as Gosport's busy harbor did business. Mary's ears picked up the sound of the waves lapping and sucking at the pier's aged pilings, contrasting sharply with the booming and bustling activities just down the beach at the naval base where craftsmen worked feverishly to refurbish the monster ship, CSS *Virginia*.

She took the three broad steps up to the wide porch of the shop where a bunch of rowdy, old mariners lounged in cane-backed chairs around tables made from upturned tool kegs. Some sat back, chewing tobacco and spitting, watching passersby hurry along. Others, in high spirits, shared friendly insults over a rousing card game of faro. They called hellos as Mary negotiated around them and entered the store to get a better earful of the usual banter between Simeon and his old friend, Norfolk's favorite barrister, Leland Keener Burrell.

"Leland," Simeon said hoarsely, "as I recall, you never liked your mother's cousin much anyway." He hacked into wracking coughs.

"Lord, son!" Leland said. "You look like we gon' lose you to the consumption. Sound worse than a dyin' engine. Had me a horse once sounded like you do."

Simeon wiped his nose with a large handkerchief and regarded his friend inquiringly.

"Shot him between the eyes. Took us both out of our misery." He made a bellows laugh, truly enjoying this pastime.

"You ol' sinner, you," Simeon said.

"Yeah, but bless God, even leaning on the back side of fifty with all of my slothful ways, I'm still here to gloat about it." He spoke like a revivalist preacher, his voice pitching and rolling and brimming with imperative.

He was a slender man with a pumpkin head surrounded by white hair that shot out like Johnson grass, which he made no attempt to control. Everyone's friend and a teller of fascinating courtroom stories, Leland was fifth in a proud line of Virginia Burrell lawyers, now senior in the small but prestigious partnership of Burrell and Burrell.

He had been tilted back against the wall in a straight chair with his hands clasped behind his head, but abruptly set it right when Mary entered the door. Eyes glistening with merriment, he greeted her effusively. "Miss Mary. One singular sable beauty, undeniably. A true gentlewoman of the South, in yet another gorgeous kufi. That's what you call it, isn't it?"

"Yes," Mary said.

"I want you to know, it is my honor and privilege to say I have you as my acquaintance."

"That and a dollar still won't buy you a new suit of clothes," Simeon said. "She's way too busy preparing for the show."

"Can't blame a man for tryin'," Leland said. "It's gonna be some whang-dang-do around here that night—that is, if Simeon lives."

"He'll live," Mary said, chuckling.

"He babbles. It's a birth defect," Simeon said. He was speaking from behind a long oak-topped counter across the wide central lobby. "Poor soul can't help himself."

Mary shook her head, looking at Simeon's pale complexion. "You look worn out. Hungry?" She held up her basket to him.

"No," Simeon replied.

"I could stand a l'il somethin'," said a stumpy, gray-bearded customer.

"Herman, where do you think you are?" Leland said. "Coolie's?"

Herman guffawed. "Ain't got enough whiskey in here, ladies, to fill my lap, music or dancin', and ain't no platters of fried catfish comin' out the kitchen with Miss Coolie's special sauce on top. Nope, this sho' ain't her place."

Simeon held out Herman's change and he slid it into his pants pocket. With purchase in hand, he ambled to the door. The brass bell tinkled overhead as he swung it open to leave. He tipped his battered hat. "Miss Mary, don't let these rascals corrupt you."

Laughter ringed around.

Usually reserved, Simeon Louvestre was more gregarious when mischief-maker Leland was around. A robust man, Simeon was a head taller than his lawyer friend at nearly six feet three or four, with abundant silver hair worn combed high and back, giving him a leonine appearance. An attractive brown mole to the left of his upper lip was provocative under a straight, aristocratic nose, and direct lively blue eyes set in bronzed skin seamed from years at sea. More formal than his friend, he looked crisp in tan trousers, pale-blue shirt, muted red silk tie, and navy blue suit coat. Despite his years, his was still the arresting face of an aristocrat, even today when he was obviously low sick with something.

Mary hefted her basket from one hand to the other and inhaled the pleasant smell of leather goods, oiled woods, hemp, and tobacco smoke. Dismissing her apprehension about Gates, at least for the moment, she scooted past Leland, who puffed billows from a fat stogie as he spoke casually.

"It is my sage opinion that people are going to seed, eating too much and doing too little work. We're becoming a Commonwealth of piglets sucking on the tits of our own predilections."

"Now where did that come from?" Simeon rested his head in his hands. His lips were dry and his throat raw. "I swear, if nobody talks to you, you'll talk to yourself."

"No better companion," Leland acknowledged drolly.

"You two never quit. I'll have food on the table in a minute," Mary said as she skirted another counter and made a short jog to the right. She glanced left down the hallway to a smaller showroom with specialty items of shoes and clothing—some of it made by herself. She pushed through a door into the inner office where two sets of wide-paned windows opened to the water.

Behind her she heard Simeon clear his throat and say, "Join me for dinner, Leland. That cook of mine, Roguey, is a sourpuss and a rough customer, but what she puts on the table ..."

Leland chuckled. "Like she's practicing for Jesus?"

"Don't you know," Simeon said, coughing again.

"You've twisted my arm."

"Mary?" Simeon called to her. "Do we have enough food for Piglet Leland?"

She poked her head back around the door. "I've got a whole kitchen in this basket." She turned to leave.

"Mary?" Simeon said.

She swiveled back around.

"Thanks," he said. "I know you're looking in on me because of Tesh-Lucianne. Tell her I'm okay and I won't ruin her party by taking to bed or dying on her."

"Whew!" Mary said, "She'll be glad to know that."

Simeon's inner office was a disaster. Mary sighed as she looked around. To a compulsively neat person like herself, this was a horror. A massive ornately-carved mahogany desk and curved-back chair dominated the room's center, covered with unruly stacks of papers. Behind the desk, choked bookcases containing a menagerie of nautical resources overflowed to the floor. Two comfortable chairs, bracketed by narrow tables, faced each other in front of the impressive brick fireplace with marble-topped mantel crowded with miscellanea.

Mary decided the easiest place to set up was at a window table that looked out onto the side courtyard shaded by cedars. A wide drafting table and high stool squeezed into a far corner where light flickered over a stately painting depicting life on the sea. From the outer quarters, she heard Leland taking up his pace again.

"Don't get me wrong, Old Salt, but things handled poorly, all that we hold dear of our cherished South will turn to cow manure. Frankly, I'm worried." His tone was serious. "War's not really in the Southern craw, or at least, not yet. Oh, we make sounds like we're gearing up for it. But I ask you, what do most of our boys know about real fighting? Barroom brawling maybe, after getting tanked up on ale. That's not war. That's recreation. You start talking about tangling with the well-trained, well-armed Northern forces, and that's more than a notion."

Mary cleared and dusted the table and began setting it, keeping an attentive ear to the outer conversation.

"Take Jitter Conroy for instance, poor sod," Leland went on. "Or, poor us. Imagine him leading a regiment. The man's a plodder just like a lot of them coming in from the fields and outhouses."

"Jitter works in his daddy's mill, doesn't he?" Simeon said. "Leads a line of workers."

"Jitter couldn't lead a mule in a circle," Leland said. "Don't get me wrong. He's a decent enough soul but, at bottom, he's a miller who fancies himself a jewelry maker. He also happens to be the idealistic son of a successful businessman here in Norfolk who used his political pull to get the boy assigned to this dubious military contingent now parading around town. Jitter'll give you the shirt off his back if you need it. He's a good friend and a Christian, but see it rightly. Leadership and original thought just weren't bred into him."

"He's alright," Simeon said hoarsely.

"Jitter is not driven to protect the South or even his father's business. You want to know the real reason he wants a spiffy uniform and fresh haircut?"

"No," Simeon said.

"Coolie Parts," Leland stated.

Mary perked up.

"What?"

"The fool's heart done jackknifed over good sense. He's so in love with that girl he can't see for lookin'. We talkin' Coolie, the daughter Gie Atkins won't admit to," Leland said. "That's the corniest thing ever was. Who in the whole Commonwealth don't know the—beg pardon—tangled bona fides of that one. We just ain't stupid enough to say anything 'cause Gie's so rich she can buy and sell us all." He chuckled flatly. "I understand. Love means different things to different people. To Jitter Conroy, it means Coolie Parts. And I have to say, she's as sublime a beauty as a promise of God." He sighed loudly. "I can see why Jitter's out at her place soon's the sun rises over the waters. Sad thing is, she won't give him the time of day."

"I know her," Simeon said. "Feisty."

"She's live ordnance all right. Fact is, she won't give any man—black, white, red, or any combination thereof—the dust off her shoes. But I do hear," Leland whispered, "she'd cut a man's throat and leave him gushing red blood over Mary in there."

Simeon guffawed. "You're a terrible liar."

Mary detected a long pause.

"That's outrageous!" Simeon protested. "You're not saying ...?"

"One thing I've learned in all my years of lawyering," Leland said, "is you never know who people are or what they'll do, even those under your own roof."

"I do know Mary," Simeon stated with some heat.

"Suit your own head. I'm entirely sympathetic. But as far as soldiers on the premises, we're clean out of our heads to depend on what we've got now. We've got Jitter and lots of other Jitters out there with guns, no less, purporting to defend our sovereign land, our Southern way of life, and our peace of mind."

"It's not like you, Leland, to take such a dim view of things."

"Listen, ailing son. I'm a Burrell and a barrister and it falls as my lot to examine the facts realistically."

"Things'll get better," Simeon said in a weak voice.

"Present state of things're scarin' the daylights out of me. These old eyes of mine ain't perfect anymore but I need to see something soon I can better subscribe to, y'know?"

The front doorbell sounded again and Mary turned back to her task.

Setting up the sumptuous meal, she bumped into a drafting table and sent large papers cascading to the floor. As she picked them up, she noticed the beautiful renderings of a large ship.

Thinking to herself, she wished she had someone as able as this to construct patterns for her. Idly, her mind reflected on the sketch of a dress she'd been working on: a light wool so smooth in texture as to appear like silk, navy blue with pleated front. On each shoulder was a line of buttons made from persimmon seeds painted gold and strung together in the intricate Peyote stitch. An easy-banded waist with a simple front fall of pleated skirt—tiny, precise stitches lining every pleat—created a crisp look. Descending closures down the bodice and waist-side were small, gold-plated bee-bees, handcrafted by her friend, Bear, the blacksmith. To the stand-up bandeau collar she planned to inset the tiniest of ferns she had collected from the woods, also painted gold to repeat at the ends of each sleeve. For a bit of whimsy, she meant to have a gold sash drop from the right side. This she would make from delicate, long horsehairs treated with umber and ash, dashed with gold sprinkles to create drama, flow, and elegance in movement. She couldn't wait to finish the rest of the details. Wrenching herself free of such thoughts, she glanced back at the ship's papers.

Mary was dimly aware that Simeon's job as adjunct naval engineer required that he help refurbish the old wooden ship, the *Merrimac*, into a new fighting monster the American waters had never known. It was to be an ironclad called the CSS *Virginia* whose mission would be to power down the Hampton Roads waterway to take on the Northern ironclad, the *Monitor*, break the Northern Blockade that had been strangling the South, and then tear into that arrogant Northern capital, Washington. Mary had heard it said that this showdown would finally teach President Lincoln the lesson he so richly deserved.

For no apparent reason, Mary's mind slipped into recalling that lately, every time she asked to hire a new helper to counteract her enormous workload, the Louvestres nixed the idea. Tesh-Lucianne told her money problems were not the issue. Rather, they were diverting money into a fund for Simeon's political ambitions. Still, it was unlike them to deny her, especially since so much was riding on this fashion show for them too. They'd derive a lot from its success. As Mary pondered, she stacked the papers and put them back in place. She smiled, looking over the dinner table. She was pleased. It was fit for a king—two kings.

She went to the outer door to announce dinner and saw Anders Tremaine, adjunct Navy man, going over some material with Simeon at the counter. He was a free black brought in by the Navy as a special mechanic on the *Virginia*, working under the direction of Simeon.

Anders glanced up at her approach and smiled.

Mary smiled back.

"Your new design work on this ship is good," Anders continued saying. "If we could just get the engine and others parts going as well, we'd be in business."

"You're the mechanical engineer."

"Machinist," Anders corrected. "But I thank you for the more august title."

"How'd you come to know so much about fixing things?" Leland asked.

"My father," Anders said. "I should say, the father who adopted me. He's a temperamental Frenchman who's nothing but excellent at his craft. Now he's the mechanical engineer. He's been teaching me since I was little."

Mary cleared her throat to get their attention.

"Mary!" Anders said brightly. "Excuse my manners." White teeth showed in his handsome face.

"In a minute," Simeon said.

"Tesh-Lucianne sent me over to make sure Simeon ate so he can feel better. Right now, he's got the look of a broken cattail in the water about to fall over."

Anders wagged a finger. "I won't let it be said I plotted a part in that." He collected his things. Good humor animated his features. "I'm cutting out."

"Okay, okay," Simeon said, "I'll eat. Ready Leland?"

"Durn tootin."

"I'll walk Mary back to the ferry," Anders said hopefully.

Simeon pivoted around and, unusual for him, spoke sharply. "She knows the way. We've got a deadline. I want you back on the ship tending to your duties."

The room fell quiet.

Simeon headed out, but stopped and turned back. "Sick men can be stupid sometimes. I apologize." He left, followed by Leland.

"I'll get my things," Mary said.

As Anders opened the door, Mary said quietly, "Just so it won't come as a surprise out there, I have to tell you a man has been following me."

Anders stared at her.

"It's the new deputy."

"Elam Gates," Anders said. "He's been making a nuisance of himself everywhere and he's only been in town a short time." He smiled ruefully. "If I were to wrack my brain really hard, I couldn't come up with one somebody I know who likes him."

"I don't like him. And I want him to leave me alone."

"I'll have a talk with him."

"No, Anders. That won't make good sense."

"Come on. Let's get you to the ferry. And if you see him along the way, let me know."

"Why?"

"Oh," Anders said blithely, "I just want to acquaint him with what could amount to fish food around here."

"Stop it." She looked worriedly at him. "I don't even want to think things like that, for him or for you."

"Hmm," Anders replied, looking concerned.

"C'mon," Mary said, heading out. "Gates is a bully. He likes to start a good rumpus, but he scuttles away from a bad finish."

Anders regarded her a moment. "You've got a lot of sides to you. Lady. Fashion Designer. Friend. And, uh, fighting cock, not one to trifle with."

"That'd be my guess," Mary said.

They laughed as Mary's mind rolled back to the time when she became not one to be trifled with.

———

She was young. That day was warm and pleasant and she stood on the docks with two of her friends, skipping pebbles across the gentle chop. The white man's voice over her shoulder had been harsh as he spoke to her. Before she caught herself, she snapped back sharply. The man's face loomed so clear in her mind she could still see the stubble on his chin and smell his rank odor. A brickhouse of a man, maybe ten years older than she, his face had an unkempt look despite a morning shave. His eyes glowed with pure hate and his bottom lip twisted cruelly. His partner said, "You gonna let a nigger wench get away with back-talking you like that?"

In a flash, the younger man grabbed Mary, lifted her off the weathered pier of the small harbor, and threw her legs over one of the handrails. Mary's panicked friends screamed and ran. "Don't you move, gal!" he ordered as her body dangled over the dock. When he yanked off a long piece of the rail wood, she put her hands over her eyes and squeezed them tight. The last she remembered was the howl that tore from her throat as his crude weapon bludgeoned her left knee.

Days later, Mary regained consciousness. Visiting friends told her the other girls had come back and dragged her home, where her father, Tug, went nearly crazy at the sight of his daughter. Mary's mother died when the girl was very young. So Tug sent for Miss Effie, a medicine woman, who doctored on her day and night. Mary would never walk right again, Miss Effie said, but at least she was alive.

For weeks she lay sick in bed more from reliving the torment of what had happened to her than the agonizing stabs of torture to her leg. To that, she generously added feelings of helplessness and pity for herself. Then Tug arrived home early one morning from making a large haul of fish for the farm, yanked the covers off her, and ordered her to get up. It was time to be well, he said. "No daughter of mine gon' be a cripple!"

Just after the sun eased out of the crimson-gold bed of horizon and began its job of soaking up curdles of fog, Tug took Mary into the thick woods where he presented her with a polished-oak walking stick he'd used all his skills to carve. Into its round head, he'd etched the letter "M." "Not a cane," he insisted, "a walkin' stick 'cause that's what you gon' do." Mary squatted on a flat stone, complaining to the ground. Tug put his hands under her arms and lifted her up. They stared at each other for long minutes, saying nothing. Then he stretched out to her the tapered column of walking stick again. She could hear the calls of nameless birds and feel a light wind blowing out of the trees. She gulped and inhaled the sharp, clean smell of pine. Slowly and painfully, she reached out and grabbed hold of the walking stick.

The moon shined full and directly overhead when Tug carried her home on his back. The next day, after breakfast, was like the first—Mary and Tug in the woodland clearing. At first, she leaned on the walking stick awkwardly, scooting and galumphing about, falling and crying and swearing. She crawled on hands and knees, panting for breath, begging her father to have mercy on her ruined knee. Tug's reply was to lift her up and hand her back the walking stick. Then one morning, to her surprise, Tug had set her paces. He had taken stones and placed them at various distances—this one on a nearby tree stump, that one on a distant rock, another in the crook of a tree over yonder, another on a log far off set in the azure riffles of a burbling stream. Using her walking stick, Mary was to traverse them as fast as she could while he counted from one to twenty-five. Each day she was to break her previous pace time.

When Mary accomplished that, Tug began teaching her to fight with her walking stick. Her initial problem was balance. With his own wooden cudgel, he attacked nonetheless. She was astonished at how quickly and deftly she fought back. He made a small circle of stones and told her she could not cross them. Shrieking like a banshee, he came at her again and again and again, moving about the inner circle. One blow caught her in the ribs, another exploded off her shoulder, tearing her blouse loose and sending a spurt of blood—red and shimmery—into the sunlight. His next blow was aimed toward her neck when she countered and threw him off. After another while, she tired of defending herself. Now she was on the attack. She wheeled around with a warrior's scream and came at Tug like lightning spiking out of the sky and shattering to submissiveness anything in its path. Next day, Tug tied her legs to two small trees, leaving her arms free with the walking stick in hand. His blows toward her crisscrossed the moisture-laden air of the forest, ruffling the wind with his force. Mary fought off blow after blow and even sent a few his way. The following days, Tug pinned Mary to the ground with her arms tied over her head. The only way she could fight back was with her legs. She cried out in pain when his blow connected with her inner thigh, tearing open an angry gash.

Lightning cracked among the trees and thunder cannonaded along the metal-gray sky. Heavy rain began to pelt the ground and pock all in its path. Winds shifted in spirals, gullying water in surges. With a fierce, primal howl,

Tug launched out of the woods' darkness, arms high, wood staff in hand, ready to strike when Mary fell to the wet mess of ground and caught him up in a pincer hold. Both legs held him so tightly, he screamed bloody murder. After the rain let up, the smell of jasmine filled the air and clutches of low-hanging clouds gave way to extraordinary streaks of sunlight. That was when Mary and Tug wearily trudged home arm in arm.

CHAPTER 5

The gleaming glass knobs on Mary's salon double doors turned and in charged a thin, diminutive woman. Tesh-Lucianne was Mary's owner and benefactor. The older woman who bowled in, trailing scents of lavender and lemon, was her best friend. A straw hat with astonishing bright flowers attached to its wide brim led her way.

"Christ! This heat! And it's still early!" boomed the voice of Eugenia Atkins, affectionately known as Gie, as she threw up her hand in greeting. Yanking off her headwear, she sent it sailing in the direction of a side table where it ricocheted off the corner and slid under it. She abruptly halted, eyes wide and blinking behind silver-framed spectacles in the room's bright light.

"Tesh-Lucianne, will you kindly make yourself useful for a change." Gie screwed up her face, groping out with her hands. "You see me standin' here, blind as a bat in glare. Help me to a chair. Got these new glasses and I could just as well've bought another chamber pot for all the good they're doin' me."

"As I live and breathe," Tesh-Lucianne said, huffing over to her friend. "Now you're an invalid!"

Mary chuckled as Gie played a deadpan, sag-and-shuffle walk to one of the two large sofas in the center of the room and flopped down, landing bumpily, hands splaying out. "Don't dump me for gawdsakes! I'm not a sack of potatoes," she complained.

"You're no kin to somethin' that substantial," Tesh-Lucianne said, observing her.

A mass of curly brown hair well on its way to being gray and parted in the middle stood out from Gie's head like a halo. Cutting quite a figure, she sported a linen dress that suited her perfectly, bestowing upon her the image wealth wore with definite aplomb. Made on the order of a coat, it was closed in front by three crocheted buttons, and its wide three-quarter-length sleeves were comfortable for this time of year. Her outfit was peacock blue, with touches of amber hand-embroidered in an abstract pattern stitched into the sleeves, skirt, and back, and echoed in the simple jewelry she donned at her neck and ears.

"Aren't you polished up like the Lord's spittoon this mornin." Tesh-Lucianne said.

"Mary's to blame," Gie said. "She dyed this dress fabric herself and put me in such a fashion sensation that I'm too happy to strut the streets of Norfolk and make every wag wish they were me."

They laughed.

"Proud to see you, Miss Gie," Mary said. "What you know good?"

"Every day above ground is more than I can ask for."

Though small in stature, Gie had a strong presence that commanded a room. Mary had always liked her, liked her irreverence, liked that if she had to put a word on her it would be "bold," so bold that, even when Gie left a room, her essence still lingered.

"Lodestar," Gie addressed the ancient colored manservant who followed her, his twiggy, brown arms laden with packages, "dump that stuff over there somewhere. Doesn't really matter where in this mess." She cocked a look at Mary. "Not your mess, dear. I dare say you never make a mess. It's Tesh-Lucianne. She has a talent for it."

"You're tetched," Tesh-Lucianne cried out as she watched Gie let her tatting-string purse clatter to the floor and flick off her smart tan pumps with the shiny blue toes. She held up her feet, wiggling her toes, looking forlorn. "I just don't know what's going to become of me. I'm deterioratin'. Feet spent, done swole up the size of tree trunks. Eyes gone. A blind man can make out better'n me. And I'm ugly still, though I must say, I carry it off a little better than my daddy."

Mary's soft chuckle followed her to a deeper corner of the vast room, near the flagstone fireplace and marble mantel, where she sat down at her Queen Anne desk to make some notes.

"Don't get all down in the mouth about somethin' you don't have the slightest control over," Tesh-Lucianne said.

Gie removed her spectacles and peered at Mary, fixing her with subdued mirth. She drawled thickly, "My best friend in this whole wide world and you see the sympathy she musters for me." She rested her head back on the couch, speaking in tragic stage-theatrical tones. "Does it take nearly dying to get some refreshments around this dratted hen house?"

"What do you want, old woman?" Tesh-Lucianne asked.

"I could start with a tall, cold drink. And make sure your hand lingers liberally over it adding a smooth import from one of those heavy cut-glass decanters over there at the bar."

"Sot!" said Tesh-Lucianne.

"Bully," Gie said.

"You two have got to learn to play well together," Mary teased, admonishing them.

Mary knew Gie was putting on as usual but she did believe there was something to her eyesight comments. Over the last five years, Gie worried aloud about fading colors, blurred images, and a sense that her eyes were simply shutting down. She was not the type to dwell on it in conversation like other customers. They'd want to talk it to death, whatever the ailment—headache, hangnail, sore bunion, digestive disturbances. Not Gie. Yet Mary did notice of late that the woman's eyes had become almost opalescent.

"Here," Tesh-Lucianne said, handing Gie a cup and saucer. "You drop anything on Mary's new oriental rug and I can't think how she'll assist your earthly transition into the Great Void."

Gie sniffed her cocktail and smiled. She turned hound dog eyes to Tesh-Lucianne, "This'll do for starters. Bless you, my child."

Eugenia Atkins was not beautiful. She hooted when people charitably referred to her as interesting-looking. She accounted for herself by explaining she favored her maternal grandmother who, even in dim candlelight, could have passed for a tree root. Hers was a formidable, almost intimidating face with a strong jawline, a wide, jutting nose, and intelligent eyes set a bit off-kilter under craggy brows the size of small caterpillars.

Reputed to be tough as tenpenny nails, she wore her authority openly, naturally, and fairly. She was successful in her own right, apart from Daddy Enoch's thriving barrel business. As a child, she'd learned to make essential oils from her mother, who she was able to train with for two years before the fever took her. Gie made up batches in her barn and started out selling them using catchy newspaper ads, first local, then broadening out. That proved hugely effective and now, many years later, the name "Lady Gie" was synonymous with the finest perfumes, sold mostly to the exclusionary world of wealth and privilege. "No woman will pass up a lovely fragrance; no suitor of that woman can afford to," Gie often said.

Gie sipped her toddy and uttered, "Umm." She sighed. "Mary, you're a saint for allowin' me and my cohort here to commandeer part of your fine quarters for our little soldiers' project." She sipped again. "Now that I'm here to actually get this party into gear, we'll get organized and send those boys a little something they need before the war closes." She shot a look at Tesh-Lucianne.

"How you talk," snorted Tesh-Lucianne.

Stacked in the back of the shop were tall piles of shirts, pants, socks, and scarves donated to help clothe soldiers.

Gie grinned at Mary, her small white teeth gleaming, eyes sparking devilishness.

"You and your help group are the Norfolk Redeemers?" Mary said.

"My brilliant idea," Gie said, running her hand lazily through her hair. "Every cause needs snappy names and labels to rally around, don't you think?" She leaned out, snatched a nearby ottoman with her feet and parked them up on it. "Does that name sound too, oh I don't know, self-serving?"

Mary appeared thoughtful for a moment. Amused, she answered, "Yes."

"Then it's perfect," Gie said. "I think we should go with something really pompous. I think that one does it. It'll give folks in this town more to gossip about." The look on her face said that idea appealed to her enormously.

Gie dug into her purse and extracted a small gold snuff case elaborately inlaid on the top with mother of pearl. She pinched the tobacco with thumb and forefinger and started to pack it between her lower lip and gum. She caught Tesh-Lucianne's look of disapproval, stopped, and snorted, "What?"

"Put that away for a minute," Tesh-Lucianne said, joining her on the couch and placing a plate of Roguey's goodies on the low table in front of them.

"I declare," said Gie, "I thought it might take an act of God to get some food around here! Tantalizing me with all those marvelous fragrances. You know how keen my nose is. Yet you withhold when you could have the graciousness to give. My grievance is ..."

"Shut up, Gie."

Mary, back at work at her drawing table, relished listening to the constant carping and good humor between these two. She knew there was no point in trying to referee. Long experience told her Gie was going to pick, pick, pick, and Tesh-Lucianne was going to complain, complain, complain—neither meaning a bit of it most of the time.

They'd grown up together on adjacent working farms when their parents were still trying to establish part of the Commonwealth. The flourishing, self-sufficient Louvestre tobacco holdings made up enough in property and stock to nearly be called a plantation, and their eminence in shipbuilding and imports mostly supported it all. Not far away, years of poor output from the hard-packed, clay parcel owned by Gie's parents, sapped the energy for farming out of her dad by the time he was thirty. That's when he decided to develop his skill and trade in barrels. He constructed such high-quality watertight vessels that soon distillers and winemakers from all over were placing so many orders, he and his staff were sprinting to keep them in supply. Then Enoch and Daddy A.B., Tesh-Lucianne's father, went into a side enterprise together that made them wealthier still, importing fine spirits and liquors from Europe and the islands.

When the love of Enoch's life, his wife, Eula, died just two months shy of her twenty-seventh birthday, Gie, their only child, was just twelve years old. A short time later, he was sent to prison for taking a pair of pliers to the tongue of a whiny distributor who wailed out an unsatisfactory explanation for why his last order for copper rims was short. The court said Enoch needed to be taught a lesson about the consequences of his unbridled anger. He was to serve five years and Gie was placed with a severe couple in town, who had four prissy daughters, all appalled by the likes of her.

"You ornery, girl!" birdlike Judge Curtis had chirped after young Gie appeared before him for running away for the fourth time. "Ornery! Ornery!" he declared, shaking a gnarled finger at her. "Just flat-out ornery! Go on out there in the cold, cruel world then, missy. See just how easy it is to bring yourself up all by your lonesome." Gie had whirled on her heel, thrown the judge a backward glance, and strode out the courtroom door on her way back to the farm her parents had given her, with a mission to create a new destiny.

"Mary, we've got the hall secured," Gie said, smacking her lips over her drink, little finger up, "though we're going to have to clean the riffraff out of there a few days in advance of the show so we can air the place out and get it decorated. Some sort of travelin' theater company is in there now doin' a play, though I do wonder about them."

"I heard that every time they perform in different towns, a bank gets robbed," Tesh-Lucianne said informatively. "Last Sunday afternoon, they recited parts of a play by Shakespeare and I poked my head in for a minute. The lead is handsome as all get-out. He's tall and blond, with captivating, velvety brown eyes. He spoke in a deep voice that put me in mind of a sound rolling under water." She swept the air with her hand, then clutched it to her breast. "Most of what he was saying didn't make a lot of sense to me. Folks back then talked a little strange, didn't they? But this man sounded real good, sayin' what he was sayin', you know. He was fascinatin'. Not that the rest of them weren't. There were four others." She placed a finger to her bottom lip, considering. "But if they were all on stage, how do you suppose they pulled off robberies? Clever bunch if they did. Hmm. I guess that says, if we know what's good for us, we won't bring any of them home for Sunday dinner. Right?"

Gie and Mary exchanged pained glances. "Thank you for not telling us all you know," Gie said.

Tesh-Lucianne snapped her lips closed with her fingers and sat back.

"I'll continue," Gie said.

"Nothin' stoppin' you," Tesh-Lucianne retorted.

"You've got the world at your feet, you know that?" Gie said to Mary. "Folks've had a sense that something's in the air, something bringing a change. I'm not talking about the war. I'm talking about Mary Louvestre. You've been doing that inch by inch over the years. People listen to what you have to say regarding fashion. You've got them excited about your unique styles, colors of your own making never worn before, even getting women to give up their corsets to sport your designs. Not only have you made people look good, you've made them feel good about themselves. That's a gift. So now you're rich, maybe not in dollars and coins, but in a greater currency—resource. Now things are primed for whatever is this 'hugeness' you're ready to launch. Do you feel it?"

"Mary knows she's important," Tesh-Lucianne said. "What is this speech about, silly girl?"

Gie turned to her friend and patted her hand, no foolishness in her voice now. "I'm talking about something really important. I'm talking about readiness, potentiality, the kind of irrepressible life force so strong that when a flower bud is supposed to open, you have to almost kill it to keep that from happening." She snapped her fingers. "Mary is somebody now and going to be greater." She turned back to the designer. "There's a saying that applies to you, Mary: 'Nothing is more powerful than a thing whose time has fully come.'"

Mary said nothing for a while as she reflected. "I know I've got a lot in me that wants to come out. But special as all that?"

"Yes," Gie said, "flat-out. Acknowledge it. Work with it. I believe when you've been given a gift like you have, it's your responsibility to control it and guide it. Doing less is an abomination. Look, you're a pathfinder, emerging at a time when the common ground under everything is shifting. Change charges the air; it has no judgment about good or bad. In these days, who knows what's going to happen next in advances for this or that. We just know something will. And you're in place to set a new standard in fashion."

Mary shook her head in wonder. "I'm a child of slaves—a fisherman and a cook."

"And the talented daughter of the Louvestres of Norfolk. Protégé of the world," said Tesh-Lucianne proudly.

"I'm here to tell you," Gie said, "that time does not care about your station in life, what color you are, or what you decide to do with it. Day'll become night and back again no matter what. Take courage, Genius, and get on with what you've been put here to do or stop wasting my time."

"You've never known me to be shy about anything," Mary said. "I do feel like I'm on the verge of something significant." Her hands made circles as she struggled for the right words to convey her thoughts. "For the first time, I admit I feel uncertain as to which direction to take."

"Then stand," Gie said. "I'm not a religious person but I can remember my father quoting passages from the Bible about preparing yourself in the best way you know how. Then just stand. God will give you the answer. He'll take it from there."

Mary's face blossomed in the golden light. "Why is it that sometimes you need people to tell you what you already know?"

"See what happens, Gie, when you drink a lot and lush-up before supper," Tesh-Lucianne said. "You get all preachy and squiggly."

"Squiggly?"

"Yes. A right-headed person can't get the clear of nothin' you say. Squiggly. That's you."

Gie laughed and winked at Mary. "Then squiggly is the word for the day." She held up her cup and moaned, looking sorrowfully at Tesh-Lucianne.

"I'm not doin' it," Tesh-Lucianne said.

"Okay, Chief," Gie said to Mary, "my ladies—a host of them—are all excited, raring to go, awaiting your instructions, including me."

"Decorating the hall will be the easy part," Mary said. "On the front doors I want two panels posted. They're to simulate the entrance to a regal palace, creating the mood right away. As people enter, they'll walk down a runner I've woven in the same theme as on the sides of the aisle chairs. It will carry along the front wall and up three stairs to the platform where the showing will be held. The backdrop for this will be simple. The fabric I've been working on for months will drop down from the ceiling. It's a gold filament embedded with majestic monarch butterflies I caught, treated, and arranged in a pattern. When light hits it, colors burst out on the order of a rainbow gone mad. I think you'll like it."

"Anything you do, everything you do—I like," Gie said.

"You let us know when, where, what, and we'll be there."

Mary nodded. "Give me another day or so and I should have everything worked out."

Gie lifted her cup in mock salute, sipped, then looked sadly inside. "How come I can see to the very bottom of this vessel? Could it be there's no more liquid inside?" She inclined an expectant face toward Tesh-Lucianne.

"Woman, you've gone 'round the bend! You're already blind in one eye and can't see out the other. Can't half-walk on swole feet. Talkin' out your head, makin' grand speeches and it's not even three o'clock in the afternoon. I couldn't sell your ol' carcass for two cents. So, you want another drink, you know where it is."

Gie glanced at Mary. "We ignore her." She struggled up from the couch, feeling air with outstretched hands. She made it to the two-tiered caddy of crystal decanters and, fingering them like a blind man might, she added, "What's this world coming to?" as she poured liberally from the one labeled "bourbon."

"I wouldn't hazard a guess," Tesh-Lucianne said huffily, and crossed her arms across her chest.

Gie returned to the sofa and held up an index finger, pausing for dramatic effect. "I have some news."

Tesh-Lucianne brightened, clapping hands, exclaiming, "Oh, goody!" She settled back and gestured that her lips were sealed. She crossed her legs at the ankles and waited.

"Thurston Stone got shot this morning."

Gie was gratified at their concerted gasp. She had their rapt attention.

"What I heard was Deputy Gates walked up to him at his wagon, pulled out his pistol, and blew a hole the size of a quarter," she indicated with index finger and thumb, "into his arm right then and there."

"What for?" Tesh-Lucianne said.

"Nobody knows for sure. He was muttering something about how Thurston had to pay for his sins."

"Don't you just hate it when people get on their high horse about sin, like they've got the inside track on it," Tesh-Lucianne said with rising heat. "Who are they to talk? Most people don't have a clue what sin is much less how to get it back right. We're not God. The dickens how we fathom that great mystery! You know, we could correct a whole lot of what folks want to call up as sins if we'd spend six months tendin' to our own daggone business and six months leavin' other folks' business well enough alone." She took a breath. "Is Thurston dead?"

"No," Gie said, eyeing her talkative friend. "They took him to Doc Sloan's. Then Bear carried him back to Stonehaven in the buggy. Nobody's heard anything since."

Tesh-Lucianne said, "Is Gates a relative of Sheriff Bridges or somethin'?"

"Or something," Gie said. "Lots of stories been circulating about him. One particularly gruesome tale is that he's the son of a poor white trash cousin on Clara-Jean's side from a nowhere wide spot in the road out Kentucky way. Nobody knew who blew out of town faster in the dead of night, Gates or his shadow with the law fast behind him. He made it to Norfolk and into Miss Clara-Jean's keeping where she hid him out until his trouble settled down. Gates supposedly tied his father down, stuffed lye soap chunks down his throat, and hammered pine knots up the old man's butt. Other stories are going around too."

"Why'd he do it?" Tesh-Lucianne said.

"Well, seems the old drunk got plastered again, flew into another violent rage, and whaled a cast iron skillet up side his wife's head. Beat it to mush right there on the pine deal table where she'd set out the flatware for evening supper."

Tesh-Lucianne pressed disturbed fingers to her lips. "That's gruesome."

Gie took another sip of her beverage, cleared her throat, and continued. "Say Gates came home with a rabbit and a squirrel he'd killed for supper only to find his mother lying on the floor in a widening pool of blood. He said, 'She was the onliest somebody I ever meant anything to.' His father, stinking in soiled long johns, sat slouched over the kitchen table drinking hooch from a Mason jar and singing bawdy songs. Gates asked him what happened and the old man had nerve to say, 'That heifer sassed me. So I beat her head in with that there cast iron skillet.' To let Clara-Jean tell it, a purely righteous anger rose up in Gates."

"Then he killed his own father?" Tesh-Lucianne whispered, screwing up her face.

"Supposedly, Gates lit into him. Brought him down though the old man was twice his size. Tied him up and proceeded to choke him 'til he turned blue. That's when Gates calmly walked to the lean-to by the house and got hammer and nails. He came back and crucified the poor devil over the hearth above where his mother had been cooking stew. But Gates wasn't through. Then he poured the old drunk's liquor all over him and set him afire."

"Jesus paid it all," Tesh-Lucianne declared.

"All that may or may not be true. There are other Gates stories. Some, I believe, he put on the wire himself to add to his mystery. Gets a kick out of it, I'm sure."

Mary wondered about a man who started a future by wrecking the past like that, assuming the story was true, of course.

"I sure wouldn't wish anything bad on anybody," Tesh-Lucianne said, "but I've been worried a long time about Thurston Stone. He's got a few admirers; others hate him with a passion. Not much in the middle."

"I know," Gie said, sipping her drink. "Stonehaven's got a lot of folk mad or jealous or both."

"I hear it's quite a place," Mary said.

"I've seen it firsthand," Gie said, "and it's special alright; a huge farm. Negroes not only run it, but live better than most whites. You know the rumors about it."

"It's a free black community, isn't it?" Tesh-Lucianne asked.

"Well, Thurston freed his own slaves years ago and many of them still live there. I suppose some runaways have managed to get in too. To stay there, he has two rules." She ticked them off on her fingers. "Number one, no lying. He believes if you'll lie, you'll cheat, and if you'll cheat, you'll steal. Number two, take care of one another. Some Negroes own property out there. They all share the work and the harvests. Others who only get a good wage have been known to pool their money and buy freedom for another, then bring them back to Stonehaven. As a result, Thurston's got some of the best of everything out there—carpenters, a blacksmith, wheelwrights, cobblers, farmers, weavers, domestic workers galore. Arnetta Bost, a white woman and a teacher from New York, arrived on the train a couple of weeks ago. At Thurston's invitation to educate the folks at Stonehaven, she's joined them too. And what with Thurston's gift for inventing all kinds of things, the place is not only completely self-sufficient, it's downright astounding."

"How many would you say live there?" Mary wondered.

"A hundred, maybe a hundred and fifty, including children. Thurston invited me to lunch once and showed me around. Truly, I couldn't believe my eyes." She described the scene: "After driving through a long tunnel of trees, the place opened up into a luscious womb of beauty. There's a two-story, brick dormitory with wings and porches sprawled in the center of maybe three hundred and fifty acres of waterfront property, set off by spreading oaks on either side. Cobblestone walkways fan out from it like spokes of a wheel to other buildings. Set back under enormous magnolias and weeping willows swaying in the breeze are neat brickhouses trimmed in white where well-dressed Negroes sit on their porches or work in the flower beds in their yards and children laugh and pump high on slat-bottom swings roped into the trees."

Gie went on to tell that in the distance coloreds worked abundant fields of crops. A couple of barns sat on a rolling knoll, surrounded by a sizeable herd of horses—some stood in shafts of sun eating from the greenest grass, others drank from a babbling creek as tree leaves overhead fluttered like thousands of brilliant butterflies in the dappled light. There were stables and red-brick wells with cups hanging off the side.

Gie waved her arm absently as she remembered, "Bear—I don't know what you'd call him—not manservant, because Thurston wouldn't hear of that. 'Assistant' might be the word. Anyway, he's the blacksmith and the one in charge of everything. He also put in a sanitation system, something we don't even have in the city."

"Progressive," Mary said.

"Heaven," suggested Tesh-Lucianne.

"Radical would be the word I'd use," Gie said, "given the times and all."

"Thankfully, there's never been any trouble out there as far as I know," Tesh-Lucianne said. "Live and let live, I always say."

"That's a touching sentiment, but naïve," Gie said. "Many folks've been itchin' for a reason to burn that place down. They believe if they can't have it, Negroes certainly shouldn't. Its very existence is kindling to a torch."

CHAPTER 6

Coolie's place was a rambling, two-story, clapboard house with a red, slanted roof and wrap-around balcony tucked in among large cypress and weeping willow trees in a section of sweet riverbank off the worn path where fishermen sold their day's catch. The restaurant connecting to it was reached by a flagstone walkway. It was a Coolie add-on featuring pan-fried bass, trout, any other fish in season, heaping helpings of shrimp, and fresh clams and oysters bursting out of their shells and onto a plate.

One day, she had taken up a brush and joined a few happily misted patrons who agreed to work for drinks and a meal. They painted the entire house such a pristine white, Coolie suspected that God would have been stunned to see it when He said: "Let there be light." Yet there it was. Later additions were sassy green plantation shutters made by an itinerant carpenter she'd bested in a late-night game of poker. She offered he could further work off his debt by constructing a large sign for her place out of interlocked slates of white oak onto which he burnt the name in bold letters: Travelers Rest. The inn hosted many a wayward over the twenty years since she first opened her doors. Travelers Rest offered good liquor, good food, clean lodgings, and, in a building out back, entertainment of the horizontal kind if a man had need of it—at no judgment and reasonable prices.

Flower beds around the main building sported azaleas, hibiscus, and jasmine that charged the air fragrant under the azure sky. Ducks could be heard out on the water just out of sight or forming V-shapes in flight. Knots of men and women of all descriptions lazed about in chairs or along the balcony on the porch. Others sprawled on the grassy front lawn or eddied along the lengths of paths to the outbuildings in the rear. Accommodations were such that a man could unload his dirty laundry back there and, according to the weather, throw down a few drinks, squeeze the weasel, dig into some good catfish while playing a hand of cards, and soon be packing clean, freshly-ironed togs with the fresh smell of lavender as he went his merry way.

Laughter spiked the air as Mary approached. Strangers eyed her, interested, no doubt, in the lovely, well-dressed colored woman, but others who knew her greeted her with hearty, "Miss Mary" and "How do?"

She stepped inside the cool of the main building, her open palm letting the tall double doors close softly behind her. She looked into the large room on the right of the wide hallway and could barely distinguish the figures through the tobacco smoke drifting up through the pale-yellow light emanating from wall lamps above the flocked red and tan wallpaper. Though she couldn't make them out, she could hear the music of the piano and guitar players blending in a lively tune.

Sharp smells of whiskey, spittoons, soap, greasy food, shrimp boiling out back, unwashed bodies, and the sea assaulted her nostrils. Many patrons, consisting largely of white men with a sprinkling of blacks, sat on wooden stools, feet propped up on the brass footrest underneath, along the curved mahogany bar that took up most of the room. Above the shelves of sparkling clean glasses on the wall behind the bar was the distinctive sign for Coolie's place. It was two tall, bright blue intersecting crosses Coolie took proud credit for designing. Just out from there filling the rest of the room were small round tables where other patrons congregated, swigged hard shots in short glasses, beer in thick mugs, or tankards of wine.

These travelers filtered in from road and riverboat to rest a spell, or sometimes, after they were all liquored up, to roll up their sleeves to let off steam in a good tooth-jarring fight.

They were an odd mix of humanity searching for a niche without condemnation for the way they had to make a living. Most hosted knives, guns, and razors in pockets or tied to their ankles, and in a by-your-leave could sever a man loose from fellowship and into a six-foot hole in the ground. Others, decent sorts too, just wanted to sit at the bar, nurse a stiff drink, and enjoy the revelry. Coolie took them all in and took care of them, though she never laid down for the most lustful soul. For the most part, she did good by them and they did good by her in return; they liked and respected her enormously. They were what they were, by God. That was her feeling. And, at bottom, the simple fact was, they were hers.

From somewhere toward the back of the room, Mary could hear Coolie's smoky voice chiding, "Jitter Conroy, get your new soldierin' boot off'n my table! Act like you got some home trainin'!"

Jitter, thirties, with curly hair the color of sun blaze framing milk-white skin and angular features, jerked as if hit by lightning, and thunked his boat-sized shoe to the floor. He groaned aloud and stared down forlornly, cursing the hard leather of the new footwear. The boots were a dubious gift from his parents, proud of his enlistment. The odious footwear was made from unyielding black leather called kip, structured calf-high. Built to last and formed without regard to the shape of left or right foot, they tortured the feet until continual wearings finally broke them in. Jitter's had the added value of being shiny black.

"I'm 'bout hobbled," he complained to anyone who'd listen.

"But you look good," Coolie said, plopping a shot of whiskey on the table in front of him. "To ease the pain."

Jitter smiled as he swung a fawning expression toward her. Pools of red brightened his cheeks as he flushed, mooning for all to see that his heart belonged to this stouthearted inn owner, whether she wanted it or not.

"Home trainin'? How's he gon' to do that?" piped a high-female voice from a corner table. "Wasn't the boy raised by coyotes or bears or something like that?"

"Get it right, Verona, if you're going to tell it at all," said a gaunt man with a pockmarked face, sitting at a window table playing solitaire. "It was bats. Now we really got to worry about protecting the honor of our great Commonwealth of Virginia since the man's only fit to fight at night."

Laughter erupted around and the man threw up a friendly hand. It was Elroy Pickett, the man who had spoken. Pickett was a saddle maker out of Georgia who wore his thick gray hair pomaded and combed back from a hatchet face the shade of paste. He was thin as a sapling and odd-shaped, with one shoulder hiked higher than the other from a twist in his back.

"The good news is, ain't nobody died from new shoes, son," Elroy said.

Jitter's look was poignant. "That's 'cause they ain't never had to wear these."

"Careful, y'all! A man with hurtin' feet bear watchin'," Coolie teased, returning to her work at a small alcove near the bar.

A stronger drift of banjo music rose as Mary inched further inside, taking in the many different characters. Raffish-looking, beefy Hoyt Wesson sat facing her at the table, wearing a brand new military uniform of the Virginia Sharpshooters, with beer mug at his eager lips. Verona Banks and Sweets Filpot, admitted po' whites who also did double-duty as loyal employees of Coolie's, perched at his side. Both were peppy sorts but worked like dogs for Travelers Rest, their home. Mess with Coolie and they turned raging beasts. Meddlers were hasty to remember the ladies meant what they said: "I'll claw your eyes out!"

The bartender, Theron Latt— a powerfully built black man—exuded a palpable sense of danger. Dour-faced, he was reputed to hold his patrons responsible for their behavior. And he could do it too. Many a transgressor had met the ground, head first, like he'd been poleaxed. And if they mouthed off to him, the trusty club he kept under the counter cut that discussion short. Today, wearing a white apron around his waist, he leaned casually behind the bar drying glasses with a white cloth. His alert eyes were hooded, but they watched everything protectively, especially Coolie.

Coolie let out a great belly laugh when she caught sight of Mary. She chased off, arms outstretched to greet her. "Shut my mouth! If you ain't a sight for sore eyes!" Her face beamed. "What you doin' out here? You ain't got enough work to do?"

"Let me put this package down," Mary said, smiling and turning to a vacant table near the bar, where she placed it. She sank into one of the wooden curved-back chairs. "Open it."

Coolie stared at her like a delighted schoolgirl. "For me?"

"Open it," Mary waved a hand at her.

Coolie's eyes were mischievous and in another moment she had torn the brown paper wrapping off to reveal a gorgeous black dress. "Lawd I say!" she exclaimed, holding it up to herself. "You done done it this time!"

"It's got the three big pockets you wanted and is black as tar like you wanted. I had to add some touches to brighten it though. Why, as young and pretty as you are, you want to wear dark colors, I can't figure."

Coolie stopped prancing around and stared warmly at Mary for a long moment. "Y'all really think I'm pretty?"

Amusement danced within the depths of Mary's cat-green eyes. "Brat! Your sign says 'Travelers Rest.' What do I have to do to get some of it, dance on the table?" she asked.

The young woman barked a laugh. "Ha! I'd sell tickets to that, and wear my new black dress!"

Coolie Parts, even in her thirties, was, hands down in everyone's estimation, the most fetching black woman in Norfolk. She had flowing, copal-colored hair that spilled in curls well below her shoulders and framed a heart-shaped face the color of rich cream. Her large hazel eyes, always seductive, twinkled with mirth, and her Cupid's bow lips stayed upturned, especially when Mary was around. Blessed with the best of the white Atkins' line, she had a curvaceous body, full bosom, and firm hips. Her black father, killed shortly after her birth, endowed her with that amazing patina seen in beautiful paintings rendered by the masters.

Her mother was Gie Atkins, whose substantial fortune and good works to the town bought Coolie large pardon regarding her bloodline, though mother and daughter had been estranged forever. Her mother's father, Enoch, insisted that either Gie keep the baby and move out of state—putting considerable distance between her and the family—or give up her child to be reared by kindly Aunt Viney, the black nursemaid who doted on the baby girl from birth. Without a fight, Gie had packed up infant and foster mother, bought them the house Coolie had since turned into a barrooming house-restaurant, and didn't look back.

Coolie never spoke of her parents, and no one else who had a lick of sense did in her hearing, but folks decided that because she felt she didn't belong to anyone, she took in every stray who needed belonging and made them family.

Coolie pulled the skirt of her navy dress between her legs and squatted in a creaky wooden chair across from Mary, her hands dangling between her knees. She called over her shoulder to the bartender. "Theron, bring Miss Mary some refreshment, will you? It's hot as the dickens in here."

"Coolie, how many ladies have you seen sitting like that?" There was no reproach in Mary's tone.

Coolie turned a crooked smile, sat upright, straightened her dress primly, and crossed her feet at the ankles. White socks showed above heavy brown work shoes well scuffed at the toe.

In a moment, Theron slid a sweating glass of dark beverage onto a napkin in front of Mary. "Thank you, I think," she said, glancing up at him, then down at the drink. "What is it?"

"Somethin' to pick up yo' step." His dark eyes smiled and he sauntered back to his station, taut muscles rippling.

"If you ain't laid out with quarters in your eyes by mornin'," Coolie said, "the drink was good, that's all." Fun lit up her face and tone.

Coolie clasped Mary's hand. She was plainly happy to see her. "I feel swelled up and silly when I'm 'roun you. Like I can't half-think straight."

Mary's face held a certain magic. "Maybe you're coming down with something. Needing a tonic?"

"You!" Coolie bit her bottom lip and glowed.

Mary inhaled deeply. Smells of fresh sawdust on the floor filled her nostrils. "Look here," she said seriously, "What's this about you and the new sheriff's deputy? Heard you two had words."

"Gates. Humph! He come in here actin' a fool. I don't play that."

"Coolie," Mary said with caution in her tone.

"I ain't studyin' him," Coolie said in her attractive rough-hewn drawl.

Mary peered around the room as if simply taking in the day. Her eyes fixed momentarily on the large blue crosses over the bar. She turned. Through the wide front windows, she could see through cypress trees down the bank a passing riverboat far out on the water. "You better study on him and mind your P's and Q's."

"Why?" said Coolie, looking down, fiddling with her fingertips.

Mary scooted her chair closer to the young woman and let her eyes roam about the room. The other occupants were involved in animated conversations, mindless of her and Coolie except for Jitter Conroy who kept staring in their direction. Mary sensed his expression was more curious than jealous right now. She glanced at him and he dragged his eyes away, then she leaned forward in her chair and placed her arms on the table, lacing her fingers together.

"What're you going to do about that one?" Mary asked, nodding toward Jitter.

"Oh, he don't mean no harm." Coolie swatted air. "He dream 'bout me, I know it. But when it come right down to it, he gon' find him a blonde Miss Jane. I ain't stupid."

Coolie absently started to scratch her butt, caught herself, and glanced over at Mary. "Why you askin' about Jitter?"

Mary stared at Coolie until the younger woman got her meaning, blinked, and looked away. "That's why," Mary said. "I worry about you."

"For cryin' out loud!"

"Coolie," Mary said patiently. She took another sip of her drink. "Listen to me. Do what you want about Jitter, but I believe Gates is dangerous. He's slipping around watching. I have a bad feeling."

Coolie's eyes widened. Her fists clenched. "Hey! He done done somethin' to you?"

"Not so's you can make a point of it," she said.

Coolie looked at her suspiciously, made a negative grunt. She let silence hang, then, appearing to consider the matter, glanced at the lively crowd around them. "Folk lie somethin' terrible but word is Gates was sittin' around drinkin', lyin', and showin' off for his partners outside The Pig Trough Bar when he spied

Bear 'cross from them at Gordon's. Mindin' his own business, Bear was loadin' up the wagon long with Mr. Thurston. Gates called him over, challengin' him to arm-wrestle. Bear didn't want to. Gates commenced to insult Bear, makin' him mad. Gates took offense 'cause he'd been braggin' about how he could take down even the strongest in the parish, could lay down any comers, anytime, anywhere. The man's a fool but can't nobody stop him from bein' who he is. He been grudgin' after Bear. Leastwise that's out there."

"What happened last night?" Mary insisted. "Roguey told me you had some trouble with Gates."

Coolie flapped her hand. "That ol' blowhard come out here with his attitude on his shoulders. By the time I got through readin' his character, he stood here red in the face breathin' like a bellows. I told him to get on out before I left him fartin' out his nose."

"Coolie!"

Coolie grinned. She surveyed some newcomers. A motley crew of white and black, poor and gold-cufflinked, surrounded the bar. They laughed louder the more the bartender poured brown liquid into their shot glasses.

Mary glanced again at the large trademark. "That's very creative. It looks good up there, the way you've got it lighted and all."

Coolie looked over at it. "Come to me in a dream. Sure rankled Sheriff Bridges though. He say, 'Gal, I got a bone to pick with you 'bout usin' them crosses. Don't seem right. Then you went and painted 'em blue too.'" She laughed. "I fixed him right up. I give him some of my catfish, collards, potato cakes, and corn bread with sweet tea I laced with something to improve his mood. The old hand dragged off back to town belching, ready for a sleep, aimin' to get Miss Clara-Jean my recipe for bourbon bread puddin'."

Coolie ran counter to Sheriff Bridges too many times to count. Running afoul of the law seemed to be a favorite pastime. Sheriff Bridges threatened, "I'm gonna haul your pretty little ass to prison, you keep on. Niggers and whites ain't need to be mixin' in with one 'nother." But he never did, run her in, that is. His appetite for her good food got the best of him. Coolie never changed nor did her clientele.

"Folks sniffin' 'roun, think they know what's goin' on around here, but they got no idea."

Mary regarded her a minute. "Meaning?"

Coolie waved a dismissive hand. "Meanin' nothin'."

Mary sipped her drink, then said, "Coolie, your mother was in the salon yesterday. Her eyesight is getting pretty bad."

Coolie huffed. "I should care?"

Mary stared at the young woman. "It's not my business but—"

Devereaux's voice startled them both. "Mademoiselle?"

"Man, you's as sharp as a tack, clean as a pot of greens," Coolie admired.

He gave her an acknowledging smile. "I am handsome too, yes? And so are you." He bowed.

"Hey, say your name." Coolie cackled. She glanced at Mary. "I love it when he says his name." To Devereaux she said, "Go 'head. Say your name."

"I am Devereaux Rainier Leodegrance de Perouse."

Coolie whooped and slapped her thigh. "Again."

"Devereaux Rainier Leodegrance de Perouse."

She mimicked him. "Devereaux Rain-Leo-de-Grass-Per-oo." She shook her head. "How come you ain't never used Louvestre? You belong to that family."

Devereaux whirled. "Never! I am never that. Perouse is who I am, son of Michael Blafford Perouse and Marie-Louise, of the New Orleans Perouse."

"Hey, I'm sorry," Coolie said. "Didn't know you were so touchy on the subject."

"You are forgiven, mademoiselle," Devereaux said. "Louvestre would be a slave name to me. I am Perouse. Any man call me out of my name will not live to see tomorrow."

Coolie glanced at Mary. "You got time for me to get this man a drink? I believe he needs some coolin' off."

Devereaux looked gentled by her. "It is over, my friend. Not to worry."

Mary stood. "Coolie, you're impossible. I've got to go. I have to do an errand for Tesh-Lucianne." She turned to leave, then spun back. "Coolie, I have no idea what you're involved in, but please, please be careful."

The younger woman grinned at her. "Watch my wicked ways." Jitter Conroy's eyes followed her, seeing Mary out.

As the carriage was driving away, Mary looked out the window to see Coolie staring at her, smiling, with her hands theatrically pressed over her heart.

"You're a pisspot, Coolie Parts," Mary shouted and ducked her head back inside. Hearing the younger woman's laughter as they proceeded down the lane, Mary chuckled.

"Long as I'm yours," Coolie called back.

Mary looked out and saw Coolie grinning. "You don't have right good sense!" she hollered to Coolie. To her conscientious driver she pleaded, "Help me take care of this wild child, Devereaux Rainier Leodegrance de Perouse!"

CHAPTER 7

The Louvestre parlor was one of Tesh-Lucianne's favorite rooms. When she and Simeon had designed the house, she knew she wanted this room to be especially comfortable. In it was a cozy seating arrangement of couches and chairs with side tables and lamps that gaily chased away shadows. Here she had put one of her favorite possessions—her six-foot grand piano. Given to her as a recent birthday gift from her father, it was a remarkable work of art: hand-carved rosewood case, intricate veneer scrollwork, tapered legs, music rack, and scalloped ivory keys. She had placed it near the bank of wide windows that looked out onto the blooming gardens and ancient oaks, sycamores, and magnolias, and played it as often as she could.

Tesh-Lucianne sat demurely, looking with eager eyes at the two young lawyers, new in town, who had come to see Simeon, now playing host at the bar. While pouring bourbon into crystal glasses for the men and a small sherry for Tesh-Lucianne, he asked, "So, what can I do for you gentlemen?"

"My name is Sampson Longhouse Withers." Withers, maybe twenty-five, was round. Though fashionably dressed, twin rolls of fat stretched his white shirt. He had a boyish face, splashed with freckles over his small nose and anxious eyes the color of wet moss. He sported a thin mustache and his quick smile blossomed a wholesomeness over all his features.

He introduced the angular man who sat tall on the sofa to his left. "This is my partner, Obadiah Lumley. We have recently established a law firm in town, Lumley & Withers." He coughed into his pudgy fist, cleared his throat, and continued. "As a way of getting to know folks, meet people around, we've learned you are a man of parts in town to help make that happen. We wanted to make your acquaintance and see if we might elicit your assistance in getting connected, so to speak, with the right people."

His heavy accent put him out of Mississippi most likely, Tesh-Lucianne guessed. He was obsequious in manner and her initial assessment of him was of a gentle soul.

Simeon passed around drinks and settled in a chair opposite them next to Tesh-Lucianne, who kept her sherry in hand and focused on the visitors.

"But I don't know you," Simeon said politely.

Withers spoke in tones of fine breeding, not a feature missed by Simeon. "We're not without letters of introduction," he said. "I believe, once reading them over, you'll find your sponsorship of us might be of some mutual benefit."

Where Withers could be described as fleshy, Lumley, late thirtyish, was so thin as to appear chiseled on a lathe. His hair was black and sheened; his delicate, rather beak-nosed face had the color of sun-bleached bones. Hollow cheeks bore deep skin distresses, and curved lines along his profile were parentheses to astute, narrowly placed eyes the color of fish scales. Disconcertingly, his lips were as attractive as a hatchet blade. On his chin was a trim goatee, and the tiny wrinkles around his mouth were clearly not laugh lines. He gave no impression of one who did a lot of that.

With each one speaking in turn, they explained that, while new to Norfolk, they represented a wide range of people throughout the Commonwealth, some who just might be helpful in Simeon's bid for high office in the Confederacy's new government.

Simeon cradled his drink, cupping the glass bowl like he would a woman's breast. He swirled it, appreciated the aroma, sipped, and looked over the rim at them, waiting.

Withers went on to add that, while Simeon had many influential friends, any rising political figure must promote his advantages. He and Lumley were prepared to offer him the support of a group of loyal men, patriotic adventurers willing to put their lives on the line to provide goods most people, including the wealthy, were indisposed of at present due to the Northern Blockade.

"Like what?" Tesh-Lucianne asked.

Lumley smiled ingratiatingly. "Why, nearly whatever your heart might desire."

"Fabrics?" she asked.

"Alas, no," Withers said. "That is one of the few commodities unavailable to us at this time. Nearly anything else, though. So, let us say, you wanted to make a gift to friends of coffee—real coffee—fine cigars, the best bourbon, salt, and other luxuries. In fairly short order, we can see to it that you have them."

"How?" Simeon said.

Withers fairly hummed through his fat lips. "We're not at liberty to discuss that. But, we can assure you prompt service. No questions asked."

"Such benefits, in these difficult days, could go far to cultivate even more earnest patronage among your old friends and new ones, wouldn't you say?" Lumley offered.

"Go on," Simeon said.

"In addition," Lumley said, finishing his drink, "we are aware of how important it might be to your image as a true son of the South to take a strong stand on containing the nigras. They seem to be getting a bit rambunctious with all this airy talk of freedom." He snickered. "Many whites around town are growing increasingly concerned, for a variety of reasons, about things getting out of hand."

"How so?" Tesh-Lucianne asked.

"What happened at Harper's Ferry is never far from memory," Lumley said. "One whose platform contains certain assurances to fight against that kind of rebellion and restore a greater sense of security to our Southern way of life would go far, I'd imagine."

"That doesn't answer the question," Simeon said.

"That's why I have aligned myself with Sheriff Claude Bridges and his new deputy, Elam Gates, who have sworn to bring into play determined practices for justice and social reform. What could be better? How timely for you," Lumley said.

Withers leaned forward, his belly pushing against his belt. "Mr. Louvestre, we can help you make some decisive statements about just where you stand on the issue of … race relations."

"We can marshal men to that service. The nigras will tremble at their core with fear, thereby squelching any attempts to, uh, get out of their places again. You get my drift?" Lumley said.

"I believe so," Simeon said. "But you see, gentlemen, I've never held to such practices. It goes against my grain."

"You might want to rethink that position, if I may be so presumptuous," Lumley said. "These days, our people—white people—want someone in office who will soothe their worried brows. If you do not want to do that, I would ask why do you want a powerful political placement? Fun and games? Just what do you stand for?"

Flint animated Simeon's face before he mastered his emotions and tidied his features. He fetched a sigh, then spoke calmly, "Peace. I stand for peace."

"But at what price?" Lumley's tone was cold, his eyes accusatory.

Silence fell over the room.

Simeon was hit with a fit of coughing. "Sorry."

"Are you alright?" Withers asked.

Simeon ignored the pleasantry. "Let me ask you a question, two questions actually. Why have you come to Norfolk? And why now?"

Withers glanced at Lumley. "I'll take this one."

Lumley nodded.

"The enemy is at our gates. Lincoln has already targeted us. Northerners are closing off our goods and services. Military preparations are gearing up. Norfolk is key. We have to make a stand, right here, right now. We, as faithful defenders of our way of life, must come together lending all of our strengths to the task. The Bible tells us that a house divided against itself cannot stand. So, we unite together and *stand*. This is not the time for vacillation. This is not the time for equivocation." He turned fully to Simeon. His speech, sparked by emotion, was nonetheless slow and deliberate.

"I am convinced there are times in our lives when, because of who we are and what we are, we are inexorably drawn into being the best of who we are.

We have to accept that there is a greater plan for us, a plan God has ordained that could bring about—does bring about—a greater good."

Palms open, Lumley interjected, "Influential Southerners see something substantial in you. They are wooing you to come and serve. People like you, admire you, look up to you, Mr. Louvestre. More importantly, people trust you. As we have learned, people know you to be a reliable man, responsible, honorable, and because of your farseeing eye, one who gives clear guidance. Again and again, people say, 'Simeon Louvestre, in good times and bad, is a friend who's there.' I would say to you, be there now. Our people need you. Your destiny could be great. I would appeal to you to accept it, embrace it. This could be the greatest calling of your life. We can and will help, if you'll let us."

Tesh-Lucianne saw that Simeon was captivated.

Simeon took a gulp of his drink. His mind trolled for reasons to disagree, but found none. His eyes traveled from Withers to Lumley and back again. "Your argument is provocative, sir," his voice, though hoarse, was resonant. "Let me think about this and we'll talk again soon."

They rose.

Simeon said, "My dear wife here is hosting a birthday party for me in a few days. Many people of the type you want to meet will be there. I ...," he looked to Tesh-Lucianne, who smiled, "would like to extend to you gentlemen an invitation to join us."

Withers nodded. Lumley grinned and extended his hand to shake. "We'd be honored."

When the men left, Tesh-Lucianne said, "I'm not sure about them."

"Neither am I. But they could prove to be very helpful," Simeon said, pouring himself another drink. "Political office requires that you have to deal with all sorts of people. Can you stand by my side?"

Tesh-Lucianne, surprised, took her first sip of sherry. "I am your wife. I cast my lot with you years ago. Would you ever doubt where I'd be, no matter what?"

Simeon smiled at her. "This is bigger than both of us. It's bigger than the views we have long held regarding a lot of issues. These are changing times and we have to change with them."

Tesh-Lucianne suddenly shuddered. She looked out the window. "I wonder what this will all mean."

"All good things, my dear," Simeon said, holding his glass up in toast.

"Put that down," Tesh-Lucianne said. "You've had enough and you're still not well. I'm taking you to bed right now."

"Hmm," Simeon said playfully. "A most interesting proposition."

CHAPTER 8

Mary was at her worktable sketching another dress when Mrs. Nollie Thatchcock arrived for her fitting.

"Lord! This heat is sure a misery," Mrs. Thatchcock said as she waddled into the room. "Most nearly takes the fun out of trying on new dresses."

"Let me get you a fan," Mary said, picking up an ornate folding fan made of sandalwood. "Every time it's waved, its sweet perfume fills the air."

"Whew! I've got to catch my breath," Mrs. Thatchcock said as she sank into a parlor chair that protested her weight. She took the fan in her beefy hand and fluttered it like a bird on a wing. Hers was a hag's face complete with a large ochre mole to the right of her upper lip. She wore a hectic attitude even before complaining another word.

Mrs. Thatchcock was nigh fifty, built like an egg, with mottled skin the texture of fried pork rinds. Her thin, gray hair was pulled tight and high on her head, secured in place by a plethora of wooden combs. Rheumy, gray eyes rooted around in search of any morsel of information to set rumor in motion. Her jowly face twisted up in a perpetual bad mood—her forehead knitted, wet lips pursed, her pug nose turned up like she'd whiffed a dead cat on the line. She was boorish and critical, with a wicked tongue.

Mary recoiled from this woman but tried her best to hide it. Word was she got poor, weak Edgar Thatchcock to marry her on the promise that her money would finance his many harebrained business schemes—not one of which ever materialized—and sustain the pathetic, hole-in-the-wall place where he hawked small religious statues carved and garishly painted by beleaguered Indians who didn't fathom the difference between Jesus and Jones, the shoemaker, or care. She was an angry woman, angry about being fat and a slave to her appetites and for lacking the kind of husband who could elevate her to the status of doyenne or chatelaine that would allow her to fully wield her capricious temper over others.

It also was no secret that she drank like she had a hollow leg. From the odor emanating from her today, Mary had no doubt the woman and whiskey were on solid terms. Mary catered to her as a client, but privately she had the same regard for the woman as that of a feral pig.

"Elmerel Hanks is telling it that Clara-Jean Bridges is near-about frothin' at the mouth you didn't ask her to model in your fashion show. You put that Coolie Parts in it but not her?"

Mary said nothing. She kept her hands busy, eager to get this fitting over with.

"Coolie Parts in a show for white people! A nigra?"

Mary tensed.

Mrs. Thatchcock waved the fan vigorously at the beads of perspiration lining her forehead. "I know. I know. She's Gie Atkins'... what would you call her? Not 'bastard daughter'—her consortin' with a slave at that. Issue, I'd guess you could say of her. I can see you wantin' to put Coolie in the show to curry favor from Gie since she's so rich and all. But the very idea of it just makes me taste chicken gall."

Mary had to steel herself not to lash out. "Coolie's a beautiful woman. Why would you object?"

Mrs. Thatchcock scoffed. "Even Gie doesn't want anything to do with her, you know that's the truth. A blight on the Atkins family, I tell you."

"Coolie?" Mary said.

"Of course, Coolie. Then she has the nerve to take that grand home place Gie gave her and turn it into a bar and whorehouse! Scandalous!" Undone by emotion, she gave over to chuffing when she breathed. Moisture shined her upper lip.

This woman's mind was a ferret, always digging up dirt, making detritus when she couldn't find it, Mary thought. She thrived on it. Mary's innards boiled.

"Be a dear, chile, and fetch me a couple of those big cinnamon rolls off the buffet table over there. Your cook, Roguey, is such a prize. There's about nothin' she makes I don't absolutely love!"

Even flies have to watch out for you, Mary thought as she went for the delicacies.

Mary didn't believe she owed this sow an explanation, but as she opened the big armoire filled with finished dresses, she spoke patiently, "I deliberately chose fifteen women and five men from our local community of different ages, sizes, builds, and personalities to best show off my new line."

Little finger in the air, Mrs. Thatchcock smacked her lips over another bite of sweet roll and, speaking with her mouth full, said, "If you want my opinion ..."

Mary didn't.

"... you best not get on Clara-Jean's bad side. She's going to be in production of her new play at the town hall. Wrote it herself. Said she was thinking to ask you to make the costumes. So I wouldn't cut off my nose to spite my face, if I were you."

"Why do you think Mrs. Bridges would want to be in my fashion show?"

Mrs. Thatchcock licked her fingers. "If you don't know that this is the event of the season, you've got no more brains than a brood hen. The fact that she's not in it, even as an usher, tells her she's not important enough for you. It's a pure d-insult. The mother of the sheriff? You're either ornery or ignorant."

"Something you'd know a lot about," Mary stage-whispered to herself.

"What?"

"That's something to consider, Mrs. Thatchcock." Mary bit the inside of her jaw.

Mrs. Thatchcock belched loudly and looked self-satisfied for the effort. "Say, you wouldn't have anything to drink back there, would you? Just to give me a leg up on the day?"

Mary's cool green eyes regarded her. "Of course. What would be your pleasure?"

"Well," Mrs. Thatchcock said, licking her lips and tarrying over the thought as if she needed a moment to think about it, "a mint julep would be nice, but on second thought," she brightened with certain conclusion, "whiskey, straight."

Mary smiled mischievously and made a suggestion. "Mrs. Thatchcock, you wouldn't believe this, but just yesterday a client brought me some moonshine. Said to be so pure angels sing at the sight, and strong enough to melt chest hairs off a black bear. You think that might do the trick for you?"

Mrs. Thatchcock placed a hand over her chest and fairly swooned. "I ... I ... think it might. I can give it a try."

Mary poured a liberal tumbler of the lightning water and handed it to the woman, who threw back a big swig, coughed, and swigged again. Eyes glistening, she said, "I'll pray for you, Mary. You've blessed me this day." She smiled, her tiny, brown-stained teeth showing.

Mary turned away in disgust and hummed from a hymn, "and the burdens of my heart rolled away." She busied herself for a bit, giving time for the liquor to do its work. She hoped it might redeem Mrs. Thatchcock's nicer disposition. But, in a few minutes, the woman was in rare form again.

"I'm sorry about your father," she said.

Mary whirled around. "Tug? What about my father?"

Mrs. Thatchcock took another sip of the drink that dizzied good sense, going straight to her head. Beginning to slur her words, she continued, "My first cousin, Nancy Bledsoe, you don't know her. She lives not too far from Sam Hodges's farm, where you're from."

"No, I'm from the Clairoux Plantation, owned by Daddy A.B."

Mrs. Thatchcock went on as if uninterrupted by the facts. "Well, the poor man really fell on hard times. Lost everything. His wife, Jenny, left him too. Went back to her people in Kentucky. Shame," she intoned sadly without meaning it. "For a while there, folks thought he'd got his gamblin' demon under control. But his good friend Wire Sims got off the riverboat, came to visit him, and they went off on a weekend excursion doing the most sinful things." She paused over the deliciousness of those possible events. "Finally, when Hodges woke up in an alley, he had nothing; had gambled away everything he owned." She studied her glass. "Everything gone, including Tug. Sorry. Thought you knew."

Sure you did, Mary seethed.

Mrs. Thatchcock's eyebrows rose in disdain. She laughed pointlessly, then glanced around as if trying to see who else might be listening in the empty room. "Oooh! Eee!" she wailed. Her beady eyes looked hopeful. "Have I let a cat out of the bag?"

"How could I know?"

"Simeon was at the slave auction. Held it right up in town square at the Customs House. Could have bought 'im. Decided the old fisherman was too played out and he cost too much to boot." Mrs. Thatchcock was well into her cups now, her tone growing haughty.

Blood roared in Mary's ears from this news about her father.

"Don't y'all worry yourself though. Tug—that was his name? He got sold off to Gilbert Montague who owns a bunch of shrimp boats down Louisiana way." Her wily eyes darted to Mary's face for a reaction. "Say he suck every ounce o' life out of 'em. Work 'em hard on those boats. They don't have much longevity— what all they got to do if the alligators don't get 'em first. Wonder what it'd be like, big, sharp alligator teeth chompin' on your insides? But," she shrugged, "your father's old anyhow. He's done pretty well as slaves go, wouldn't you say?"

Mary felt blood congealing in her face and fought for composure.

"Nigras like you have your run too, y'know?" She giggled drunkenly. "Ain't meanin' to hurt your feelin's none." She waved her hand in the air and sang, "'Y'all come and y'all go. Y'all come and you go.'" She continued, "The truth shall make you free, leas' as free's you gon' get. You jes' ain't white."

Mary jerked.

Mrs. Thatchcock giggled again. "Listen to me. Blab. Blab. Blab." She flicked a pink tongue across her lower lip.

"How about another tad of this deli ... marvel ...," her tongue struggled, "really good beverage for your best client in Norfolk—no, Virginia. Hell, the whole damned worl'—Mrs. Amy Bell Courtmire Thatchcock!" She pointed to her chest.

"Don't you think you might want to hold off a minute," Mary offered tactfully.

Mrs. Thatchcock's eyes widened. Flushing red-faced, she was instantly belligerent. "Say! Who the Sam Hill do you think you are to tell me anything? I swear, all y'all nigras' the same." Her heavy-lidded eyes batted slowly, then she focused on Mary again. "Get the damn drink, girl!" She emphasized each word.

Mary's thoughts were brimstone, but she said placatingly, "Sorry, Mrs. Thatchcock. Right away."

She retrieved another glassful of the liquor and thrust it at her.

"Oh, goody!" Mrs. Thatchcock said, seizing it and recovering her good humor. "Ahh! That's a good girl, yessiree, a good girl." She pulled down another slug, held the liquid in her mouth a moment, swished it about, then swallowed in a gulp. Her following belch could have won prizes. "'Scuse me! Now, skedaddle over there somewhere, wherever you stash beautiful dresses, and fit me up with one to make me look like whashernamenow? Cinnerella."

Humpty Dumpty, Mary thought.

The salon doors swung open, and Tesh-Lucianne swept in. "Mary, I'm so excited." Then she stopped. "Mrs. Thatchcock. Hello. I didn't know you were here. So nice to see you."

"So nice to see me too," the woman slurred, agreeing.

Tesh-Lucianne glanced at Mary, who shrugged.

"Was telling your girl here, sorry about her father. But he's gone to a far, far better place."

Tesh-Lucianne threw a worried look at Mary. "I, uh, I was going to tell you. But I knew you would be disappointed and I didn't want that for you."

"That Simeon wouldn't buy my father?"

"Listen, it's the times. Everything's dear these days and the asking price for him was so high."

Mary stared at her in disbelief.

"See, you're upset. I knew this would do it. I ache for you, but Simeon felt it would be a bad investment, especially since we don't need a fisherman around here or any more drag on our budget."

Thunder pounded in Mary's ears. She stared at Tesh-Lucianne, a maelstrom of emotion beating her heart. Still she said nothing.

"Well," Tesh-Lucianne said, embarrassed. She ran her hand over her hair, smoothing it. She grinned real big. "I do seem to be at a loss for words about that. So I'll proceed to other more pleasant matters. What I came in here to tell you was I really, really, really need you to put all your creativity to work on helping me to make Simeon's birthday party just the absolute sensation—like nothing Norfolk society has ever seen." Discomfort dispensed with by other things, Tesh-Lucianne babbled on. "You just won't believe all the wonderful things happening for Simeon, for his political career. And, of course, now more than ever we want to show you off." She grew more enthusiastic, hooking her arm into Mary's and sauntering to the buffet. "We have to talk tablecloths, and settings, and flowers, servants."

"Tesh-Lucianne, I've never heard you use that word before." Mary was disturbed.

"Oh? Silly me. I'm just gettin' with the times." She picked up a sweet roll, took a bite, and rolled her eyes heavenward. "Is this just the best?! That Roguey! Anyway, I want you to make sure the girls are here to serve."

This was so unlike Tesh-Lucianne. Mary paused to wonder.

Both women pivoted about when Mrs. Thatchcock suddenly boomed, "Fee. Fie. Fo. Fum. I smell the breath of an Englishman. Hey diddle, diddle. Fiddle. Fiddle. The cheese stands alone. Poor cheese. Tha's me. Alone." She began to whimper. "All alone. Little Amy Bell, in her pretty pink dress and her shiny black patent leather slippers, sitting all alone." She hiccupped. "She is afraid. She calls out 'Mother. Father.' All alone. And the cat jumped over the moon. Or was it a cow?"

Mary thought hotly, it was a cow all right. Most definitely a cow.

After Mrs. Thatchcock had been troweled up from her supine position on the divan and packed into the carriage for Devereaux to see her home, Mary returned to the salon, reeling from what she had learned. She didn't know what to think and her feelings were slippery cobblestones.

Frantic knocks on the salon door jarred her. Gray shadows were lengthening around the room as she opened it to Roguey, whose full face appeared bloated with rage.

"What?" Mary said.

"It's Coolie," Roguey panted. Her expression was grave. "She bleedin."

"What's happened?" Mary's alarm mounted.

Roguey had run from the kitchen to the salon and was winded. Finally she wheezed out the answer. "Gates. Elam Gates."

Mary stared at her. "Where is she?"

"Kitchen," Roguey panted. "What we gon' do?"

Mary grabbed her walking stick and pushed past her without another word.

CHAPTER 9

Mary launched herself through the kitchen's swinging doors and saw Coolie, wild hair thrusting out in a shock, her head lying between arms splayed on the table. She rushed to the younger woman, and hugged her shoulders.

"Coolie?" Mary shook her a little.

Slowly, Coolie lifted her head and Mary bit her bottom lip. Anger flushed within her as she gazed at a face ruined by someone's fists.

"Not so pretty anymore, huh?" Coolie was not able to say the words clearly. Her bottom lip was cut to the cleft of her chin, her right eye swollen shut and purple.

Mary felt a cold knot in her chest as she pulled out the chair next to her. "Roguey, will you get me some water and a clean cloth?"

"Sho," the cook said, eyeing her, then Coolie as she moved away. "I could yank his teeth out, one by one."

As Mary's eyes examined Coolie, she could hear Roguey dipping the cool liquid from a bucket by the back table. In a moment, the thud of Roguey's work shoes told her she was bringing it back.

Mary thanked her and began to dab the soothing dampness to Coolie's face.

Coolie winced. "Ow!"

"Shh-hh," Mary said, holding her face in her hand and tilting it to the light while she searched for injuries.

Roguey returned with a crystal glass and inclined her head to Mary as if asking permission. Mary nodded and she handed it to Coolie.

"Umm. This is almost worth gettin' beat up for," Coolie said, trying to smile. She downed the liquid, squinting a little. "Don't worry, Miss M. I be fine."

Mary chose not to correct her grammar as she usually did. She also didn't smile at Coolie's antics performed to disguise her pain. This was serious, though she didn't believe Coolie would admit it as such. She dabbed the cloth around the younger woman's eyes, cheeks, chin, and around her mouth to remove dirt and blood crust. All the while, Mary was livid.

"Can you tell me what happened?"

Coolie made a small lopsided grin. "Sho', if I can have me another one of these."

"Don't get too comfortable with that, young rascal," Roguey chided.

Coolie shrugged and began to tell the story.

"Gates come swaggerin' into my place already red-faced, two sheets to the wind and mean. You could tell he was prospectin' for trouble. Everybody'd been laughin', havin' a good time. Then he parked hisself up at the bar. Two guys on either side of him slid away. 'Hey,' he bitched to Theron, 'I stink or somethin'?' He farted and laughed like he thought that was a fine joke. Nobody else did though. He say, 'I want me a shot of bourbon, none of that watered-down rotgut. Gimme the best in the house or I'll shut y'all down. I mean it too.'

"I was back in the kitchen fixin' to bring out a mess of collards and fried catfish, but I knowed the sound of his voice right away. I eased up around the corner and saw all he done." She caught Mary's grimace and corrected herself. "I seen all he done."

Mary let it go.

"Gates throwed back his drink and say all loud an' everythin', 'Sweets, get your raisin-face ol' broke-down, lazy-butt self up, and come on with me. Earn yo' keep, gal! Sweets say in her squeaky voice, 'You ain't got enough money or nothin' else for the likes of me.' He say, 'Whore! For two cents, I'd pour the contents of this here spittoon down your gullet and make you like it.' Well, you know Sweets, she can talk it good's the rest; she's hard to control."

Roguey chuckled at that one. "Lawd! Talk about the pot callin' the kettle black."

Mary waved a hand for her to go on.

"Sweets say, 'Yeah? You and who else?' That done it. Coolie made a derisive noise with her lips and regretted the pain.

She cradled her weary head on her hand. "I come out and set the food tray on the bar just about the time Gates stood up off the barstool. Sweets wasn't backin' down. She say she ain't goin' nowhere. Her job's to keep the books for Miss Coolie, not for pleasurin' the customers between the sheets. Folks commence to laughin'. Gates grinned too but not in a good way. He say he ain't hearin' that. He gon' lay his good money down and he want somethin' for it." A new tide of anger rose in Coolie and she sat up again. "I knowed he was spoilin' for somethin' and wasn't gon' stop 'til he got it. That's when I got 'twixt him and Sweets. I could look at her and tell she was scared, though she kept a-mouthin' off. I says to Gates, what you want don't cut no ice with me. You want to shake yo' thing, shake on 'roun back where they's plenty back there to he'p you do it right. Not that layin' with you would be any bed of roses." Coolie glanced from Mary to Roguey. "See, I was still tryin' to be nice."

Roguey clucked.

Coolie's pink tongue ran along her bottom lip, fretting the beginnings of a scab. Her breath rasped in the back of her throat and she cleared it. She began to ape Gates. "Gal," he say, "I'll kick your righteous behind into the next state. I wasn't even talkin' to you. Get on somewhere." She waved her hand and Mary saw the raw, red knuckles.

She took Coolie's hand and dabbed it with the wet cloth.

Coolie chuckled darkly. "Shucks! I got up in his face like this." She leaned within inches of Mary's, mugging, then leaned back. "I say, 'I'm obliged to tell you you ain't nothin'. You wrong an' you got to go through me.' His hand come up faster'n a whip. Blood went roarin' through my head and I went flyin' into the side of the bar. Sweets jumped on his back, whalin' his hard head with her fists, but he knocked her off so's she landed hard with her legs speared up like tongs. I wanted to help her but I was on my hands and knees tryin' to get up myself when I saw Gates's muddy boot swingin' back. I knowed the hurtin' I was gon' get likely would chase away the promise of my unborn children."

Mary said, "Hmm," and lifted Coolie's blouse, running her hand along the purple whorls of battered rib cage.

"Da Jesus!" cried Roguey, standing under a cache of pots and pans hanging from the oak ceiling beams. She looked over Mary's shoulder at the young woman's ugly bruises. "That man gon' git his someday, sho' as they's a God in heaven."

"I b'leeve he done collected on some already, Miss Roguey."

Mary spoke to Roguey. "She's busted up pretty bad. I'm going to have to bandage her very tightly."

"You needin' some medicine herbs from your shed out back?"

"I think I have enough in my bag upstairs, thanks." Turning back to Coolie, she said, "Go on. Finish the story."

Coolie swallowed, her breathing labored. "I was hotter'n a bucket of fresh horse patties when I bulled up sluggin'. I caught sight of a thick beer mug sittin' on the bar. I grabbed it and brought it up 'side Gates's temple with all my might. He reeled sideways but didn't go down. Blood roped down his head, running off his chin like some scary haint, but he looked up at me and grinned. His fist split my lip 'fore I could move. I took it and grinned right back at him. He reared his head and squealed like a stuck pig.

"Theron tore out from back of the bar with his bat and Jitter Conroy lit out from the side, but I didn't want no trouble for them. I snatched the bat, pushed Theron out of the way, and laid all I had into Gates like I was beatin' down snakes in the long grass. His stupid eyes bulged outten they sockets. He couldn't b'leeve it. I hit him 'til he fell in the sawdust on the floor and stayed down. His mouth hung open like his jaw was broke. I know I took out a few teeth too, way he was spittin' blood. I didn't care. I wanted to send him to hell so I kept hittin' him 'til Theron yanked the bat away and held onto me whilst I tried to get some breath back. Gates squinted up at me before he passed out and I think I saw fear in his eyes like he might a-been lookin' at a lunatic." Coolie sighed.

"A couple of Gates's buddies dragged him out of there, then Theron practically threw me into the buggy and Jitter carried me over here. Jitter was 'bout cryin' 'cause he say when Gates wake up, he gon' be fixin' to get me. A black woman done done that to him whilst his frien's stood around laughin'." She sputtered her lips. "I ain't studyin' no Gates. He the one better worry."

Roguey made whooshing sounds in the background as she hauled an armload of vegetables from the pantry, thumped them on the counter, and for the want to feel useful, began to chop down hard with a knife that could have passed for a small machete. "Coolie, I'm makin' you some soup," she announced.

"Yes'm," Coolie said.

"You can't go home tonight," Mary said. "In fact, I'm not sure when I'm letting you go. You've got a lot of healing to do."

"I got a business to run."

"Theron can take care of things, along with Sweets and Verona. That's what they're there for," Mary said.

"That cracker ain't gon' run me 'way from my place," Coolie said with a determined tilt of her chin. "I ain't a-scared of no Gates."

"You're crazy not to be." Mary patted Coolie's hand. "You'll stay in my room. You'll be comfortable there. I'll clear it with Tesh-Lucianne, but I'm sure it'll be okay." She stood and gingerly angled Coolie up from her chair. "We'll get you cleaned up and tucked into bed. In the morning we'll decide what to do."

She looked at Mary with her one good eye. "You ain't mad I come, are you?"

"I'd have been upset if you hadn't."

"I'll bring up the soup soon's it's ready," Roguey said.

"You know," said Coolie, trying to smile at Mary, "there's one good thing come out this beatin' I got."

"What's that?" asked Mary.

"I'm here with you, ain't I?"

Mary returned to business. "Can you walk?"

Coolie placed her hands flat on the table and listed a bit. Mary reached out to brace her. Coolie's dress hung in strips on the left side, showing skin underneath. The right side had dried blood spray. Coolie took a couple of steps and toppled. Mary dropped her walking stick and picked the girl up in her arms, carrying her through the door.

Mary glanced back at an astonished Roguey.

"Will you bring us hot water?"

Roguey immediately pulled down a large pot.

Coolie sank in the clawfoot tub filled with steamy water fragrant with herbs and healing oils. Mary bathed her until she felt the younger woman relax. Then she dried her with a big towel, dressed her in a soft nightgown, and helped her up into the big four-poster bed, covering her with fresh white sheets and a colorful summer coverlet.

The curtains in the bedroom were white and gauzy. They puffed and coiled in a breeze that blew through the trees in the yard. Coolie's face glowed with a yellow luster from the light of the table lamp. Even in this condition, she radiated the boldness of a rose in the fullness of its time.

"I like it when you put your eyes on me," Coolie whispered.

Mary said nothing, but she smiled.

Roguey knocked quietly and let herself in with a tray, carrying a bowl of delicious smelling soup.

"Po' baby," the cook said, looking worriedly at Coolie.

"Let me help you sit up," Mary said, propping her up on two plump pillows.

Coolie tucked into the soup and had soon finished it.

Mary handed Coolie a cup. "Now drink this."

"What is it?"

Mary lowered herself to the edge of the bed. "Something to help you heal, and to sleep."

"Ugh!" Coolie mimicked savaged faces. "Tastes like swamp water."

Mary indicated with her hand for Coolie to continue drinking, and when Coolie had finished, she took the cup. "Now scoot under the covers." When she did, Mary leaned down and kissed the young woman's forehead.

"You gettin' in with me?" Coolie murmured.

"In a little while."

Mary turned around and closed the bedroom door behind her. She shook her head and chuckled at Coolie's antics as she proceeded back down the hallway.

———————

Soon after Coolie had snuggled under the lilac-scented sheets and closed her eyes, Mary pushed through the hedges to the carriage house where Devereaux lived. She hustled up the side stairs and banged on the door. The driver answered in an instant, looking even at this time of evening as crisp as a fresh new day. He took one look at her and stated, "Mademoiselle?"

"It's Coolie," she said. "She had a bad run-in with Gates this afternoon. I'm worried."

"What can I do? Count on Devereaux."

"Take me out to Bear's," Mary said gravely.

Devereaux stared at her. This was indeed serious.

A rider on horseback galloped toward them. Mary peered down at him. "Jitter. Jitter Conroy. Is that you?"

He jumped off his horse and approached the circle of light near the carriage house. Yanking his hat off, he turned it around and around nervously in his hand. "Is Coolie all right, Miss Mary? I was thinkin' she might a got hurt bad."

"She's bruised up pretty good, but she's going to be okay." Mary watched him sigh with relief.

"Is there anything I can do?" His voice pleaded.

"Let her rest right now. We'll let you know."

Jitter stomped his foot into the ground and yowled from the pain of his new boots. "I could kill Gates, I swear."

Mary descended the stairs. "Jitter, you won't be helping Coolie if you do that."

"Is her face ... I mean, she's so beautiful."

"No wounds that won't heal in time," Mary said reassuringly. "The best you can do is let her rest for a couple of days. Then I'm sure she'll be glad to see you."

He looked up. His face brightened. "You think so?"

Mary was having trouble following this. She knew Jitter was sweet on Coolie, but this was something else again. "Give her a couple of days and maybe you two can have a little lunch out in the gazebo. Weather cooperating, you'll enjoy yourselves."

Jitter shifted from foot to foot. "Thank you just the same, but I'm fixin' to take her into town for a sit-down at a restaurant."

Mary frowned.

"You see, Miss Mary, Coolie's a lady and I aim to treat her like one, same's I'd do if she was white."

Mary said ruefully, "But she's not."

Jitter had defiance in his tone. "I'm sick of folks treatin' her second-class. High time she gets the respect she deserves."

Mary nodded. No use to argue the point.

"Well, uh, thank y'all an' everything." Jitter seemed to stall. "Guess I best pull on outta here and let y'all get on with whatever, uh, y'all was doin'." He smiled awkwardly, mounted his horse, touched his hat brim, and charged off into the night.

Devereaux shook his head. "That man has got it bad."

"Bad won't be the half of it if his father, Harper Conroy, gets wind of this. He's not widely known for his 'liberal attitudes,'" Mary said.

"Poor Coolie," Devereaux said, shrugging into his jacket, "one man loves her to death. The other would like to see her that way."

—————◆—————

As day deepened, a low red band flamed across the horizon casting a sultry glow on the woody expanse along the road. Devereaux drove the horses down the streets of Norfolk, trying not to seem frantic and draw too much attention.

Where Main Street bisected country roads at the edge of town, Mary could see that a tent minister, the fire and brimstone brand, had set up in a clearing. As they passed, she could hear him inside, hooping and blatting to an appreciative audience of plain, hard-working whites who clapped and called back "Yea, man!" and "Thank you, Lord!" in response to whatever he said. Then a strong-voiced somebody inside raised a rip-roaring hymn just as Mary and Devereaux pressed onto the gravel road where tall oaks, maples, and pines gathered with low hedges, rangy scrubs, and spots of wildflowers.

A cool breeze drifted off the water, and cicadas sang loud and plaintively. The quarter moon shined faintly, rousing a generous peppering of twinkling stars appearing in the breezeway of gentle sky not day, not night either.

A confrontation with Bridges's posse or Gates just wouldn't do tonight, Mary thought as she tried to keep herself calm. They had begun a regular patrol of the roads during the evening, making themselves a nuisance and a threat to anyone out there who had the bad luck to get stopped by them. Gratefully, in another five minutes, Devereaux skirted the sharp turn that took them back a ways, following a road thick with tall trees and boxwoods hanging over both sides. Just ahead were two brick pillars where the initials "TS" hung in weathered wood over a white-painted fence. This was Thurston Stone's compound.

Fortunately, the fence was still open—an unusual occurrence, Mary knew.

From what Bear told her, Stone liked to keep most folks out unless invited. Devereaux raced along a side road past Stone's three-story, rectangular abode on the left. Sounds of the carriage startled quail that shot up like buckshot into the sky, stuttering and cawing into the gilded light. They emerged through a tunnel, thick with beech, sycamore, and elm trees, into a wide complex with rolling waters just beyond it.

Seeing it herself for the first time, Mary could now understand why some whites who had learned about this place spread the word that it was something to be upset about, Negroes living this way. Even in the moonlight she could see white-painted fences flanking cattle and grazing horses, their coats shining in the reflected light. Long, bountiful fields lay in precisely cultivated rows. Swaying corn stalks rose tall from fecund, black earth. Mary stirred with smells of manure, rich wet earth, and a multitude of fruit and vegetables heavy with nature's magnanimity—undertaken and maintained by the labor of blacks.

As they veered to the right, Mary caught sight of several neat log cabins set across a rolling knoll. There were equipment sheds, a few small outbuildings, two sturdy barns with wagons filled with hay in the doorways, and the tall edifice Gie had described as the dormitory—home to many blacks and their families.

Mary could see it was ingeniously designed. A large brick building dominated the center from which a series of handsomely landscaped breezeways led like wagon spokes to smaller structures. On a nearby slope, in a surround of hickory and loblolly pine, a red brickhouse with white wooden shingles nestled in the bosom of huge trees. It also had a rock chimney and a low, generous porch that ringed three-quarters of the expanse set off by a white rail fence and flower beds in a bustle of color. Mary knew this had to be their destination.

Throughout the ride, Mary fretted for Coolie, who acted oblivious to her present danger. Gates could, and likely would, be bent and bound on taking revenge. That girl! Mary reflected as she mused on the start of her friendship with "the wild one." Years ago, Coolie had come to the house to help out with one of Tesh-Lucianne's many community projects. She had taken an instant liking to Mary, who had to admit she liked the pretty girl with so much spunk as well. From that time on, Coolie made it a point every week to bring Mary a bouquet of fresh flowers and a bottle of fine imported whiskey from a shipment given to her by one of her favorite riverboat patrons. Afterward awhile, as they came to enjoy each other more and more, Coolie arrived with all sorts of pleasures: wines, imported cheeses, smoked meats, seafood, and a variety of useful things from all over the world that Mary could use in her fashions. Then, as Mary designed dresses for her in return, they spent time together in the salon while Coolie spun out one outrageous yarn after another from her daily life at Travelers Rest. They would laugh truly 'til they cried.

Mary liked that Coolie, untended and untamed, would take on anything she set her mind to and succeed at it. The inn was one example. With a hodgepodge of illiterates like herself, she had built the most popular business of its kind in the Commonwealth and quite probably in the South.

Mary also liked that Coolie liked her so much. It was a good feeling. Who else but Coolie Parts would look at her, eyes gleaming, and pronounce, "You a silk purse and I'm a sow's ear. But we's all right together jus' the same, I reckon."

"My friend," said a soft, deep voice from the shadows as Mary stepped up on the plank porch. "Good to see you."

"Bear?" Mary caught her breath. Putting a hand over her frightened heart, she scolded, "Are you trying to scare me out of a few years of my life!"

Bear stepped closer so she could see him. Everything about him was big and as solid as a mountain. His head was a small boulder and his neck as broad as a tree stump, but the wide features of his face were kind. His manner was gentle in his collarless shirt and denims, worn with suspenders, a raw tear at the knee. He combed his tight brown hair back from a wide forehead.

"Once't evening come, I like to sit out here, put my feet up on the railing and rest in peace," he said. "Sometimes I stays out here 'til sunup. C'mon over and make yourself comfortable." He ushered Mary to a square oak table with four straight back chairs. He pulled one out for her. In the center was a Mason jar filled with wildflowers.

Bear caught Mary looking at the arrangement and said, "Poochie loves doing that, you know. 'Keepin' things beautiful,' she tells me."

"How is your wife?" Mary asked, settling into her seat across from him.

"That woman don't never slow down. I swear, I don't know where she gets the energy from. Cooks in the dormitory every day for about fifty people. She do breakfast and supper, then hauls back here to take care of me and the kids. Where she still finds time for her flower gardens is anybody's guess," Bear said with pride and humor. He spread his hands outwardly. "Just look around."

"How are the children?"

"Max'll be ten in October. He helps with my blacksmithin', say he want to be one too when he gets big. And Alder ..." He opened his hands and shook his head. "What can I say about a five-year-old girl who wants to be a fairy? Teacher read her 'bout them in a book over at our school, now thar we got one. Chile even talked me into makin' her some wings, gold-like, 'cause that's what true fairies got she say." He chuckled. "Now she runs around here, pretty as you please, makin' like she can fly. Even sleeps in the daggone things."

"So it's good out here at Stonehaven?"

"Better'n anything I ever could've imagined. Mr. Thurston, he ain't like no white man any of us ever knowed or heard about. Decent work, decent pay, good friends, good life. He don't make no difference 'twixt us and him. We go to the fields, he go to the fields right 'long side. When we eat, he eat with us. Say all the time, we his fam'ly and he don't never change 'bout that. Where else in this worl' when white folks tryin' to kill each other in they war you gon' find such peace as this? Especially for black folk!"

"Yes," Mary said, looking off into the distance. Moist heat, not uncomfortable, closed in around them.

"While back, Elam Gates come out here tryin' to make trouble. But Mr. Thurston wasn't havin' it. Sent him packin'." Bear sighed and picked up a corncob pipe. He didn't light it, just held it between his teeth. "You got to know Gates messed with me in town. We had us a tussle and he wasn't happy with the outcome. Ended up shootin' Mr. Thurston and tried to bluff me sayin' for his friends' sake: 'It ain't over.'" Bear wagged his head. "But see, I ain't said it's over neither."

Mary sighed. "Bear, that man's as dangerous as a rattler."

"Not if you take a hoe to his head." Cows lowed and harmonica music drifted on the air from one of the log cabins. Bear stared at her. "Okay, Miss Mary. What's goin' on?"

Mary took a deep breath, let it out. She recited the facts of Coolie's encounter with Gates. When she finished, Bear leaned back in his chair exclaiming, "Jesus paid it all!"

"Time and time again, I've cautioned Coolie about that temper of hers," Mary worried.

"The girl's live fire, true 'nough." Bear scratched the day's stubble on his chin.

"I'm thinking that she can't get loose from Gates now. What he won't do, I just can't guess."

Bear leaned forward, hands dangling between his legs, staring out in the distance. "You got to give her credit for standin' up to the likes of him, though."

"Not if it's going to get her killed."

"Sheriff Bridges won't do nothin' 'cause of his mama, Miss Clara-Jean. Gates done charmed her. And everybody know Bridges ain't going up against that woman no way. She's a war horse."

In the evening's cool and quiet, Mary could faintly make out the whitecaps hitting the beach, feel the salty air, and smell the night-blooming flowers on the wind rustling through the leaves and grasses. She stared out into the gathering darkness toward where night birds chattered in the trees.

Bear studied his pipe a long minute, his brow furrowed. "Miss Mary, don't want you to worry 'bout this none."

"Why?"

Bear smiled wanly. "Preacher told in a sermon once about what Love couldn't do to fix a trouble; Duty failed at it too; Responsibility didn't make a dent in it. You know what finally done the trick?" He looked at her.

"No."

"It was Right Time with a little he'p from his friend called Do Something."

Mary shuddered. "Look, I'm not trying to hand this problem off on you. I'm just frantic to know that Coolie's going to be safe, in spite of herself."

Bear smiled, showing uneven teeth that somehow flattered his face. "Miss Mary, if she somewhere 'round you, she be all right. I ain't takin' lightly these troubles. But you worth more'n gold in her eyes. Ain't a soul 'round here don't know that, 'ceptin' maybe you."

Mary's expression kept her feelings to herself.

His breathing made a hoarse sound as he studied his big hands in his lap. "Coolie growed up without no mother who'd claim her. Aunt Viney done brought her up bes' she knowed. But somethin' in that girl got a fever for the love she ain't never had." He blew breath out hard in a long gust. "Fact is, we love who we love. Some folk die parched as dry groun' hungerin' for just a little taste of it."

Mary felt embarrassed and answered more sharply than she intended. "She's got to stop acting like a willful child."

"If that day ever happens," Bear chuckled, "we'll notice everybody we know."
They both laughed.

"Maybe send a telegram!" he hooped.

Devereaux advanced from the shadows along the side of the house. He nodded his head and bent formally. "Bear."

"I knew you was out there somewhere, Devereaux."

The driver smiled briefly, then addressed Mary. "We must return. Danger threatens the streets at night."

"You mean, threatens us," Bear said.

"Oui," Devereaux said. He held out his arm for Mary.

"Remember what I said, Miss Mary. You and Coolie got friends."

CHAPTER 10

Mary was very concerned as she watched her old tutor, Miss Effie, minister to Cecilia, whose condition had grown worse. The patient lay swaddled in ragged sheets and as many blankets as her daughters were able to rustle up from neighbors. Yet she shivered and shook. She was out of her head uttering grunts and unintelligible words. The old medicine woman regarded her with anxious eyes but soothed her brow with soft hums and gentle fingers.

"Miss Mary, we thank you for bringing Miss Effie to us," Pluck said with burdened eyes lowered.

"Miss Tesh-Lucianne must be somebody real special to help us like this," Fortune said.

"How's that?" Miss Effie stood up. Her thick lips scowled. "Mary the one brung me here."

"I knowed it!" cried Pluck. "I knowed it in my heart." She started to say more, but Mary held up her hand. "Are you girls forgetting folks are waiting out here for food!"

Fortune and Pluck bore down on the task of frying up dinner—four sizeable catfish. Along with that, Mary brought green beans and potatoes, a roast chicken Roguey prepared, as well as loaves of bread fresh from her oven. From a street vendor, she also picked up salted fried pork rinds for a treat. Soon, the group joined hands and Miss Effie blessed the table with a prayer. The old medicine woman, stalwart though she was, looked tired. She'd been up with Cecilia for the last three days and nights.

"Mr. Devereaux," Pluck began, "where he at?"

"I needed him to pick up some fabrics for me in town," Mary said. "He'll be back to take me home."

"He a fine man," Fortune said, blushing. "So handsome too."

"He do have a way about him," Pluck said.

"He married?" Fortune queried.

"No," Mary said, smiling to herself. "Though I believe he has someone special up near Richmond."

"Well," Fortune said, spearing another bite of fish, "if he ever don't, put in a good word with him about me, will you?"

Mary laughed. "For sure."

The delight that she was, Pluck soon had Miss Effie telling how she found herbs for medicine. She was a serious woman by nature, but her stories regaled the kids with adventure and mystery, and for a time they were carried away, seeing themselves in the stories as Miss Effie fended off snakes and bears with her walking stick—sort of like Mary's—as she filled her basket with leaves, twigs, flowers, and roots to make her homemade apothecary.

Mary told about some of her training with Miss Effie in the medicine way. She was eight years old when, one day after months of working together, Miss Effie took Mary into the woods. The old woman had been teaching her about how to move silently, leaving no imprint. Mary had looked up to find herself alone. Where was Miss Effie? They had just been together under a thick canopy of trees, in foliage so dense, day had turned to night. The river raced and tumbled its way in the distance. Miss Effie, Mary called. No answer. Miss Effie! Suddenly Mary was afraid. A chill raced up her spine. She was alone. Tears came. Did the old woman fall and Mary not notice? She could see no trail, no path. Where could she be? Miss Effie! Miss Effie! Nothing.

The children's eyes glowed brightly in the light of the tiny fireplace. They were rapt.

The "child" Mary stumbled around trying to get her bearings. Birds sounded shrilly above her. She was standing in waist-high vines, her feet in undergrowth. What had Miss Effie taught her about being lost in the woods? First, don't panic. Calm yourself. Look around. Look at the vegetation on the trees. That will help orient you. So that's what she did.

A crash sounded ahead of her. What was that? She hadn't paid enough attention to determine if it was a tree branch falling, an animal making its way home, or worse, someone pursuing her. Every horror she could imagine came to mind. Should she run? Run where? Which way was home? She missed the secure feeling she always had when she crawled into the lap of her protective father, Tug. Would she ever see him again?

Came a scream—high-pitched, loud, angry. A razorback? Those ugly creatures could tear a little girl into slivers with sharp, curved horns. Were there razorbacks? She couldn't remember. She dropped her collecting basket and ran.

Her crippled leg caught in thorny brambles and she nearly fell, her walking stick shooting away from her grip. She couldn't go far without it. Where had it landed? She groped through thick bushes and tall fan-like ferns, her eyes scanning for her stick. There, she spied it lying atop a spreading bush. She went to reach for it, stopped. What were those red berries on the bush? What had Miss Effie told her about them? Why couldn't she remember? Something told her not to push her hand in there. So what must she do? Came the loud scream again and sounds of movement. She had to get away.

Casting around for something to help her, her eye fell upon a length of dried stalk. She grabbed it, used it to leverage her stick off the bush; but still, was it safe to touch it? How frustrating she had abandoned her collecting basket. Inside was a rag she could have used to wipe off the walking stick. Her eyes probed the green dimness. A plant with wide green leaves was close by. As far as she could recall, a leaf that looked like that was all right. She yanked on it. No give. She tried to bend it. It resisted. And she had left her knife in the collecting basket!

Movement again, this time approaching. She was frantic now. She turned to go back to the bush and her foot hit something so sharp, she cried out. She looked down. The rock was almost as sharp as a knife. She rocked it back and forth in the ground until finally she was able to wrench it free. Using it, she was able to cut the broad leaf. She cast the rock aside and, leaf in hand, made her way back to where the walking stick lay on the ground. She picked it up gingerly and wiped it down with the leaf. A yowl! My God, it was almost upon her. Her walking stick pounded the ground as she lurched between trees, scratched herself on thickets, sogged her moccasins in mud, and still could find no way out.

She stopped, her heart beating wildly. She made herself close her eyes and take slow deep breaths. After a moment she told herself to pay attention to where she was. Suddenly she became acutely aware not only of her surroundings but herself as a part of them. They would show her the way out.

She pushed her way along. Think, Miss Effie had told her. Another scream and she was sure the thing—the huge creature with terrifying red eyes, sharp yellow teeth and white fangs—would be on her at the next instant and tear her apart.

Crying but pressing forward, ready to use her walking stick as a weapon, she could see light. Was she almost safe? The circle of light grew larger and she half-walked, half-ran toward it. Then a blow to her shoulders landed her face first in the dewy vegetation. She saw stars. In another moment, she looked up into the smiling face of Miss Effie.

Mary was shocked. She didn't know whether to laugh or cry.

"I made all that noise for you to find me," Miss Effie said, giving her a hand up. "Took you long enough." And she walked away.

The kids in Cecilia's kitchen laughed and laughed.

Miss Effie looked at Mary with kind eyes. "She was young, but she became my best student. Got so even I couldn't lose her in the woods."

Mary left the house to be alone for a while. Out in the woods where she collected plants for her dress dyes and medicines, she worried about Cecilia's condition. But she believed in her heart that Miss Effie could bring her back. Mary would keep herself busy so as not to worry excessively, for that surely wouldn't mitigate her friend's illness.

Ever since she was very young, Mary had sorted out her problems by cleaning and keeping to tasks. Her father always told her, "How to see your way out of a problem is first clean it up." She started out as neat and orderly, but as the years wore on she became almost compulsive.

After returning from the woods, she got bucket and rags and scrubbed her salon until every surface shined. She followed that with liberal applications of linseed oil and turpentine to make everything lustrous and smell good. All the while, she speculated and measured her reactions to the storm of events that had cascaded on her like cold buckets of rain. She felt betrayed by her white family and worried about the survival of two women whom she both loved and felt responsible for.

Mary finally settled down and was able to listen to Tesh-Lucianne prattle on about what she needed her to do for Simeon's birthday party.

Mary told her that she was pressing as hard as she could to finish everything for the gala, but she still needed more help. "Work is going well with Fortune and Pluck, but what with Cecilia fading, the girls are doing all they can under tremendous duress."

Tesh-Lucianne interrupted to be reassured that the girls were also going to serve at the party. Mary told her that not only would they be there but she made new party dresses for them. Tesh-Lucianne sat back and sighed with relief. Mary continued to stress that she needed to employ at least one more weaver and two more seamstresses. Also, she had to pay the various artisans who were making special accessories.

Tesh-Lucianne looked concerned. "Why would you commit people to do work who had not been approved for payment?"

"I had not thought to do so because this has never been a problem in the past."

"I'm not sure Simeon will agree to more help with the current state of things."

"What is that?" Mary looked troubled.

Tesh-Lucianne assured her they had not gone poor, but she did sound miffed that Mary questioned her about Louvestre money. "Need I remind you that Simeon is indeed providing a good deal of funds for the fashion show's success. In fact, its success is something he is counting on."

Mary watched as Tesh-Lucianne palmed her hands together prayer-like, pleading, "Oh God, make Simeon all better from his bad cold right this very moment. Get him well, pl-ea-se. He's got so many important things to do. This party could help him like nothing else. Mary, you will see to his lunch tomorrow, won't you?"

Mary nodded. How strange, she thought. What was going on with Simeon, and she didn't just mean what had turned out to be a bad cold. Why did she also have the persistent feeling that Tesh-Lucianne was, uncharacteristically, hiding something?

CHAPTER 11

Simeon Louvestre was considered a man's man. From boyhood, his father saw to it that he learned from the best to hunt, fish, trap, and hold his own when guzzling whiskey. Fixing him with cold eyes, the old man had constantly reproached his only child that the world owed him nothing and if he was going to get anywhere in it, he'd better be prepared to take what he wanted, assuming he knew what that was. "People drivel about love and passion driving a man to achievement," the old man had scoffed and snickered, "but the simple truth is, single-mindedness and dedication to purpose are what will get you there. Don't forget that."

Where his father was ruthless with a take-no-prisoners attitude, Simeon was focused, never afraid to broker a fair deal. The old man was always thinking the worst of folks. Simeon was even-tempered and willing to judge a man by his actions. If he was unethical, Simeon never did business with him again.

Generally, people deemed Simeon a good man, a true Virginian, somebody to be counted on. And he liked people. His personality, though pleasant, was typically aloof, tending to observe more than comment. But his neighbors had learned if they needed him he was Johnny-on-the-spot, even more than the Bible-spouters who could quote chapter and verse what the Good Book laid down about being a good neighbor.

The Louvestres had met at a church social when Simeon was finishing his last year at The College of William and Mary. Their marriage took place one week after graduation, and they set out immediately for Norfolk to take possession of the generous wedding gift from both fathers: prime waterfront property and a noted architect to erect their dream house.

In the years that followed, neither of the Louvestres mentioned the concern of his family when the sprightly young bride bore no sons. Nothing issued from her more than a positive attitude. Both Simeon and Tesh-Lucianne had desperately wanted children but were not so blessed. They treated each other with smiles and affection.

The added wedding present of Mary brought as much joy as a child of their own. The couple immediately embraced her as kin, even bestowing her with the family surname, a rarity for slaves who typically had first names only. Mary lived with the Louvestres and was educated by them. She had tasks, but not of the menial sorts. She showed a knack for making and mending clothes, which her adoptive parents encouraged as a trade. She mixed with white guests, and both wives and husbands were charmed by her elegance. Not all, however, approved of Mary's preferred status. "You can't treat a darkie like white folk," Tesh-Lucianne's father, Daddy A.B., rasped. "Have you gone simple?"

Mary deposited her basket on the pine floor in Simeon's chandlery, near a small table she thought might be a good place to set up lunch since it was near a window with a nice breeze. As she cleared a place, she heard Leland, Simeon's barrister friend, taking up his pace again.

"The nigras are simply getting out of hand. Getting brazen, let me tell you. Just the other day, a couple of hire-out nigras I had sashayed up to the *front* door, halfway finished with the job I was paying them for, and informed me they got a better opportunity with more money and they were leaving on the spot. Just like that, leaving me high and dry," he complained. "They even gave me an attitude like they were entitled to do just what they did. And they're not the only ones who believe this war business suggests a different balance of power to the labor force. Take the immigrants swarming into the city these days, believing their numbers alone justify new terms of negotiation in pay and status. I swear, the whole thing's gone cockeyed." He paused.

Simeon said nothing, staring out to the sea.

"You with me?" Leland said.

"Worrisome," Simeon finally uttered.

"Indeed," Leland said, sounding sad. "Abolitionists roaming around stirring up trouble. Filling nigras' heads with concepts they simply can't understand. And Thurston Stone, that scandalous lowlife, is escalating that aspect fast as thunder. Now, I don't abide violence for violence sake, but if we're lucky, what Gates did might've been therapeutic, maybe knocked some sense into the old fart."

"I agree," Simeon replied. "Reluctantly, I agree."

"What's happened? I've not known you to go along with me so easily before. You and your madam are almost always on the side of the darkies."

"You think we might be priming for another Harper's Ferry?" Simeon said.

"Pshaw!" exclaimed Leland. "The nigras around here don't want violence any more than we do."

"Change is in the air. You've as much admitted that. Yet what change? How far-reaching?" Simeon sighed. "I've not much concerned myself with the colored people in my employ. I've done well by them. They've done well by me.

But in today's climate ..."

"Has something happened?"

"Not really. Mary's fashion show is coming up. That seems to be auguring in a curious change right in my own house."

"Like what?"

"I don't know how to describe it. For me, it's mostly a feeling like Mary is becoming the master of Louvestre Manse. How petty and silly is that?"

"You've never been able to decide whether you want to own slaves or you don't—as a moral question—humanitarian that you are. But let me clue you in on something." Leland lowered his voice and Mary moved to a discreet position to hear better. "Take Mary, in your office there. You treat her like family, but let's face it, she's nothing but a commercial product. Yes, she's well-spoken, respected, and liked, with talent up the flagpole. She's made you a lot of money through her sewing and all. And you like her a lot. Yet, the hard reality is, my friend, if something happened—God forbid—to you and Tesh-Lucianne, that girl'd be sold quicker'n you could say burnt biscuits. And do you think for one second her new owners would regard her as anything more or less than prized property, bought and paid for? She lives in lovely quarters provided by you and your sweet missus. Where would she be if the buffers to her life were taken away? So, the question is, are you helping her or hurting her by the pretense of having a silken cushion? Are you falling guilty to promoting false expectations in her mind? If so, just how humanitarian are you?"

"Careful of your back now, Leland," Simeon said sarcastically. "You don't want to hurt yourself with all that weighty speculation."

Mary was surprised to hear this from Leland, a man she had known for many years and held in high regard. And Simeon? Why, this was startling. She'd never heard anything come out of his mouth like this. His words felt like betrayal, even though she knew whites generally felt that way. Mary remained stoic, arranging two lovely place settings. "Thurston Stone built that big—I don't know what to call it—dormitory-like on his property, out by the river," she heard Simeon say. "Told it right out, almost like he was bragging, that he built it for the blacks who work for him."

"Got their whole families squattin' up in there," Leland said. "And if gossip's true, it's right nicer than a lot of homes 'round here. That rebel put in all the latest conveniences for 'em. Gas lighting. Heating stoves. Real beds, not cots, with nice quilts on them. Sofas. He even put in bathtubs. His boy, Bear, is the one supervised the building of it. That was another thing that got Gates so riled."

"Better housing upset him so?"

"No, no, son. Matters stack up between those two. This time, it was the fact that Thurston put a black man over a team of white contractors. Gates didn't like that one bit. Plus a black man earnin' more money than them. Shoot! To Gates and the men, that qualified as a sin, first-rate. So he lodged this complaint with Thurston, but all he got for his trouble was Thurston shaking his head. Told Gates Bear was the best blacksmith in these parts, and furthermore, Bear was his friend. So, if Gates wanted something different, take his men somewhere else. Thurston said, 'Not my problem.'"

"You think that's what drove Gates to call out Bear the way he did?"

"Hell," exclaimed Leland, "who knows what drives Gates to do anything? But I will say this. That nigger'd better watch his ass. Thurston can't protect him but for so long."

A shiver ran up Mary's spine.

A playful breeze drifted through the open windows, lifting papers and scattering dust motes that hung in the sunlight, twinkling like stars in the middle of the room. As she placed on the table the sugar-cured ham, cold fried chicken, black-eyed peas, rice topped with raisin-thickened gravy, and cornbread made in the cast iron skillet, the cawing of seagulls eager to get their fill of leftovers floated in the distant air. She turned more toward the door to hear the talk from the outer office.

"What does Thurston's family think about what he's doing?" Simeon asked.

"Shucks, they'd as soon roll him out under a plow team," Leland snorted. "Foster, his daddy, say if Thurston gon' help blacks like he's doin' with the money he gets from him, then he ain't gon' get no more of it." Leland waved a dismissive hand in the air. "But, if he thinks Thurston cares about that, he got another think coming. Thurston has enough businesses of his own going 'round these parts to sustain a whole county. He can do what he wants."

"Why's he like that?"

"Partial to blacks?" Leland asked.

"Yes. I can't claim to know much about him or his family long as I've lived in these parts."

"It's not a complicated story, though tragic."

Leland began to tell it, a sad tale if ever there was one.

Thurston was six when Noreen, a young black girl, was brought to Courtland Way, the family estate, to look after him. She was one of those faithful hearts who wore that quality in her smile and in her devotion to Thurston. She spent almost all her time with this energetic boy who was ever creating the most fascinating and ingenious things. The feelings were mutual. Thurston wanted to be no place if not by her side. To show you just how talented he was, still early teens, he crafted a personal box for Noreen, inlaid with beautiful woods that he polished to high finish. On top, he crafted exquisite little figures that danced to the music of Beethoven when she opened it. Inside he put in mirrors and ribbons and doo-dads for her hair.

Old man Foster preferred his office in town and the relationship with his ledger books to anything with his son. The old man—bilious and friendless—happened to fall on an idea for a toiletry business that made him rich. He contracted with some of Virginia's finest silversmiths to make combs, hair brushes, mirrors and other personal items—the kind of trade geared to the well-to-do. Soon, he'd done so well he was able to build that rambling and columned monstrosity down by James River he pretentiously called Courtland Way. Turned out, for all its high-sounding name, it was never regarded as home by any of them. Rather, it was simply a large tomb—handsomely furnished—to wait out whatever time they had to tenant there, and all their sorry grievances with each other never to be righted in this life.

Thurston's mother was always feeble-minded. Maybe that's why the old man got her to marry him at all. Regardless of the season, the little slip of a thing would climb up a tree, perch there humming and daydreaming most days, drawing pictures on a paper pad she carried with her. She had no interest in taking up time with her boy either.

When he got older, Thurston was seized with a powerful desire for Noreen and wanted to make a life for them together as husband and wife. Noreen, being more realistic, told him to quit his courting foolishness, but the boy wouldn't let it rest.

One day, she was standing at the head of tall stairs while he was pulling at her trying to get her to listen to him as he declared his love. Noreen had a laundry basket in her hands when Thurston yanked on her arm. Before she could grab the banister for balance, she stumbled, dropped the basket, and went cartwheeling down to the main level, hitting hard at the bottom. Thurston ran down after her, but to his horror, blood oozed from her lips, and her neck tilted back at a deathly angle.

Devastated, Thurston screamed and wailed. He clutched her to him and wouldn't let go. Then it happened. Colored men and their children halted what they were doing, and housewives slowly dragged out on their porches and into their weedy yards, staring disbelieving at the pitiful soul who shambled down the lane carrying Noreen's lifeless body from Courtland Way down to her mother's shack. He pleaded for the old woman's forgiveness, repeating over and over how sorry he was, that Noreen was the true love of his life. But her mother stared at him with those conjurer eyes of hers and declared, "God gon' git you for this. Live as long as you can, try all you might." She waggled her forefinger in his face. "God gonna bring yo' house down."

"From that time on, Thurston has slammed a hammer or shovel with the best of them, driving for hours in the hot sun, burning his white skin the color of tree bark," Leland said.

"It's just my opinion, but I think he'd rather torture his back than deal with images of Noreen in his mind," Leland continued. "Far's anybody knows, he's never taken up with another woman. He just stays among his nigras, doesn't matter what nobody say. Maybe he's trying for redemption, I don't know."

Mary listened to the story, feeling sorry for Thurston Stone. What a sadness, she thought. Few people ever experience a love like that. Yet, she knew, that even if Noreen had lived, there was little chance they could have been together, not in the conventional sense. After all, she was a slave, he was still a white man, and this was, indeed, the South.

"Lawd," Simeon muttered. "I thought he was just a rich, eccentric inventor."

Leland laughed. "Got to give the boy his due. He's that too."

"I can see why Bear's so loyal to him."

"Hell, they all are."

Through the open windows, a loud chant rose from a group of dockworkers toiling in the sun as they rolled big barrels toward the glistening gray ship under construction. Mary watched them absently as she listened with increasing interest to the conversation in the outer office.

"So, Simeon, what kind of real difference will that eyesore out there in the harbor make for us? Tell me the truth."

"With all the refurbishments we're making, four-inch iron sheeting around it being one of them, there won't be anything on the waters that can beat us."

"Well, I want you to get that ol' tub out there fixed up and ready to do what she's supposed to, and maybe it can mean the difference between us just chasing the bastards out of our territory and summarily sending their souls to Hell," Leland said. "Don't drag your feet on this thing. Set it to rights."

Simeon chuckled. "Once this beast takes to the sea, she'll leave nothing in her wake. No Northern ship can defeat her. They're constructing an ironclad too, but from what I've heard it's small. Queer-looking, they call it a 'cheese box on a raft.' Frankly, whatever they call the thing, it doesn't stand a prayer against the *Virginia*."

"They know about our fighter?"

"Of course. There are Northern spies and journalists everywhere these days. Their balloonists fly over and can see her in the harbor. What they don't know—the secret in our hip pocket—is the innovative engineering on the inside and the extraordinary capability of the battering ram."

"She sounds nigh invincible," Leland said thoughtfully.

"You're durn tootin'. What the battering ram alone can do will turn their blood cold."

Mary glanced at the elegant drafting table to her side. Under the warm glow of the desk lamp, she again glimpsed the detailed blueprints for the CSS *Virginia*. What should she make of these now? Suddenly, they were not just pretty renderings. She picked up the corner of one of the large pages and her fingers trembled.

CHAPTER 12

Stern-faced and thick-mustachioed Hoyt Wesson, one of Gates's latest posse hire-ons, rode at the head of his band of ten misfits and miscreants. Just after midnight, they reached a tall hill, and under a pale quarter moon they could see a small settlement just outside the city where several free blacks made their home. Located on the northern end of Norfolk, this was more a village than the protected cooperative of Stonehaven.

Stands of oaks bordered neat houses edged by bright flower beds. Gravel paths led to privies out back and to proud gardens that splayed into humble rows. The hub was a commercial area where along the plank sidewalk squatted a general store, a café, and the looks of a saloon with a hitching rail out front. Angled a short length away were a blacksmith shop and a carpenter shop, and up the side stairs of another building a carved sign indicated a doctor's office. A tall, white-painted cross marked the clapboard church on the other end. A few outbuildings suggested storage and a horse barn, all evidence of a vibrant, growing community.

Everything was silent. Nothing stirred, not cricket nor frog. Wesson, a big man held in awe and respect by his company, sat tall in his saddle. Broad-shouldered and thick-necked, his large head yielded thinning, straight, ginger-colored hair. Callused fingers rubbed across his day-old stubble as his dark eyes of thirty-six years glowed studying the lay. He took his time, but finally he spoke. "Deputy Gates has ordered us to put these niggers in their place."

"Hellfire," whispered one of the posse.

"That's what we gon' do." Wesson raised his muscled arm. The attention of the ten men was upon him. Their glistening mounts anxiously sensed something about to happen. Skittering and restless, they blew breath hard into the night air. The men reined them up, patting their necks, quieting them as best they could. Wesson leaned forward in his saddle that creaked under his two hundred pounds. He turned and focused his intense brown eyes onto the line of gunmen. Holding for the count—one, two, three—he flung his arm down to commence the witching hour.

Horses' hooves beat a rising tattoo as they tore up ground descending upon their targets below. The earth shook and trembled with their approach. Muzzle flashes lit up the blackness as rifle and revolver fire shattered window shutters and splayed the wood of front doors behind which families slumbered. A few in their nightclothes braved a step out on their porches, startled and confused, trying to figure what was going on.

Half an hour later, houses had been set afire, horses set loose, flower beds ripped asunder. The village was destroyed, and nearly all who lived there—some two dozen men, women, and children—lay dead. Some homesteaders, quick-acting at first gunfire, had spirited their frightened families into the close woods where they took cover in its thickness. After a while, hazarding a glance through the dense foliage, they made out the fright of raiding horsemen, guns poised, etched blackly against the background of leaping flames whooping and hollering in a terrifying din, robbing them of nearly everything they had.

Wesson looked around. Their job was done. Norfolk's blacks needed a warning. Rumor had it that some among them might have been urged by abolitionists and other liberal whites to rebellion. However fancied this suspicion, since he did not know one of them to ever lift a hand against anybody, he believed tonight would raise enough alarm among many of the blacks that they would settle down again. He and his rough guards were duty bound to protect Southern society, especially its ladies. A prime directive for them was to squelch any possibility of another horror that lived in whites' memory like that of 1859, John Brown and Harper's Ferry.

Next day, Mary read the account in the *Norfolk Day Book* with disgust. The local newspaper reported graphic accounts of the Negroes' slaughter as told by the few survivors. Some citizens made outraged sounds but no effort was expended to discover and apprehend the murderers. Most whites just shook their heads and resignedly threw up their hands. Vigilantes were cropping up all over. With the War Between the States and the many encroaching threats of all kinds since then, nearly everyone agreed that the once harmonious seaboard town of Norfolk was forced to change. It, more than any other city of this wartime, folks said, was a citadel of Southern life under siege.

CHAPTER 13

"I don't think she gets all that involved with the common folk," Lumley mused aloud.

Withers looked up. "Who?"

"Our fashion star."

"Meaning?" Withers was shaking his newspaper free of wrinkles.

Lumley smiled derisively. "You know who I mean."

"And your point is?" Sometimes, like now, it was hard for Withers to disguise his growing annoyance with Lumley. The veils were coming off his eyes, and he was beginning to see his partner as a cad who acted like he had the inside scoop on life's mysteries and only he and God made up that exclusive club of knowledge. He watched Lumley unfold his slenderness from the leather-tufted desk chair, saunter to the casement windows, and lean his elbows on the ledge, looking out as if lost in profound contemplation. Withers bit the inside of his jaw, trying to say nothing more, but he hated a dangling sentence. "What does that have to do with anything?"

Lumley reached inside his jacket pocket and fingered out a large hand-rolled. He sniffed its blend like a connoisseur, held it up to the light, and studied its rich color of cured tobacco leaves. "You're not quick, mentally, I mean. Did anyone ever suggest that to you before?"

"This sounds personal," Withers said, laying the paper down on the hand-tooled, walnut partner's desk.

"You would say that." Lumley observed the busy street below. He struck a match and lit his cigar. Puff, puff. "I'm trying to assess the situation." Puff, puff. "The woman could be a money maker for us, but she must be kept under control. If this show goes off with even the modicum of success anticipated, she could get a bit unruly, falsely believing she's the celebrated star who has now arrived. She already has a way about her I don't like."

"That's called confidence and the last I knew, she *was* the star," Withers replied. "A big article in today's paper confirms that. And, by the way, who is this 'us' in what you're saying?"

Lumley did not answer right away. He enjoyed the feeling of power he derived from making others wait on him. His eyes rummaged the humdrum of pedestrians—the commoners below—his expression seeming negligent but, at his sides, he clenched and unclenched his hands.

Withers said nothing. He waited.

Lumley returned to his side of the partner's desk and settled into the large chair. His drawl inflected a chilly contempt. "I thought we were supposed to be trying to manage the Louvestres. This includes Mary, does it not?"

"How, pray tell, are *we* managing Mary?"

"Let me tell you a secret, lawyer. She's a force to be reckoned with. Don't ask me how I know. I do. What I also know is the way to control someone is to give them what they want. Allow them time to get used to having it. Then be prepared to take it away or threaten to take it away."

"You're all heart," Withers said, suddenly feeling as if he'd just been planted into a moral crossfire.

Lumley was puffing like a smokestack while regarding his partner from the corner of dangerous eyes. "We agreed we wanted to take over this town or at least pull its strings. Heart wasn't in the contract." He held the cigar out with thumb and index finger, studied it, then flicked an ash into the ashtray. "You backing off the plan?"

"Which one?" Withers asked evenly. He was liking this association less and less. At the moment, Lumley was insufferable.

"You gone daft or stupid?" Lumley was now plainly irritated.

"Ever since we came away from the Louvestre home last time," Withers said, "you've changed. It's like you've kicked ruthless up a notch. Put permutations on the word 'nefarious.' Frankly, that scares me a lot."

Withers reached across his desk to the rack of pipes. He chose from among them—clay, porcelain, corncob, wood, and elaborately carved Meerschaum—wood, which he had since he was a kid. The bowl, well-insulated against the heat, fit perfectly in his hand and the stem, well-broken in, felt just right at the corner of his lips. Thanks to Lumley's impoliteness at not offering him a cigar, he'd enjoy his own pleasure. What he wasn't aware of at the time was Lumley's sooty gray eyes on him that had turned from watchful to as calculating and sharp as a reptile.Withers was pudgy and soft, had been since he was a kid. Others used to pick on him until they realized that he was nobody's doughboy. Somebody went up against him and found they'd underestimated their enemy. His softness belied a toughness that showed in his gray-green eyes, a willingness to put up his dukes to life, whether the game of the opponent was played fair or not. People's misperception of him had helped him throughout his law career and especially in court. Ready to represent the underdog client, he'd bumble around for a while, allowing his opponent to be contemptuous of the hick barrister. Then he'd swing out of the gate with such scintillating arguments and reasoning, such well-presented evidence, that opposing counsel ended up limping off. He was now doing the same thing with Lumley.

He had to admit, the man made him nervous—often like mongoose to snake—but he could never allow Lumley to know that. He stood, went to the side glass-fronted cabinet and retrieved a crystal decanter. He poured himself two fingers and returned to his chair.

His crisp tan suit, light-blue shirt, and polka dot tie made him the picture of Southern gentry. "Uh-uhn! Lord, lord, lord!" He smacked his lips over his drink. "The son-of-a-gun who made this batch ought to be arrested. So good it ought to be against the law."

"Better leave that smoke and drink to the grownups, you know what's good for you."

Withers raked pudgy fingers through his hair, reflecting that Lumley manipulated people, scared them if need be to get power over them. Yet he'd never known the man to be in a physical fight. His scheming might cause them, but he usually found someone else to do his dirty work. Well, he could be a sly fox too. The question: Did he really want to be?

"Every man to his own, don't you think?" Withers returned to the decanter. "I'd say this goes with a good smoke right nicely."

Lumley's eyes trailed him.

He sat back down into his padded leather chair. A couple more of these, he thought, and I won't give a damn what Lumley's up to. The thing was he believed he had entered troublesome waters with the man from the time they visited the Louvestres. He never aimed to be a part of anything but a clever plan to get ahead. So soon as he felt something amiss with Lumley, why the devil didn't he get out right then and there? It wasn't that he didn't know that Lumley's past, as the man admitted, was checkered with fools who had been useful. Withers shrugged. The Louvestres could fend for themselves because he had the insistent notion that Simeon, in his own way, was as ambitious as Lumley, for whatever his reasons. He just hadn't found his way out of the box yet. Well, Lumley would help him and they'd be brothers. Shame on Simeon if he didn't remember the Cain and Abel story. As for Mary, he planned to seek her out personally and, at least, give her a heads-up. He'd help her all he could; he didn't want to see her harmed. He could alert her to danger.

"What's your angle with Louvestre?" Withers asked, examining the bright red glow in the bowl of his pipe. "The two of you really seemed to get on well together."

Behind Lumley's smile was preoccupation. This time could be the big one. His past was littered with small towns, small minds, small successes. But it was going to be different now. He could just feel the bigger opportunity with Simeon Louvestre. In the past, he'd always bottomed out or hit the ceiling and could go nowhere. He thought, when he met up with Withers, together they could break through. Withers had money, if not family connections and social influence. He, Lumley, didn't have even that. Came up poor. Scrabbled for everything he got and held on dearly. What he did have was grit, and he planned to use it for all it was worth.

From young years when he worked with his father on a little patch of ground, he studied the ways of the rich, how they talked, walked, dressed, everything. Decided that he really was one of them, just misplaced among poor crackers.

One day, he'd make good for himself, though he knew under his birth name he'd never be accepted. Nobody'd ever have a good feeling for one named Everette Dobbs. So he remade himself as Obadiah Lumley, of the rich and powerful cattle Lumleys out from Austin, Texas. Once he left home, he continued to reinvent himself to suit the situation, always refining his background, putting everything in place in case someone decided to check up on him. His aim was politics so he knew there was always the possibility that some reporter would go rooting into his past. He covered his tracks well.

He'd counted on the last old political dog he worked with in Mississippi. Lumley never wanted to be out front himself; power-behind-the-throne kind was best. Put a lot of time and effort into that political hack, Judge Creassy, but the man had a great weakness—he couldn't leave the women alone, had to bed as many as he could whenever he could. The more popular he became, the more women. Then when it looked like he was going to be elected to the top seat in the state, he got ill. Syphilis. Stupid worm! But Simeon Louvestre was different. Quality. Someone you could count on if you played your cards right. And he would.

Lumley could tell that Louvestre was motivated by something other than being a big man. He had researched him. Learned about his angry wretch of a father, how Simeon wanted—no craved—the old man's approval but never got it. This situation could be just the ticket to use on him. Driven by his own ambitions for power and wealth, Lumley would make it his personal mission to herd Louvestre. Lumley would hold the reins.

"What?" Lumley said. "What?" He felt irritable that the man had wrenched him from his thoughts, mumbling about something else. "Dammit, if you have something to say, speak up!"

Withers was reading the newspaper, interrupting Lumley's thoughts with banal concerns over the Negroes' plight in Norfolk.

"What are you driveling about now?"

Withers read him the account of the attack on the free black community and the murder of all those people.

"Tsk, tsk," Lumley said, dismissing it. "So what do you want to do, take mysterious white riders—assuming they were white—to court and sue them for reparations? Or maybe an apology?"

"You can be quite reprehensible, you know that?" Withers was beginning to smolder inside. "Those were human beings."

"*Three-fifths* human beings," Lumley corrected him. "The rest is monkey or some such that live in trees, scratch bugs off themselves, copulate at will in front of God and all, and can hardly understand complete sentences much less make them."

Withers sat forward and stared at Lumley, who stood, drove his hands into his pockets. Withers vaulted out of his chair, squawking. "I don't hold with this kind of inhumanity! Whatever they did or were, how could they possibly provoke this? Doesn't this act of downright cowardice and murder disgust you?"

Lumley watched him. He was coming to believe he misjudged Withers as a suitable partner. He was turning out to be a pansy and a royal pain in the ass. A man, if he was a man, knew to clean up his mistakes.

CHAPTER 14

Theron Latt had brought himself up in the streets.

Trying to stay clear of slavery, he became very clever at being everything to everybody. He demonstrated early that he was good at ciphering and he enjoyed books, though teaching himself to read had been long and laborious. He hopped a wagon going to Norfolk, figuring that his skills might get him further along in the city than rambling between country farms and small towns. When he got off, he landed a job as a sweep—not a chimney sweep, just a common sweep. With a collection of brooms and brushes he made himself, he'd sweep a law office, a restaurant, a barbershop, a sheriff's office—didn't matter to him as long as they paid him and he could be a fly on the wall and listen to what white folks were saying, how they were feeling, and what they were planning to do about things.

Theron learned that Miss Gie Atkins was a powerhouse in town and most men and a large number of women knew to be afraid of her if they knew what was good for them. This is how he heard about Coolie and Travelers Rest.

Coolie told him right off that she didn't need a sweep, what she needed was a bartender. He said he could do that, though he'd never poured a drink in his life. He was a teetotaler. He was not much of a smiler either, but he was so creative and entertaining behind the bar, the patrons didn't seem to care that he never joined in with them. They wanted his drinks, what concoctions he put together, and were willing to help supply both him and Coolie with more of whatever they wanted from stock on their ships.

Over just a few short months in his early employ, Theron demonstrated to Coolie not only a dedication to hard work and long hours, but also a vigilance with regard to her and Travelers Rest. As far as he was concerned, he was home. He knew about everybody who came in. Those he didn't know, quickly learned his rules. He watched how hard Coolie worked. She never let down cooking, cleaning, organizing, finding ways to grow the business. Nobody was a stranger to Coolie at Travelers Rest. Even a new passing traveler got a heaping meal, a strong drink on the house, and a sit-down talk with Coolie to learn about them.

But Theron saw there was something haunting about Coolie. Even his hard heart turned soft as he gazed upon her staring out the windows to the sea. Wistful. Her arms crossed over her breast, close to tears. He wanted so much to protect her.

⊷•⊶

One night, Jitter Conroy pushed out of the shadows and approached Theron as he hauled the trash out back of the restaurant. A soft, startling sound rose and Theron drew the knife from his pocket, as ready and lethal as a snake.

"No. Hey! It's me, Jitter. Jitter Conroy." His voice was quiet.

"Jitter Conroy?" Theron repeated.

"I come to see you."

Theron waited, still poised for danger.

"Didn't want others to know about it, is all." Jitter slowly emerged out of shadow into the small circle of light behind the inn. He was no longer in uniform.

Theron watched him, primed for attack.

"Stop actin' like that," Jitter said. "You know me. Served me a hundred times in your bar. Have I ever hurt chick or child? C'mon."

Theron relaxed in stages—first his shoulders, then his arms, then his entire stance. But his eyes never left Jitter.

"Look, I didn't want to fret Miss Coolie about this, but I heard something that's got me powerful worried." His face took on an anguished aspect.

Theron was silent.

"Gates has got a bee in his bonnet over her and Miss Mary too, but it's Coolie—well, I just wouldn't want anything to happen." His voice trailed off like a wisp of smoke.

"What's he mad about now?" Theron's voice was almost a growl.

"I don't rightly know. But I know you look out for her. I would too. I mean, I would like to help look out for her, but me being white and all, I'm not sure Coolie would trust me like she does you."

"Coolie don't care what color you is—you an' nobody else," Theron said.

Jitter's eyes cast around them, looked at Theron, saw the truth. "Hell I know that. But still I thought you'd best be knowin' about this."

"Yes, sir," Theron said.

Jitter gave a sad laugh and shook his head. "I hate this part."

"What part is that?" Theron said, watching him intently.

"The part that seems to split us up all the time. You an' me. Black an' white." Jitter looked down, shuffled his feet. "Don't look like it matters what's in your heart."

Chapter 15

Saturday night, Elam Gates perched on his favorite wooden chair in his place of honor in The Pig Trough Bar, a place where nobody sat but him. He was playing poker with the boys. His beige duster hung over a chair next to him. He was waxing loud and expansively, telling yet another story of his adventures. Once a cowhand specializing in breaking the most stubborn horses, he next became a steward on a riverboat exclusive to card sharks so serious about their game that, as soon as they sat down at a table, each player put his pistol next to his hand. He spent some time frequenting Indian camps doing any kind of work they wanted if they would, in return, teach him nature's ways—hunting and tracking, how to be invisible in the forest, how to endure pain and injury, how to survive in severe weather. Now he was in Norfolk with a silver star on his chest.

"My credentials are that I'll take on any man in a fist fight, I can shoot the top off a bottle at fifty feet, and, you do something bad, I'll keep comin' after you until you're a snivelin' mess of rat shit and you're in jail or dead. I don't care, faithful son of the South that I am."

The men in the bar whooped and hollered as a compliment for him, some because they liked his bravado, others because he scared the bejeebers out of them and they wanted to show they were on his side.

"The sayin' is 'If you see crazy coming, cross the road and run.' Well, here I am. I'm Crazy! And I'm comin'!"

Another burst of thigh-slapping laughter erupted.

Handsome raconteur and popular with at least four ladies this evening, Gates felt so good about himself that he'd already covered three rounds of drinks.

"I'm a rake, ladies," Gates said in his honey drawl. "I am happy to give you babies, but don't count on me to stay around and help you raise 'em. I'm good for a bed an' a bottle an' a good time that'll make you walk funny for a week."

"You're a man of strong opinions," one card-playing buddy ventured.

"Indeed I am, friend. I don't like teetotalers. I don't like liars and horse thieves. I don't like Yankees. I don't like fathers who beat their sons. And I 'specially hate niggers." He pounded the table so forcefully with this pronouncement that the bar grew instantly quiet.

Slowly, a soft murmur stirred as the waitresses served another around.

"Gates, why do you hate niggers so much?" one drinking old hand asked.

"Well, old sod, since y'all got me tellin' tales out of school this evening, this is one to beat the band. It's a tale that goes back a ways. Had me a black boy friend name of Slow-Ernest Tilder. Everybody called him Slow-Ernest because everything he did, he did in a slow way, easy-like. Kinda glided when he walked in that way of his." Gates slid his hands together in a deliberate stroke, mimicking the gait. He grinned at the corner of his lips. "Slow-Ernest talked like butter on a hot summer's day runnin' off the lip of a glass. Sometime it'd get on my nerves and I'd say, 'Out with it, Ernest.' But it didn't make no difference. He kept his own pace.

"Slow-Ernest had him a sister, name Rochelle. Men, y'all will appreciate this. The girl had skin the color of toasted butter. Breasts the size of cantaloupes, hangin' ripe, waitin' for the pickin'. Waist no bigger'n two hands 'round." With his hands, he demonstrated. "Plump hips and a smile to dazzle you. I was about fifteen, feelin' my oats. Who could blame me? I couldn't get her out of my mind.

"Me and Slow-Ernest called ourselves brothers, tight like this." He held up two linked fingers. "Used to go snake huntin' together. Trapped all kinds of snakes, sometimes those suckers were as big around as young Maureen's thigh here." He squeezed waitress Maureen's thigh and she jumped away giggling. "We'd skin 'em and I'd sell their skins to traders. I was fair. I'd give Slow-Ernest a few cents out of it and he was happy. But when he caught me looking at his sister, he got put off. Told me I could have about anything else of his but not that. I couldn't help it. I wanted her like nothin' I ever knew. Somethin' about her just drew me in, not that she was tryin'. In fact, she was nice and all, but wouldn't give me the time of day in that department. But I had me a passion for her so hot, I was dousing myself in the river couple of times a day. I dreamed about her. Those breasts. Bein' between those sweet, liquid thighs. I couldn't think about nothin' else.

"One day, I saw her coming back from the river, carrying a bucket of water. I was happy to have a chance to be alone with her for once. Told her I wanted to talk to her. Show her some butterflies I'd just caught. But she rushed away, sayin' she had to get back home with the water. I got the clear she didn't want to have nothin' to do with me. I told her she could talk for just a minute. I'd even carry the bucket back to the house for her. She turned up her nose, said no, and left me standin' there on the path. That didn't sit well with me—made me mad.

"I ran up to her and tried to turn her around, still just trying to get her to talk to me. She swung around and hit me so hard with the bucket I thought my leg was broke. I commenced to boiling, so I couldn't see straight.

"I grabbed her, threw her down, and did my do, hard as I could. Afterwards, she got up and ran home. I just sat there on a rock waitin' 'cause I knew what was gonna happen. Soon Slow-Ernest ambled down the path. His face looked like stone but his eyes glowed with fire.

"I said, 'Slow-Ernest, I'm sorry. I didn't mean to hurt Rochelle. You know how much I like her. I was just tryin' to talk to her.' Slow-Ernest challenged me with, 'That what you call talkin'?'

"He flew at me. I never saw him move so fast, ever. We fought hard. Grunting, rolling on the ground, fists flying. When I realized he was gettin' the best of me, I picked up a rock and started whaling daylights out of him, didn't stop until his head looked like buzzard meat. Shoot! I realized that all that brother talk was just a bunch of mess."

"What if he'd wanted to lay with your sister?" another buddy asked.

"I'd have hung him on a hook and skinned him alive just like we used to do to all those snakes."

Gates looked around at the astonished faces. "I'm gonna tell y'all one more thing and then I'm through talking for the night. I'm sick of the way the niggers prance around this town actin' like they white. I got me a plan to plant a lesson on one they call their finest. When I get through with her—what does the Bible say? 'The half has never been told.'"

Nothing moved in the room. The others sat fingering whiskey glasses, thinking about Gates and Slow-Ernest. Fear had crept in even though it was not directed at them. What they saw in Gates was Crazy coming down the road.

CHAPTER 16

A black chauffeur guided the magnificent carriage of Senator Robert Short and his wife, Emma, who were nestled in the soft leather of its back seat. The rays of a September sun lowered on the horizon in flushed panels of reds, purples and mauves; heat shimmers rose up in ghostly patterns, then were swept away by a cleansing breeze off the river. The two guests stared, impressed, out the carriage's small windows. They entered through tall, ornate iron gates, negotiating past a line of spreading oaks, then pulled up by the shiny carriages of other eminent visitors in their evening finery. Their ride finally angled to a stop at a footpath leading to the palatial Louvestre mansion blazing full of light, the sounds of merriment for Simeon's birthday party spilling out. When their coachman opened the door, the Shorts gasped together at the spectacle.

On a gentle slope so arresting as to be deemed by the locals as "God's country," branching sycamores flanked the stately three-storied family structure. As if magically, it shot up from a generous tuck of red rose bushes, pink hydrangeas, and purple irises in manicured beds. A lively creek burbled enchanting sounds as it flowed alongside a right wing brick sprawl that was Mary's salon.

Senator Short and his wife joined gay partiers, taking the three steps up to the roofed, banistered porch that bordered the wide front portion of the house supported by graceful pillars, where six white-painted rockers with bright chintz padding and rattan tables were lazily arranged along the gleaming, slat-wood floor. Bright lights and spikes of laughter erupted amidst other arrivals. They did not have to use the big brass doorknocker. A white-jacketed black man, wearing gloves the color of doves, parted the graceful double doors of handcrafted mahogany. Aromas of food and fine tobacco floating on the soft summer air coaxed them further.

Some women are defined by the way they look in the prime of their lives. Tonight, Tesh-Lucianne would have stood up and off the canvas had she been a painting. The senator's jaw was testimony. He gaped and could not take his eyes off the welcoming hostess. She was dressed to be the envy of every woman there.

Mary had blended several plant mixtures to achieve the outstanding, brilliant burnt ochre on the very soft silk to accentuate Tesh-Lucianne's eyes, hair color, and fresh-milk skin. The off-the-shoulder, fitted bodice appeared to be much like a Navy captain's dress jacket, cut simply and low in the front, with three gold buttons crafted from amber set in a row down the center. It tapered to a narrow shape terminating straight across the waistband. A small gold braid rested at the top of each sleeve. Three lines of raised, embroidered gold chevrons ran diagonally across each lower wrist. Her figure had valiantly fought the softness of aging and Mary chose to make a cummerbund-style high waistband, accentuating it with tiny military insignia. The skirt hugged down a plain front with thin persimmon soutache cords. Two squares of the garment met in the front middle directly under the line of buttons. At her lower back were five broad, overlapping pleats let to fall naturally over ample hips. The effect was that the dress would sway with her movements, glide tempestuously with appeal that could try men's souls. Tesh-Lucianne was sensuous, a glory to gaze at, an alluring figure of what every Southern white man coveted and meant to protect at any cost.

"Come in," she cooed in her liquid drawl, pitched at an enthusiastic height befitting the affair's gaiety.

The senator eventually tore his eyes away and followed her. Emma, a pleasant-faced, blunt-built woman who was no stranger to wealth, oohed at the foyer with its high ceiling, teardrop glass chandelier, gold-framed mirrors, and heart-of-pine floor.

Tesh-Lucianne ushered them past the two majestic staircases that curved up left and right of the entry, egg-and-dart molding showing off in recessed light, all leading to bedrooms on the second level. The guests stopped to stare at the elaborate flourish of mahogany.

Mary stood hidden, watching, taking it all in like a child in a fantasy. She could remember, long ago, being awed by this house. She was just twelve when the Louvestres brought her here.

Mary had not been able to believe her eyes when Tesh-Lucianne first showed her the bedroom—her bedroom—completely outfitted for a young girl, as big as the entire shack she and her parents had lived in. There was a small, wood-burning fireplace with marble mantel in the wall opposite the door. It was flanked by two wide windows where delicate curtains fluttered on either side. A bay window opened to a view of the expansive flower garden below. A tall bookcase packed with books stretched from window to wall. Near it sat a comfortable armchair, side table, and lamp. A desk and chair dominated the scalloped alcove of another wall. Across the room was a large bed, which could have easily slept her whole family. Standing on ball-and-claw feet several inches off the floor, it was topped with a bright pink chenille bedspread and fluffy pillows perched against the walnut headboard; a walnut chiffonier faced that. Large beige rugs featuring delicate pink roses and green vines separated one area from another.

"This is your room, Mary," Tesh-Lucianne said, mincing inside.

"My room?" Mary said, incredulous.

"Of course."

"But I be a slave."

"A very talented one and a special gift from Amber Beauregard Clairoux of Prince William County, my father. Why, I already consider you a member of this family. And you will be treated just like that."

Mary was speechless.

The prattling white woman sank into an armchair. "And call me Tesh-Lucianne. That's what I like and answer to." Grinning and fiddling with her hair, she added that her daddy had wanted to name her Lucretia, after his mother, but her mother didn't like either the sound of the name or its bearer, so they tried out Lucy, Lune, Lorna, and other L's. Finally, when someone got the brilliant idea to name her Lucianne, he'd tacked on the Tesh in front of it to fancy it up. Her father was always trying to be different. Where the Tesh part came from was anybody's guess.

"Goodness," Tesh-Lucianne cried when the words ran out. She cocked her chin and gazed briefly at the ill-clad slave girl standing stock-still at the threshold, gaping into the room. "Come on in! Put your things in there."

Mary, holding a croker sack that contained all she had in the world, looked to where Tesh-Lucianne pointed. It was a walnut armoire that nearly touched the ceiling, with mirrors, framed in curved wood, on the face of its double doors. Mary licked her lips and sighed.

"Come, come! The party's starting without you," Tesh-Lucianne said gaily to her party guests, snapping Mary back into present day. The admirers eased down the long, floral-carpeted hallway lined with gilded family portraits. They passed the fancy living room, a genteel parlor with overstuffed chairs and grand piano, and library where a round table displayed a large family Bible.

A glimpse to the hallway's other side revealed what was Simeon's study, with its large walnut desk and glass-fronted bookcases against the walls. At a turn that would soon lead them outside, the senator poked his head in the dining room. An elaborately carved sideboard caught his eyes. There, crystal glasses glimmered on display. Finally they passed through French doors out to a breathtaking terrace where a radiance of lanterns lit a domed gazebo buffet. Candles at tables flickered and danced in the playful wind. Bits of lively conversations rose on the humid air; coiffed and glittering people drifted together, dissolved, re-established somewhere else; eager eyes searched out who to see and who should, most assuredly, see them. A few military officers in full, dazzling regalia held court in the garden center, lest anyone not have a chance to fully appreciate and admire them. A halo of blue cigar smoke surrounded them, and the pungency of bourbon, stout, cognac, and port could have been their toilette.

A beautiful floral arrangement was centerpiece in the gazebo, surrounded by sparkling bottles of Château Lafite wine, Moet et Chandon champagne, and the best Kentucky bourbon. A backdrop for platters groaned with colorful finger food, tiny chicken pot pies, steaming batter-fried trout, glistening roasted quail, braised cabbage, glazed carrots, buttered peas with remoulade sauce on the side. Heaping baskets of breads were garnished with an assortment of fruits and the finest cheeses. The china was Imari, just as from the tables of royalty. Several white-jacketed Negro waiters breezed through the congestion; musicians corded guitars to stirring songs of the South. From the side, Fortune and Pluck stood in their bright pinafores, excited to attend to the groups' any desire.

Simeon saw Tesh-Lucianne and the new guests enter. He moved toward them. "Senator Short. Glad you could come. Emma, you're lovely as ever."

"Wouldn't have missed it for the world," Senator Short said.

"Happy birthday," Emma said. "Congratulations on another year."

"Bless God to be alive," Simeon said, smiling broadly. "Please, let us get you started. Food? A drink first?" He signaled and Pluck instantly appeared.

"Bourbon for me," the senator said, "tall and neat."

Pluck stood forthright, waiting to make certain the missus and her guests didn't need anything else. Tesh-Lucianne, standing just a couple feet to the girl's side, whispered to the senator's wife: "My dear, what an absolutely gorgeous fan. Are those peacock feathers?"

Pluck overheard the comment and, smiling, made a mental note, keeping her eyes fixed slightly downward.

"I would die for one like that."

Tesh-Lucianne continued to fuss with approval over Emma's fan, then took her elbow and cast a mischievous glance back at the men. "Champagne, dear?"

"Tall and neat," Emma said.

They laughed. People nearby who didn't know what they were laughing about—but who didn't want to appear as though they missed something—laughed too.

Tesh-Lucianne said, "We'll leave the men to talk. I'm sure they'll want to go on with their boring opinions about the war and the fate of the free South. Let's us do something more entertaining like go eat too much, and ..." she turned, batted sultry eyes at her husband, "we'll put sinful strain on our waistlines."

"Sounds marvelous," Emma cried.

Mary watched as the lawyer Lumley took a position one step removed from the groups, where he could study them all. He laughed at the right times, added "uh-huhs" appropriately and "oh surely no's" as his apparent merriment added to the collective, but his eyes told Mary differently.

If the folks back home could see him now, Lumley thought. He held his glass up and regarded it in the dancing light of nearby candles; he took a long pull on the fine bourbon inside, smacked his lips in relish. A humorless chuckle bubbled in his throat. He ran a hand down his black suit, tailored to his tall slimness and befitting a nobleman. His Egyptian cotton shirt felt just right, its white sleeves ending at gold clasp cufflinks, his silk tie a saucy plaid for the occasion. He reached into an inside pocket and withdrew a hand-rolled Cuban. He smelled it, closed his eyes. After using a cutter to snip the end, he lit it with a match, letting his body enjoy the bolus of sheer pleasure shooting through him on the smoke. A man of rising power has many needs, he thought, and this was one of them. He intended to muck up some sheets sweatily attending to another later in the night. He could feel it coming on.

Laughter ripped from a group of men by the bar. Lumley cut his eyes at Simeon, who seemed adhered to the senator. No doubt the talk of these cocks-of-the-walk was politics, war, the economy, and the Navy's refurbishment of the CSS *Virginia*. Simeon was likely enjoying center stage for his participation in its improvements to knock the North out of the waters. Let him have his fun tonight, he thought. He had plans for Mr. Simeon. Oh, did he have plans.

Simeon and the rest of his ilk, for all their talk of defending Southern shores, didn't seem to have a clue that some people who looked like them—people right in their very midst, who sounded aggravated at the uppity Yankees and worried out loud about slave uprisings—actually held them in contempt. These glib, influential sons of the South, born with silver spoons in their mouths, were so trite as to be boring. And worse, they were Virginians! To let them tell it, God first made Virginia, then with idle time on His hands, created the rest of the South beneath them.

Their arrogance was one of the reasons Lumley had chosen to come to Norfolk. That sense of entitlement made them vulnerable in the world of his kind. For all their languid airs and allowances, he was aware that given the right moment, right situation, one of their membership would show private disdain for him, let the cover slip off at their regard of him as second-class.

Most of them would not remember an incident many years ago when a band of travelers had tried to set up outside of Norfolk where there were no neighbors. There, the group wanted to wrest farms out of the harsh soil, raise their families, keep to themselves, and live to old age, God willing. When others in the area discovered there were silversmiths and jewelry makers among them, they wanted to trade. But these people did not.

Gossiped about, whites came to fear them, said they came to this country as witches and whores all the way from a place called Romania. They spoke a funny tongue and dressed in colorful clothes, and their women were kept far and away from outsiders. Rumor had it that they practiced unholy ways, lied as a cost of doing business, and told fortunes cavorting with spirits. Gypsies, these people had taken Lumley in as a callow youth after he set off on his own. A daring couple from this wandering group made him their "get," an add-on to their family, and asked hardly a question about his past.

Before dawn one morning the gypsy conclave was set upon. Their homes went up in fire, their women raped, their children kidnapped and sold as slaves. Only a few escaped the onslaught. When the woman he called mother saw the men on horseback approaching, she hid him under a big iron kettle in the yard. He covered his ears with his hands but he could still hear the screaming and crying. Later, when silence returned, with the horror still living behind his eyes, he stumbled half-starved along the riverbank, for how many days he did not know. He heard a coyote howl. He whirled at the sound, tripped over slippery vines, and collided with the ground. When he woke up, he lay in bed under a quilt. A pleasant-faced woman smiled at him. A man with a long black beard peered into his eyes and patted his forehead. He slept again. These were the Lumleys, Kenneth and Marjorie. This gentle couple that called themselves barren said that God had answered their prayers. His way could sometimes be harsh but they now had the son they always wanted. They gave him their name and the boy had another new family. Yellow fever took them both when he was fifteen. They had lived so simply that Lumley always thought they were poor. But a man in a black suit came to see him after the funeral and what he revealed of his inheritance set Lumley on his heels.

He went to Charleston, South Carolina and recreated himself again. He became educated. Read for the law. Yet the hate within him never dimmed. These rich Virginians owed him a debt and he was going to see it in good return.

Lumley sipped his bourbon and glanced around. Just look at them, he thought, whirling and glittering in their evening finery, laughing, indulging themselves in the same conversations, same expectations and services they took for granted. Would that they knew just who was in their midst! In his own time, well aware of life's present exigencies, he'd make them choke. He would stare them in their shocked eyes as he shoved his fingers down their pampered throats. He'd laugh and laugh at their naïve protests and fevered pleadings. He even planned to use one of their favored to help him do it. Simeon. Simeon Louvestre. Lumley glanced over at the big man holding forth among his friends.

Mary watched Lumley's lower lip turn up in what could be mistakenly regarded as a smile. She guessed that the very people who extended to Lumley a hand in greeting or friendship had better watch out. He despised them, she could tell. The music took a different turn. Fiddlers dressed in bright red shirts stepped to the front of the platform before the other musicians. They struck a high note and began to play rhythms that encouraged people to dance. A few got started with such exuberance that others followed, and soon the whole yard seemed to be awhirl.

Tesh-Lucianne peered, concerned, out into the darkness.

"What is it, dear?" Simeon said, approaching behind her. He placed his hands on her shoulders.

"For the life of me," she said, "I can't figure why Withers is not here."

"He's a lawyer," Simeon offered. "Things come up."

Tesh-Lucianne made clucking sounds. Her furrowed brow said "maybe." "This was what he and Lumley said they wanted, to meet Virginia's fine families. It just doesn't stand to reason he wouldn't be here."

Simeon shook his head, chuckling. "I swear, Tesh-Lucianne, you adopt everybody whether they want a mother or not." He kissed her cheek. "From what I know of him, he's probably off defending some poor, needy, or criminal. He may get here yet or tomorrow he'll regale us with stories about what stalled him."

"A disappointment," she said.

"I didn't know you liked the fellow that much to worry about him."

"I didn't at first," she said thoughtfully. "But there's a kindness in his eyes. Something about his spirit that makes me feel good around him."

Simeon looked off distractedly in the direction of the dancing but was not really focusing there.

"I feel I need to look after him," Tesh-Lucianne said.

"Hmm?"

"Nothing," she said, glancing again into the dark night. "I'm sure it's nothing. Let's dance before Daddy comes in."

Mary stared out the glass doors at the party. She saw movement at the side gate. A scowling elderly gentleman, wearing evening clothes and holding a cigar, was being pushed in a rolling chair by a manservant. "Uh-oh," she said to Roguey, who was heaping high another platter of lamb.

"Somebody stormin' the walls?" Roguey asked.

"Might as well be," Mary said. "Daddy A.B. just rolled in."

"A'Lawd!" Roguey said, smiling to herself. "Things gon' heat up now!"

Mary heard the man's voice boom at Pluck when she tried to hand him a drink. "Girl, do I look like a highball to you? Bourbon. Straight. Fact, just fetch me the bottle."

The girl's smile faded as she raced across to the bar. Daddy A.B. watched a moment, then turned his attention to the guests. He commanded to no one in particular, "Where the hell is my daughter? Where's Tesh-Lucianne?"

His feral black eyes peered, rather than looked, at people and objects, as if quickly assessing them as prey. His lips wore a sour expression. His legs might not work well, but his mind was vital and he was nothing short of authority.

"That man crack the whip on everybody," Roguey said to Mary. To a young waiter she said, "Now take this platter on out there whilst the meat still hot." As he left, Roguey continued, "That old man got 'nough money, he prob'ly own Virginia. I bet you elbows-to-grease he ain't here for no birthday party. He come to see 'bout Tesh-Lucianne."

"Why?" Mary watched Roguey decorate a platter of deviled eggs.

"You know he ain't never liked Tesh-Lucianne takin' up with Simeon. He'll tell you so. He ain't shy," Roguey said, not looking up from her work.

"I thought he'd come around to trusting Simeon."

"See," Roguey said, pointing at her with a fork, "you know strong-headed Tesh-Lucianne made the old man go along with it. But sad is the future of any man Daddy A.B. think'll do her wrong."

"I still don't understand why you think he's here if not for Simeon's celebration."

"Simeon ain't gon' be the same Simeon 'fore too long. He gon' be politician Simeon. I ain't never heard Daddy A.B. say a kind word 'bout a politician."

"And ..."

"Politicians runnin' for office need money," Roguey said.

"Oh, this is like pulling teeth." Mary sounded frustrated.

"Who got mo' money than God?" Roguey said. "You gettin' onto this yet?"

⎯⎯•⎯⎯

Roguey reigned authority over the Louvestre kitchen, installed into the household nearly six years ago when the former, gray-haired cook clutched her chest and fell dead on the floor on a Monday before breakfast. This cook, whose skin was the color of ancient roots, had a build like a bull and a ready, furious temper to match, regardless of the consequences. Her face was compact, with wary eyes, large, flat nose, and tiny ears set under a thatch of short, brown nappy hair.

Roguey had toted more bales of tobacco than any slave in the tortuous fields on the Orday plantation outside Raleigh, North Carolina, and had laid claim to legendary strength. She was also reputed to have punched the lights out of any man who called her out of her name. Later, she watched over each of the five Orday children in their huge house while her own three young ones had to fend for themselves on slave row. Widely regarded for her expertise in mouth-watering cuisine, admirers trumpeted she didn't just cook a dish, she took mastery of it. Friends of the Ordays came from all over to their many social functions expressly to enjoy the latest Roguey creation.

The maverick cook also had it in her to run away. "I'd jes' get sick and tired," Roguey told Mary one day when they were on the back porch snapping beans together. "I had to aim for somethin' better. That was befo' I had my chilrens, though."

Problems had set in when Master Felix Orday decided to punish her for what he called willful insubordination after she ordered one of his prestigious guests to "act like he wasn't a fool and get his fat feet off the table." Next day, Orday sold Roguey's three youngsters to a slave broker, sending them off to places unknown. "When he done that," Roguey related to Mary, "I wasn't no mo' good. Didn't matter then what they done to me."

Roguey was inconsolable after that incident, Orday had explained to Simeon Louvestre during business travels, and he began to have concern for his life. "Despite Roguey's reputation as the best cook in Virginia," Orday said, "I paused every time I'd sit at the table."

"Sell her to me," Simeon had said.

"She could be a troublemaker."

"My wife has a way of soothing such types," Simeon told him. "Even ones who are a handful."

"I'm afraid you don't rightly know what you're getting," Orday declared.

They had laughed in genial understanding, and two weeks later, Roguey was transplanted to modest quarters off the detached kitchen of the Louvestre home.

———•◆•———

An enormous birthday cake arrived to the party. Four waiters carefully rolled it out on a white-clothed cart along with several bottles of champagne. Tesh-Lucianne took the platform, the music died down, and revelers took their seats. "What a beautiful night! You've made this a simply gorgeous affair!" she gushed.

The crowd applauded and cheered. When the noise subsided, Tesh-Lucianne continued.

"I was a young girl of seventeen when I first laid eyes on Simeon Louvestre. We were at a lovely dinner party. He was every girl's dream, so dashing in his Navy uniform, so full of duty and purpose. This was a man who was going somewhere, I told myself." Sotto voce, she said conspiratorially, "Of course I didn't let on a thing to him. What I did not know was that he was in cahoots with the hostess to meet *me*. We stared into each other's eyes that night and no one else existed in the world. I knew then and there, like Ruth said to Naomi in the Bible, 'Whither thou goest, I will go. Your people shall be my people.'" Tesh-Lucianne smiled brightly at Simeon, who stood off to the side.

The crowd "oohed" and grinned at each other, then turned back to Tesh-Lucianne. "I don't want to tell you how many years ago that was, but to me it was yesterday. Nothing has changed since then. I consider myself to be one of life's lucky ones. I found my husband, my completeness, my timeless love in Simeon Louvestre."

She beckoned for Simeon to join her on the platform. He did so, looking out sheepishly as she put her arm through his. The partiers erupted with applause. He nodded to them in appreciation.

Tesh-Lucianne beamed as she continued. "Tonight, I thank you for joining me in honoring this great man on his birthday. The day he was born was the day God hung the sun, and every year since we've been together he's added another star to the constellation of my sweetest night sky." She placed a hand over her heart and looked to the heavens. "For all of this, I give thanks."

"Whoo!" someone yelled.

Someone else cried. "My goodness! I've got to write this down!"

People laughed.

"We better cut that cake before I start to cry," Tesh-Lucianne said.

"And don't forget the bubbly," someone shouted.

"Pop those corks!" another voice cried.

"And the birthday song," another piped up.

Tesh-Lucianne lifted her soprano to lead the singing. "For he's a jolly good fellow ..."

Waiters began to pass around slices of cake. Seven tiers of Simeon's favorite sweet potato cake were layered with cream cheese filling, light as air. The frosting was made of tea and homemade caramel. Tiny florets of chocolate, interwoven with petals of fresh strawberries, adorned the outside of each layer. Roguey had outdone herself, all admitted. On each plate was added a scoop of rich, creamy vanilla ice cream.

Then music began again. Tesh-Lucianne lightly kissed her husband as he enveloped her in his arms. A thunderous clapping and cries of "Happy Birthday!" rose on the gentle night breezes.

After a time of dancing and drinking, Senator Short stood and raised his glass of champagne. "Ladies and gentlemen! To Simeon Louvestre, a man among men, a friend to us all!"

A hush fell over the group.

"I have the distinct honor to reveal a secret here tonight."

People exchanged expectant glances.

Senator Short continued, "Those of us who serve our South as politicians, as well as myself ..." That earned him a chuckle from the crowd. "We've long seen Simeon as a man of great character. A man of vision. A man of action. A man for the people. I couldn't be more pleased to announce to you that we are joining forces to see this man to the new capital!" He swung his arm and pointed a finger at Simeon, whose face was turning red. "We need this man working shoulder to shoulder with us as we bring about a new South, a stronger South, a South that will not know defeat! Simeon's own roots grow deep within this precious land of ours, and we can rely upon the fact that he will use every power within him and without to protect it—and us!"

Men hooted loud praises.

"We congratulate Simeon tonight as, in toast, we quaff down his best champagne and bourbon, some of the finest I've ever tasted!" He looked to Simeon and gave a conspiratorial wink. "Can I get your source?"

People laughed.

"To Simeon Louvestre, truly Virginia's finest!" Senator Short had to yell the last phrase to be heard over the din of applause and cheers. He held up his glass. "Ladies and gentlemen, I give you the next senator of the Confederacy! May God bless us all!"

Lumley pumped Simeon's hand. "I knew it," he said. "I knew it."

Simeon grinned.

Tesh-Lucianne beamed. She blazed with happiness at the vigorous congratulations of their friends on this magical night for her husband.

Later, Tesh-Lucianne took to the platform again and tapped a glass with her silver spoon to get everyone's attention. "Friends, I don't want to stop the drinking and debauchery for too long." When conversations and music paused, she continued, "I just want to announce another special person tonight—one who helped to create the beauty of this evening, the very one who designed this marvelous dress I'm wearing. She's the woman the whole South will soon turn out to see at her upcoming fashion show. She's none other than Norfolk's fashion designer extraordinaire. I give you our own Mary Louvestre!"

Mary had been standing inside the kitchen, just behind the glass doors. She had been bracing for this moment. She took a deep breath and glanced at Roguey, who was grinning at her. "Here goes," Mary said.

"Strut yo' stuff!" Roguey called after her.

Mary's entrance was nothing if not amazing. From one of the tables, a woman's voice put it succinctly: "I declare!"

Mary stepped out in the light of many flickering candles, wearing a classic-line, lightweight cotton black dress, understated by design. Being a slave, she could not afford to upstage her mistress or the other whites gathered there. Her skirt was cut on the bias, trimmed at the waist and hemmed with thin black purse twist. The bodice was a rounding one-piece with the tiniest of almost imperceptible embroidery stitched within. At her neck was a collar crafted to look like overlapping white Phalaenopsis orchid petals. A thin, blood-red line ran down the center of each leaf. Loose sleeves drew close at the wrists where Mary had repeated a small line of purse twist. Her black pumps gleamed at a high shine along with her elaborate gold-headed walking stick.

As she strode the long wine-colored runner, laid from kitchen door to platform, she approached Daddy A.B., who sat at the aisle. She bent down deferentially to greet him. He put up his hands, fending her off, and swung his wheelchair away from her. She felt the snub but continued forward with a smile.

Light from the candles dazzled her auburn hair, shimmering along its fall to her shoulders beneath the matching kufi perched atop her head. Dignity carried her to the center of the room, where she bowed and smiled to polite applause.

Tesh-Lucianne said, "While you gentlemen continue with your talks, we ladies want to visit with Miss Mary to see what she can do to make us look as lovely as she is."

Lumley was again at Simeon's side. "You didn't tell me you had such a winner in your household."

"She is that," Simeon said.

"Such talent must be exploited to its highest potential," Lumley said. He lifted his drink, "And profits." He gave what Simeon thought might have been a smile.

"I already have plans in motion," Simeon said.

Elegantly-attired Lumley, his pitch-colored hair gleaming, linked his arm with Simeon. "Do tell," he said in a drowsy drawl. "Let us walk, not among the common folk." He led Simeon out toward the beach. "Let's explore these intriguing plans of yours."

CHAPTER 17

Earlier that evening, Withers, dressed for the party, mounted his horse. It was dusk as he turned at the end of the street. When he hooked a right, he heard horses behind him but paid little attention. There were always horses, always wagons, always noise. Soon, he pricked his ears as horses seemed to be approaching him. He turned in his saddle and was surprised to see Deputy Gates and a couple of his men at his back. The men leered at him and called out taunts.

Withers pulled up and challenged, "What's this about?"

One of the men spat on the ground and said, "Nigger lover, we know who you are."

Withers cast a surreptitious glance over his shoulder. These days it didn't make much sense to be well-dressed and traveling alone at evening, but Lumley had suggested that Withers ride horseback and follow what he described as the quickest route to the Louvestre home. Lumley said he was going to meet Simeon early to discuss business and that he would see Withers at the party.

Withers had met Lumley many years earlier in a Mississippi bar. Over a few drinks and good conversation, he thought they had mutual political interests. Lumley had talked a good game. What Withers did not know then, but later learned through a friend, was that Lumley had researched and had sought him out. At the time, Withers had just ended his engagement with his longtime fiancée, Alcamera, whom he had never fully loved. Alcamera was pressuring him to marry. She wanted to make plans for the fall. They'd been engaged for two years, but he just couldn't bring himself to think of the rest of his life with her. She was a daddy's girl, a whiner, with a bit of a hook nose and weak chin, traits he did not want to pass on to his children, God willing. She also displayed a sense of entitlement and was too quick to punish a slave. When he spoke to her about that, she acted surprised.

Once, a remarkable episode of violence began with a slave woman serving them tea.

"Slaves are nothing but green flies on cow dung," Alcamera said airily. "They are noisome irritants, totally expendable. You swat one and three more spring up."

The slave woman had gathered up items on a tray to return to the kitchen. When Alcamera spoke sharply to her, a cup from the tray fell to the floor and broke. She quickly apologized. Withers watched stunned as Alcamera rose from the divan, went over to the girl, hauled back and slapped her so hard in the face he thought he was listening to bacon frying. The girl slumped dejectedly, but Alcamera was not satisfied. She screamed that the cup was part of an irreplaceable set, and what was the girl going to do about it? The girl did not answer. Her lowly attitude seemed to make Alcamera even angrier. Just when Alcamera was about to hit her again, Withers stood and stopped her fist. He held it in the air while Alcamera, red-faced and puffing, turned on him, spittle flying from the corners of her mouth. Something died in him that day for his wife-to-be.

"Withers," she hissed. "How dare you chastise me, especially in front of a nigger."

Alcamera shrieked for the slave to get out of there, and the girl fled.

Alcamera turned steely eyes on him. "You, young hero, just sealed that girl's fate."

"Come on, 'Camera." Withers tried to placate her, using her nickname. "Let me buy her from you. If she's that sad a state of affairs, let me take her off your hands."

Alcamera settled herself on the divan, her lips screwed up as she thought. "I thank you for the offer, but I have my own plans."

"Out of human decency!" Withers put out.

"No," she said, calmly.

Two days later, when Withers learned of the girl's horrible death, he immediately visited Alcamera and called off their engagement. She swore vengeance on him, screaming and wailing like a shrew as he left her house. "I'll see you dead!"

These were his ruminations when he realized that Gates and his men were following.

Gates leaned over the knob of his saddle, the leather creaking under his weight. "Mr. Sampson Withers, esquire and nigger-lover. Sheriff Bridges told me although you're relatively new in town, you've been busy." He chortled. "You're a bad fellow. You're a tick, really. Like them, if not taken out, our balls can be infected."

Withers had reason to worry. "I've got no idea what you're talking about and I've plans for the evening. I must get on."

Gates lifted an upturned hand. "Hold on. Hold on a minute." He kept a casual feel to his end of the conversation. "Sheriff told me that you're bringin' suit against Stoley Upchurch, one of Norfolk's finest residents and leading tobacco planters. Said you're making him a test case." The lawman pushed his hat back a little on his head, and grinned.

Withers did not respond, though he did cast glances at the other two men, who seemed to be enjoying themselves.

Gates went on, "Seems Mr. Upchurch sold Cincinnati, that free black still living on his property, back into slavery. Sold him to a good friend down in Georgia who needed a cobbler. You put it out that Upchurch informed Cincinnati if he didn't go along with being sold, Upchurch would turn around and sell his whole family. Why, friend, you're making like free blacks are a vital part of our community. This could scare other whites and frighten the poor darkies. Said you plan to argue to the court that white people don't have a right to do that. What a lot of bull! Let me school you here. Whites were still in charge when I got up this morning. Don't you know you're sabotaging just what makes the South the absolute best place to be?"

"For whom?" Withers asked scornfully.

Gates leaned back and exchanged glances with the men. He grinned wider. "You got to ask me that question, Mr. Withers, you too dumb to be a Southerner. And we don't want you here."

Withers's back stiffened. He took a deep breath and tried to explain that it was a clear case of extortion.

"And what do you get out of this?" Gates asked, scratching his ear. "Something for the good white folks or something for the nigras?"

"Just trying to do the right thing," Withers answered.

Gates shook his head sadly. "That's just crazy. All nigras will get to thinking they can take their cases to court, when we know courts were created for white folks."

Withers realized with these men there would be no reasonable talk or satisfactory explanation. "Haaya!" he cried and kicked his horse to a gallop. He raced through the back roads and whipped onto a dirt path through a thicket of bushes and ancient trees. Just when he reached a bend in the road, Gates and his men closed him off.

Gates made a mocking face at the panicked Withers. "Lord, man, that was wild. Who taught you to ride like that?"

"Listen," Withers began.

The men laughed loudly now. "Look at that mutt's face," one of them said. "I think he's gonna shit a load."

"Okay," Gates said, "that was fun but I've got someplace to be. So if you would be so kind, Mr. Withers, get down off your horse."

Withers's head filled with dizzying fear. The sky and earth spun around him. "I told you, I've... I've got someplace to be myself," Withers stammered. His throat was dry.

"Up at the Louvestres'?"

Withers nodded.

"Gonna meet Mr. Lumley?"

Withers's eyes were wide. He did not move or speak.

"Now see," Gates murmured, "you got to be careful who you call friend these days."

Withers's fright was a torment now. Sweat beaded his forehead and his body began to quiver. "I ... I'm leaving."

Gates smiled. "Yes, you are. Our business together won't take much longer." He took the reins of Withers's horse. "You do have two friends who asked to be remembered to you. One said to give you her special regards."

Withers hardly had a voice at all. "Who?" he managed.

"Gal by the name of Barlow," Gates said, sucking his teeth.

Withers looked perplexed at him. "Alcamera?"

"Seems she has a score to settle with you. Your other friend does too." Gates now stood over Withers, who was being forced to his knees by the two men. "This man said to tell you he was sorry, but you got in his way. Irritated the hell out of him. Told me to make sure his name was the last thing you heard."

Gates bent down and whispered into Withers's ear as one of the men struck. Withers looked up and his scream sent night birds bursting from their nests and careening into the dark sky.

Gates repeated the name that trailed Withers into blackness. "Lumley!"

CHAPTER 18

For Simeon, getting to sleep had been easy. Staying asleep had been the trial. Dreams, more like nightmares, had tired him out and made him feel uneasy. He sat up on the side of the bed.

"What is it, dear?" Tesh-Lucianne asked, putting a gentle hand on the small of his back.

He turned and looked at her in the blue light of pre-dawn. Hopeful eyes looked back at him. How lovely she was. That hadn't changed after all these years. He took her hand and patted it.

"Too much stimulation." He chuckled softly. "Go back to sleep."

"No, there's something," she said sitting up. "I can tell."

He sighed. "My thoughts are muddled, but I guess I'm concerned about the future."

Tesh-Lucianne propped herself up on the many pillows at the headboard and did something uncustomary for her. She waited.

"In my selfish love for the sea, I always thought I'd be on it in some way. When I stupidly fell while on the last ship, I knew the Navy was going to retire me on the spot because the doctor said my heart wasn't the best. But they didn't. Said I was a great asset to them and gave me this adjunct capacity to help with various projects without having to leave land. Thus this consultation I now have, refurbishing the CSS *Virginia*."

Simeon ran his fingers through his tousled leonine hair, and it fell pleasingly back into place. "What if the North continues its stranglehold on the South, despite everything? What if a fight between our ironclad and theirs does nothing but provide entertainment of an afternoon for the onlookers? I won't have done what my father harped on for years."

"What's that?"

"I haven't made a back door for myself, a contingency plan, so to speak."

"Is this where politics comes in?"

"It does. But sometimes I feel like a huckster, up on my high horse pitching snake oil for bunions."

"Why?"

"The issue for most Southerners of our quarter is about land, how to hold on to our piece of it. Everything else we do is a consequence of that—slavery especially. For all my talk, coached expertly now by Lumley, most of what I say doesn't mean a hill of beans to the average person."

"You're forgetting you're not addressing the average person," Tesh-Lucianne said. "It's the moneyed class whose ears you have. They're your constituents. They could not care less about anything other than keeping the slaves in check in order to protect their profits on tobacco, on cotton, on the sale of liquor. That's why they're all het up about law and order. It's about their ledger books, dear. And they know that you know about such things. What's more, they know you don't want to lose what you have, any more than they want their things threatened. If you win, so do they."

Simeon went to one of two comfortable armchairs and a Hepplewhite table, across from her, where he poured himself a glass of water. "How'd you get so smart?"

"I've been married to you all these years," she said. "I've learned a few things."

"Frankly, I don't know what all the new government of the South has up its sleeve for the people. I'm just out there talking, throwing out issues and possible solutions. Who knows if the Confederacy will back me on what I'm saying? The real fact is I'm out there trying to build a platform to make a more solid place for ourselves, come what may."

"Just what everybody does, if they can," Tesh-Lucianne said.

"The thought that I'm driven by personal self-interest, and maybe a little greed, seeing what I can buy in these down times—well, that's troubling for me. I feel a bit diminished as a person."

"Ah, well. That you can do something about."

Simeon looked up from the cut glass tumbler in his hand. "How?"

"Change your thinking," she said. "It's just that simple."

He smiled and rolled his eyes.

"Seriously," she said. "You want something different, think differently. If you feel like a huckster, then decide to run the show. That's what they, our people, want you to do. That's what you want to do. So?"

"And what about you, Tesh-Lucianne, the heart of this town, doer of good works?"

She looked at him directly, intensity in her eyes. "That image wouldn't help you in your endeavors?"

He sat upright. "I don't understand. You've aided the sick, ignorant, downtrodden, and slaves when it certainly wasn't the socially advantageous thing to do. You did it anyway." He sipped from his glass. "I'm confused. You'd foster that just to help my new career?"

Tesh-Lucianne sat in the lamp light, bright on her face, illuminating the best portions of it. She smoothed the crocheted collar of her lovely bed jacket for sweet effect, radiant in the dawn. "Your new word for the day is 'prudence.' Women have made friends with this word for a long time. It means to do whatever it is you have to do. Isn't that fun?" She smiled brightly.

Simeon leaned back and surveyed his wife, her long hair drifting over her shoulders. Her gown lay softly over mounded breasts rising and falling with her breathing. Suddenly, he felt something stirring in his pants. Nothing down there had suggested life for a long time. Well, he laughed to himself, a rising manhood. If this is what politics can do for me, I'm all for it.

"You might consider Lumley a sort of godsend," Tesh-Lucianne said.

"Oh? Tell me why."

"He thinks he's not, but he's transparent. He's obviously a very ambitious man. He would be regarded as a second-seater. He doesn't want to be in the lead, out front, so to speak. What he wants is to control the lead. In this case, that would be you." Tesh-Lucianne gestured at the table. "Pour me some water, won't you?"

As Simeon retrieved a glass and poured her drink, she went on.

"His strengths are that he gets things done. He's a weathervane that sees which way the winds blow. With hard eyes he reads the directions well. He knows that people in this town are het up over the issue of law and order. They're afraid of the changes coming on and the new manner of things coming with them. The winds of war blow on the good and the bad. The strange thing about wind is, if it blows on you too long, it can drive you mad."

Simeon handed her the drink. She thanked him with her eyes and took a swallow. "If that happens," she continued, "the good people don't know if they're good anymore. And the bad can carry the illusion of good. In other words, life gets distorted and intentions get twisted in the wind. People make bad judgments just to save themselves from personal mistakes they didn't set out to make. Arrogance and defiance carry the day. That's when an awful thing can happen."

"Worse than arrogance and defiance?" Simeon said.

Tesh-Lucianne sighed, turned a contemptuous lip upward, and sipped her drink again. "Forgetfulness. A cruel loss of mind. People don't remember who they really are. All sorts of things can get borne on the wind then."

Simeon looked at her directly. "Are we still talking about Lumley or me?" he said.

Tesh-Lucianne blinked twice, seeming to come out of a trance. She looked back at him full-eyed. "What?"

"That did not sound like the voice of Tesh-Lucianne."

"What do you know?" She swatted air at him, scoffing. "Beware of Lumley. Keep a watchful eye on him or what I'd call the Humpty Dumpty fate could befall you. He would not hurt you. He'd make you hurt yourself."

The room was quiet a long moment.

Simeon turned to her. Her sensuousness exuded not from body alone. "I think I like this new you. Did you happen in this wind when I wasn't looking?"

"A long time ago, my father produced a distortion, no, two distortions. Me and—," she stopped. "Oh enough! I sound impassioned and I'll quit this very minute." She handed him her glass.

"I take it you're not going to reveal the other distortion?

"Forget about it. It's old business."

Simeon rose, took off his robe, and climbed into bed with his wife, taking her into his arms. He kissed her and murmured into her ear, "I'll let it go for now. The wind has compelled other things to lift too."

Tesh-Lucianne giggled and pressed herself to him, wanting to in a rush, needing to, in the haloed flames of lamplight while the frogs and crickets outside played a melody.

CHAPTER 19

"I never get tired of this place," Mary said wistfully as she gazed at the profusion of trees turning autumn yellow and wildflowers that carpeted the rich earth. She was standing at the riverbank where a lively tributary fed into the cobalt waters of the mighty Chesapeake. "Creation is eloquent here and nourishes the soul. This is truly God's country."

"Shame we don't have any fishing poles," she said, turning back toward where Anders was lounging on a large blanket under a spreading sycamore.

"I don't think we need one," he said. "The way those fish are leaping, we could just hold the frying pan out and they'd jump right in it." Taller than her by a head, his was an angular face, glowing and glistening under the sun's demanding rays. Wide, powerful shoulders and taut, muscular arms bulged under the rolled up sleeves of his red-and-white gingham shirt. His chest plunged toward a flat stomach where a wide black-leather belt cinched a small waist above narrow hips in black trousers creased knife-sharp. He exuded a mellow energy that resonated within Mary whenever they were together. This machinist, a free black man, had an inner confidence without boastfulness.

She went to the picnic basket. "I hope you brought your appetite." Her green eyes, flecked with umber in the bright sunlight, were teasing.

"Always," he said, "for more of you."

Smiling, she swatted at him. "Stop that kind of talk. It's unseemly."

"To who?" Anders looked around. "Not a soul out here but us chickens." He jumped up, folded his elbows back, and strutted around looking so much like a chicken that Mary had to laugh.

"Stop clowning," she said, motioning him to sit. "Compliments of Roguey, we have spiced ham slices, roasted game hens, okra, fried green tomatoes, and fresh-baked sweet potato biscuits with butter." She eyed him playfully. "For dessert, her famous pound cake with rum sauce."

"Seems like a celebration."

"It is."

"For what?"

"For your completing all the hard work on the new battleship. Or ..." Mary, filling his plate, paused thoughtfully. "When we discussed it some more, we weren't quite sure if we should be paying you compliments or not."

Anders had his back propped against the tree. "I've definitely got mixed feelings about that." His eyes gleamed as he took the heaping plate Mary handed him. "God, girl! You fattening me up for slaughter?"

"That'd be futile," she said.

"Anyway, I work too hard to put on weight. Like you, I don't seem to gain or lose. And on you, it looks beautiful." Anders eyed Mary more hungrily than his plate.

Mary was wearing a heavy copper-colored silk dress cut V-necked and slightly off the shoulder. She had used Algerian embroidery to set off the neckline of lightweight white silk, working slanting lines of lattice-pattern in crimson threads. A fleur-de-lis edge was composed of two rows of chain stitch and French knots twisted with threads of pearl. The bodice was close fitting and a simple belt-like waist fastened the skirt with a cording button. The plain skirt fell in an easy drape, with the same embroidered patterning repeated in a thinner line down one side. On her middle finger was the ring with the carnelian gemstone in a gold setting that Tesh-Lucianne had given her.

Anders became self-conscious that he still wore his work clothes. He picked at the food on his plate. She read the frown on his face.

"What is it?"

"Things are coming to a fast conclusion."

Mary waited.

"The ship is going out for one last test next week, even though I keep telling them that the engine still needs work. She's very heavy now with that four-inch iron plating crisscrossed around her bow. With all that weight, she'll ride dangerously low in the water. She needs power underneath her, and well, I don't know. I should keep my mouth closed."

Mary said she had heard more about the Northern ironclad. "From the looks of it, people are calling it a 'cheese box on a raft.'"

"The engineers say it has an iron-plated turret that revolves all the way around. I've never heard of such a thing."

Mary replied, "I'm sure they didn't want you to hear that."

"Either way, we're in for a battle to be remembered."

"No doubt."

Anders paused a long time, staring into the middle distance. "Ours is a monster ship, frightening to look at. Even more scary to be fired on by her. Yet for all that, she's not invincible."

"Could another ship wound her?" Mary asked.

"Typical ordnance against her will only frustrate the shooter. It'll bounce right off without a scar. Those in charge are pretty smug, but she can be hurt to the point of going down."

"Really? How?"

Anders looked at her. "Pound her at the waterline. That's where she's weak. No plating."

"Why wouldn't they protect that area?"

"Because they're pretty sure no ship can shoot cannon that low or would want to."

Mary had put her plate down while Anders was talking. "Why do I want to feel good about that?"

"You know, while I am working on the ship, I feel proud to be there, proud that I could show them that a Negro can be a skillful artisan. But now that the job is about over, my mind is getting low."

"I know," Mary said. "My feeling is if I do a good job in my craft, I'm helping the South, and that may mean I'm working against myself in the end. If I don't do a good job, I feel like I'm betraying my God-given gifts. Sometimes I feel trapped."

"Yes," Anders said, his gaze far away. "You know, in a few short months, they won't need me anymore."

Mary didn't want to admit it to him, but she too never felt more expendable. That seemed contradictory to what was happening in her life, with the fashion show coming up and the greater possibilities for developing a name for herself. For reasons she couldn't put her finger on, she felt as if she were on sinking sand.

"I've been racking my brain what to do."

"Have you?" Mary said softly. "Did you think of something?"

Anders sadly shook his head "no." "Nothing that wouldn't eventually get us in trouble or killed."

"These days, everything feels tissue-paper thin, hardly with substance."

Mary stared off, not knowing what to say.

He wanted to hold her, feel her softness against him.

Mary wanted to be held, to wrap her arms around his taut, muscled body once more.

Anders stood. He held out his hand to help her up and moved close, not wanting to immediately pack up to leave. He smelled her femaleness and moved closer to her. She arched toward him. That was the sign he wanted, that she wanted to be near him too. He caressed her cheek, then dropped his hand down the side of her throat and around to the back of her neck. She lifted her mouth up to his. She fingered his face and pulled him to her as they kissed. She held him and pressed herself against him in a way that revealed her desire. He saw she had closed her eyes, and at that moment he realized she reflected all of the needs within him and was as hungry to fulfill them as he was.

They made love on the blanket, heedless of the late afternoon cool. They wanted all of each other now—smell, taste, touch. They gave in to their all-encompassing desire beneath the few leaves that hugged the trees, for what sustenance they could receive before autumn died and they had to let go forever. Afterward, Anders lay his head in her lap. She touched his forehead, his hair, his ears, finally the space over his heart, a space she knew she would also occupy in her absence.

Later, evening lowered over the valley when the startling sound of horses pounded on the road behind their wagon, kicking up clouds of dust. Anders glanced over his shoulder and clicked at the horses to angle the buggy out of the way. Mary looked back to see the riders. One of them wore a duster; she knew a headache was coming on. When they came abreast of the buggy, Mary swallowed hard.

Gates grinned at them, tipped his hat. "Evenin' y'all."

Neither Mary nor Anders spoke.

"Where y'all comin' from?"

"Mr. Gates," Mary said deliberately, "what is it you want?"

"I'm tryin' to pass a civil moment with two of Norfolk's finest darkies."

"You ran your horses like bats out of hell to visit with us?" Anders asked.

Gates pasted on a wider grin, then spoke menacingly. "Where y'all comin' from or goin'? It ain't often you get to see such a sight as you, Miss Mary, dressed up in what I have to say is even more beautiful than usual, ridin' in a fine buggy, beau at your side," he said and glanced in the back, "with picnic basket and blanket. But you didn't answer my question."

"We're coming back from an outing," Mary said. "Just an afternoon outing, that's all."

Gates hawked and spit, wiped his mouth on his sleeve, and returned the smile to his lips. "Well now, seem like Junior Wooford had him some trouble out to his place. Somebody, just for spite, let his horses out of the corral and his pigs loose. He's still chasin' the pigs. Might be out by St. Louis around now, the way he was runnin'." He chuckled. "Mad as a hornet he was. Swears if he gets wind of who done it, he gonna ..." Gates slapped his hat on his thigh. "Well you can imagine what he said. You know Junior when he gets riled."

Mary and Anders exchanged anxious glances.

"I wouldn't expect y'all have any notion who might'a done such a dastardly deed as that?"

"No," Anders said. Mary said nothing. Eventually, she shook her head.

"I surely wouldn't think that of y'all. But somebody said they saw a couple of coloreds out by that way," Gates said, his eyes taunting, his tone feigning politeness.

Mary heaved a sigh. "Mr. Gates, do we look like the sort of people who would look for entertainment like that?"

Gates guffawed. "Oh heck no. Y'all quality niggers." He wagged his head sadly. "Never can tell about people though, can you? I just ask direct."

Mary pursed her lips and stared at him. Gates had something up his sleeve, she thought. She would just wait him out.

"By the way, y'all got any passes to be out this late?"

Anders snorted, surprised. "We've never had to have passes before."

"Before? Before what?" Gates said.

"Before being accosted on the road this evening for nothing," Anders said with heat.

Gates leaned forward to look Anders in the eye. He held the stare, as did Anders. "You better keep up with the rules around here. All nigras got to have passes any time they're out and about, especially toward evening."

"Since when?" Mary said, challenging him.

"I fixed notices around just this mornin'," Gates said. Then he wagged his finger at them. "Ignorance of the law don't make you less guilty. Why, I could run y'all into jail right this very minute."

Mary looked at him, and said nothing.

After a minute, Gates hooted. "Hellfire! I like 'em rumble-tough, don't you, boy?" He was addressing Anders.

Anders's jaw tightened, but he said nothing.

"Well, hell, I tell you what I'm gon' do," Gates said, having fun. "It's such a lovely evenin'." He turned his face up and sniffed deeply. "I'm gon' turn a blind eye to your outright abusement of the law and let you go this time. I don't want to throw Miss Classy-Spitfire into no nasty jail cell, leas'ways tonight." He rode off laughing, then turned around as if he forgot something. "Boy" he called to Anders, "you better pack up an' git on back to where you come from, you know what's good for you." Then he rode off, whistling a ditty tune.

Anders was practically panting. He felt impotent against Gates and his like.

Mary put her hand over his forearm and touched his face with her fingers. "Don't let Gates get to you. He's a ruffian and he likes to bedevil people."

"I wanted to slug him," Anders said. "I wanted to get down from this buggy and drag that fool off his horse and whale the tar out of him. And I wanted to read him his character, what little he has of it. But all I could do was sit here in front of my lady and that white man and hang my head. I hate it! I hate it that he is one of the people I help build that ship to save." His expression was pained. "It's not right. It's just not right."

Anders's passion hit Mary like a sledgehammer. She felt exactly the same way.

CHAPTER 20

The next day, Mary awakened, stretching and luxuriating in her four-poster bed. She knew she had to get up, get going for the day, but burrowing under the freshly-ironed sheets and soft chenille bedspread for a few more minutes felt so good.

Lavender fragrances from the garden wafted into the generous space that was her room. The sun dawned dramatically in yellows and golds out past her balcony over the trees below. Her eye traveled around the room. She had loved this place since she was a girl. The stained glass lamp glimmered on the small table near an easy grouping of parlor chairs and a Chippendale glass and wood bookcase where she kept her beloved collection of newspapers, magazines, and books. Her present favorite book featured Eulalia, a Northern woman who came to the South as the bride of a plantation owner. Mary smiled, thinking on the woman's spunk, and hoped there'd be time to read today. She gave silent blessings to Tesh-Lucianne for having taught her to read even though this was against the law. Books gave Mary such pleasure. Studying the problems characters encountered, she challenged her mind to see solutions quickly.

Okay, enough indulgence, she told herself. Up, the day was wasting. Birds chittered outside. She sat up, pulled the dainty housecoat over her gown, stuck her feet into matching Chinese slippers, and yawned. She let her eyes wander along the bottles filled with Hungary water—a blend of scents and alcohol—and a mixture of mountain laurel, witch hazel, and water she applied to her body for its sweet, refreshing fragrance. She sighed in the morning's laziness and looked over at the basin and white pitcher trimmed with delicate blue flowers that sat on the mahogany bureau. She decided it was time to go downstairs to fill the pitcher with fresh water to wash up. Mary had been so busy preparing for the party that she felt neglectful of Coolie. The young woman's body had healed from the beating inflicted by Gates, but her mind was still anguished and couldn't sleep. Coolie had convalesced at Bear's home at Stonehaven and was now back at Travelers Rest. Bear, Jitter, and others were keeping a close eye on her. Mary stretched as she rose from bed, deciding that she would pay her friend a visit.

She had finished dressing and was enjoying a final spritz of fragrance when a scream tore the air.

"This is just terrible," Tesh-Lucianne cried. She held a page of morning paper in her hand.

Mary quickly banged down the stairs.

"You're going to make yourself sick, you keep this up," Simeon said, patting her hand and looking at his wit's end. "Mary, thank goodness you're here. Can you see to Tesh-Lucianne?"

"What's the matter?"

Roguey looked about to curse.

Tesh-Lucianne, flush-faced, thrust the paper at Mary.

Mary read the headline out loud, "A Life For Peacock Feathers." She looked up, puzzled.

"Read on," Tesh-Lucianne said, blowing her nose into a handkerchief.

Mary sank down into a chair as she tried to absorb the news story of a young Negro named Pluck who was shot along the river's edge while foraging for peacock feathers on Emmett Crawthers's property. Tears of anguish began to well inside her. Pluck dead? Shot? For feathers? It didn't make sense. Why?

Tesh-Lucianne cried, "It's all my fault."

Mary looked up, both irritated and confused. "What are you saying?"

"When she was here tending to the party," Tesh-Lucianne sniffed, "We ... I was admiring a hand fan carried by the senator's wife. Pluck was serving us and I mentioned how much I admired the fan. She must have gone looking for some ... feathers." Tears teetered at her lower lids. "Now this."

Simeon tried to comfort her. "There, there dear, how could it be your fault? You couldn't have known this would happen."

Tesh-Lucianne's eyes appealed to Mary. "Do you know anything about Crawthers and these ... these dratted birds?"

Mary's emotions had her frozen for a moment. She wrapped her arms about herself and spoke flatly. "Crawthers." She cleared her throat. "A trader brought in a few of them years ago. They're peacocks. Mr. Crawthers liked their colorful feathers and decided he wanted to breed them on his farm. Local kids would sometimes steal onto his property to fish or swim and pick up some of the bird feathers. I don't know much more than that." She sighed ruefully. "I can't imagine how this happened with Pluck. Everybody knows how Mr. Crawthers feels about trespassing his property."

Tesh-Lucianne collapsed into another fit of tears.

Mary flinched when she glanced at Roguey. A vein pulsed hard and fast in the middle of the cook's forehead; her eyes were cold and hard. "You're on your way to the girl's house now?" Tesh-Lucianne asked Mary.

The girl, Mary thought. Now it's the girl? Her name is Pluck. "Yes," she said.

"Well, you tell her mother not to worry about a thing. Simeon and I will pay for the burial." Tesh-Lucianne's voice was now composed, the hanky put away along with any tears.

Mary rose. She spun around carefully to avoid another glance at Roguey. Instead, sickened unto death in her own heart, she replied with teeth, "I'll be sure to do that."

As she moved in a controlled hurry to leave, she heard Tesh-Lucianne brightly opine, "Goodness me!" She clapped hands. "Burden lifted."

Roguey made rumbling sounds in her throat.

Mary and Devereaux rode through the narrow inner-city streets of Norfolk to Cecilia's tenement building. Beside herself with worry, she burst through the door to see Miss Effie administering a compress to Cecilia, whose skin was the color of clay. Her face held no expression.

"Miss Effie, I'm so glad you're still here. What can I do? How can I be of help?"

"Nothin' you can do, Mary. She fell over when neighbors come with the news," Miss Effie said. "I gave her somethin' to make her sleep."

Mary felt helpless, knowing it was best to let the sick woman rest. Fortune was weeping uncontrollably into her hands in a corner of the dim room. Mary went to her and wrapped the girl in her arms to offer comfort. Pluck was laid out on the kitchen table. Two pennies lay on the table. Mary knew they would cover her eyes.

Fortune's anger blazed through her tears. How could Mr. Crawthers shoot her for taking feathers?

When Mary asked if Miss Effie needed more medicine for Cecilia, the old teacher shook her head. "Let's give her through the night. She was rallying well before this happened. She's gonna have to grieve now. That's gon' take its toll."

Mary realized she could do nothing more right now. As she and Devereaux left, she placed several Confederate bills on the kitchen table.

CHAPTER 21

Simeon knocked on the door to Mary's salon and entered. "Hello, hello," he said heartily. "Came to check on your progress."

"Really?" Mary said, still in a snit. Emotions from her visit to Miss Effie from just a few hours earlier still resonated. She sat stoic at the shiny Chippendale mahogany table that served as a workspace, continuing with her hand stitching.

"The fall line—well." He sucked on a dead pipe, looked at it surprised, and rested an elbow on the marble mantel above the fireplace. "A lot's riding on your newest creations."

Mary kept her mouth shut.

"You have nothing to say?"

Mary wagged her head, trying to distract herself from thoughts of Pluck and the pile of work in front of her.

Simeon pulled up, put off by Mary's attitude. He put his pipe to his mouth and spoke jerkily until he was able to light it again. "Everything going off ... without a hitch. I know you need more help ... so ... I'll allow for two more seamstresses. That suit you?" He grabbed the poker with the duck's head and prodded the fire. Leaning on the mantel again, he continued, "The business has grown immensely in the past couple of years. You and Tesh-Lucianne have done a great job bringing in new customers, counting money on your fingers and toes." His short laugh and sorry attempt at humor fell flat on both of them.

Mary stopped sewing and regarded him quietly.

Simeon went to stand beside Mary, and placed his hand on her shoulder. His own sense of importance so filled the room that he did not notice the involuntary shrink Mary gave his touch. "One of the problems I have as leader of this household and business operation is knowing when to use the word 'no.' Up to now, we've never had to say that to you, but things have grown almost out of hand."

"Oh?"

"I believe the business has outstripped homemade ledgers and Mason jar cash drawers."

"That's good, right?"

Simeon puffed, tilted his head ever so slightly and eased away. Stalled in answer, he made a to-do at tapping the contents of the pipe bowl into the fireplace when came a verbal knock on the door.

"It's only me," Tesh-Lucianne said. "The two of you with your heads together could only mean something interesting."

"Oh," Mary started before Simeon held up a restraining hand.

"Come in dear."

Tesh-Lucianne's eyebrows arched playfully. "What could the two of you possibly be dreaming up?"

"Little or nothing."

"Right you are."

The Louvestres laughed, exchanging companionable glances with each other as if they didn't have a clue about Mary's upset. Mary watched them take each other arm in arm.

"Tell me something," Tesh-Lucianne said. "Why do you have a fire going in September, hot as it is?"

"Roasting bugs," Mary said lowly.

"Ugh!" Simeon exclaimed, glancing down at a pan of dead insects he'd not noticed before.

"Not so bad," Mary said, "not when you're making buttons out of them."

"Well, I for one am glad to see you back at work," Tesh-Lucianne said, "and things proceeding along. I sent invitations to the fashion show to every important person in the Commonwealth and points south. And each and every one has penned a note back that they're coming. We want to do all we can to assure that this event helps launch The House of M into the common parlance of everyone of resource and influence. In other words, the rich and voting public."

Mary watched as Simeon and Tesh-Lucianne crossed the salon to the doors that opened onto the veranda. "I'm going to hoodwink my husband into strolling the evening shore with me before bed," Tesh-Lucianne said, winking. Mary squeezed the bone needle in her fingers so hard she snapped it in two, drawing a little blood. Her eyes stared straight ahead, the rise and fall of her breath coming in bursts, the wind off the veranda fingering her hair. She muttered angrily, "Not a word about Pluck."

Mary's mood changed when she reached Travelers Rest and found Coolie in her expansive apartment above the inn. Coolie had been brushing her hair, and Mary quickly took over.

"You're coming along all right."

"Evidently," Coolie said.

"Your hair's beautiful."

"Yeah well, Mama give me somethin' worthwhile, huh?"

"Coolie, Gie gave you life, whatever else she may or may not have put up is for grabs."

"That the way you think about yourself, Miss Mary? I mean, you got long hair too, almost straight. Ever wonder where that might've come from? Ever wonder how come you got the hair you got?"

As the two women talked, Mary realized there was something different about Coolie today. She seemed to have some of her old fire back. Coolie told Mary how upset she was about Gates, the slaughter of Negroes in Norfolk, the murder of Pluck, the increasingly agitated talk of whites. Mary said she too was growing concerned and felt threatened, even among the Louvestres. Mary admitted that she was being followed. Coolie's brow pleated. "Why ain't you said nothin' 'bout this before?" Coolie's anger flared when Mary said she hadn't wanted to worry her.

"See," Mary said, "that's just the reaction I didn't want to cause. I don't want you going off half-cocked again and getting into trouble over me."

But there was a look in Coolie's eyes Mary had not seen before.

"What have you got on your mind, girl?"

Coolie grinned slyly. "Why?"

"I don't get it. For days, you went along so low you were looking up to the belly of a snake. Then I come in here today and you're different, like you could take on the world."

Coolie hugged Mary and danced around the room. She stopped and uttered mysteriously, "People can change and I'm a people." She giggled, but Mary was not fooled.

Mary returned to her salon later in the day but found it impossible to concentrate on her work. Taking up her walking stick, she went in search of Devereaux, who was grooming the horses.

He saw the dark concern on her face.

"I can't get Coolie out of my mind. I need to go back out there."

"Yes, Mademoiselle," he said smartly. If Mary was concerned, Devereaux was concerned. "Ten minutes will see us on our way."

CHAPTER 22

"So when is Daddy A.B. returning to Richmond?" Simeon asked.

"Tomorrow sometime," Tesh-Lucianne whispered. "Right now, he's on his head to see you in your study. Lumley is waiting with him."

Simeon sighed heavily.

Tesh-Lucianne put a hand to his chest. "Y'all be nice, now. You can put up with him for one more day, whatever he's got to say."

"Your father can be so demanding," Simeon lamented, glancing toward his office door.

"So? Let him demand away and then return to Richmond. He's an old man in a wheelchair. He certainly can't chase you around and make you do anything, can he?" Tesh-Lucianne was teasing her husband.

Simeon bent down to her and said in a low voice, "Your father will find a way."

Tesh-Lucianne chuckled and shooed him on with her fingers. "We'll have lunch when you're done gladiating each other in there."

On the large desk in front of Daddy A.B. was a single piece of white paper with a list of names that were numbered. He glanced at it distractedly, then pushed himself toward the blaze in the fireplace. It was an annoying fact of his life that even on warm days his intractable limbs required even more heat to keep from aching intolerably. He poured himself another tall bourbon—that helped when nothing else did. He didn't care that he'd had two already. This was one of the pleasures of an old, invalid man, that and the fun of scaring the daylights out of his son-in-law cum politician and his major cohort, Lumley. The door creaked.

"Daddy A.B., I'm delivering to you my sweet Simeon," Tesh-Lucianne said, sticking her head in the door. "I want him returned to me safe and sound, you hear?"

"Scoot, l'il darlin'," Daddy A.B. said, not unkindly. "The men folks got things to talk about."

When Simeon and Lumley had drinks and settled on the sofa across from the fireplace, Daddy A.B. said, "You're a failure, Simeon."

Simeon raised a surprised eyebrow at the old man. "What?"

"Don't look so startled. We're not foolin' each other. I know you threw that fancy shindig the other night to encourage votes, right?"

"The idea was Tesh-Lucianne's," Simeon began an explanation.

The old man held up a staying hand. "She's shrewd. She picked up that you were losing ground and you needed a little lift." He smiled mirthlessly. "You've barely begun your campaign and already you need more support."

"Political campaigns don't just happen," Lumley offered, leaning forward, drink in hand. He bent his head as if in supplication, let his shoulders slump, but he was really only playing to the old fop. "The election to senatorial office requires a lot of work. Not only by us but by the many volunteers who need a headquarters. Influences have to be persuaded and highly-placed allies encouraged."

"Oh," said the old man, "let's see if I've got this straight—influence, soap boxes, finessing, and money. That right?"

"In a word, yes," Lumley answered as if repeating the obvious to the slow-witted.

"I see," Daddy A.B. said, puffing the cigar clenched in his teeth, as though deep in thought. "Well, my bankers tell me that the two of you have been moving a lot of money into this and that. But other of my informants say you're not gaining that much political ground as a result. You've been doin' a lot of speechifyin', makin' noise about law and order and all." He grunted. "I think people take you for a patsy. After all, what would a ship's chandler know about governance?"

This was priceless, Daddy A.B. thought. He was tweaking Simeon and enjoying it immensely. He could see the younger man, who always prized himself for being in control, losing it by degrees.

Simeon grimaced and arched an eyebrow. "I take issue with that. My platform has, at its heart, a safe Norfolk. It declares a hard line for law and order to reinforce and protect it. I'll call forth the men who might be left behind, the ones unacceptable as soldiers and sailors for any reason, to enlist with us to protect our sovereign land." He looked hard at Daddy A.B. "You couldn't possibly know all I've already done toward those efforts, but we're sure they will gain us victory."

"Really?" Daddy A.B. assessed him over his drinking glass. "So what, specifically, have you done?"

"It's enough to say, a lot. No one needs to be privy to details but me. And, of course, Lumley here."

"Lumley! Balls!" Daddy A.B. cried. "You two are a pair to draw to. That much I know."

Exasperated, Simeon stalked to the bar and poured himself another stiff one. He wanted this old coot out of his life and his house in the worst way, but

Tesh-Lucianne adored him. That meant he couldn't tell the self-righteous cud to hit the road.

Daddy A.B. pulled long on his drink and smacked his lips. "Fact is, I think you'd do yourself a service to hire another manager. This one," he poked his cigar in the air toward Lumley, "well, what do they say about a dried mustard seed? It's got heart, but ain't much promise in it."

Lumley angrily shot up. "Wait just a minute! I'm no novice to this business. I know what I'm doing."

"And I have ultimate faith in Lumley," Simeon stated adamantly.

"I could put my faith in these old bones in my legs working again, but that would be ridiculous," Daddy A.B. said. "With this rheumatism, I know that simply is not going to happen. All I'm saying is, we have to be certain about where we put our trust and ability, to make things happen." He opened his palsied hands. "I don't care about your campaign and I don't care about you. Bottom line is, I care about the happiness of my little girl. When you don't win—and the likelihood is you won't—all of these new so-called friends dancing around you will dissolve like heat shimmers over a hot road. She's going to wonder where they all went, what did she do, how did she let you down? I told you when I let you marry Tesh-Lucianne that you were never to make her cry. Well, she's being set up to cry now." When he looked over at them, his face was red with spleen. "Get this right, young fellows, or I promise you the future will be your worst enemy."

"Is that a threat?" Simeon asked. "I'll not have you talk this way to me in my own house. Tesh-Lucianne is your daughter, but she's my wife. I'll take care of her the way I think is best."

Daddy A.B. waved his hand. "I'm a sick old man. I don't have to threaten anyone. I'm rich, so rich I don't know a soul in the Commonwealth who doesn't want to make me happy—whatever that takes." He smiled at the men and lifted his glass in salute. "No sir, I don't have to threaten at all. I just say the word." He held up gnarled fingers. "Life and death are in the power of my hand."

"Sounds like a threat to me," Lumley said. Still, he knew Daddy A.B. might be an old man decrepit in body, yet his mind was a steel trap. He was indeed one to bear watching—and using, if he could, down the line. "Threats don't sit well with me."

Daddy A.B. laughed. "You politicians. How you can turn a phrase."

CHAPTER 23

Gie Atkins appeared at the door held open by her maid, squinting and batting her eyes behind thick bottle-lens spectacles. "Mary, is it? Come in."

She wore a green silk dress Mary had designed for her last season. Worn simply over small shoulders, it had a V-neck with a tiny yellow ruffle in teasing descent along her slope of breasts and repeated from the easy waist flowing at angles down the right side to the hem. Her riot of hair was parted in the middle and barely contained in braids folded over each other and pinned on top of her head. A gold choker accentuated her crepey neck.

"To what do I owe the honor of your appearing unannounced at my home this morning?" she asked. "But come in."

Mary followed Gie through the wide wainscoted hallway where portraits of dour ancestors lined the walls, past the library on the left filled with leather-bound books and pleasant seating, to the parlor where wide windows looked out on a green lawn trimmed with showy hibiscus. Sunlight streamed through the branches of ancient pines and into the room to dance on the rich oriental carpet on the floor.

Uncomfortably, Mary sat on the edge of a damask-covered chair. The maid set a cup of hot, fragrant tea in front of her.

"I brought your dress for the gala," Mary said. She felt like a coward. Why couldn't she just come out with it? Borrowing time, she took a polite sip of the unsatisfying liquid. It tasted like gall to her tongue.

Gie sat in a tapestry-covered chair across from her. "Thank you, but seeing as how you knew I'd be at your house later today working with Tesh-Lucianne on our help-the-soldiers project, I assume something is on your mind of a private nature."

Mary was silent, ill at ease.

Gie gave a dark chuckle, though laughter did not reach her opalescent eyes. "I heard what happened with Coolie. Who hasn't? But if you're here to beseech me for maternal concern, forget it."

Mary swallowed hard, mastering a calm exterior. "Is that so wrong?"

"Look, by now, both you and Coolie are acutely aware I have no maternal interests. Had I, I would not have pretended over the years that I do not have a daughter. What I have is money and social standing that I'm not willing to trade for the issue of a ten-minute dalliance I had once in bed. Even though that hard-bodied slave did give me more pleasure than I'd ever admit in pleasant company."

"But Gates is a dangerous man."

Gie's eyes were hard on Mary. "And what would you have me do in light of that?"

"Do?" asked Mary, confused.

"Sheriff Bridges's mother, Miss Clara-Jean, is one of my closest friends."

Mary shot her a look, then put her attention on holding her teacup on the lap of her mustard-colored dress. She restrained herself from fingering the thin red and gold piping tweaked around her neckline, knowing to fidget would reveal her nervousness.

Gie continued. "Gates is a cur. So what? With the riffraff filtering into Norfolk these days, we unfortunately need his type."

Mary tried to keep herself from wincing at that remark. "Right now, Coolie could use a little mother—"

Gie snorted, interrupting, "Mother-love? Don't make me laugh! And don't try to give me any guilt that she needs me. She's a wild filly who will find her way back to the corral—some corral, anyway." She leaned forward, chin up. "And from what I hear, it's your corral she wants to be in. Is that right?"

"Gie."

"If I ever had feelings for her," her tone was scoffing and she waved her hand in the air, "lies told to myself in the dark of night, by morning I had my head on straight. I'm sorry if she doesn't understand and you think me a heartless, cold stone. The plain fact is, when I gave birth to her, I may as well have been passing gas. She is a simple consequence of pain I caused my father. Like bad decisions, critical comments, and sad deaths, one must simply walk away from them."

"Couldn't you just talk to her?" Mary heard herself practically begging.

"Haven't you heard a word I'm saying?" Gie spoke deliberately. "To me, Coolie Parts is nothing. I tried to give her a leg up in this town. Got Aunt Viney to bring her up. Gave her darn near a mansion out there on prime waterfront that she turned into a den of iniquity. Fortunately, in this town, if not my money then my social and political influence gives me a buffer, makes people want to ignore the fact of that trash because they need what I have to offer."

The cup of tea had turned cold in Mary's hand.

Gie chuckled. "Anyway, from what I hear, she wants less of me than she wants of you."

Mary's head jerked up. "I'm so tired of hearing that accusation."

"If you're trying to give me an innocent act, try it on somebody else. You know the score."

"Gie, we're talking about your daughter, your own flesh and blood. Her life could be in jeopardy. Do you really not care at all?"

Gie stood and shambled toward the window, looking out.

Mary hoped she might be reconsidering.

She turned back to Mary. "Hear me on this one last time. 'My daughter' is a false sentiment that, together with a Confederate nickel might buy a cabbage that would make my farts stink. Pardon me if I am indelicate, but I didn't get to be who I am by pulling punches. Coolie doesn't want me, she wants the illusion of me—the accepting mother who will hold her to the breast. The milk of human kindness and all that crap. Fact is, she wants you. She wants your breast. She wants to be enfolded in your arms, unholy alliance that it is. If she is to be saved, God help you, that will have to be your doing."

Gie's voice was clipped and flinty. "I have helped you to become who you are, Mary Louvestre. But if you ever bring up Coolie Parts to me again, I will exert everything in my considerable power to render you nothing more than pig middlings. Do I make myself clear?"

They locked eyes on each other. Mary rose. "Thank you for your time."

"Sit down," Gie said forcefully. "I'm not finished."

Mary sat.

"While I'm making myself clear, let me add this. I am a steadfast friend to Tesh-Lucianne. Someday she may be a favored senator's wife by the side of Simeon. As the new South is being designed, he may be a powerful point of the plow in the Confederacy. Tesh-Lucianne is a sweetheart, devoted to Simeon—and to me. As a close friend, I will be the beneficiary of their largess. They will tout me, and more people will know the name Eugenia Atkins, a woman who would stand tall at the pinnacle of business tycoons. This will rid me of all the stain of my youth. That, my dear, is what I want. And will have."

Mary trembled. Hiding her growing anger was becoming almost more than she could bear.

"Don't get me wrong," the woman continued. "I will continue to support you because it is in my best interest to do so. Norfolk will become the new Paris because of you. A destination for singular fashion. But my advice for you right now is to remember that there are no honest men—or women. As I have hard learned in business, there are only people with personal agendas who'll do anything to achieve them. Beware when their triumphs are at hand. There is always on the tally sheet a wins and losses column. You do not want to be crossed off as a liability."

Mary was stinging from the threat and surprise from this woman she had known almost as long as Tesh-Lucianne. Gie had encouraged her talents and supported a heightening career. Yet right now Mary could not have felt more disappointed in her or frustrated for Coolie. She wanted to scream. Instead, she composed a pleasant face. She set her cup down with great care. What she really wanted to do was fling it with all her might onto the wall.

She looked up to see Gie amble toward the door, obviously concluding this meeting. A sharp smile blossomed on the older woman's withered face. Mary's eyes cut away to the grandfather clock in the corner, its heavy pendulum swinging.

The thick eyeglasses made Gie's eyes look owlish. Her lips were a sneer. "I really am being your friend here. No doubt you don't believe that now. But there are sins of commission and sins of omission. Whatever are my sins about love are mine. Yours are myopic. You can't see for looking. What do you know about love in the Louvestre house? Have you ever wondered?" Gie paused. "I don't expect an answer but I will ask the question: Who do you think Tesh-Lucianne really is to you? She's got a pert nose. So do you. She's got billowy, straight hair. Yours is more on the red side. Hers is caramel with those same tones. I could go on."

Mary stared at her. Baffled, she had no words to say.

Gie shook her head. She squinted at Mary, who was now standing motionless outside the front door. The woman's face contained a malevolent light, her lips in a jaundiced screw. The spectacles magnified her eyes grotesquely.

Mary watched as Gie shut the heavy door with a thud in her face.

CHAPTER 24

Fortune had made arrangements at the small black church, Mount Zion Baptist, for Pluck's services, but it soon became clear to Preacher Alonzo Macawayne that there would not be room for the unexpected large turnout. This was the place where Pluck's mother, Cecilia, had sung in the choir, the place where Pluck had portrayed Mary in the Christmas play, the place where they had regularly worshiped. Quickly, Preacher Macawayne had the deacons set up chairs and benches in the wide wooded area out back. He'd also had them carry out the church's rickety piano, where Miss Agatha Givens was now softly playing hymns that struck Mary as inextricably sad. And because Pluck liked it so, Miss Bertha, a robust woman who played her tambourine like a virtuoso, accompanied.

Bear, dressed in a black suit and starched white shirt, wanted to seat Mary up front where the family and Coolie were sitting, but when she looked up to see Anders, she gratefully took his hand and they scooted in among those in the back. Mary had always hated funerals, wanted nothing to do with them, believed they were crude ceremonies more for the living than for the dead. Yet now, as she looked out at a sea of dark people and a smattering of whites, she felt a certain comfort. Preacher Macawayne had just the right look for his job. He surely had to be taller than any man present, including Bear. Big in stature, inky- black, he had a gentle, open, friendly countenance that beckoned for all who would come to the fold to do so.

The service opened with the singing of *O How I Love Jesus*. Mary was sorry for herself when she saw the tracks of Cecilia's tears; the sight uncapped her own hard-fought emotions. She swallowed hard. Mercifully, Preacher Macawayne began to speak.

Bouquets of wildflowers adorned the simple cypress wood coffin. The children had placed around it corncob dolls and a few marbles. Startlingly, four peacock feathers were perched against it.

Mary barely heard the minister's deep voice in the background. "How can we bring comfort to those who have lost someone they loved from their home?" His fiery glance focused on Fortune and the tearful weakened figure of Cecilia sitting under the protective arm of Miss Effie. "Home is the one place we're supposed to feel comfort, warmth, acceptance, identity, and safety. We're supposed to feel at home among friends. We like to believe that Pluck felt at home here with us. Aren't we all prodigal at some time or another in our lives? We go out into a world which can bring us low. Have us practically starving in spirit until we remember that we are a child of a rich God and we can go home.

"The father is so happy to see us, to welcome us back. 'Bring quickly the best robe and put it on him; and put a ring on his hand, and shoes on his feet; and bring the fatted calf and kill it, and let us eat and make merry.' This is our father's house, our home."

Silence was a pall upon the mourners. Where before there had been punctuating cries of "Don't you know it, Preacher!", "Tell it like it is!", and "Amen!", now not even a cricket was heard.

Preacher Macawayne's voice rolled on as resonant as a church bell. "That's where Pluck has gone, to her Father's house. There, she wants for nothing anymore."

"Ain't right! Crying shame!" mourners cried.

Preacher Macawayne's voice grew to a pitch. "One little brown girl doing a good deed. Did she call out in her fear and pain when the bullet pierced her chest? When she fell in the bracken and mud of the riverbank, was she calling out for you?" He sighted one after another in the congregation. The people grew quieter.

"Or you?" He looked at Mary. He paused and held her gaze. "And would you have come? There are overpowering forces at work. Life-threatening. Ask yourself. Will you come?"

Preacher Macawayne held his arms wide, his black robe giving them the look of eagle wings. He slowly let his worn brogans take the steps down from the makeshift pulpit. "If anything at all, our daughter Pluck brought us a message: Take a chance to do some good! Take the risk for others! Do it out of love, come what may."

He brought his arms forward, palms up, hands outstretched. "Take a chance." He whispered softly with a clutch in his throat. "Take a chance!"

Standing on the ground before them now, Macawayne bent his hoary head, closed his eyes, and brought his palms together in prayer. "Repeat these sacred words with me: 'Our Father who art in Heaven ...'"

Mary turned her eyes from the minister to the great black seabird that appeared in the azure sky, wheeling overhead, cawing and crying out, and her tears welled up as the congregation prayed.

"I tell you, my friends," Macawayne said evenly now, "Pluck was the wake-up call we needed. We gonna take her body home to her resting place. But we know her spirit is not in this coffin. Her spirit is on its way to Heaven."

He made his way past nodding heads and waving hands to where Mary sat.

"But just like Jesus, who said he would not leave us alone, he left us with a protector, a spirit-lifter." His piercing look was on Mary.

Don't do this, she thought. Don't do this to me.

"Miss Mary," he said, hands outstretched, "won't you lead us? Your little Pluck is waiting. We are waiting. Take us on home."

Mary looked around. All eyes were on her. "He'p her, Lord," an old mother exclaimed. She glanced at Anders and then slowly stood, her walking stick in hand.

As Mary eased out into the center aisle, people called out to her. All these years she felt she was not of them, didn't really know them, yet here they were embracing her, bearing her up. Her shame was overwhelming. She looked into Preacher's smiling face.

His deep bass voice struck a chord as he sang out: "She's on her way to heaven!"

The congregation responded, "So am I!"

"She's on her way to heaven!"

"So am I!"

Mary felt his words coming strongly now, joined by the congregation, hefting it up in song:

Glory, glory, hallelujah! Since I laid my burden down,
Glory, glory, hallelujah! Since I laid my burden down.

Preacher Macawayne fell in behind her, the congregation moving out of their seats behind them, old, young, infirm, those as mind-weary as she was. She turned and watched as Cecilia, frail and overcome with grief, was collected by the ushers who helped her. She was followed by Miss Effie, Fortune, and Coolie. Moved beyond words, Mary pressed the crown of her kufi into place and stepped lively using her stick.

The minister's voice picked up the rhythm and a hundred voices came to life, feet patting, hands clapping in syncopated sound that took her attention away from her aching leg, from everything that absorbed her in herself.

Preacher's voice was more commanding now.

I feel better, so much better,
Since I laid my burden down.
I feel better, so much better,
Since I laid my burden down.

Mary heard her own deep contralto roll out. Where did the words come from? How did she know them?

Burdens down Lord, burdens down Lord, Since I laid my burden down.
Burdens down Lord, burdens down Lord, Since I laid my burden down.

"Lift those knees, my friends," Preacher's voice exhorted. "We got somewhere to go! We're marching. We're marching. We're marching home!"

"Hallelujah!" vibrated the air from the crowd.

Mary sang from deep within her now, giving her sound the steady beat of a joyous march. She turned to see the casket on the shoulders of four men behind her.

I am climbing Jacob's ladder, Since I laid my burden down,
I am climbing Jacob's ladder, Since I laid my burden down.

Anders, smiling, walked a little behind her. She was their leader. He was her strong right, his own rich voice raised high with the rest of them. The hundred pairs of clapping hands and feet accompanied Mary as her voice broke away and soared high above the treetops.

Ev'ry round goes higher and higher, Since I laid my burden down,
Ev'ry round goes higher and higher, Since I laid my burden down.

They were not just with her. She was with them.

People milled about the church grounds after burying Pluck. Each person seemed to have a disturbing new story to tell about trouble around town. After a while, Coolie took Mary off to the side. Bear was there. He asked if she would come to Coolie's bar that evening. "There are some people we want you to meet up with," he said. "Things are heating up for us black folk 'round here."

Coolie nodded, watching Mary carefully as Bear continued, "You hear about that young Mississippi lawyer who came to town? Turns out he was an abolitionist. Was helpin' slaves escape north. Somehow Gates found out. His body's been found." He paused. "Name was Sampson Withers."

When Mary heard that, she almost fainted.

CHAPTER 25

Mary took Simeon his lunch at the chandlery. While setting up, she once again glimpsed the large drawings of the new Southern ironclad. She didn't question herself now. She just unfolded the large papers and took a good look at the renderings, first because of their beauty, and second because of the comments in the margins. They noted that the ship had a major weakness at the waterline, just as Anders described. If the Northern ship hit her there repeatedly, she was as good as sunk. But what the North didn't know would hurt them. Simeon's notes suggested ways of shoring up the area, but another's scribbled hand had added, "Alas. No time to fix this. God bless us anyhow."

Mary put the papers back and began to tidy the office, deciding to push her concerns about the ship to later when she could give full vent to her deliberations. Rather, she now let herself be preoccupied with clients scheduled at the salon the whole of the afternoon and with dress fittings for the show. There were accessories to pick up from various workers. She had to recheck the decorations for the hall. Swan, the carpenter, was presently at the Mechanic's Hall constructing the raised, crescent-shaped runway she wanted. It had to elevate from the dimly lit floor to the majesty of the glittering proscenium. That meant she had to check on the lighting. If it was not perfect, the effect would not be perfect. So many details! She had to get back.

Mary waved to Simeon on her way out. "Your nose knows Roguey's good food's on the table," she said.

Simeon barely paid her attention. His face was as white as nowhere and he was making stabbing motions with his finger to Lumley's chest. As the door of the shop was closing behind her, Mary heard Simeon growl, "He wasn't supposed to die, goddammit!"

Mary didn't know the last time she heard Simeon say a curse word. As she reflected while rushing down the path toward the ferry, she realized Lumley's face had been mottled red with anger. She swung looks left and right, listening hard; she wanted no trouble with Elam Gates who, like dirt, seemed to be everywhere.

The boat's horn sounded. Mary could see the ferry just ahead. Passengers called and waved to her to hurry. Mary dashed on board. Two black laundresses made a seat for her on their bench. Once she sat down, Simeon's words came back to her. "He wasn't supposed to die, goddamit!" What on earth could he have been referring to?

On the ride back, her nerves settled and the murkiness cleared over her brain. She gasped with understanding and appall. This secret would have to remain buried inside of her or else she would see a similar fate. Mary entered her salon steely-faced and further crushed by disappointment. She feared that these people who seemed so genteel and conscientious much of her life, the couple who had lovingly raised her, capitulated to the swelling mob mentality. She feared that the Louvestres, who had always abhorred violence, now rationalized it for political gain. Were they really that duplicitous? Could they be such shallow opportunists? Mary felt like a cog with no choice but to roll with her benefactors or risk being cut loose like a broken spoke.

The sheen of being a Louvestre had dulled, Mary thought as she stepped through the magnificent doors that no longer felt like her own.

Tesh-Lucianne danced from one foot to another during the last-minute fitting before her tea.

"You've got to hold still for me to do any good," Mary scolded.

Tesh-Lucianne craned her neck over Mary's shoulder to get a full view of herself in one of the salon's long mirrors. "Ooo-ee!" she squealed.

"You could get arrested for disturbing the peace," Mary said, watching her mistress primp.

"So what do you think?" Tesh-Lucianne adored what she saw.

Mary had made an exceptional design using fine handkerchiefs she had sewn together to make a diaphanous fabric, then dyed it daffodil yellow. She examined the result and approved. It became Tesh-Lucianne and, she had to admit, was stunningly unique.

"Mary, you're just outstanding! And to think, you're all mine."

Mary was quiet, pensive. She liked that she had created a version of the Garibaldi shirt, with its placard front and easy long-flowing sleeves fitted at the wrist. "You don't want to outshine the governor's wife, so I've kept it simple."

The skirt was gored, narrow at the waist and flaring out to the floor. It was the belt accessory that was especially eye-catching. Thin, twisted cords of hemp had been intricately woven into a wide band, looped and fastened by two small hooks hidden under a small lacquered tortoiseshell.

Tesh-Lucianne gushed. "I look amazing! How do you come up with these ideas? I'm the envy of all the girls." Mary knew "the girls" were the newly established set of Norfolk's social elite, so bluenose as to be entirely lacking in singular distinction. "I don't have enough fingers and toes to count invitations from the governor's circle alone—luncheons, dinners, and parties." She hugged herself. "So many parties."

That very afternoon, Governor Letcher and his wife were to be the honored guests at the Louvestres' for tea. Lumley was to attend also.

"God does work in mysterious ways," Tesh-Lucianne said.

Mary waited, crossing her arms.

"You know, about Lumley," Tesh-Lucianne said. "I feel we've known him all of our lives. He appeared out of nowhere at just the right time. A manager. Just what we need right now."

"A manager?"

"Oh, but he's so much more than that, Mary." Tesh-Lucianne seemed to have lost years as she tripped about the room like a peppy girl and danced on tippytoes in front of the mirror, pleased with herself. "It's more like we're on this journey and he's the seasoned guide. Because of him, we won't have to worry about getting to our destination."

"Which is?" Mary asked, regarding her with interest.

"We're going to be king of the hill." Tesh-Lucianne stopped twirling and stared into the mirror. A bright shiver of excitement ran through her. "We're going to be a senator from the great Commonwealth of Virginia."

Mary paused for a long moment, thinking the woman comical. Then she muttered, "Hail to the king."

Tesh-Lucianne smiled, visualizing herself and Simeon walking the red carpet to ascend the throne. Crowds cheered and, resplendent in their gold and jewels and pretense of humility, they waved to their peons. In the present, she slowly bowed grandly.

Amused, Mary coughed. "Lumley's going to be pope-counselor then."

"Oh you," Tesh-Lucianne said, coming out of the moment. "Undoubtedly, Simeon will award him a government post to keep him by his side."

"And Withers?" Mary probed.

"The man's disappeared," Tesh-Lucianne said with a wave of her hand. "Who's to say, a man like that."

"Like what?"

"Like—I don't know. Him going off somewhere without a word and leaving Lumley high and dry. Why, he didn't even have the decency to send his regrets for missing Simeon's party."

Mary cleared her throat. "Tesh-Lucianne, just the other day the man's body was found nailed to a tree, his eyes plucked out by birds."

Tesh-Lucianne's fingers flew to her mouth. "My Jesus Lord! I surely did wonder what happened that he didn't come to the party."

How shallow, Mary stared at her incredulously. She coughed again.

"Oh no, not you too," Tesh-Lucianne complained. "I'll never forgive you if you come down with something dreadful."

Mary went to the sideboard for a glass of water. "I'm fine."

"You don't look fine. You've gone all putrid in the face like I just told you your dog died, if you had a dog."

"Your tea is at two," Mary said, ignoring the inane comment. "I've a couple of things to finish on your outfit. It'll be ready for you by noon so you'll have plenty of time to get dressed. But right now I've got to go see Roguey."

Tesh-Lucianne clapped her hands. "Mary, I'm sure they'll want to meet you too."

Mary's hand was on the door. She turned back around.

"I was thinking," Tesh-Lucianne said, "you should offer to design a dress for the governor's wife. That should put him firmly behind Simeon, because from what I hear, he's head over heels for her. Whatever she desires. So, we barter."

"You barter me now?

Tesh-Lucianne wrapped her arms about herself and squealed with glee, ignoring the question. "I'm nothing if not a quick study. I'm going to do Simeon proud as a senator's wife. This is better than anything!"

Mary was so disgusted she could not form words. What had happened to the Tesh-Lucianne she had known and loved all her life?

———•——•———

Mary was amazed at the sumptuous dishes Roguey arrayed on the counter for the tea—thick slices of honey-glazed ham with red-eye gravy, pan-seared soft shell crab on rolled onion pancakes stuffed with cheese, collard greens, cinnamon-baked yellow squash, stewed tomatoes, a fresh fruit compote, and ice cream. Sweet potato biscuits were nearly ready to come out of the oven. Tesh-Lucianne wanted dazzling. Well, Mary thought, be careful what you wish for.

After the meal and drinks on the verandah with the Louvestres, Governor Letcher's wife wanted to meet the woman who made Tesh-Lucianne's stunning dress. "I've heard nothing but great things about her."

"She's been up to her eyeteeth with one thing or another, getting ready for the fashion show," Tesh-Lucianne explained.

"John and I will definitely be there," said Mrs. Letcher, "with bells on!"

Tesh-Lucianne sent for Mary, who quickly appeared on the porch.

After introductions, Mrs. Letcher said cheerily, "Mary, your designs are to die for. Are you expensive?"

Mary cut her eyes mischievously at Tesh-Lucianne and replied, "Yes. But maybe we can barter." Mary excused herself, grinning like a Cheshire cat as Tesh-Lucianne sucked breath.

CHAPTER 26

Mary limped down the path to Travelers Rest, conscious of the steady ache in her leg.

As usual, the place was busy, bustling with colorful patrons in a flow. Music was lively. The air was pungent with smells of tobacco smoke, food, beer, whiskey, human musk, and the sea.

Mary looked around for Coolie, who emerged from the hallway and beamed when she saw Mary. Coolie's face was restored to its former splendor. Coolie seemed to be her old self again, light in her eye, spunky. She gave Mary a big hug, took her hand, and gingerly negotiated them through the maze of tables. They arrived at a plank backroom door.

Mary glanced questioningly at Coolie as she opened the door, and was surprised to see a number of her friends—Anders, Roguey, Devereaux, Bear, Theron, and other black professionals from town. Some sat around a large table in the center, others on stools and kegs. Theron rolled a small barrel around and perched atop it near the door.

Bear spoke first. He told Mary they'd come together to talk about happenings in Norfolk. Racial tension was growing high.

Mary looked around the group. "We're missing Scoots. Scoots Dunham."

Uncomfortable glances were exchanged between the others. "We didn't think it wise to ask him," Bear said.

"Oh?"

"See, his business is ... expanding, so to speak." Bear threw out a meaningful glance.

Mary regarded him a minute. "Okay, what's this about?"

"Seem like Brother Dunham done got hisself caught in the crosshairs. Hear tell, he double-dealin'. He trade with black folk and trade *in* us too. He been sellin' us out up one side and down the other. Man who own Scoots's boat pay him a quarter for every Negro he turn in for somethin' or other. Say Scoots gittin' fat on our lard."

"No!" Mary cried. "I've done business with Scoots for a long time and he's been nothing but good to me. He makes buttons and other accessories for my fashions."

"You pay him?" Anders asked.

Mary nodded.

"You got yo' answer," Bear said. "Long's his palms greased, he fine. Just don't get on his bad side and don't let him in on yo' business."

Mary was appalled.

"Sad to say, some folks say he done turned lap dog for Gates too, if you can believe that. What he don't know is Deputy Gates is the one with bite."

"Growin' cloven feet too," Coolie jeered.

"Don't you worry. He gon' get his. It's owed to him in a matter of time," Bear said.

Coolie waved her hand in the air dismissively. "Don't pay that rascal no min'. See, his bowels ain't been reg'lar in a while, y'know?"

"And just how would you know that?" Mary asked.

Coolie danced her eyebrows up and down. Laughter rounded the room.

"Gates likes to work alone but he has a growing group of devotees at his disposal who are the hands-on type, doing the dirty work, calling it law and order," Anders said. "What they have is a license to kill."

"What with the war coming on," Bear said, "many slaves are trying to get out of the South, running to Union camps, some with the help of whites."

"Abolitionists?" Mary said.

"Sampson Withers was one of them," Anders said. "He was a Quaker, a liberal-minded man. Hated slavery. His cover was as a new lawyer in town, filtering around, getting to know people, quietly finding out what was really going on and how to help slaves. He even took up with Obadiah Lumley to set up a law office."

"So Lumley's an abolitionist too?" Mary asked, puzzled.

"Not even close," Bear spat. "When he discovered he was in partnership with someone who held views opposed to his, I suspect he felt duped, highly offended. Couldn't hardly wait to distance himself from Withers after he used the man's money to set up shop here. I'm sure Lumley would not like it known to Simeon and others he's trying to woo now, but we've heard some stories about him."

"Really?" Mary said.

Bear nodded. "Slave grapevine is a powerful thing."

"One we heard," said Anders, "was that Lumley came out of Georgia, where he was also known as Scythe. Reputation was he'd cut down anything in his way to clear a path."

"He prides himself on being a man of the times," Devereaux joined the commentary. "He reads all the newspapers he get his hands on every day. He attends theatre. He is ingratiating himself with the elite. He's a man who is always looking at the world and what it offers him and how he can take it."

"Lumley's an ambitious man, a manipulator," Anders agreed. "He gets close to the right people, groveling to provide what they want. But even as he's on bended knee before them, his eye is always roving, trying to get a bead on ways to undermine them, bring them down, and take their power and position."

Coolie looked directly at Mary and said, "Frankly, we should worry for Simeon. Lumley, this 'Scythe,' calculates competitors to his ambitions, convinces them he's what they need and all they need for their careers. Then when they least expect it, he cuts their throats and they don't even know they're bleeding."

"And now these rotten Black Codes," Devereaux declared. Elegantly attired as usual, his hand flashed a red lace hanky in the air.

Mary's eyes were questioning.

"You didn't hear?" Bear asked. When she shook her head, he said, "Sheriff Bridges just posted new do's and don'ts we're to abide by. One is, no two or more coloreds may congregate on the streets. 'Nother is, if we're caught doing that near dark, the penalty will be especially severe."

"Why?" Mary asked. "Most of these white people we've been knowing all their lives. They know we'll do no harm."

Wheelwright Noble Bridgewater spoke. "Doesn't matter. We used to have protection because they needed us for our specialties. Like Bear's blacksmithing. Or Titus Rupert," he said, pointing to the robust gentleman sitting in the corner, "for his barrel making. Finest anywhere. None of that counts with this new bunch. They believe we got wrong thinking in our heads, that we're planning something against them. That could have us strung up a tree as fast as an outright insult could. And far's our trades are concerned these days, they'd find 'em somebody else."

Mary looked around the group. "They can't replace us all that easily."

"No," Bear agreed, "but the new codes are a worry. Any of us could be rousted up and hauled to jail just for coming together in town to say hello."

The group murmured assent, heads nodding.

"Them codes give Gates all the right he want," Coolie added, "to parade his men around, hassle us for no good reason. I, for one, am sick and tired of that reprobate."

"Kindly tone it down," Mary said. "And do not say that to his face."

"You know that cracker is lookin' for any reason at all to turn us to ashes under his new law and order campaign," Bear said. "The question is, how can we prevent that?"

After a moment Mary said, "Gates is under the sanction of both the town council and Sheriff Bridges, who doesn't want to get his hands dirty. More importantly, he's got the endorsement of Miss Clara-Jean, who doesn't fancy blacks beyond field hands and domestics, and nobody is going to go up against her."

"If we don't do somethin'," Coolie said, "he's only gon' get worse."

Mary, thinking about the coming fashion show, said quietly, "I'm a seamstress. I am not a troublemaker."

"If the South wins this war," Coolie continued, "we'd better be makin' trouble."

Tension eased as they shared a hearty, though nervous, laugh.

Aldous Briley, a soft-spoken ferryman who typically kept to himself, spoke up. "Miss Mary, in case you don' know, Simeon was on the streets publicly endorsing the sheriff and new deputy. He says he agrees with the sheriff's new reforms for law and order."

"What?" Mary was surprised.

Aldous bobbed his head. "And that's not all," he added. "The men in this room have our suspicions that Simeon ordered Gates to make an example of Withers and, as usual, things got out of hand."

Mary stood up, shaking her head. Her mind replayed the earlier scene between Simeon and Lumley. "No, no, not Simeon. That's outrageous!"

Anders wagged his head sadly. "Word has come to us that Simeon didn't order that by his own hand. Rather, Lumley convinced him it would demonstrate that Simeon was firmly on the side of the South. We heard that Lumley told him he needed to clean house of white men who would dare to help Negroes in any way."

"You watch," Aldous said. "Simeon won't come right out and admit he had Withers beaten, after which he 'accidentally' died. No. He'll make a point of saying the act was horrible, but this should be a lesson to others of his kind. Lumley was behind this, surely. He likely paid Gates to make an object lesson of Withers. Such a man to Lumley was expendable anyway."

Usually jovial Exie Campbell, the barber, added, "This could be one thing Lumley can hold to use against Simeon, all the while seeming to be moving heaven and earth to help him. He wants Simeon to rise so he can come too."

"Blackmail?" Coolie asked, eyes wide.

"If that's what it takes," said Exie.

Mary's mind cast back to a recent kitchen talk with Roguey. The cook had told about when she served rolls and coffee to Simeon, Tesh-Lucianne, and Lumley out in the gazebo. Roguey had related what she overheard. "The bunch of them was excited 'bout some man comin' from 'cross the water. I can't call the place. Somebody they's expectin'. He's a big shot over there in the fashion business."

Mary's interest had been piqued. She asked, "What's his name?

Roguey shrugged. "Didn't get nothin' more'n that."

"What are they bringing him here for?" Mary wanted to know.

Roguey shook her head. "Didn't get no more than what I jus' said. But I knows somethin's up. You know how sly Lumley can sound. Well, all whilst I was servin' 'em, they lookin' out the corners of they eyes, and he's whisperin' to 'em and carryin' on."

Anders's voice shook Mary out of her reverie.

"Next thing you know," Anders said, "things'll get really bad around here— more lynchings, more houses burned to the ground, more families split up and sold away. We don't want that. We want to get control of this situation and provide order for ourselves. We need a plan for all of us to follow."

Bear outlined his idea. They would organize into a covert group. Each would provide certain specialties. He, as blacksmith with his wide network of contacts and informants, would call upon them for various supports, especially Thurston Stone. Coolie, who knew everybody and all of whom owed her a favor, would begin to call those favors in. Theron would keep his ears open at the bar, listening to news from travelers as they came and went. Devereaux, as driver for Simeon to parts all over the South, would use his eyes and ears, like none of the rest of them could, to scout and gather information about whites and their contrary operations. Roguey and Mary had a unique inside track to keep them posted on the doings of Simeon and Lumley. Anders would keep them informed on the progress of the ironclad, do military reconnaissance, and let them know about the military press of the North against the South.

He then looked to the rest of the group. "Y'all know how you can best help. We got to do constant surveillance to protect our homes and families."

"If we all work together," Bear said, "we can outthink the Gateses and the Lumleys, get out ahead of them, and outmaneuver them. We'll train our people, young bloods included, how not to overreact but to watch out for our old folks and the women and children, and get them out of harm's way. We'll have to figure a plan for the men, both on foot and horseback, to silently patrol against Gates's white posses so another colored settlement won't be massacred. We got to keep the hotheads among us from further agitating whites, gettin' them stirred up and playin' right into Gates's hand. If we don't, no one would turn a hand to stop him if he and his bands sweep in and kill us all where we stand. We're not armed. They are."

"I'll start a tally," Anders said. "And horses. How many horses do we have? That'll tell us how many riders we can put out on patrol."

Bear looked directly at Mary. "Miss Mary, I don't believe anybody here would argue that you're about the smartest and most respected of our bunch. Can we count on you?"

No one moved or spoke. Lively sounds from the outer bar and restaurant infiltrated the room.

Mary was slow to respond, then said, "For what, exactly?"

"I can lead and they'll follow." Bear glanced about. Heads nodded. "But I sure could use a counsel in my head. You'd keep my thinkin' straight."

"I got a thought!" Theron cut in. "We can call ourselves The Travelers, 'cause that's the name of Coolie's place, where we gittin' started. An' we sho' got some travelin' to do." He grinned.

Mary didn't smile back. Mary had studied every book and magazine on fashion that came into the Louvestres' home. Now she was considered a haute couturier and the spectacular fashion show coming up could vault her to greater heights. She wanted that success so much she could taste it. Once she achieved that, she believed no one could harm her again. Were Bear and the others asking her to give that all up? Jeopardize her future?

The room remained still.

Bear waited for Mary's reply. After moments of her silence, he collected two bowls from beside him on the floor. One was empty. The other held small pebbles. "For everyone who is with us," he said, "put a pebble in the empty bowl."

Aldous's spindly fingers picked up one and the others followed. When the bowls reached Devereaux, he threw up his fist and proclaimed, "I, Devereaux Rainier Leodegrance de Perouse, will see us to victory!" Then he cast his pebble to the bowl with force.

Anders had his eyes on Mary as he reached for a shiny stone. The bowls soon reached Coolie, who took up hers and dropped it into the other now nearly full bowl. Then the bowls came to Mary. She looked down. There was only one pebble left.

She swallowed hard. All eyes in the room were on her. Coolie leaned over and whispered into her ear, "Remember what's been done to your father."

Mary gulped a big breath. After what seemed like a lifetime, she slowly and deliberately took up the last pebble. She clenched it in her fist. Silence hung in the room like a pall as she felt it grow hot in her hand. When it seemed to sear her skin, she dropped it onto the pile of pebbles.

CHAPTER 27

Mary tended Anders's burned hand by putting it in a bowl of cold water. "Yikes!" he cried, trying out a little-boy face to get more sympathy. They were in Mary's salon and Mary was all business.

"Couldn't you have gotten here sooner—I mean like right after the accident happened." She tsked and lifted his hand to examine it closely. "It's a wonder you didn't lose your index finger. This burn is almost down to the bone." She gently slid it back into the cold bath.

He winced. "Too much else to do."

"Like what?" Mary said, "Single-handedly save the Confederacy?"

Despite his anguish, Anders smiled. "Don't grouch. Can't you see I'm an injured man?"

Mary went to the corner Chippendale highboy she used for storage, lifted from the bottom drawer a large bag made of beaver skin, and brought it back to the table. She pursed her lips and dabbed a white cloth around Anders's burns. "Doesn't the Navy have a doctor at the ship who could've treated this wound for you?"

Anders grinned sheepishly. "Sure, if I'd let him. But I thought coming to you could buy me a few minutes. You've been so busy lately, I hardly see you at all."

"The show is just days away, that's all," Mary said. "Truly, I need to be two, maybe three more Marys these days." She glanced out the window toward the long driveway. "Right now, I'm expecting a runner from the factory to come pick up dresses I need the seamstresses to add one thing or another to. Already they've worked twelve hours today, but I know they'll be there until the work is done."

"I'm sure they could use the extra pay."

"It's not just that. Most of the ladies have been with me for years. I trained them, even trained some of their daughters I've brought into the shop too as we've grown."

"Heck, I'd work for you."

"Your foot couldn't fit under the sewing machine!"

"I thank you to know I could pump that pedal like a pile driver," Anders said, looking down at his boat-sized feet. "Well, maybe I couldn't."

They laughed companionably.

Anders watched Mary at her task. "You're lovely," he said.

Mary did not look up as she retrieved his hand again from the cold water, dabbed it dry, and opened another of her pouches.

In the flattering light of evening, Anders silently watched Mary treat his wounds. A zephyr played with the loose strands of her hair and he saw it glow in copper highlights, falling like a burbling stream along the side of her face.

"Anders," Mary said, "I'm sorry, but this is going to hurt like the dickens. I'll be as quick as I can."

His hand stung at first, though her touch was like a feather. He used stronger language than "hurt like the dickens." Then, in another moment, the pain, gratefully, began to recede.

Mary pursed her lips as she dressed Anders's raw, open wounds. She always enjoyed seeing him, but the multitude of lists rang back-to-back in her head with things she needed to do. Stop it, she told herself. He was hurt and he needed her. That should have been enough.

She found herself reflecting that she had done Anders a disservice. Yes, she was fond of him, loved him, in the capsule of the present. But early on she told herself he was too young for her, that she shouldn't get involved with him for his own good. He should find someone his own age, a free woman, so they could marry and make a life together. But he'd worked his magic on her with his persuasive words and charisma. Until Anders, she hadn't allowed herself to acknowledge just how lonely she'd been for that kind of contact with a man. Lord!

"I have to wonder, my sweet, what if the North wins this war?" Anders pondered. "I'd like to hope they'd come in here and kick Southern butt with a sharp toe, unshackle every black person, and more than set us all free—make us equal citizens under the law."

"You've been giving this thought, I can tell."

"But even if the South wins, Mr. Lincoln will have put such a hurtin' on them that they'll have to reorder things, giving Negroes a chance to help the economy get better. Face it, the war has already started, even if the shooting hasn't. When these two ships go at each other out there in Hampton Roads, nothing is going to be the same again. I believe, even if these cornpone, hamhock-eating, bourbon-guzzling Southerners win, we stand a good chance of getting a piece of the pie down here, so to speak. Whites won't like it for a long, long time, but all we want is to do something for us.

"Shoot!" he continued, trying to keep his mind off the pain of his wound. "Reason things are heating up around here now tells us, loud and clear, just how much they need us, though they don't want us to know that. As my wife,

I'd want you to sit down and rest for a minute. I know the importance of your career. I want that for you too. But I want you to sit with me in our house, in our kitchen, on our land, and have coffee of a fresh morning. Say a little prayer of thanksgiving. And, by the way, I want children." He flashed her a grin.

Mary squawked. "I'm getting old, Anders! My womb's more than two score and already shriveling up like an old root!"

"How you talk! Plenty a women with a little age makin' babies. Anyway," he said, getting serious again, "unless I miss my guess, when this time of trouble is over there'll be a lot of homeless kids who need a place to be with people who want to take care of them."

"I'm sure," Mary said, though her back-mind shouted that this man might just as well be howling at the moon as setting her up for motherhood.

While she put finishing touches on the intricate wrap on his hand, she reflected on the first time she met Anders. She had just come from the chandlery, beating a fast pace back to catch the ferry home. He had come up beside her. "I think if I put you next to the most beautiful rose in the garden, that rose would feel sorry for itself."

Recalling that time, Mary glanced over at the stranger. He glided along in a smooth gait, wearing expensive black boots spit-shined to a glisten that could reflect his face in the tips. She was a bit undone at his approach and stammered, "Who ... who are you?"

He touched two fingers to a wide-brimmed straw hat set rakishly low on his forehead. "I'm Anders Tremaine, a machinist working on the CSS *Virginia*."

Mary kept her pace.

"And you are Mary Louvestre."

She flashed a sharp look at him. His smile was brilliant. His extraordinary, luminous eyes were set above high cheekbones and below brows so thick they looked like caterpillars stenciled on skin the color of stained wood. "How is it you know who I am?"

"Who hasn't heard of you in these parts? You'd have to have mush for brains not to know Mary Louvestre is famous in Norfolk."

Mary found his soft, slow manner of speaking bewitching. She gave him an intrigued glance and kept walking. Anders kept apace.

After a bit she asked, feigning a bit of annoyance, "Can I help you with something?

His generous lips turned up in a lopsided grin, showing milk-white teeth. "Why, yes, ma'am. You could do me the honor of going a little slower. Even with that walking stick it's hard to keep up with you."

Mary barked a laugh. "And why would I want to do that?"

"So I could give you the good news. You've just met the man of your dreams."

"What?" she giggled, captivated by him. "If you're not full of yourself."

"No," he said that day. "I took one look at you and knew I'm the man to wake up next to you each morning. I'll turn and ask this question. What can I do this day to make you happy?"

"Whoo!" She darted a quick look around as if seeing who might be listening. "I know you didn't just say any of that to me, a total stranger."

He stopped. His expression turned sober. "We're each other's destiny."

Mary scoffed with a dismissive wave of her hand. "Seems like when some of our people learn to speak proper words, they love to string them together with the greatest of—what's the word?—oh, yes, bombast."

Anders chuckled and gentlemanly offered his arm as she climbed the stairs to her ferry. Sweat jeweled his forehead. "Say what you will. There's something to be said for yearning and waiting. When you return, and I'm certain you will, I'll be here yearning and waiting, just for you."

She remembered that day often, like a delighted child remembered the first taste of a special piece of candy. Now that sweet man sat before her, tempting with his eyes.

"Mary," Anders began tentatively, "I have some money put by."

Mary blinked herself back to present.

"I'm thinking to offer to buy you from the Louvestres."

She was startled, not sure she heard him correctly. "You what?"

"Well, I'm a free man. And I believe Guillaume will allow me to buy a parcel of his many acres in Chester County to build a home for us. He's a good man, Mary, saved me from a cabin fire that took my parents when I was only three. He brought me up in his big house and taught me every skill I have."

Mary leaned back to collect herself and wait out Anders's spate of enthusiasm.

"I've been over it and over it in my head. I know the land I want us to have. It's rich land set up on a high rolling slope. You tell me what kind of house you want, me and Guillaume and our friends would have it up for you like that." He snapped his fingers. A light burned in his eyes. "No matter how fancy—promise. If you want heart-of-pine floors, marble mantels, big kitchen—it will be yours."

She thought for a moment. "At such brashness my father would say, 'Lawd I reckon!'" She sighed. "Don't think I'm putting you off," she said, though she was. "I can't cram anything more into my head right now than this show."

Anders looked crestfallen.

"If we're supposed to be, we will be." She looked at him, watching his mouth take on an enigmatic turn at the corners. At times she believed that Anders was a missing piece of her. She enjoyed the look of love in his eyes and had to admit to herself that when she knew she was going to meet him, she went out of her way to look the best she could, to look alluring. He was young, good-looking, with the kind of infectious laugh and warm personality that drew people to him. She liked being on his arm, receiving complimentary looks from other women. Yet, Anders never noticed the others as they trailed everywhere she went, letting her know that to him, there was no one better.

Mary convinced herself to enjoy her time with Anders and that future matters would take care of themselves. Yet every time she tried to envision a life with this man, reality swooped in like a breeze pushing away morning fog. Truth is, she belonged to the Louvestres, and he was a free black. It was impossible.

She hadn't gone out of her way to let this man capture her heart. She'd never looked for that with him or anyone else. Times had been, over the years, when she'd share an evening's walk with a man who called courting her, but she never let it come to anything. In fact, until Anders, she considered her life could only be that of other black women who had work, family, and friends. Men could come and go, and did.

"A penny for your thoughts," Anders whispered, calling her back to the moment. When Mary didn't answer, he said, "Too cheap? Well, a nickel then."

"What?" Mary said.

"You were here, then you weren't for a long time."

Mary busied herself needlessly, rechecking his bandages until he placed a restraining hand over hers.

"Hey," he said, making cheerful tones in his voice, "whatever it is, it's all right."

Mary watched his lips tremble a little as he worked up another smile for her.

"Look, whatever happens, I want you to know I love our time together. People can search their whole lives for one moment of the kind of happiness we have—making a picnic, fishing in our favorite spot, searching the woods for your herbs or things for you to create your fashion accessories, or being in my arms." He made his eyebrows dance playfully over the arms part.

"Soon your show will demonstrate what all of us who know you know— that you're going to be way up there in a place few whites and almost no Negroes can go."

"There's no way of knowing ..." Mary tried to interject.

"God has been preparing you for this for a long time." Anders leaned so close to her that she got a good whiff of the musky aftershave she had made for him. "I will step aside, for now. You've got to do this with a clear mind."

Mary looked down at her hands in her lap. "What if, after folks see my fashions, they think I'm nothing special?"

"Do I detect a bit of doubt from one Mary Louvestre? Who never has a whit of doubt when she puts her mind to something? Well, I'm here to tell you right now—stop it. From what people tell me, this is your time." He stood up in the middle of the salon, his arms up like an orchestra conductor. "Ladies and gentlemen, I present to you tonight the fashion star of the Commonwealth. She is the one, the only legend of style and taste and quality! I give you, from The House of M, Miss Mary Louvestre!"

He clapped his good hand on his other forearm and made crowd sounds. Together they enjoyed a good laugh.

Later, Mary was in her salon working as Tesh-Lucianne prattled on about the possibilities of being a senator's wife and all the new dresses she would need. Mary's mind was too full to think. So many thoughts flew back and forth like a shuttlecock—the meeting at Coolie's, then the talk with Anders earlier in the day, all while she was trying to concentrate on costume details. More to stop Tesh-Lucianne's stream of talk than anything, Mary said, "I was just wondering if you were going to continue helping out at Mount Zion Baptist?"

"I won't have time for that anymore," Tesh-Lucianne said. "And for Simeon's sake, I can hardly allow myself to do the work there I had done in the past. Continuing to teach slave children to read would be considered subversive. I cannot afford to jeopardize his political chances by flaunting such illegal activity. I have our image to be concerned about now."

Tesh-Lucianne's response registered on Mary in stages. She had been so engrossed in her work that when the woman's answer finally hit her, she could not believe she'd heard right.

A pounding on the door made both of them jump. Roguey rushed in and stopped when she saw Tesh-Lucianne. She stood, wringing her hands.

"What is it?" Mary said.

"You got to come now. We in the kitchen." Roguey cast a quick angry glance at Tesh-Lucianne on her way out.

Mary looked to Tesh-Lucianne. "I'd better go and check on whatever this is."

"Fine, fine," Tesh-Lucianne said airily, seeming to ignore any problems but her own. "You go ahead. I've got plenty to keep me busy working on ideas for my new wardrobe.

When Mary entered the kitchen, Golen, the Louvestres' ancient gardener, was seated across the table from Devereaux, who was rocking back and forth, weeping like a child, and crying, "Bon Dieu! Bon Dieu!"

Mary put a hand on his shoulder. "Devereaux, what's the matter?"

A clenched fist to his lips muffled another hoarse cry.

Mary moved quickly through the large dining room and the broad hallway. At the study she turned left. In seconds, she whipped back into the kitchen. In her hand was a short glass with a stout pouring of dark-colored liquid in it.

"Drink this," she said to Devereaux.

"We puttin' a hurt on Massa's brandy," Roguey said.

Mary's look said, so?

No one spoke until Devereaux took three gulps, then finished it. Roguey grabbed the glass, rinsed it quickly, and whisked it back to the study.

Mary said, "Now, tell us what's happened."

Devereaux looked away from them, out the window at the tall magnolia in the backyard. After a short while, he sighed heavily and began.

He said that after Simeon had finished his business in Richmond earlier in the day, he drove him to the Wharton home, as on no trip to Richmond did he miss an opportunity to see his longtime friends. Devereaux couldn't have been happier. While the white folks had their drinks and talked, he could be with his lady love.

"They call her Louise," he said with a wan smile. "She is no one's Louise. I change her name myself. She is my Ann-Marie. Being with her is like coming home again.

"Before we reached the Whartons' and still talk in privacy, I became a bold man. I asked that this might be time for Mr. Simeon to buy Ann-Marie. So that we could be together. In return, I said, that I have given him many, many years of faithful service."

Tears fell as Devereaux said Simeon answered him bluntly—no. The Louvestre household did not need any more staff, what with the war shortages and all. Devereaux was crushed. After a moment of silence, he had told Simeon then he wanted to be sold to the Whartons. Simeon became angry, declaring that was absolutely impossible.

Simeon had told him that, from now on, whenever they were at the Whartons' home, Devereaux was to stay with the carriage. He was never to see Louise—his Ann-Marie, again.

"There is more." He told how he had done as ordered when they reached the Whartons' and stayed with the carriage. "When Simeon returned, told me Mr. Wharton agreed he would sell her. My heart again leaped with hope I could not believe my ears. Then he say Mr. Wharton's trader will take my Ann-Marie away when-some-ever he next come to get slaves."

"Never have I hated a man more." He sought Mary's eye. "Simeon say to me, 'You are too important to my household. You think I'd risk you doing something foolish? I don't care a whit about that girl.'"

Suddenly, he began speaking in French to Mary, then he turned to the others and repeated his words in English, "Now I will lay in eternal labor awake in the night trying to birth pictures of how she is, what she is doing. Is she missing me as much as I am missing her?"

At the table, they all sat quietly, then Mary spoke. "Cela te surprend-il vraiment, Devereaux?" She continued speaking French to him, then turned and said to the others, "Does this really surprise you? Did you really have illusions that go against a way of white life that is so deeply entrenched?"

Roguey looked astonished. "I knowed you understands his 'culiar talk, but I ain't never heared you speak it."

"Devereaux began teaching me French years ago. We speak it when we're alone."

Years ago, the Louvestres had glowed about acquiring Devereaux, who they believed was quite a find. Self-contained with a touch of arrogance, he was pretty much a loner, keeping his distance from the rest of the household staff. He was regarded as a misplaced nobleman with a lot on his mind. For sure, no one thought more of Devereaux than Devereaux himself. Elite by his own account, he was the son of a successful white shipping merchant in New Orleans and a beautiful quadroon mother, the man's mistress.

Mary's mind slipped back to the past, remembering when she'd first learned the story of Devereaux.

After a stressful day of business transactions in New Orleans, Simeon had been relaxing in the Sang Froid Bar, a favorite among habitués of the French Quarter. There, he sipped a cognac and watched people until it would be time to leave to meet friends for dinner. A conversation at the next table grew boisterous, drawing his attention. He heard a man recount how he came to be in recent possession of a most remarkable slave, for whom he'd ask top price.

The storyteller recounted the tale of one Devereaux Delaflote, a brash young Negro—a bastard from a slave row tryst—who ran afoul of the man whose seed gave him life. At fifteen and with wild notions of joining the man's shipping business, working side by side with the older man as mentor, Devereaux claimed he would never disappoint him, never be disloyal, never be anything but dutiful. The boy was stunned to learn the old man didn't want him around, that he was to depart on a work-gang made up of common laborers. Their jobs were to do such menial labor as lay ties for the railroad, haul refuse from the streets, and bus chuck buckets from the hospital for the poor. Devereaux railed at the elder, growing increasingly irate, pleading at first and then insisting that the man do right by him. The elder Delaflote had looked at Devereaux like he was piss. Devereaux became so enraged when the man turned his back that the boy drew down a wooden club on his neck, nearly killing him. Then he ran.

Reeling from it all, sunset found Devereaux throwing back his third bottle of bourbon in an alley beside a dry goods store. Nightfall saw him in jail after that whiskey told him he could fight all five of the Tippideaux brothers, about the worst bunch of scut there was. Next day, pattyrollers rolled up outside the jailhouse and declared they wanted the pretty-boy nigger, saying they had a rope necktie and a stout tree branch with his name on it. Simeon listened as the man went on to say how the sheriff had called him to whisk the terrified boy out. "Better we should make money off the good-looking fellow. I got him locked in a hotel room in the French Quarter. Just the first pleasure he'll be knowing." The men laughed.

Simeon listened with avid interest, clearly suspecting that this new jailer promised more torments to young Devereaux than being sold into slavery. Where profit was to be made, the boy didn't stand a chance. Simeon signaled the bartender to send a round of drinks to the man's table, and was promptly waved over to join them. In less than an hour, he had made arrangements for himself and Devereaux to leave for Norfolk.

On the ride out of town, Simeon asked the dispirited youth if there was anything he could do to let him know life with him was going to be better. Devereaux told him the first thing would be to allow him to change his name. He wanted no reminder of his father. He did not want to be known by the name Delaflote; he wanted to be Devereaux Rainier Leodegrance de Perouse.

"All of that would make you happy?" Simeon said, amused.

The young boy brightened. "Yes."

"Then so it is."

—————

That had been ten years ago, to Mary's recall. Since then, Devereaux had worked as driver as well as caretaker for the horses and carriages. He lived in a spacious apartment over the carriage house, ate the best that Roguey's kitchen had to offer, wore fashionable clothes care of Mary, and when he wasn't working, had a ready pass and a few dollars in his pocket to do with as he wished. Still, for all of his ways, Mary knew Devereaux was a man filled with unquenchable fire. She recalled words he had said to her only once but with an anger she could not forget: "Never. Never, dear one, no matter who they are, trust a white man."

CHAPTER 28

T esh-Lucianne had turned the fashion show from its initial thrust as a gala to instead benefit Simeon's political ambitions. To the thrill of Tesh-Lucianne, powerbrokers from all over confirmed their attendance. Mary had been working feverishly, long into the nights, to complete her line, to meet new orders for the upcoming event and to create the special gifts of her designs pledged by Tesh-Lucianne as favors to the wives of political contributors. She'd split herself every which way, trying to run to the warehouse in town to supervise work there, get her own tasks done in the salon, and carry Simeon's lunch to him at the chandlery. He seemed more standoffish with her than usual. But Mary wrote it off that he'd been as pressed about things as she was these days.

The activities of The Travelers had to take a back seat to her imminent demands. She wanted to help them but just couldn't get to Coolie's for meetings. Roguey told her that Devereaux was volunteering for whatever they needed.

"He actin' like he don't care what risk he take," Roguey said in hushed tones. "He doin' mo' of everythin'—patrollin' with the men to protect they camps, usherin' slaves from place to place, stayin' out all night as watchman. Some of the men wonderin' if he don't have a death wish." Roguey scooted closer and dropped her voice. "Bear say to ax you, should he let some of the boys shed steam by ruinin' some white folks' farm equipment?"

Mary stopped for a moment, having to shift gears from her design work to consider the question. "No, it'll only make things worse. Ask him to be patient for a while longer."

"How come I knowed you'd say somethin' like that?"

"I'm only being conservative until I can finish this show. Then I might have more time to actually work on what's happening around here."

Mary finally complained to Tesh-Lucianne that she was simply spread too thin. Taking lunch to Simeon at the chandlery cut too much time out of her day. Tesh-Lucianne told her she'd been having the same problem and would insist Simeon work in his home office at least for a few days. He agreed.

One day Mary stopped in the kitchen for coffee and had to laugh. Roguey might just as well have been a general heading up a special contingent. She'd gotten three old sisters from the Baptist church to help her prepare some of the food dishes. She was directing each one to a certain task. "No, no, no!" Roguey sputtered as Mary entered. One of the old sisters had challenged her on what ingredients to put in. The very idea! They meant no harm, but Roguey allowed no one, no one, to question her about anything to do with her kitchen or her food. When Mary told Roguey how much she appreciated all she was doing to make the party after her fashion show so special, Roguey ordered her out of her kitchen. Mary grinned and placed a brown paper-wrapped package on the counter where she was working. "It's a gift. For you."

Roguey didn't let on how moved she was, only repeating that Mary was to get out her kitchen. "Cain't you see I got things to do?"

Mary, carrying a tray with a silver coffee pot, was proceeding down the hall to her salon when she ran into Tesh-Lucianne escorting a handsome, elegantly dressed gentleman to Simeon's office.

Tesh-Lucianne, playing Southern belle and hostess, introduced him. "Mary, this is Monsieur Claude Delaclaire."

He bowed to Mary. "Charmed, mademoiselle. I have heard many great things about you. It is my pleasure to meet you nearly on the eve of one of the biggest social events of the South. I will sit in the front row where I am sure I shall make myself an idiot as I cheer every one of, what I know will be, your unique creations. Bonjour, mademoiselle." He bowed again.

As the two turned into Simeon's office, Tesh-Lucianne peeked from behind the closing door and whispered, "Isn't he simply marvelous? Aren't Frenchmen just enchanting?"

Before Mary could reply, the door was shut.

Mary returned to her salon and was joined not long after by Tesh-Lucianne, who needed a fitting. "Mary, I will be so glad when the *Virginia* is finished. Thankfully Simeon's work is nearly done. He and Lumley have so many wonderful plans."

Mary was glad there were straight pins in her mouth, making it impossible to speak.

"That Lumley," Tesh-Lucianne said with glee, "he couldn't be more devoted to Simeon than if they had been best friends since childhood. Why, they're practically inseparable. Lumley may as well have a room upstairs as much as he's here. He works diligently on helping Simeon's political career. The man schedules every task he's set himself to do. Newspaper interviews for Simeon. Speeches at different places. Even the parties he wants us to attend." Tesh-Lucianne looked positively radiant as she gushed, "I couldn't have guessed he was so smart and so focused. And I want you to make him some new clothes, Mary. He does have to keep up appearances, you know."

Mary listened, saying nothing as she kept her fingers busy basting trim on the dress shoulder as Tesh-Lucianne continued to blather. Simeon told her that the Confederate Navy wanted to throw as much weight as possible against the Northern ships at Hampton Roads to break the blockade and steam right into Washington, up to the door of the Capitol. "'We want to win this war. Get it done!' he said. "Put things back in our lives the way we like them."

"Does that include keeping slaves?" Mary asked. She was curious to know if Tesh-Lucianne's feeling about this issue had changed too.

"Hmm," Tesh-Lucianne said. "Well, we, personally ourselves, don't *keep* slaves. All of you in the Louvestre household may not have freedom papers, but I don't believe you could be any place else in the South where you could *feel* more free than you do here."

Mary quietly asked, "Did you ever wonder what might happen to us if, God forbid, something happened to you and Simeon?"

Tesh-Lucianne dismissed the notion. "Nothing is going to happen to us." She chuckled. "I have to be around. After all, my rose gardens need me."

Mary pressed on. "Without our freedom papers, our lives could turn to shambles in a second. To put it gently, I could go from my beautiful four-poster bed upstairs to the lice-ridden mattress of any redneck who could afford to buy me. You've brought me up in this mansion, as you've told me over and over, like the daughter you never had. Would you want that for me?"

Tesh-Lucianne looked uncomfortable. She obviously didn't like the tone and topic of conversation. "I don't want to talk about this. It is unpleasant. President Lincoln is a fool if he thinks he can browbeat us into freeing the slaves. If the South does so, we'll do it in our own time, in our way."

Mary took the direct approach. "Would you consider freeing me?"

Tesh-Lucianne guffawed as though Mary had told a funny joke. "Why would I do that? We love you. We want to protect you. What kind of owners would we be if we didn't do that? Just think about it, Mary. You've had a place with us since you were twelve. We've tried to give you a good life." She suddenly became misty-eyed.

Mary chewed on the inside of her cheek. She didn't know whether to laugh, cry, or run screaming down the street.

"The world is a harsh place, Mary, difficult enough for white women who have good husbands like Simeon to take care of them. You have no one like that."

"I have Anders."

Tesh-Lucianne made a rude noise. "Really? Well, Mister Anders Tremaine will be sent packing very soon."

"What do you mean?" Mary asked, a chill running up her spine.

"Well, Simeon tells me that they'll soon start trial runs on the ship. Anders's work is to secure the engine and boiler. If all goes right, Anders is gone."

Mary felt stricken and her face showed it. Tesh-Lucianne made an idle attempt at comforting. "Look, Mary. Things are going to be very different for you too very soon. You need to think about that, not about Anders."

Tesh-Lucianne blinked down at Mary, who was still working on the hem. "Your place is right here. Right where you are. So we can protect you from the real world." Then she brightened. "Who knows, I may be first lady of the Confederacy one day. Wherever would I find someone of your abilities to design and dress me? What do you say to that?"

CHAPTER 29

A̲t six o'clock, the prestigious three-storied Mechanic's Hall was brilliantly lit, impressive against the deepening pastel sky. A broad rug in patterns of red, black, and gold stretched across the wide verandah and down the marble steps to the walkway. A crowd of stupefied locals gawked at the staggering procession of power and influence that arrived. They came by elegant carriage. They came by shiny surrey. They came by sturdy wagon and bold black trains belching smoke as they rumbled into the town depot.

Flowing up the walkway in all their finery, they passed a huge red sign posted on the spacious lawn. Its black lettering announced the evening's event: "Design from The Fashion House of M." They ascended the steps and entered through the magnificently carved walnut double doors into the vast hall where two notable and irrepressible spirits, Tesh-Lucianne and Gie, sponsors of the affair, were the welcoming hostesses at the door.

While excited scrums of magazine and newspaper reporters zigzagged through the crush of people, the sophisticated gatherers shifted in knots around the wide mezzanine of the hall, redolent with night-blooming jasmine and sprays of tall orchids in clear vases. Others drifted into the glorious atmosphere of the grand inner hall, which shimmered in the light of a hundred brilliant candelabras.

A bevy of white-jacketed Negro waiters attended the guests, bearing crystal glasses of the finest champagne and trays stacked high with hors d'oeuvres. Along the walls, long tables groaned with cheeses, mounds of breads, fresh oysters, shrimp the size of small lobsters on beds of lemon and ice, and smoked meats galore. From a corner, a gowned and jeweled harpist filled the air with classical renditions. In the brace of two tall Ionic columns, tables set in white linen tablecloths and napkins engraved with the letter M, fine china, and gleaming crystal awaited all, along with a show to remember.

The mayor mounted the podium to give a glowing history about Mary Louvestre and the rise of The House of M. From backstage, Mary peeped out at the huge audience. The main floor was a sea of happy faces. The second and third level galleries were packed. As she listened, she was tingling all over.

The mayor went on. "I have a very special announcement! The eminent Parisian designer, Claude Delaclaire, is present to bless this event. He came all the way from Paris, France, to join us in celebration of this night's remarkable achievement. I hereby declare Norfolk, Virginia the new Paris, France. The fashion capital of the Confederate States of America!"

Loud applause erupted.

Mary saw Monsieur Delaclaire smile demurely at the mayor's mention of his name. Impeccably attired, he turned in the crowd and nodded. For this man the word "class" was an understatement. He was debonair, the epitome of elegance and refinement, with a bit of the devil-may-care about him.

Then the mayor introduced Mary.

Mary didn't dally. She stepped before the quieting crowd. After a few words of gratitude, she nodded toward the musicians. To a long drum roll, red velvet curtains slowly lifted. The dramatic black background was punctuated by one single construction: an elevated, gold-painted runway, curved and glittering, slanted down toward the audience beneath sparkling revolving balls reflecting light. The audience gasped audibly as Mary's husky voice announced: "The House of M and I present 'An Evening of Enrapt Allure.' I hope you will find here the finest of new fashion." With a swoop of her walking stick toward the rising curtain, the show began.

Throughout the procession of fashion, the audience spontaneously erupted in cheers and applause, either for an outfit or an esteemed model, some of whom strutted in glory while others struggled to contain their nerves. Men and women paraded the runway in hats, vests, and coats Mary had created, while others displayed her line of shirts, skirts, belts, dusters, and parasols.

Near the end, Mary announced, "It is my immense pleasure to introduce a special lady. A living treasure of this town, my sponsor and my friend—Mrs. Tesh-Lucianne Louvestre, in a most special creation."

As the music swelled, Tesh-Lucianne strode the runway in magenta peau de soie Mary had dyed in blocks of varying hues to create the effect of a symmetrically composed mosaic. The dress was slenderizing to Tesh-Lucianne's zaftig form. An off-the-shoulder scoop descended to a low drop of the neckline, below which ran a row of small magenta-embroidered butterflies. The eyes of the butterflies were set with tiny diamonds.

Tesh-Lucianne reached the top of the runway and stopped abruptly, then turned and postured in profile to show off the bodice of shiny tuxedo pleats just under the butterflies. Then she whirled to reveal the line of corded buttons in darker magenta that Mary had fastened down the back, from the neckline to just the top of the derrière. The skirt was a matte magenta featuring three small pleats on each side of the easy waist, where Mary had embroidered double lines of the darker color and added another tasteful touch of diamonds.

Tesh-Lucianne swirled in a circle and again stopped. Next, giving her face a coy look, she slowly hiked her skirt to display matching pumps, the toes encrusted with rhinestones. Then, as low drumbeats sounded, she walked to a slump of fabric at the side of the stage, grabbed it, whirled it around and let it fall over her shoulders. It was a splendid short stole of the softest magenta mohair, tatted at the hem and outfitted at the neck and closure with two diamond braids.

The audience murmured sounds of awe.

After the models trailed a whole line of outfits, there was a long pause. The lights went off. Before the audience could get restless, a bugle heralded something new. The lights rose. To the center of the gold runway, a length of shimmering black had been added.

"Ladies and gentlemen," Mary's voice boomed. "Purple is the color of royalty the world over. No less should it be right here. Feast your eyes on the signature piece of my collection, worn by the successful Norfolk businesswoman Miss Coolie Parts."

Polite sporadic applause followed. The majestic fanfare of gleaming French horns rose in the air.

Coolie could not have looked more stunning. She stepped down the runway with presence and flair. Even those who might have wanted to be annoyed that a colored woman was in the show had to admit her beauty. Mary's showpiece was an exquisite purple silk designed to create an absolute sensation. The neckline, a deep V, was lined on both sides with two rows of intricate gold stitches interspersed with handmade knots the color of blood. This pattern was carried in a single row down the bodice to the waist. But it was the neckline that was most unusual. The fabric was woven from the roots of cattails, beaten with a rock to separate the tendrils, then partially dried and dyed in a solution of Mary's own making to produce the outstanding shade of purple. From the back of the neck rose a sensuous curve of fabric, from shoulder to shoulder, to frame Coolie's lovely face.

Coolie pranced and glided and reined up, whirling and turning, showing off, below each arm, three golden cords, also made from cattail roots, that dropped to the waist and ended with a touch of fun in tiny gold raffia bows interwoven with brilliant purples. The dress, as Coolie wore it, was spectacular. She knew she looked anointed. Coolie made this abundantly clear as, rushing as close to the audience as possible, she halted dramatically. Reaching down, she grabbed a portion of skirt created in front by overlays of four gold panels, cut to highlight the flow of body underneath. Coolie made a swooshing sound. She whirled around, turned and turned. As she did, the skirt separated to reveal under panels of intricate design and the color of spun gold.

"Incredible!" came a cry. "Breathtaking!" someone shouted.

Coolie drew forward again, stopped, put her hands on her hips, and threw her head back haughtily. Her magnificent hair became a gold-cast nimbus under the lights. She stared out at the audience. She lifted one pump, slowly inched it from under her dress, and pawed the ground first with one toe, then with the other.

She bent down then reared up, arms overhead, palms outstretched, fingers delicately stroking the golden light embracing her. She whirled around, bent over slightly and wiggled her hips. That made the audience laugh as they applauded—the women admiring the repeated pattern of three rows of gold and blood-red from waist to hem, while the men cheered their appreciation of Coolie Parts.

Coolie's grand finale came when she reached down at the edge of the runway for the last piece of this ensemble. Like a magician, she seemed to make it materialize in her hand. She moved to the middle distance of the runway and turned her back to the audience. As she rotated, she whipped out the cloak and swirled it above her head in the golden light. She let it land on her shoulders, the back crafted to fit just underneath the stand-up collar.

The audience was on its feet now in barely controlled enthusiasm.

It was a purple cloak cut in seven panels of dark silk. The collar was several pelts of silver fox. Coolie swaddled it around her, canting her neck, nestling herself inside the burrow of softness. Her face had a look of love, of passion, of ownership of something so desired and wonderful as to be wrapped in the mystery of the ages. A woman in the audience squealed in delight. Men whistled and cheered.

Coolie tossed her mane of hair. Sultrily, she turned her back to reveal the work of a master. Mary had crafted three lines of gold stitching and blood-red knots sparkling with touches of gold in movement narrow at the neck and fanning out to the cloak's hem.

Coolie threw a smoky look back at the audience and, as French horns sounded again, she lazily, sensuously sauntered back down the runway. Tension in the room was at its height, about to brink. At the end of the runway, she halted, posed, then disappeared into a blast of gold light that, little by little, faded into blackness.

The house lights went down. The crowd fell silent, then suddenly there was pandemonium. Chants of "Mary! Mary! Mary!" rang out until Mary came out on stage.

"I thank you all so much for coming." A man from somewhere in the back yelled out, "That Coolie gave new meaning to that!"

Mary reddened, embarrassed, while the men in the crowd roared with laughter.

Partiers and patrons streamed forward, calling out congratulations to Mary and The House of M. She was stalked by the press for interviews while others crushed forward to pump her hand and add their pledges for items in her new line. She was "wonderful," "marvelous," "outstanding," "incredible." Mary reeled from the flow of compliments and feeling of triumph.

Then the tone of conversation changed. She listened with varied reactions as she heard the Louvestres praised for being visionaries, for cultivating Mary's genius from a young age, for recognizing something surely rare and hard to divine among darkies. Speaking as if she weren't within earshot, Mary heard a woman say, "The Louvestres trained her well. Now Norfolk and the entire South will benefit from her. Wonder if they could do it again with another one?"

One man wanted to know where the Louvestres found her. Maybe there was another in her litter who could do the same for him? He laughed.

Mary kept trying to smile.

"You got yourselves a good one," one fellow said to the Louvestres. "It's probably a thousand to one, but you hit jackpot. My hat's off to you."

One gray-haired woman asked, "Can she be bred? I've got an exceptional stud on my property."

Tesh-Lucianne scoffed, fluttering her hand, "The girl's past that."

The woman insisted, "We can try. You never know. I'll pay whatever is your price."

Mary listened to it all silently, struggling to rein in her scalded emotions.

Lumley, meanwhile, was working the room for everything it could yield. From the looks on the faces of the wealthy and noted, they knew it and could not have cared less. On their minds was the same thing that Simeon and Lumley were thinking as they saw how everyone fawned over Mary and the Louvestres: How could they best exploit it for themselves?

On what should have been the grandest night of her life, Mary felt deflated.

Her spirits lifted a little when she caught sight of Coolie emerging from backstage. Mary beamed and silently mouthed, "I'm so proud of you."

Eventually and reluctantly, the crowd began to depart. There was the after-party to attend at the Louvestre mansion. Coolie stood offside the stage, her eyes riveted on Gie, watching the woman—her mother—mingle. Finally, Gie glanced up through her spectacles and saw Coolie, so pretty, yet still so vulnerable. For what seemed like an eternity, the old woman stared up at her woodenly, expressionless. Finally, her lips pursed and she grimaced. She pivoted and stalked away.

Tears crowded Coolie's eyes as she stumbled toward backstage. Her legs felt like rubber. She wavered, staggered. She saw Mary coming toward her and held out her arms, hands clutching air. "Please!" she cried before she collapsed to the floor. Jitter Conroy vaulted to the stage, grabbed her up in his arms, and carried her behind the curtains.

As the Louvestre party grew in scale and volume, one after another of the arrivals approached Mary with celebration and praise. In a short while, the hurt she'd felt at some of the stinging remarks spoken after the show were blunted and soothed by so many accolades. Tesh-Lucianne introduced her around, making promises that Mary would design something special for this person or that. Someone inquired as to how she was going to fill all of these orders.

Simeon replied. "I anticipated the need for such a solution. I have appointed Mr. Claude Delaclaire as president of The House of M. He has a wealth of experience in running a business of this magnitude and a vision for making it even more financially successful. This will allow Mary to design and continue as seamstress. Operating the venture this way will undoubtedly assure that all your orders, now and in the future, will be filled without delay." A smattering of applause broke out around Simeon and Monsieur Delaclaire.

Simeon's news exploded in Mary's ears. Her smile shattered as her face burned with disappointment and betrayal. How could Simeon do this to her? The House of M was her brainchild. She had worked for years to build it, to achieve this success. Delaclaire pumped Simeon's hand forcefully and then turned to the crowd. "My dear new people, mes amis, thank you for this welcome." He motioned to Mary, standing nearby. "The mademoiselle Mary, she has some talent. She will continue to make a dress here, a coat there. After the war I shall teach her even more. Now, I am here to join forces with your cause. We will clothe your men and I will revolutionize the way those clothes are made. I invite you all to our factory, what had been Mademoiselle Mary's warehouse, in a week to experience yourself my transformation of that space into the most modern and efficient of working conditions."

Stunned and upset, Mary turned to leave and collided with attorney Leland Burrell. He was red-faced. Initially she thought he was drunk, but when she peered into his eyes, she saw anger.

"Hold yourself with dignity, Miss Mary," he said, gripping her shoulders. "I heard what Simeon said and I'm going to see if I can't get the clear on this. He sounds like he's done lost his right mind." When he let her go, he did so with such force that she nearly fell over, and only her walking stick allowed her to keep her balance.

The Louvestres had never said a word to her, but clearly this was the plan they had put into action long ago, to be able to get Delaclaire from Paris in time for the event.

So what did the Louvestres plan for her? Would she be relegated to a position as employee, prized, but a slave no different than a Pluck, and maybe just as expendable?

What a fool she had been! An idealistic fool. She had bought into the whole idea, hook, line, and sinker. Not only had she trusted that someday she was to be free, that she would transcend being a Negro slave, she had convinced herself she'd have financial control over her life, real power over her future.

In reality, she was special only as a special pet of her owners. They didn't physically beat her. Nor did they board her on slave row. She didn't eat from a peck of rice and throwaway saltfish. Yet, she still felt insignificant.

Her life testified to other Negroes that, if they worked from dusk to dawn every day of their lives to "serve the South" and "make their masters proud," they got to keep on doing it for the rest of their lives. That was their prize. Regarded as second-class no matter how they tried was the message she had received. It was galling—and so unfair.

As Mary continued down the hallway, the sound of her walking stick and footsteps muted by the thick pile of the oriental runner, she reached the open door to Simeon's office. Illumination tipped the revolving brass balls on the ship's clock on his desk. The light spearing from the timepiece brought her to a halt. Her head was still awhirl, yet suddenly she focused on the big roll of paper that hadn't been there yesterday, or this morning, or even this afternoon. She wasn't sure why it held her riveted to the spot.

A wisp of wind fluttered the inner silk curtains under the heavier cordovan brocade at the two sets of bay windows. One of the large white pages of the roll blew open and slowly lowered to the side. Then another page unfurled. Mary blinked, then blinked again. She stared at the pages of what she now realized were renderings of the CSS *Virginia*. She listened to the sounds of the house, then darted a glance over her shoulder to see if anyone was around. She slipped closer to the pages. They were indeed the ship's definitive drawings, with notations of the Southern ironclad's strengths and weaknesses. She pressed her lips tightly between her teeth. She recalled Anders's words: "Her four-inch iron sheeting makes her pretty much invulnerable. But she can be hurt if she's crippled at the waterline."

Oh, my God, she wondered, what was she thinking? She turned away feeling shaky and continued to her salon. Once the door there closed behind her, she leaned against it as new urgency rose from the pit of her stomach.

CHAPTER 30

Breakfast was set in the white latticework gazebo. The weather beckoned gentle warm breezes and earthy smells under a sky so blue as to be intense, without a hint of cloud. Golden sun danced color all around the garden and sparkled on the shiny blue and white Delft plates and crystal glasses on the amber-colored tablecloth. Polished silverware gleamed on napkins a shade of putty. Birds kept their chatter to a minimum so that they, along with Roguey who was setting out the meal, could overhear Simeon and Tesh-Lucianne's discussion.

"When I woke up this morning," Tesh-Lucianne said, "I had to check myself in the mirror."

"Why? Something wrong?" Simeon buttered a thick biscuit.

"I can't think of anything wrong right now," Tesh-Lucianne said, her eyes twinkling. "I was just checking my body to see how many times I might've pinched myself since the party to make sure I wasn't dreaming all that up."

Simeon smiled and heaped his plate with big helpings of fried eggs, glazed ham, lengths of hickory-smoked bacon, grits, and gravy. He spooned apple butter on the saucer with his biscuit.

"How can you eat so much after all we had after the gala?" Tesh-Lucianne said as she dished up for herself butter to accompany two corn fritters and a ditch-digger's portion of fried green apples and a leg of roast game hen.

"You should talk," Simeon laughed, eyeing her plate.

"I *should* talk," Tesh-Lucianne said. "Near about everybody told me how wonderful the fashion show was. Some even asked if they could send a card around for me to schedule an interview with Mary to discuss their wardrobe needs. I couldn't keep it all in my head. Drivers and runners came to the door all day yesterday with thank you notes as well. Mary got a bunch of presents, as did you and I." She paused to take a breath. "Senator Short and his wife sent two men in a wagon to haul their gift to us."

"What was it?" Simeon asked, taking a sip of coffee.

"A huge silver coffee urn with cream pitcher, sugar bowl, and an enormous silver tray to set beneath it. Their note said with you as a new senator from Virginia, we'll need it for all the entertaining we'll be doing." She sighed.

"I can see you're excited," Simeon said with a laugh. "Shouldn't you eat your breakfast? Sounds like you're going to need to build up strength to carry the thing."

"Thank you, Roguey," Tesh-Lucianne said to the cook as she finished putting out all her dishes. "You can take the cart back to the kitchen now. We've enough food to sink a battleship."

"Yes'm," Roguey said, and she clomped in her big shoes behind her rolling service cart, across the expanse of lawn and through the kitchen's French doors.

"I didn't want Roguey to hear," Tesh-Lucianne said, lowering her voice, "though I do believe the woman's able to hear what's said on the other side of Norfolk."

"What?" Simeon was intent on eating.

"Lumley told me he felt like a kid amongst a slew of candy choices, meeting all of the dignitaries that came to the fashion show and party. At the end of the evening, he said he didn't believe you were going to have a minute's trouble with your bid for senator."

"He's always been optimistic about that," Simeon said, holding a tight fist to his chest and making a small belch. "The endless meetings and speechmaking and all that goes into a campaign are beginning to wear on me. But I guess it's paying off."

Tesh-Lucianne grinned at him. "That and the fact that Daddy A.B., Senator Short, and a whole mess more of powerful folk have decided that you're in. The rest is for show."

"Tesh-Lucianne," Simeon said, folding his napkin on his lap, "is there something you're tryin' to tell me in all this? I need a map to follow you already."

"Well, Lumley told me that government was controlled by men who carried a lot of weight in a lot of different areas, along with men who sometimes controlled them with their money. He plans to tell you all this himself," she whispered. "I wasn't supposed to say a thing. Swore me to secrecy and all, but you know me, bad as a leaky bucket."

"Tesh-Lucianne!"

"He said he had a chance to talk to them all at the party and what with Daddy A.B. giving you his stamp of approval, they're all behind you." She put her fingers to her lips and squealed as her eyes nearly outshined the sun. "And this is delicious! He said Senator Short's wife just loves me. Said I was fine government wife material. Told him she would personally take me under her wing and make sure she taught me everything her years with the senator afforded her."

Tesh-Lucianne glanced toward the house to see if anyone was spying. Then she went on. "Lumley said Daddy A.B. was making him *his* personal assistant as well as whatever post you give him."

Simeon's face began to darken. "Why would he do that?"

Tesh-Lucianne flapped her hand at him and took up her fork. "You know Daddy. He probably wants to help provide Lumley a good salary. Government officials don't make all that much money. He's likely doing it as a thank-you for helping your career and for ushering in just a deliriously fairy tale of a good time for us. That is," she added, making a sober face for a moment, "while you help people and do good works."

"I swear, Tesh-Lucianne, I don't know whether to laugh or cry."

"Well, if I were you, I'd choose the former. As senator, you can assign somebody else the duty of crying." She tucked into her green apples.

"So who's Lumley to answer to," Simeon said, his appetite suddenly a bit dulled, "me or your father?"

"Why, how'm I supposed to know that, silly?" She stuffed part of a corn fritter into her mouth too, chewed and gulped it all down with a sip of coffee. "You know, that woman in our kitchen can co-oo-ook! I'm so glad we have her, and Mary to make our clothes, and Devereaux to drive us, and Golen to grow bushels and bushels of good food for us. We're so blessed!" She stopped and looked over at her husband, whose own eyes had taken a far-off expression. "Simeon?"

A sea breeze lifted a hank of his hair, laid it down in its wake.

"Simeon? Is everything all right? Did I say something wrong?"

He blinked himself back and patted her hand. "Did Lumley say anything else?"

She thought a minute and brightened again. "He said he was sure Daddy A.B. was in your corner one hundred percent because of a trade they made."

"A trade?"

She giggled. "Yes. Lumley said he gave Daddy A.B. a record of your orders to him and Gates, as well as something about tallying up something. I don't know, you'll have to ask him. He did make an odd comment though, now that I think about it."

Simeon clasped his hands together. It was not a happy gesture.

"He told me that Daddy A.B. said 'They now could control the horse if it ever tried to run away.' Or something like that. I forget. Ladies came up to me then, wanting to carry me away to the dancing and eating and drinking. Anyway, are the three of you buying a horse? Maybe a race horse?"

Simeon shuddered. "No, dear. Not that kind of horse at all."

Tesh-Lucianne gave a small burp. "I am stuffed. I tell you, I am so stuffed. I've got to go see Mary now, love. If we're still talking in animal terms, I've got to smooth her feathers. I don't think she took the news at all well about Delaclaire and The House of M." She rose and kissed Simeon on the cheek. "I'll do my work, sly as a fox." She giggled and did not see Simeon's face go ashen.

"They've got me muzzled," he muttered to himself, "and not a damn thing I can do about it!" He looked across the lawn at the back of his retreating wife. He watched her turn, smile, and wave at him cheerily. He waved back as he continued to grumble. "Got the bit in my teeth, have they? We'll see. We'll surely see."

CHAPTER 31

Rain had started out gusty early in the evening as fat drops slapped city roofs and plowed fields with loud percussive thumps. By night's deepest pitch, it pounded Norfolk as fiercely as anything they remembered. Demonic winds howled and gripped ground debris, dragging it about like a whip. Its strength wrenched at thick tree branches and ripped them from their joints like dry bones, hurling them into the darkness in runaway blasts. Rocks and pebbles churned in agitated swirls that pelted and cracked windows. Thunder bawled low and menacing across the horizon, then rose, rumbling into stupendous cannonades loud enough to proclaim themselves harsh blows from the hammer of the god Thor. Lightning flashes slashed jagged blue veins into the black sky. One jolt shot hotly to the ground, causing wide-eyed horses, already terrified, to snap their tethers and race away into a headache for their owners to retrieve the next day. Anybody and anything that could take cover did, trying to wait out the worst of it. Almost anybody.

A tall black man wearing a slicker and slouch hat pulled down over his features also wore a black silk scarf that masked his face nose to chin. He peered out from behind a tall oak tree in the woods. His astonishing light blue-gray eyes carefully swept a look all around to make sure it was safe. Seeing nothing but the heavy downpour, he stepped out and plunged forward. Behind him quickly trailed eight people—three men, two women, and three youngsters—soaked to their old work shoes that sucked in mud and slipped over ground vegetation so slimy that keeping upright was a constant challenge. They hunched into the wind and driving rain, holding hands to keep together.

By instinct and frequent illumination from lightning spears, the man led the group across a wide-open field that would have taken too long to circumvent and rushed them into the thick, thorny brush on the other side. His urgency pushed them as much as their fear. They were running for their lives, he knew, as well as toward that slender hope for something better. This is why they had embarked upon this perilous journey. Now, in this dark night, they also ran from fear born of a new-felt freedom and a determination not to go back to lives as ciphers in their slave master's log books. This was terrifying for sure, but exhilarating too for the man. He loved this work, and succeeding, even narrowly, gave him the satisfaction he needed to do it again. Even if he had not been part of The Travelers, he would have done what he could to work the line.

Heavy drops pummeled their backs as they sluiced a tortuous course that wound deep into the back country. The leader occasionally made clicking noises in his throat to indicate his direction, though knowing the way in this potentially disastrous pitch meant little. Furtively, from time to time, he glanced over his shoulder. Then, he thought he heard something different in the din. He halted so abruptly that his party banged into each other trying to stop. His ears picked up even greater danger. His eyes frantically searched for a hiding place.

The spate of pines gave them cover from a distance, but close up they might just as well be standing out in the open. He turned around, looking desperately. Then he caught sight of a rocky embrasure and urged everyone in that direction. Once there, he told them to flatten themselves against the walls of an inside niche in hopes they'd not be visible. He held his breath. In another few minutes, he saw the men who were relentlessly pursuing them through the sheeting rain. They banged through the trees and stopped, cursing, their horses chuffing. The man counted five riders.

"Goldangit, Bridges," said one. "Ain't nothin' without gills gon' be out in this."

Sheriff Claude Bridges sat tall atop his chestnut ride. A wide-brimmed hat kept a little rain off his face, which was seasoned by many years in the sun. His blond, shoulder-length hair hung in wet strings that clung to his neck. He turned in his saddle, looking around. When he spoke, his was a mellow and humor-filled voice, even on a night like this. "Aw, I wouldn't complain if I was you, Briny. You're getting a much needed bath."

The other men brayed a laugh.

Bridges, a handsome, confident man around thirty, who wore command easily, paused another minute, his blue eyes scanning for signs of escapees. "They're out here all right," he said. "Can't see no evidence, but I feel it."

"You feelin' the one they call 'Brother,' ain't you," Gates said. "If I could get to him, I'd gut him like a chicken."

The sheriff ignored the comment and he scanned every tree and then looked up at the dark sky. "Y'all c'mon," he said. "We're goin'." He clicked at his horse and moved back through a gap in the copse of trees in the direction of the road.

The specter of trouble so raised, the black man did not move for a full ten minutes after the pursuers disappeared. He knew Bridges to be both smart and clever and did not underestimate the sheriff. So he waited a long hard time to see if the men doubled back.

All of the black man's senses were alert but finally, detecting nothing, he again plunged his party into the savage wetness and pressed on even faster than before. Another mile. Then another inhospitable mile, zigzagging, circling, never traveling in a straight line. His exhausted body sloughed on. His arms scissored through shrubs that tore at his clothes and skin. His boots dug into the mud and tangled weeds. Leaves and branches slapped his face as the fecund smell of earth filled his nostrils. His mouth sucked in air with a rasping noise but he willed himself to keep going. The slaves at his rear struggled behind him. But they too would not quit.

At last, they staggered over a hillock down to the edge of a rushing waterway where patches of seaweed and flotsam threw themselves at the base of willow trees shagged close to the water. Stands of tall cattails danced wildly in the wind. The crescent moon was a dingy smudge in the night sky. He strained to see out past where ocean waves churned, whitecapped, their frothy fingers stretched along the beach. Nothing. Not even waterfowl. All he could hear was wind and the water slapping. Questioning eyes swung to his face. He cupped his hands around his mouth and made a bird-like call. He strained to listen. In a few seconds came a responding call from a path of reeds in the shallow water to his left. He could make out a small boat in there but saw no one on board.

A black man the size of a small mountain appeared out of the mist and marsh weeds. Covering the lower portion of his face was a black scarf. He spoke in a low voice, "Can't go nowhere in that mess tonight." He hooked a finger, indicating where lightning crackled over a purling spread of sea.

A small child began to cry, and one of the women clutched him to her.

The man sighed. His mind began to race, considering what to do.

"We got us another way," said another black man, slipping up behind him. He too wore a black scarf. He was thin, with skin so dark he almost blended into the surrounding night. But his angular face held kind eyes and his liquid bass voice was as soothing as a mother's heartbeat. "We take 'em now, Brother."

The man who had conducted them this far put out his pecan-colored hand and shook hands with both men. As one of the huddled group said, "Thank you, mister," he turned to them in the lashing rain. A smile flicked at the corners of his mouth. His startling eyes glowed brightly, his face beamed. He was proud of them. What they were doing was not for the faint of heart.

"Adieu, mes amis," he said. He pushed back into the reeds, disappearing into the gloomy weather's unearthly madness, tired, but thinking to himself with a laugh, "A few more gone off the books."

———◆———

Next morning, the sun shined brightly. The skies had cleared. It was a gorgeous day. Crawthers stomped his beat-up brogans onto the damp earth. He was angry. He was always angry. But this morning, he had good reason to be. Despite last night's heavy rain, his barn was all but cinders. Somehow, thankfully, the horses were saved. They had gotten out of their stalls, and he'd have to go search for them.

"We got us somebody who likes to play with fire, friend," Gates said, examining the mess that once was Crawthers's barn.

"I'm a light sleeper, but the thunder was so loud I didn't hear a thing, not even the horses running," Crawthers said.

"Slick," Gates said. "And of course, none of your slaves heard anything either."

Crawthers shook his head, turned his slate-gray eyes onto the deputy. "This is about that nigger girl, isn't it?"

"I reckon," Gates said.

Crawthers paced a little away, then came back. "I swear to the living Lord, I ain't aim to shoot her. I was down by the river hunting wild turkey. Way I figure it, the girl saw me before I saw her and hid in the bushes. Everybody around here knows how I feel about trespassin' on my place. So I figured the sounds I heard meant I was one shot away from my dinner. I saw movement in the bushes and fired."

"Folks said she was looking for peacock feathers is all," Gates said, eyeing Crawthers, a man about fifty with pale skin like the underside of a frog. "You wouldn't know about that?"

"Nope." Crawthers scratched his paunch and hiked up his patched trousers, only for them to slide south again. "I keep some of the birds on the place but I never know where they are. They wander. Foxes and hawks always trifling with them, so I gotta keep 'em under watch." Gates turned and watched the old man open his mouth, start to say something else, then close it again. Crawthers retracted thin lips into a gap-toothed smile. He scratched his gray beard stubble with dirty fingernails.

"I wouldn't worry about this too much," Gates said after another pause. "One less nigger is one less problem."

CHAPTER 32

"Come on in," Tesh-Lucianne called lightly as she, Gie, and Mary looked up. In strode two men.

The tall one sported a pronounced belly that hung low between two bright-red suspenders. The rest of him wasn't fat; it was just his ample middle that people ribbed him about, saying he loved his mother's vittles more than the slew of eager matrons plotting to tow him to the altar. Good-looking, his long blond hair fell casually around an open and inviting weather-beaten countenance. His lapdog eyes were the color of sky at soft light. His jowly cheeks were spotted with rosy circles. At the neck of his rumpled white shirt, he wore a string tie, the type his mother favored, cinched by a carved buffalo horn. In his hand was a slightly shabby wide-brimmed hat. Though he wanted with all his might to appear a tough two-fisted gunslinger, most people agreed he came off more like an inviting rocker by the fireplace on a cold night.

"Well, look who the cat dragged in," Tesh-Lucianne bubbled in greeting. "Sheriff Claude Bridges. You lookin' good. To what do we owe the pleasure?"

"How do, ma'am?" he said, his shy smile turning fleshy cheeks into parentheses. "I think you know my deputy, Gates?"

The character who ambled behind Bridges was younger by an easy ten years. He was a few inches taller, gangly, with the look of a scruffy crane. Blond hair surrounded the boyish features of his oval face and curled at his long neck. Full lips pulled back into a grin.

As he shambled in and the coat flapped open, she caught sight of the holstered Colt slung on his skinny hip.

"Yes, of course," Tesh-Lucianne said, giving the man a measuring glance.

"My friends call me Gates," he repeated with a slow drawl.

"Yes," Tesh-Lucianne said, eyeing him curiously. "Y'all come and sit down.

You want coffee?"

"No, thank you—"

Gates interrupted the sheriff, "That'd be mighty hospitable of you."

Tesh-Lucianne led them to two comfortable armchairs and a settee near a wide bay window opening onto a small balcony and the garden below. Both men, with their calloused, large-knuckled hands, appeared clumsy and ill at ease holding the delicate cups. She smiled inwardly.

"Sorry to intrude on you ladies," Sheriff Bridges said, blotting sweat from his forehead with the back of his hand. As he did so, his hangdog eyes flicked a look across the room and saw Gie. "Oh, beg pardon, Miss Gie," he said in his soft, deprecating manner. "I didn't see you over there." He chuckled. "And you're the one with new glasses."

"Nothing's secret in this town," Gie said.

Gates snorted and sipped his coffee, his eyes never leaving her face. "It is my heartfelt wish that your new spectacles let you see forever. Or, failing that, provide vision into your life's purpose before Fate might dim your eyesight for all time," he said, smiling with a veneer of politeness.

"I want you to stop talking," Gie said sarcastically.

The others all laughed, except Mary, who watched Gates set his cup on the polished side table with exaggerated care, then casually lace his hands across his thin chest and cross his legs at the knee.

Bridges looked around self-consciously, then down to study his dirty boots planted on the sumptuous rug. "Well, I'll come to the point of our bein' here. We, uh, had us a little trouble last night outside town. I was just wondering, Miz Louvestre, if your boy Devereaux had a pass to leave the property. Say, around eleven o'clock?"

"What?" Tesh-Lucianne said. "Why on earth would you want to know that?"

"Y'all might be harborin' a criminal," Gates blurted out while gawking at the room's luxuries.

Tesh-Lucianne stifled a squeak as she regarded the men.

Gates showed one tobacco-stained front tooth overlaying another that gave him a slightly bucktoothed appearance. Raking the tip of a pink tongue along his cracked bottom lip, he stared directly at Tesh-Lucianne through lively blue agate eyes.

"We come here seekin' a nigger meetin' Devereaux's size and description. Boy who played a major hand in divestin' Mr. Emmett Crawthers of rightful property," Gates said.

Tesh-Lucianne swung toward Sheriff Bridges. "What in the Sam Hill is he talkin' about?"

"What I'm—" Gates started.

"Thank you, Deputy Gates," Sheriff Bridges cut in, quiet-voiced. He swallowed hard, causing the cleft in his chin to deepen. "Miz Tesh-Lucianne, we have reason to believe Devereaux's assisting fugitive slaves. It is likely he's tied up with a bunch of nigras calling themselves 'The Travelers.'"

"The heck you preach!" Tesh-Lucianne scoffed. She tightened her grip on Gie's hand, still on her shoulder.

"Ri-i-ght," Gates drew out theatrically.

Tesh-Lucianne pushed her chin up and spoke more forcefully. "Sheriff Bridges, I assure you our Devereaux is a fine, upstanding person who'd never be involved in such activity. Everybody knows him on sight anyway, debonair as he is. I wouldn't think that, even if he tried, he could get away with doing what you said."

"Yes, ma'am," Sheriff Bridges said. "But they wear all black with black cloth tied around their faces, only showin' their eyes."

"Then how'd you suspect Devereaux?" Tesh-Lucianne asked.

Gates answered. "Boy we're lookin' for has distinctive eyes. Conjurer eyes, like they got magic in them. Not unlike those over there." He jerked a thumb at Mary, then spoke directly to her. "Yours are more sultry though. Could make a man turn fool under your gaze. Uhn-uhn-uhn. Out-and-out fine." He shook his head. "Anybody ever tell you that?"

Mary did not respond. She felt herself flush under his offensive, smug sitting-on-the-porch-in-the shade manner.

"Sheriff, kindly put your man on a leash," Gie said huffily.

"Yes'm," he said, and held up a restraining hand to Gates.

Mary appreciated that Gie chastened Gates, even though there remained tension between her and Gie over Coolie. Things were different between them now. Harsh words had been spoken that could never be taken back. Despite Gie's standing up to Gates, Mary knew it was as much for Tesh-Lucianne's sake as for hers.

"The Travelers," Gie now repeated. "This is the first I've heard of them."

Mary kept her fingers busy with needlework. She kept her ears tuned to listen between the men's words.

Sheriff Bridges worked his shapeless, sweat-stained hat around in his chafed fingers. "Rumors are it's a secret organization of clever darkies, willing to do whatever it takes to aid runaway slaves. They're even suspected of protecting nigras around town."

"What does that mean?" Tesh-Lucianne said.

"It means," Gates said, picking imaginary lint off his trouser leg, "sometimes they shoot to kill—whoever killin' suits their purpose at the time. They might even burn a man's barn down in revenge." He shot a look at Mary.

"I don't believe that," Gie stated flatly as Tesh-Lucianne gasped.

Sheriff Bridges quickly continued. "Largely, they provide temporary shelter, food, clothing, doctoring, disguises, and transport as they assist slaves running north. What with all this war talk going on, it's unsettling how more and more slaves are risking escape from their duties and obligations to their owners."

Mary tightened her lips, taking care to reveal nothing through her silence.

"Probably the work of Yankee abolitionists puttin' ridiculous notions into their heads," Gates spat, "working them up with notions of having all the rights and privileges of white people. What rat turd. Pardon my French."

Sheriff Bridges scowled darkly at Gates, then turned to the ladies. "We gettin' worried the nigras plan on graduatin' into greater hostilities."

"Like what?" Gie asked, her eyes blinking behind her thick glasses.

"Like what was done to that lawyer man Withers," Gates added.

Mary had all she could do to keep herself from peering into the deputy's eyes in search of what might be behind this lie.

"Found him deader'n a doornail," Gates continued. "What he looked like after they got through with him—why, I wouldn't want proper ladies like yourselves ever to catch sight of such. Nightmare lookin', I'd tell it." Gates shuddered for effect.

Mary glanced up quickly, then down again. She saw Gates's lips turned up at the corners in a crooked smile. He was having a good time.

"Their leader's supposed to be a colored right here in Norfolk," Sheriff Bridges said. "Some say it's a woman, but nobody in their right mind would believe that. It's gotta be a man. I just don't know if it's Devereaux or not. It wouldn't hurt to ask him about it, though, if you don't mind."

"We do mind," Tesh-Lucianne said flatly.

"Sorry, ma'am," the sheriff said. "I'm afraid I have to insist. This is the kind of thing we've got to get a jump on. We don't … well, there could be hell to pay."

"Sheriff and Deputy, you're taking great pains to vex us," Gie said.

These men were much, much more than a vexation, Mary thought. They were as dangerous as a cocked pistol. Aware that Gates had his sights on her, she held her face unreadable and kept her hands busy, tacking the seam of a skirt she had in her lap. She regarded him from under lowered lids.

"Devereaux's not your man," Gie said with emphasis on the word "man," not that the sheriff or his sidekick seemed to get it. "I'd stake my name on that."

Bridges looked chastened. "Yours is a name to be reckoned with in these parts, Miss Gie. I know. But why would you want to? Stake your name on this, I mean."

"It is my opinion that good sense is running amuck these days, fear overriding everything," Gie said. "As a result, too many colored men have already been wrongly accused and severely punished, some to their deaths. I just don't want the Louvestres' Devereaux to be among them."

"Yes'm," Bridges said, shifting. He was perplexed about how to proceed.

"Wouldn't you think," said Tesh-Lucianne, "with all the times he's had to be out in that buggy by himself going everywhere, that if he was going to pull such a stunt, he would have done it already? Why, he's been nothing but dutiful and loyal."

"That's well and good," said Sheriff Bridges. "But I've never seen it to fail. You put a lot of stock in them, even the good ones, and you're headed for trouble." He threw a glance at Mary, then looked down at his scuffed work boots.

"Yeah," said Gates. "That be my view." His eyes hardly blinked as he watched Mary. "Even the so-called good ones."

"That'll be enough," Tesh-Lucianne scolded, rising to indicate that the visit was over. "I'll see you out."

"Yes, ma'am," said the sheriff. "But before we go, I need to ask your girl here a question."

"Her name is Mary," said Tesh-Lucianne, clenching her jaw. "How long've you been knowing her now?"

Sheriff Bridges looked abashed.

"Excuse me, there," Gates interrupted with a cock of his chin toward Mary.

"What is that striking hat-thing you've always got perched on your head? I've seen you about town and I don't believe I've seen you in the same one twice. Why is that?"

Mary blew out a slow breath before responding. "It's called a 'coo-fee.' Spelled k-u-f-i. It's African. It means crown and cap. I make and wear them simply because I like them."

"Hmm, so you can spell," Gates said, then continued without a pause. "They do make you look—what's the word?—royal. Like you should be sitting up on a throne. Making decisions about life and death." He smiled wryly. "A force to be reckoned with. A leader. That'd be you, wouldn't you say?"

The sheriff spoke before Mary was forced to respond. "Mary, you know a man named Bear?"

Mary's manner was cool, thoughtful "I'm acquainted with him, yes."

"Big man. About six foot-something. Two hundred pounds if he's an ounce. Thurston Stone's right-hand man?"

"Thurston Stone," said Tesh-Lucianne. "What does he have to do with Devereaux or runaway slaves?"

"Maybe more'n you might guess," Gates said, picking up the empty china cup again.

Tesh-Lucianne ignored him, as did Gie.

Gates leaned one elbow down on the chair arm. The odors of his lazy hygiene soured the sweet outside scents. He didn't notice or if he did, he didn't care. He openly ogled the room. "Whooee, this here's some grand room."

"This is the fashion salon of Mary Louvestre," Tesh-Lucianne said haughtily. "This is the heart of The House of M, which is our business, not yours."

Gates nodded dreamily. Simulating a smile, he said, "You don't say? A nigger got all this?"

"You'd do well to stop that," Gie snapped.

Gates dispensed to her a gaze of lurid coldness. She jerked, and he liked that she did.

Sheriff Bridges cleared his throat. "What do you think of this boy, Bear?"

"I don't know how to answer that, Sheriff," said Mary, happy to frustrate him.

"You see, like Miss Gie said, it'd be an awful shame if I was to roust a good man to the hangman's rope. I certainly don't want that on my conscience. But if he's to carry some blame for this, well ..."

"My life is here in this salon, Sheriff," Mary said, her husky voice measured. "I tend to my business and don't much mix in with anything outside those responsibilities."

Gates chuckled and wiped his sweating face with his sleeve, then picked at a callous on his hand. "Lord, how you talk." He turned to the sheriff. "Clearly, this is an educated nigger. Don't you hear refined tones of somebody who can read and write? Why, even a cracker like me can detect it. Last I heard, that was against the law, am I right?"

Before Mary could say anything, Tesh-Lucianne spoke up. Her backbone was up and she'd become testy. "Enough! You understand this. Mary's a lady of high character and we won't allow her to be insulted." She glanced at Gie, who nodded in agreement. Turning again to Bridges, she added, "Sheriff, the very idea that you have this bad-mannered 'associate' dragging around with you is something I will definitely take up with your mother, Miss Clara-Jean. You ought to know better."

Gates laughed. "I just love it when people remind other people what they already know about themselves. And do it with such good manners it doesn't hurt their feelings. Now, that's an art."

Tesh-Lucianne went to the door and held it open. "Out," she said. "You will kindly leave right now."

The sheriff bit on his lower lip. "We have offended you and I want you to please accept my apology."

"That we'll have to think about," shot Tesh-Lucianne.

As the two men walked out, Gates turned back over his shoulder to look at Mary, a crazy light in his eyes, his face cruel. "Be seein' you, fashion lady. Someday I might just want you to make me a fancy new suit of clothes. Give me the look of a proper gentleman." He flashed a fulgent smile.

She stared back at him despite a fear that was crawling up her spine. She did not believe in blinking first.

"Well, well," Gates said, "'til we meet again." He placed his hat on his head and touched the brim. He bowed to Tesh-Lucianne and Gie. "Ladies."

Chapter 33

Mary and Devereaux had made a midday herb-collecting trip to the woods. When they reached home, a concerned Roguey met Mary at the door. "Missus went to town whilst you was away. Said she wanted to surprise you with some supplies."

"Yes?" Mary said, impatient for the real news.

Roguey looked down and shook her head. "She got what she went after but she had a bad time of it."

"Why? What do you mean?"

"A bunch of drunk sailors gathered 'roun' her an' she couldn't pass. One of them pushed her into an alley an' was hoisting her skirt and lowerin' his pants when one of them women they call 'Bouncin' Bettys' heard her screamin'. Big woman, Missus said. She come tearin' out of a nearby tavern. Cold-cocked the man. His frien's ran away."

Horror was in Mary's voice as she asked, "Is she okay? Where is she?"

"She's here, but okay is somethin' else again. Missus been up in her room since she been back. Axed me to bring her some tea. I took it up there, but she wouldn't say word one. She just starin' into space. Thank God you come home."

"I'll go see about her," Mary said, already halfway up the staircase.

On the landing, she turned left and knocked on the big wooden doors. No answer. She waited a minute. She decided to go back to her salon for her medicine bag. After retrieving it, she stuck her head into the kitchen. Roguey was slicing potatoes into a pan of cold water. "I'm going to need some hot water for a medicine tea. Will you bring it up?"

"Sho."

Mary went back to the bedroom door and knocked again. Still no answer. She opened it slowly. Tesh-Lucianne was sitting on the edge of the bed. She looked forlorn, lost to everyday things.

"It's me," Mary said softly. "I'm going to take off your dress and get you into something more comfortable."

Tesh-Lucianne still did not respond but compliantly stood as Mary pulled her up. Mary undid the buttons and gently slipped the dress over her head. Then she eased off the crinolines. When Tesh-Lucianne was undressed, Mary eased her back onto the bed. She pulled a jar of lemon balm from her bag and, using her forefinger, applied a little under Tesh-Lucianne's nose. Still no response. Then Mary put a nut of the potion into her palm and began to massage the woman's neck and shoulders. After a while she turned to Tesh-Lucianne's arms to work in a healing tonic of rosemary and chamomile. Only when she was massaging her feet did Tesh-Lucianne begin to whimper. Finally, tears began to stain her cheeks. This was precisely what Mary wanted, what Tesh-Lucianne needed. A few tears dropped at first, then she fell weeping into Mary's comforting embrace.

Roguey knocked and quietly entered with the hot water. She placed it on the table by the bed, looked ruefully at the two women who did not look back, and closed the door behind her.

"I can't believe it," snuffled Tesh-Lucianne after she had taken some tea. "My very own people did this. To *me*. If that tavern woman hadn't come, I don't know what would've happened." She sighed heavily and looked off into the middle distance. "Oh, yes I do."

"Don't think about that now," Mary said. "You're safe."

Tesh-Lucianne's eyes went blank once more. "I don't know that I'll ever feel safe again."

⸺⸺

Mary was restless, keyed up. Her mind was bothered by thoughts that jostled each other for attention. She passed an exasperated hand across her forehead. It was evening and so far she had forced the troublesome noisemakers in her head, by sheer will, to be quiet.

First there'd been the visit from Sheriff Bridges and Gates. Then Tesh-Lucianne's trouble. She'd had to leave her to deal with clients, the last of whom had finally left. She had tried to be patient, listen attentively, and ask good questions to garner information that would help her design the garments they wanted. Yet time and again her mind sailed off to a gossamer somewhere, thoroughly engrossed in itself. Then she'd be startled out of her reveries, wondering what in the world her client had been talking about. Her last one had been particularly difficult.

"For crying out loud! Is my ordering a new dress distracting you?" Lydeah Bondourant had demanded.

Mary jumped. "Oh! I apologize, Miss Lydeah. My mind is acting like paper in the wind."

Lydeah scowled and peered down her nose at Mary. She arched an eyebrow. Lydeah was an attractive free black who thought more of herself than God did.

She was a woman of independent means, a slave owner herself, and had been a regular client of Mary's for years. In two weeks, she was hosting a soiree at her rambling house where she would feature some of Mary's clothes. Mary did not want to give Lydeah cause to put the word out that white patrons got more of her attention than free colored ones.

"Since me and my friends were not invited to your fancy show, we decided to have a do amongst ourselves," Lydeah said, still snippy. "I, myself, personally, want the absolute latest thing."

Mary simply smiled and said nothing in response to Lydeah's chatter. She knew that Lydeah would like nothing more than to get into the matter of why free blacks had not received invitations to the show. That had been up to Tesh-Lucianne, not her.

"It's going to be fun, fun, fun," Lydeah stressed. "And if the evening's outcome happens like I think it will, you'll just have to hire more folks to fill our orders."

"Exciting," Mary said quietly. "Then the best thing is for you to look at some fabrics." Mary ushered the woman to the shelves where she kept samples.

When Mary was finally alone in the salon's quiet, she straightened things up before passing through an inner set of doors to her bedroom suite. There she slipped out of her dress and underclothing, hung them in the tall chiffonier, and stood naked for a moment on the thick hooked rug. She examined herself in the long oval mirror above the marble-topped console. Turning left then right, she had to admit she wasn't in as bad a shape as she felt. Tall and lean were qualities she shared with her father. Even now in her maturity, she still had wide shoulders, a solid body, narrow waist, flat stomach, tight hips, and long legs. The left leg bowed a bit from the long-ago injury and arthritis, but nowhere was there any fat.

She filled her washbasin with water from the pitcher. With all of her might, she fought the urge to give in to her scattered thoughts. Not now, she commanded herself, as she tried to focus only on the refreshing, cool washcloth. Using a gelatin soap the fragrance of lavender from Gie's toilette collection, she stroked her face, neck, breasts, and back, then traversed herself again with rinse water. Finally, she dried herself and sat down in a tufted side chair. From a selection of tall dark-blue bottles arrayed on top, she chose lemon verbena lotion to shake into the palm of her hand. She massaged it into her skin, adding camphor oil to rub into the sore muscles of her legs. She liberally applied rosewater and glycerin to her feet before sliding them into soft slippers. Then she donned a leisure robe made much like an Asian happi coat, tied the side strings of raffia, and spritzed herself with Hungary water.

She finally felt better. She finally could think. She leaned back and began to consider the plans for the CSS *Virginia*.

CHAPTER 34

A soft tapping played on the salon doors.

Tesh-Lucianne poked her head in. "You decent, or at least trying to be?"

"Over here," Mary said without getting up.

"Can I come in?"

"Anything I can do to stop you?"

"True, so true," Tesh-Lucianne said lightly. She stepped near where Mary was relaxing. "Is that a drink in your itsy-bitsy fingers?"

Mary smiled. "Ask me no questions, I'll tell you no lies."

Tesh-Lucianne went to the decanters and poured a stout drink, then came back to curl up in a chaise near Mary.

"You're feeling better, I see." Mary regarded her mistress closely.

"Yes and no. The memory of those damned scalawags still makes me want to spit on their graves."

"Nothing like a righteous mad to make you feel better."

Tesh-Lucianne held up her glass. "That, and good bourbon." She suddenly grimaced. "Ooo!"

"What?"

"I've still got a powerful headache."

"A few more sips will take care of that."

They laughed and were quiet a moment together.

"I see you've got my new outfit up on the dress form," Tesh-Lucianne said. "This one's very important, you know. Confederate President Jefferson Davis personally sent an invitation to Simeon and me. We've been invited to dine. He hasn't endorsed us yet, but we hope we can woo him into doing so."

"So what're you doing here this late? Shouldn't you be having dinner with Simeon?"

"He and Lumley went to Richmond. Some speaking engagement he couldn't get out of."

"I thought he liked that sort of thing," Mary said sluggishly, hoping not to be drawn into further conversation.

"He does, but he tried to get out of it because I asked him to. I haven't been feeling myself at all since ..."

"Since what happened in town?"

"Yes," Tesh-Lucianne said, and in a stupendous feat, chugged half the glass of whiskey. "I feel better when he's in the house."

Mary turned her head. "What's going on?"

"I don't know," Tesh-Lucianne said, driving hard fingers through her hair and dislodging combs that had held it in place. "I—I've started hearing things. Voices." She paused, then asked, "You know anything about that? In your medicine work?"

"Sure. But it could be caused by a number of things. Tell me more and maybe I can help with a remedy."

"Well." Tesh-Lucianne kicked off her slippers and flexed her toes as she sat down on the end of the chaise. "They started the night of the attack. They say all sorts of things. One voice scares me badly."

Mary sipped her drink and listened.

"It's a little boy," Tesh-Lucianne whispered. "He says he's my child."

"That one's far-fetched."

"Not so much as you might think. You see, I've been wandering this house for a while this afternoon." Tesh-Lucianne propped her drink in the middle of her stomach. "Do you have any idea how many rooms are in this house?"

"You're asking me?"

"Yes. I'm asking you."

"Oh, what does it matter?" Mary asked dismissively. "Twenty, thirty, fifty."

"Wrong, and the prize does not go to you. There are exactly twenty-three rooms in this house. Not counting outbuildings." Tesh-Lucianne threw back another slug of bourbon, and again rested the drink on her stomach. She fingered the glass, turning it around and around in the light. "Most people in the city, even other wealthy ones, have much smaller houses and less land than we do. But Daddy A.B. and Simeon's father decided that wouldn't be fine enough for their grandchildren. Which is why they bought us all this land so close to the water. I used to love it here."

Mary held a long pause before asking, "Used to? What's changed?"

"Lord! So much!" Tesh-Lucianne sighed. "You know that I had five—count them on your fingers—five miscarriages. With the last pregnancy, Simeon sent for a special doctor from Boston. He told us I had to stay in bed for the last half of my time. We just knew this was the one to make it." Tesh-Lucianne looked off. "You were still fairly young then and you might not have known much more than I was sick."

"I slightly recall," Mary replied.

"No, you wouldn't have known everything. I had your room down the hall from us at first, then we made that nice apartment for you in the attic where you spent most of your time, studying everything we could find for you about sewing."

Mary listened.

Tesh-Lucianne went on. "I piled into the big four-poster and let myself be waited on hand and foot by Nivea, the cook before Roguey. Daddy A.B. was down visiting. You know how dotey he can get."

"Hmm," Mary said, stifling a yawn.

"I woke up one dawn feeling squishy between my legs. I knew that wasn't right. I threw back the covers and was horrified. There was an awful puddle of blood. I screamed like something biblical. Daddy and Simeon and Nivea all tore into the room. Nivea helped me up against the pillows. When I did that, my insides contracted and I pushed like I don't know what was happening. The most ungodly-looking thing surged out of me onto the bed. It was so horrible. Its tiny face was twisted. Little fists bawled up in the air. Its thing stuck up for all the world to see. What looked like a mouth was open, as if to tear off a scream just like I had."

She took a breath and gulped more drink. "I don't know what happened after that. I think Daddy A.B. gave me something. Or maybe it was Nivea. When I woke up two days later, you'd never have imagined that a woman had tried to become a mother in that room. It was scoured cleaner than the Lord's lobby."

Tesh-Lucianne took another pull on the bourbon. "Friends told me that Daddy A.B. had chomped on his cigars and drank and paced around and fumed the whole two days. He believed Simeon was to blame somehow. He told Simeon—and this was told to me verbatim—'If my daughter ever cries again in this house, you'll be the worse for it.' Simeon knew he meant it too. Daddy A.B. always has had a reputation for taking the direct approach in intents and affairs."

Tesh-Lucianne sat up. "I'm getting sloshed, I hope." Her words mushed into buttery slurs. "Goin' for another. You?"

"No," Mary said, "thank you."

"You're so po-*lite*," Tesh-Lucianne said, her drawl thick and lazy as she filled her glass with another drink. "Jus' like your mama. And you do take after your daddy."

Mary's senses perked up and her mind rummaged for the right thing to say. Instead, she experienced a kind of mental eclipse and could only stare at the woman who was making herself comfortable again, folding her legs under her on the chaise.

"I couldn't believe that me and Simeon wouldn't have a dozen stairstep children running through these massive rooms."

"Where does my mother come in?" Mary pressed as she nervously fingered a lock of her hair. "What do my parents have to do with this?"

"Well, it's a long story," Tesh-Lucianne said with an ironic smile. She gulped more of her drink and raised her glass. "Gonna need more of this to tell you. See, I was four years old when one day my mother, Ardella-Plusse, went to town. Nothing special, just her usual. She stopped at Culpepper's, did some window-shopping, and put her packages in the carriage. That's when she was accosted. By three white men. Jus' like me. She managed to get away, but she was beat up bad, and when she pulled up home she was talking gibberish. She caught a fever that night. Daddy A.B. and the doctor were doing everything they could. But the doctor said, 'It's the beatin'est thing. I ain't seen nothin' like it afore.' When the sun crowned over distant mountains, Mama said to Daddy A.B., 'Take care of my baby. Let her know white men can be awful mean too.' 'Honey, don't leave me,' Daddy A.B. wailed. 'I can't hardly make it without you.'

"I was hiding behind a chair in her room, but I heard every word," Tesh-Lucianne said. Her words were halting and fuzzy. "Mama died right then."

Mary waited silently. After a moment, Tesh-Lucianne went on.

"I cried forever and a day. Your mother, Evangeline, tended to me like I was her own. She was one of the sweetest women God gave breath." Tesh-Lucianne got up again for more drink. "'Scuse me. I need to get my head really bad to tell you the rest."

Mary sat up straighter and swung to face Tesh-Lucianne, who had managed an unsteady return to the sofa, sloshing another glass of the potent old-stock whiskey.

"Every day after we put Mama's body in the ground, Daddy A.B. got more hot around the collar saying, 'Somebody gon' pay if I live.' I wasn't but waist high to him, but 'while later he told me he dealt with those bad white men. Said he got 'em real bad."

Running her fingers through her hair and knocking more ebony combs out, her red hair released and stood on end. Tesh-Lucianne's eyes darted about like a cornered animal's. Her face was haggard and she tortured her bottom lip with her teeth. "I so remember this, though I hate to remember. You know what I mean?

"Daddy A.B. stormed back into the house that day and I ran up to him, lifting my arms up to be hugged and carried like always. Instead, he all but backhanded me and threw me aside. 'Get me a stiff one,' he growled as he stomped back toward the kitchen. Glancing back over his shoulder, he saw me moving slowly, hugging the wall. 'Get on with it!' he hollered at me. Young as I was, I knew to pour him a water glass of bourbon. Then I raced after him."

Tesh-Lucianne's wide eyes blinked back tears as she continued. "When I got to the kitchen, Daddy A.B. was whalin' tar out of your mama. Evangeline commenced to screaming, trying with all her might to hold him off her. But he was a big man, and strong."

Mary held her breath as Tesh-Lucianne paused for a long time. Finally, she said, "I hate to tell it, but I didn't go to her rescue. I wanted to. But I was just so little. My eyes were glued on the two of them whilst I slid down 'side the doorjamb. I couldn't believe what I saw. Daddy A.B. threw her on the floor by the long counter where she'd been shuckin' corn for supper. He hiked up her dress. Then he jerked her up so she was on her hands and knees and it looked to me like he was slamming himself up against her from behind. He had one hand on her head, pushing her head into the floor. He was grunting and swearing and sweating and bucking like a wild horse. Evangeline, sweet soul that she was, just bit her lips together and turned her face to look at me. There was nothing in her eyes. Daddy A.B. beat her with his manhood for I don't know how long. Then he fell over, panting to get his breath. When he got up he was still as angry as before. He spit on her and told her to get up and get her black ass back to work."

Mary's face was inscrutable, but her heart beat a tolling in her chest, and her soul sizzled as she tried to make sense of what she was hearing.

"Evangeline never came near the house again. Not a year after what I saw Daddy A.B. do, word came a baby girl was born to Tug and Evangeline. That infant was the talk. Said she was the color of unstained teak and had incredible hair. They said it was fine as down, tawny-colored like the underhairs of a swan. That was the good news. The bad news was that Evangeline took sick at the baby's birth and died two days later. But Tug and Evangeline had time to name the child. They called her Mary. After the mother of Jesus."

A whole long moment passed before Mary's brain comprehended the fulsomeness of what Tesh-Lucianne had just revealed. Dumbfounded, she looked around. "You're referring to me?"

"Who else?" Tesh-Lucianne stirred her drink distractedly. Her speech was still mush. "Daddy A.B.'s mostly bald now and what hair he's got is gray, so you couldn't much tell. Maybe you've forgotten, but when he was younger, people always commented on his long mane that was the color of rusty cornsilk."

"So how ... how did I happen to come here to live? I mean, wasn't I ... I a bride present?" Mary stammered.

"I was ashamed, never wanted anybody to know what happened. But night after sleepless night after I was grown, my conscience beat hell out of me until I brought you here to the mansion to bring you up. I just let you think Daddy A.B. gave you to me as a wedding present. But I was hoping to make amends somehow. I knew Daddy A.B. never would."

Had this woman gone daft, Mary wondered. Did she really know what she was confessing? She fingered a curl of her hair pensively. "Why do you want me to know this? Why now?"

"I just wanted to make things as right as I could. Especially after what happened to you. When the man smashed your knee, Daddy A.B. said if you died, so much the better. If you lived, he was going to sell you so he wouldn't have to know about you anymore. I believe his conscience was beating him too. But I pleaded with him to give you to me as a wedding present, let me bring you here."

Tesh-Lucianne threw back the final two fingers of whiskey and sat staring into familiar landscapes of the room. "I'm sick. Don't ask me how I know. I just know. The doctor's got me het up on laudanum so I can try to deal with the world. But I'm slipping. I'm goin' to get worse."

"Tesh-Lucianne ..."

She held up a halting hand. "I know what I'm talking about, Mary. Maybe, before I lose my mind, I wanted you to know where you came from. I don't know where that might lead you, but you have something." Her cheeks were tearstained as she turned a pitiful look at Mary. "Selfishly, maybe I wanted my sister by my side, hoping she wanted me too."

Mary stared, stupefied, at Tesh-Lucianne. Then she glared at the drunken woman on the chaise as the information gathered purchase on her insides. She set her unfinished drink on the side table.

Silence grew huge in the room like a manifest entity.

Tesh-Lucianne wormed herself off the chaise and slid to her knees. She tried twice to speak before she actually could. "I can't hardly stand up. Help me, sister, please?"

Mary finally rose and maneuvered Tesh-Lucianne to her feet. Tesh-Lucianne then grabbed Mary's hands and put them on either side of her waist. She laughed and leaned into her as she began to hum a waltz. She swayed a little.

"What? What are you doing?"

"Shh-hh," Tesh-Lucianne pouted. "I know I've upset you. But when we can't do nothin' else, think nothin' else, we can dance. That's what we're doing. We're dancin'."

Mary tried to pull away, but Tesh-Lucianne held fast. "No!" she screamed. "I'm a sorry excuse for a sister, God knows. But ...," her voice trailed off and she began to hum again as she grasped Mary tighter.

Bewildered, Mary let herself be staggered in a small circle. Her head was reeling with the news, and at the same time, without her walking stick for balance, keeping the two of them upright was a challenge.

Suddenly, Tesh-Lucianne pushed away and blurted, "Leave me alone! Just leave me alone!"

Mary stepped back. She watched Tesh-Lucianne crumple to the floor, her face contorting as if in a conniption.

Tesh-Lucianne flung her hands in the air before her face. "No! I'm not Ardella-Plusse! You can't do this to me! My husband'll fix you! He'll fix you good! Don't do that to me! I'm white!" she wailed as she crawled on her knees to the salon doors. She clawed at the handles and tried to pull them open. When she couldn't, she pounded with her fists, screaming, "Let me out!"

Mary dashed to her side, but Tesh-Lucianne turned and snarled, teeth bared. "Don't touch me. I'll kill you dead." Mary had to half-drag Tesh-Lucianne up the stairs to her bedroom. Almost like carrying dead weight, she hauled the woman to her four-poster and dutifully helped get her into a nightgown, although she felt that at any minute her own head was going to explode. Mary finally got Tesh-Lucianne settled in her bed, but only after giving her a big dose of laudanum.

Back in her own chambers, Mary slammed the door and allowed full vent to her emotions. Tesh-Lucianne's words echoed in her head. What was it she had said? Mary remembered she'd had to get two sheets to the wind to tell her that Tug is not her father, that Daddy A.B. is. Daddy A.B., the man who has never been shy to let her know he thinks her a no-count no matter what she does. That Tesh-Lucianne is her sister. And she had known all along. Yet another deception!

She turned and caught a glimpse of herself in one of the tall mirrors and stopped. Light shimmered off the wavy hair that hung to her shoulders. Staring intently, she thought she could see Daddy A.B. in some of her features, and she hated what she saw. Her anger boiled up, and she snatched the kufi off her head and whirled around. She wanted to destroy it. Up to now she had felt so regal in that headdress. Bunching it, she threw it on the floor.

She cried bitterly as the pain of disappointment and disconsolation rose up over her in wave after wave, until finally she was spent. She crumpled to the floor, curled up in a ball until darkness and sleep kindly overtook her.

CHAPTER 35

When Mary woke later that night, she could hardly breathe. She loosened the robe around her waist. A metallic taste was on her tongue. Her face burned and she knew no amount of cool water would stem the heat. Settle down, she told herself. Just settle down. She reached for her pincushion to set it aright on the table and inadvertently pricked her finger. Blood oozed out. No way could she tackle the muddle of consideration and concern that Tesh-Lucianne's disclosure brought up right now. It was too much. Rather, she let her mind drift off to safer thoughts. She remembered the idea that had been brewing since she'd seen the plans for the CSS *Virginia* in Simeon's office. Not knowing why, she wondered what was so important about them that they kept coming to mind. And especially, why now?

She had tried not to think much about the war. She'd gone along with the prevailing attitude that "we" wanted the South to win. As she thought about it now, she wondered if that was actually what she wanted. If the South did win, would there be more dependable, yet inescapable, chains upon the Negro forever?

In all the talk she'd heard among whites in Norfolk, not one indicated anything good for colored people if the South was victorious. She again heard Anders's words in her head: *The Virginia's not invincible. It can be crippled at the waterline.*

The plans kept haunting her. She kept thinking she had to do something with those plans—if she could get her hands on them. But what? Could she hand them off to somebody who could be trusted to secret them to the North, but who would not chafe under the weight of that mantle? Maybe one of The Travelers? They were helping slaves escape to the North. They knew the routes and the people who could help them along the way. But who? Bear? He had a family and a responsibility to everyone at Stonehaven. No, she couldn't ask him.

She couldn't stand it if something happened to him.

Who else? Anders? He too would do it if she asked, but he had his hands full with the cantankerous ironclad's engine. Furthermore, suspicions would arise if he were absent for more than a day. Devereaux? He was still rankled enough at Simeon that anger would tempt him to do it. But emotions might not sustain him.

Her mind had calmed, but with these thoughts she was getting a headache. Focus, she told herself. First things first. How to get the plans? If she stole them, that would cause an uproar. Copy them! That might be safer in the long run. Nothing would be missing so there'd be no reason to suspect anything. Yes, that's what she could do. She'd copy them.

But how? As she continued to straighten up the salon, she realized her hands were on one of the partially completed patterns for Lydeah Bondourant. Of course! She could use the tracing paper on which she made her patterns. She could cut the big sheets of tracing paper down to small pieces, small enough to hide and carry on her person easily. Often, when slaves were caught smuggling papers of some sort, what gave them away were the bulging secret pouches in hems, bosoms, and sleeves. What could she do instead? She could make a secret section in a bracelet or in the pleats around her kufi. Maybe now her hats could be put to good use. That might work.

Even though Simeon's home office was a short leg away from the salon, she couldn't afford to let anyone in the household notice anything different about her comings and goings if she decided to actually do this. She took a deep breath, squared her body, and pushed back her hair. How could she make this work?

As she thought about it, usually Roguey was the first to rise, starting her baking before dawn and shuttling between the summer kitchen and the house. Simeon and Tesh-Lucianne didn't filter around until about eight for breakfast. Mary couldn't afford for Roguey to suspect what she might be up to. There was no way she could take the loyal cook into her confidence, for fear of jeopardy to her. Just knowledge of Mary's potential betrayal would be cause for serious repercussions. That meant if she were about her business around three, before Roguey rose, she stood a good chance of accomplishing a lot. Then, if Simeon had visitors during the day, as he often did now, maybe she could slip back inside to do more. But she wouldn't count on that. Then, she'd have to decide how and where to hide the pieces. Details. Details.

What if Simeon moved back to his office at the chandlery? The fashion show was over and his cold was all but gone. Lumley was setting Simeon's schedule these days, so his comings and goings could not be measured or planned. Tesh-Lucianne had asked him to stay around more. Mary wondered if Simeon would be able to handle her growing neediness along with his career demands. Excusing himself to the chandlery might be just the ticket for a little breathing room. Yet Mary considered, even if he did, that change wouldn't have to affect her plan much. She certainly could resume taking Simeon's lunch to him there.

Of real concern were the new ruffians patrolling the streets, as well as Gates and his posse. She'd have to make sure there was not a hint of suspicion about her. If Gates could find something amiss, he would eagerly make sure she hung from the nearest sturdy tree.

Her back snapped straight up when the next thought hit her. If she could do all of this, why couldn't she be the one to see the plans to Washington? No, no, no, she thought, pushing the notion away.

Why not? her mind asked again. Despite her infirmity, she'd been able to do just about anything she'd ever put her mind to. The Travelers could help with directions and contacts along the way. Others less seasoned than herself had done it with their help. But no—if anyone knew what she was considering, they'd have more trouble than the law allowed.

She remembered that Anders had dropped a package by for her—some of his things to hold onto for him as he was moved from camp to camp. They included his favorite blue shirt she'd made him, a pocket brass compass, and several maps. She began to study the maps and plan out a route for herself.

To get to Washington, Mary would have to cross major rivers. She would have to avoid maintained roads, instead weave through woods and fields well out of sight of the main waterways. Each of the rivers was a major trade route with a network of small towns, villages, enclaves, and farms. It looked from the maps that she would first have to navigate marshes and bogs near the coast before hitting higher ground. But that was all guesswork due to her infrequent travels outside of Tidewater, Virginia.

There was so much at stake, so much she would lose. She managed a sour harrumph at that thought. What did she really have to lose? And if she actually reached Washington, no way could she return. She couldn't come shambling back expecting the Louvestres to let bygones be bygones. Why, she couldn't even count on Northerners being grateful for what she planned to do. Would she be a fugitive to both sides?

Well, whatever the consequences, she thought, she knew now what had to be done. What was it about human nature, she wondered, that didn't provide motivation to act until things became very personal? She felt almost ashamed that she had not been previously inspired by more altruistic reasons, like the betterment of her own people. But facing the situation honestly, she realized what had motivated her in the past was personal achievement. Until now the urgency in her life had been about reaching a place where she could be her own person, with a greater sense of security in the world. For most of her life she lived a deception.

※

Mary loved this place of her birth and these people. Of a spring morning there was no more beautiful sight than ribbons of dawn playing over the majestic horizon of interlacing trees, the cockscombs of rich tobacco fields, the rolling greens and blazing color of a multitude of shrubs and flowers, grasses dancing in the fragrant wind, and the azure blue waters of the Chesapeake teeming with life. Even a winter Virginia landscape, where light snow powdered fields and icicles cloistered together along rooftops and barns, was a delight of grandeur for old and young.

Her thoughts went to Tesh-Lucianne and Simeon. She was angry at them now, and disappointed. But, admittedly, most of her life, she had loved them. They were her family. Now, in the face of inexorable circumstances, she realized her privileged life with them only took her so far. Hers was a glass ceiling, topped by the color of her skin. Somewhere in the South, she reflected, was another talented youngster with dark skin who also envisioned achievement and success. The mighty operative word was *chance*. How might she help that child have a better chance? How might she help provide more opportunities for them, if they but only had a chance? Future plus chance for all people equaled more than anyone could know.

Mary saw clearly now. Little would change if the South prevailed, given present attitudes. More than likely, life would end up far worse for blacks. No way would she ever betray the South, even in thought. But President Lincoln had it right. No man should live under shackle to another. To raise up the South to greater heights, her cherished land had to be brought to a different perspective.

CHAPTER 36

By three in the morning, Mary was ready. The night had passed swiftly. When the grandfather clock gonged three times, she bolted upright. She had been deeply engrossed in every detail regarding her next move, down to adhering a soft velvet cap to the end of her walking stick so as not to be heard slipping down the hall into Simeon's office on a trial run.

She already had plotted how to quickly sketch portions of the renderings, put them aside, and stitch them back together later. A system of code had revealed itself to her during the night. Simple. But success would depend on quickness. Stealth.

The double doors to her salon did not make a sound as she opened them just far enough to slip through. She was down the hall quickly and almost to Simeon's door when something stopped her. Floorboards squeaked from a near place in the house. Who could be moving around this time of morning? She flattened herself in the shadows, hardly breathing. Another squeak echoed down the hall, advancing from the staircase. When she thought she could risk it, she peered into the gloom. There Tesh-Lucianne appeared in her white nightgown, tiptoeing forward like a wraith. Mary sighed deeply, frustrated, and retreated silently.

Roguey sat on the back porch with a tin pail filled with fresh pea pods settled between her legs. The breeze was warm off the water and smelled sweet and clean with the new day. When Mary stepped out onto the plank boards, Roguey glanced up at her and continued shucking peas. "You needin' mo' coffee?" she asked.

Mary sank into the reed-back chair opposite her and looked out onto the palette of horizon. "No." She lifted her chin and breathed deeply. "It's beautiful out here, isn't it?"

"It's all right." Roguey shrugged. "If you wasn't here, I'd be other places."

"Like where?"

"Tennessee, where I got a sister."

"Roguey, in all these years you never told me you had a sister."

"Wasn't no need. Didn't think I'd ever see her again. Then Jewel Baxter come sutlerin' around. I knew him back in Mississippi. Had him a little store, but he lost everything and started his travelin' around business. Now, he sell to the Army, Navy, anybody. He come 'round here recently. Heard the Louvestres bought me. Took a while for that word to get aroun', I guess. Like him."

"Yeah?"

"He git all over. He say he seen my sister, Pensy-Lane. She runned a long time ago. Made it to Tennessee where she be with some Cherokees. I'm goin' there someday. You'll see."

Mary's eyes were big as saucers. "You're going to ..."

Roguey glanced around to make sure they were alone. "You bet. I ain't sho' when, but I'm goin'. Baxter say he'll take me. He ain't no-count, but he got his price. Say he'll take me if my money's right."

"Is it? Is it right, I mean?"

"By-and-by will be," Roguey said. She glanced up at Tesh-Lucianne's bedroom window. "You tend to yo' business, I'll let you know 'bout mine when I'm ready. I ain't stayin' here. All this craziness. If they'll take yo' business out from under you, all you done done for them, ain't nothin' sacred." The cook scowled. "You get yo'self straight. Roguey gon' be all right."

Mary sat open-mouthed for a moment. She thought, what else could happen around here?

Roguey handed her a pan. "Make yo'self useful."

As Mary began to shuck peas, she smiled, remembering how she and Roguey became friends many years ago. It had been hard going between them at first. Roguey did not trust her. But Mary liked the hard-surfaced woman and persevered until finally they were friends.

"Coolie all right?"

"She's finding her way," Mary said.

Roguey's fingers were quick and expert and before long peas made a large mound in her pot. "Bread comin' out the oven in a minute," Roguey said. "Made fresh butter too."

"Mean old woman. You try to feed me like I was a stevedore."

"You too skinny anyway."

Silence breathed between them for a while.

"Ain't right what Simeon done, taking yo' business."

Mary said nothing.

"You mad?" Roguey asked.

"What I am is beyond any feeling I've ever had."

Roguey looked up into the distance. "What's that over yonder?"

Mary shaded her eyes. She saw a plume of dust rising. "A rider. He's coming fast."

Soon, Theron pulled up at the porch and jumped down from his horse.

"Miss Mary. Roguey," he said breathlessly. "Y'all seen Coolie?"

Mary and Roguey exchanged concerned glances.

"No," Mary said.

"We got trouble."

Theron told what he knew. The night before, when everyone was gone, he was cleaning up the bar. Then something hit him on the head. All he could remember was the floor rising up to meet him. Coolie was bathing his face with water as he came to. She was beside herself, talking crazy. The blue cross over the bar was gone. Coolie was sure it was the work of Elam Gates.

"No!" Roguey exclaimed.

Theron nodded. "I wasn't all there, staggering around trying to get my bearings. Next thing, I looked out the window and saw Coolie packing rocks into the pockets of her dress. She ran inside, had this funny look in her eyes, and grabbed the bat from behind the bar. She said, 'That cross is mine. I'm gon' get it.' Then she was running out the door. I hollered, 'Coolie, that man could kill you.' She said, 'Not if I kill him first.'"

Mary grabbed her stick and was on her feet. "Where was she headed? Did she say?"

Theron shook his head. "I was hoping reason took over and she came here."

Mary turned to Roguey and spoke in measured tones. "I'm going to change my clothes. Please tell Devereaux to saddle me a horse."

"But—" Roguey said.

Mary's look stopped her cold. "Do it."

"If you're going to look for her," Theron said, "I'll go with you."

Mary was at the door. She turned back. "You get to Bear. Tell him what you told me. Tell him to drop everything and get The Travelers together. We've got to find Coolie. There's no time to lose. Do you understand?"

Theron was on his horse, wheeling away before she finished.

Tesh-Lucianne was upstairs in her bedroom, delighting in her new dress to wear at the next fundraiser for Simeon. She held it in front of her in the mirror and sang a childish song. "See sigh, Mary won, but I'm going to dance 'til the day is done." She dabbed a hanky across the sweat beads on her forehead. She was still feeling the effects of last night's liquor binge. Sounds of hoof beats brought her to the window. Was that Mary riding out like that? She hadn't seen her on a horse for years. Oh well. No matter. Mary hadn't been herself since the party. Completely forgetting her personal disclosures of the previous night, she conjectured that Mary was probably sulking over Simeon's decision to bring in Monsieur Delaclaire. But she'd see in time. This was the best thing. For Mary. For them all.

Mary'd been so good at what she did over the years that The House of M had simply outgrown her, as Simeon had said. It was big business now. After all, what did Mary know about the ins and outs of a business this size? Her talents lay in designing, and with Delaclaire taking over, she could have the freedom to do what she did best—design. All she needed was time. Change was hard for some people. Mary would come around and see that she and Simeon were only doing what they'd always done—protect her. And she'd see how important this business was to Simeon's career.

Tesh-Lucianne shrugged. Negroes were strange people sometimes. For all the time Mary had been a part of their household, she was seeing that people were who they were, didn't matter whether they lived on slave row or in a mansion or dressed in rags or fine clothes, they were who they were. She'd have to remember to mention this to Simeon later. For now, she'd turn to what was truly important—her morning toilette. Mary had made a concoction of soapwort and lemon to make her hair soft and shiny. Where had she put that bottle?

———•—•———

Mary did not see Coolie anywhere.

The wind off the river roiled dust in the road and fluttered the hats and dress hems of busy town folk. Characters of all sorts promenaded the streets. Seagulls cawed in a cool breeze fragrant with cedar and pine. Every day, more and more people adopted Norfolk as their home. From backwoods and plantations they came, high excitement in the air. War was on and many were eager, lining up single file, to sign up.

Mary trotted her horse into the settlement, covered with dust from her journey, the horse lathered and blowing. She reined up and swung down. She peered into store windows and down streets and alleys looking for Coolie. No sign of her.

Mary caught sight of a band of street urchins plying their trade as pickpockets. Had her eyes not been on them she would have missed it, the boy was so quick. A gentleman had bent down to help an old woman sit on a bench. The white boy didn't even bump into him, he was so smooth. He had the man's wallet in a flash and handed it off to his colored friend, who ran down the walkway in Mary's direction. When he reached her side, she stuck out her walking stick. The boy tripped and fell, sprawling to the sidewalk.

Mary said to the gentleman, "You might want to check the boy's pockets for your wallet."

He felt his side pocket and looked startled at Mary, then took off after the thief, hollering, "Nigger, if I get my hands on you!"

As Mary continued her search for Coolie, she heard the boy yelp behind her.

Yelling in protest, the boy's motley crew of pickpocket friends dashed back to help him get away from the man, who was practically jerking the boy's arm out of its socket trying to haul him down to the sheriff's office. The disturbance drew Gates out of The Pig Trough Bar.

Coolie, rounding the corner, saw Gates and dug into her pocket for a stone. Mary spied her and intercepted her, pulling her into the alley out of eyesight of Gates. Coolie yanked away, running after Gates who was crossing the busy street after the boys.

"I want my cross, Gates," Coolie screamed.

"Cross? What cross?" He had no idea what she was talking about. Too bad he didn't have time to find out. He liked that nigger gal's spunk. She was a hoot who got his juices going. And when she was angry, something about her flushed to a fullness that made a catch in his throat. When she was mad, she was beautiful, a glory true. He glanced back at her, but did not lose sight of the boys who had darted down the street. Duty called.

Coolie started to chuck a stone at him when Mary used her walking stick to catch her hand and divert the aim before Gates could notice as he continued after the boys. She calmed Coolie down by stroking her hair, and together they rode to the Louvestre home. Coolie, sitting behind Mary, wrapped her arms tightly around Mary's waist and rested her head on Mary's back. More than once, she resisted the urge to kiss Mary's neck.

Coolie flared again once they entered the kitchen, which, Mary thought, would be the safest place to let her friend vent her rage. Pacing the kitchen floor, Coolie rambled angrily about Gates. How dare he steal the cross from her place? She knew he did it. Who else could it have been?

Mary worried that things had escalated to the point that it was only a matter of time before Gates made short work of Coolie. He'd likely trump up some charge to take her to jail, where none of her friends could get to her, and then, who knew? Coolie was behaving without any reason at all. Foolhardy, she seemed bent on heating things up, to make something happen.

Roguey whispered to Mary that Coolie was on a mission to do herself in.

Mary jerked. "Meaning what?"

"Like she wants Gates to kill her. Somethin' she can't do herself."

Mary knew Roguey might be right. She knew Coolie had still not gotten over the slight from Gie at the fashion show, though she wouldn't admit it.

"Onliest thing keepin' her foot on this side of the grave is you," Roguey said. "If she didn't have you, well, no tellin'."

Mary's stomach curdled. Before she could reply there came a soft knock on the kitchen door.

"That be Bear," Roguey said. "Devereaux found him and told him to come. I thought you might want 'im to take Coolie to Stonehaven."

"If she'll go," Mary said.

"And stay," Roguey added.

CHAPTER 37

Fall was setting in. Russet and gold leaves now made a thick carpet on the ground, crunching and crackling underfoot. People rubbed their hands together for warmth and pulled wraps and coats snuggly around them. Mary and Anders stood close together, arm in arm, in a cove hidden from view near a stand of giant willow trees near the riverbank. Mary watched the blue-green water, the light capping the gentle rises in bursts of bubbles and foam. She wished her insides mirrored its tranquil beauty.

"I worry about what you're telling me, Anders. As lumbering and forbidding as the *Virginia* is, I still don't hear that the ship's all that seaworthy," Mary said. "I especially don't like the idea that you're going to be on it for the next trial."

"Her, not it," Anders corrected. "Ships are called 'her.' Yes, the engine is temperamental. Doesn't take very much to upset her."

"Meaning?" She turned and looked into his face, which was uncharacteristically somber.

"When everything is up and running and we get out of dock, it's not long before the engine coughs, blows steam in places she shouldn't, and gets all of us in the engine room a little nervous."

"You've informed the captain?"

"No. My boss has been there every day and seen the problems himself. But he's reluctant to complain more to the higher-ups."

"Why?"

"Because he's been given his orders to comply. He's been told if he can't, they'll replace him with someone who can. If he's let go, we all go."

The wind lifted Mary's hair into a glowing nimbus around her.

Anders eyed her appreciatively. "May I?" he said, pulling her cloak back a bit.

"It's cold out here," she protested.

"I knew you were wearing something lovely. I just want to look."

Over her lithe figure was a silk and wool dress the color of heather, cut V-neck and slightly off the shoulder. What Anders especially enjoyed was the dress's softness as it defined her figure underneath. He put his arms around her and hugged her from behind. "You're too beautiful for me to be worrying you."

"This situation has to be worrying you too," Mary said as she drew her wrap closed.

Anders lowered his hands and dug them into his pants pockets. "The men have been talking about safety precautions. Ways to protect ourselves. I mean, we're literally in the bowels of the beast."

"So, if it—I mean, she—blows, can you get out okay?" Her brow furrowed.

"Not easily. That's part of our worry. If she blows and we can't fix her with sweet coaxing, a couple of hammer blows and a kick, we do the next best thing. We scramble up to the next level and lock the hatch beneath us. Needless to say, that's not something the authorities would want to hear."

"You'd be among the last to get out, right?" Mary began to pace.

"There are not many of us down in the hole. We'd have to move fast." Anders tried to make his voice reassuring.

Anders put his arms around her shoulders, pulling her face into the crook of his neck. "Do you pray?"

"What?"

"I'm kidding," he said, fingering her hair near her kufi. "What concerns me more is that, if all goes well, my job is done and I'll still be gone. They'll send me home on the next tidewater."

Mary stood still. "Home for you seems so far away."

"It is."

"You know, for all our being favored by our masters and deemed so special in our talents, we're no better off than Devereaux and his Ann-Marie."

"Devereaux?" Anders questioned. "What do you mean?"

She related the story of Devereaux and his beloved Ann-Marie. She ended by telling him what Simeon had told Devereaux, and how devastated he was.

"My God! That's awful!" Anders said.

"You and I have not been forbidden to see each other again, but we may as well have been."

Anders picked up a few pebbles and began skipping them over the chop. "We do have one option." He turned and took her shoulders in his hands, looking intently into her eyes. "We could run." He watched her eyebrows rise. "I mean it. As Travelers, we've helped others do it. Why couldn't we?"

"I don't know."

"We could do it," he said with some urgency. "We'd get The Travelers to help us. I have some money saved. I could get horses from someone who'd keep quiet about it. Look, far's I'm concerned, we pick a date and go."

Mary stared at the dancing light in his eyes.

"We could do it," he restated firmly. "Bear would help us on our way."

"You've thought this through," Mary said.

"Actually, no. But I don't see a good reason why not." He pulled her to him and kissed her gently, then harder, holding her close. "We could do it," he whispered into her ear. "Will you study on it? Consider it? You've got a lot to lose."

"And you don't?"

Mary walked a few steps and stared out at the busy waterway. She felt torn not to be able to tell Anders about her plans, but she couldn't. She did not want to put him in danger by having that knowledge. She also didn't want to further upset him with fretting that she might not want to be with him. She had to keep her secret to protect him. "Hey," Anders said, putting his arms around her and snuggling. "You went off somewhere and didn't take me with you. No fair."

Mary looked into his bright smiling face and chastised herself. She was being a coward with him. Just a little more time was all she wanted. A little more. Sometimes love can be so hard. She drew her thoughts back. "You could leave Guillaume? You said he's like a father to you."

"True," Anders said. "I couldn't have been more than a baby when he rescued me from the flames that burned down my parents' cabin. To this day, I don't know why my father and mother died. Guillaume won't give me much detail. But he and my father were friends, and from the day he saved me, he brought me into his house and raised me like I was his own."

"How did the fire start?"

"Nobody seems to know for sure. All I know is it was in the wee hours of the morning."

"Well, how did it happen that Guillaume was there to rescue you?"

"I don't know. Over the years I've tried not to think about my parents since the only father I've had has been Guillaume. When I got older and experienced with fixing things, he let me hire out. I began asking around if anyone knew my folks. An old fisherman told me once that people talked about that fire, said something was suspicious about how it happened. He told me that people repeated over and over again that the one thing Guillaume wanted in this world was a child, especially a son. And that's what he got."

"But you don't look white," Mary chuckled.

"That wouldn't bother Guillaume. Just let somebody call me a nigger and you'd have that crazy Frenchman doing jumping jacks on them."

"I've heard of Negroes being raised by Europeans who didn't care about color, but I never knew if that was really true."

"Take it from me," Anders said. "It's true. I didn't grow up in the luxury you did, but I never wanted for anything. The best he had, I got."

"What do you think will happen when you go back?"

"Guillaume has had it in his head that he wants to start a father and son company for us—you know, building and fixing just about anything with moving parts." He smiled at the thought. "Wants to call it 'Guillaume and Anders, A Deux.'"

"Be sure to get that in writing," Mary said, then clapped her hand over her mouth. "Forget that. I was just being bad."

She and Anders laughed.

Mary was somewhat relieved to hear that Anders had plans for his life after Norfolk, but asked anyway, "And you could just leave him?"

"I'd turn on a Confederate note. Especially for you. I've had a sense of security and he trained me well in what I do, but I also know that my world is flimsy. I'm a free black but I still live by white men's caprice. I have no inheritance to speak of to build my own life upon. In this strange time and place of war, who knows what can happen? If you get right down to it, I'm his son so long as he wants to feel that way. I'm not listed as family on the front page of his Bible. I'm on his ledger book as part of what he owns. He could turn around in a moment and sell me to the fields and what could I do about it?"

"You didn't just find this out," Mary said.

"No. But now, what with some Union soldiers actually harboring slaves, helping them get to safety up North where they can build a better life, I believe it's time to do something different. We're not going to fare any better here. Maybe worse, the way some whites are getting all het up, scared we're going to turn on them with knives in their sleep. If they decided to shoot one of us or all of us—Gates in the forefront—well ..." He opened his hands.

"If nothing else, Pluck's death brought that home," Mary said.

"If you thought Crawthers or anyone else around here lost any sleep over the murder of that child, you've got another think coming. I lay on my bunk at night, and the ghosts of everything we're talking about haunt my sleep." He looked deeply into her eyes. "Anyway, you do want to be with me, don't you? Tell me you do."

Mary returned his gaze and smiled. Eventually she said, "Of course I do."

"So?"

"I still need some time," Mary hedged. Conflicted, she couldn't put everything together just then.

"I've already left some things with you, but officers are now talking about moving the hire-ons to an even more distant camp. Would you mind if I gave you another package? It has a letter I'd like you to mail to Guillaume if something happens to me. It'll also contain a few more of my personal items and more maps I've recently collected."

"Yes. But surely nothing will happen."

"Anything goes wrong, give my clothes to some worthy soldier."

"Stop it!" Mary said.

"Bless God, you really do care about me," Anders said, looking at her with delight. He pulled her tight to him. "I don't have a life without you." He kissed her. "Not anymore." He kissed her deeply.

Did she really believe that? she silently questioned. If she continued with her plans, would it ever be possible for her to return to the South again? She couldn't let herself think about that now. She just wanted to hold Anders and have him hold her.

CHAPTER 38

Mary worried that Tesh-Lucianne was watching her carefully. She was watching everyone carefully.

Tesh-Lucianne was growing more erratic each day, her mood swings becoming more frequent. She couldn't sleep, was short-tempered, less and less her lighthearted self. Nightmares tormented her. Nearly everyone in the house heard her screams. She had begun to move about the house around the clock. On cat feet, she slipped in and out of rooms, hiding behind curtains and doors. Once, Mary had heard a soft sound in her salon and found Tesh-Lucianne on her hands and knees under a worktable. Mary gentled her out and wiped drool from her mouth. She was like a child as Mary talked her up the stairs and back to her room. But when Mary was about to leave, Tesh-Lucianne screamed, "Don't leave me! They'll get me!" Mary didn't want to, but went to the side table for more laudanum.

All of this had been making Mary more anxious. Tesh-Lucianne was following her around like a puppy. Simeon asked her to change plans about reporting to the warehouse each day so she could attend to his wife. Simeon heaved a sigh of relief when she said, "You know I'll always look after Tesh-Lucianne." Mary did not let on that this greatly aided her own plans.

Days had passed since the aborted dry run to copy the ship's renderings. Mary would rise in the preternatural darkness before dawn, and urged silent footsteps across the floorboards of the hallway into the corridor that would lead her to Simeon's study. The first day, just as she got near the door her instincts made her pause. She turned to see, well back in the shadows, Tesh-Lucianne's eyes staring at her.

"Tesh-Lucianne," Mary said, "what are you doing out of bed so early?"

The woman didn't answer, her eyes wild, darting looks around.

"Come on," Mary said soothingly, "let's get you upstairs where you can rest."

The second morning this happened, Tesh-Lucianne clasped Mary's housecoat saying, "Something's come into this house. Something ugly, horrible, not safe." Despite Mary's reassurances, Tesh-Lucianne cried, "It's trying to destroy us. Haven't you seen it?"

"There's nothing here, Tesh-Lucianne, to harm you or any of us," Mary had coaxed.

Tesh-Lucianne jerked away. "Then you don't know. You really don't know?" And she wept bitter tears.

On the third morning, light rain pattered the roof and fuzzied the outlines of trees and garden. Through open windows, Mary's nose caught the faint smell of smoke and creosote from fire barrels the railroad workers used to warm themselves. From behind her came the faint sounds of the house: the creaking of boards settling into the wet weather; soft staccato thumps of a drapery tie hitting a window ledge; droplets of water pecking at the wood planks of the verandah.

Mary was aware that Simeon planned to return completely to the chandlery in a few days. She had to make a move now. For added insurance, last night she had given Tesh-Lucianne an herb tea to settle her down. She hoped that, together with the laudanum, it should keep her out for several more hours.

Mary reached the doorknob to Simeon's study, and her heart nearly stopped when the clock inside chimed three times. She panted and made herself slow her breathing. She peered down the hall again into the familiar subdued lights and shadows as her hand quickly turned the knob. The door opened with a small squeak. The room was dark, as she knew it would be. The desk clock ticked steadily. She listened intently for other sounds. Hearing nothing, she glanced over her shoulder and edged into the room.

With each step, the empty pouch slung over her shoulder slapped softly against her hip. Inching toward the desk and the roll of large papers, Mary slipped her hand into the pouch and withdrew a pencil and a small square of tracing paper. Her hand shook a little and she ordered herself to calm. She placed the items on the desk and pushed open the roll of ship's renderings. They made a crinkling sound as they unfurled. She slowed, listened.

She took a moment to rein in her apprehensions, even out her breathing, and let her eyes grow accustomed to the dimness. She chastised herself for not remembering that it would be too dark at this time of morning to make out the drawings well, much less copy them. But she had little time for such recriminations. She squinted in her efforts. She had to draw fast and get out.

Vague objects in the room began to resolve themselves into features as she had memorized them—the chairs, tables, lamps, doodads. She could not afford to be clumsy and knock anything over. She couldn't risk lighting a lamp. No matter, she had passed the open office several times over the past days and made herself commit to memory everything in its place. She had finished her first drawing when her walking stick, which she'd perched against the desk, slipped and fell to the floor with a slap. Fear seared up her spine. She didn't move a muscle. A breeze from the window stirred the pages and cooled the beads of sweat on her forehead.

In a while she leaned forward again, pressing tissue paper over portions of the renderings and tracing as swiftly as she could press her fingers into action. Five pieces of tracing paper—five pieces of the puzzle she would put back together in the safety of her room. She slid them inside the bodice of her dress, the pencil into its slot in her pouch. She fingered the papers. Three more to trace. But not now. Now she had to get away.

She leaned down and gripped her walking stick. Making her feet splay again, she scooted herself in the direction of the door. She stopped abruptly. She could smell something. What was that odor? Her instincts were firing off blasts to her brain, yet her senses could not detect anything out of order. She eased forward, first her stick, then slid one foot and then the other across the smooth floorboards. But something still wasn't right. She knew it. But what? She stopped again.

She heard, rather than saw, something curled in the tiny space between the far table and side chair. It was moving toward her, an odor swelling like a cloud of stench all around her. She was faster, aiming her body sideways, flattening against the wall. The thing slammed against the desk with amazing force.

Mary's bowels just about opened up right then and there. She clasped a hand over her mouth to keep from screaming, and yanked open the door just far enough to escape and shut it behind her. Her heart pounded in her chest and ears. Bile boiled up into her throat as she tried to breathe. Her whole body shook like she was in the throes of a raging fever. The one thing she had not counted on had flown into her face, nearly derailing her in every way. Somehow, an enormous raccoon had climbed through the office window and was hiding in the shadows.

She glanced up and down the hallway and forced herself to get to the salon before she had any more company.

CHAPTER 39

Mary sat on a stool in front of her drawing tripod. Just beneath the dress sketches she was working on for Lydeah Bondourant, Mary hid a couple of the maps from Anders's pack. She had been studying them closely, trying to plot a walking path from Norfolk to Washington that would keep her far from main thoroughfares and towns.

Gates had implemented a program of sealing off the waterways to Negroes, making it tough to even get a dingy across the Elizabeth and James rivers. He also kept the piers feeding into the Chesapeake Bay under guard. Anyone suspected of sailing coloreds off would first have to submit to a search of themselves and their vessel, then pay a fine if they were lucky, only to later discover major damage to their water craft if they weren't lucky. The railroad was also off limits. Gates allowed the one car that was used to haul colored workers to their sites to be employed by the military to haul supplies. A Negro on horseback could also find himself in trouble with the pattyrollers who answered to Gates. A slave with written permission by a white person could find his pass ripped up and tossed into a road bank, summarily followed by himself. These men marshaled out an arbitrary justice with impunity. If they wanted to say a Negro had stolen a white person's horse and was traveling with no pass, they could whip the poor soul 'til his guts ran out in strings or drive a stake up his back and leave him impaled by the road to be eaten by the birds. The Negro had rare protection from the authorities. Stories of brutality abounded daily on the Negro grapevine.

Mary's ears perked up when she heard wagon wheels and the driver's "hupp" to the horse, bringing them to a stop at the front of the house. She looked out the window to see the driver helping Gie disembark the carriage.

"Don't let my arm go, Lodestar," Gie ordered. "I can't see a blame thing out here."

Goodness, Mary exclaimed to herself as she retrieved the maps and put them away. Gie wasn't supposed to arrive until two. She glanced at the clock.

It was one-fifty. Where did the time go? In another few minutes, Mary heard Gie and Tesh-Lucianne in the throes of their usual racket. The salon doors flew open.

"We'll let Mary settle it," Gie said, groping air with her hands out in front of her.

"Settle what?" Mary asked pleasantly.

"In a whole line of smart people, one can apparently turn plain stupid for no apparent reason," Tesh-Lucianne quipped.

Mary held up her hands, palms out. "I'm not getting into this one."

"And I came on an errand of mercy," Gie said. "See what I get for my trouble to see about a sick friend?"

"So what'd you bring me?" Tesh-Lucianne rasped. "Sick people get presents. I'm nearly out of violet water, and I could use some talc."

Gie held up a long package and Tesh-Lucianne tore into it. She squawked in surprise, "A sausage? A sausage?"

"Mary dear, help me to the settee," Gie said in a theatrically bleak voice. "Tesh-Lucianne is worth half a cent waiting on change."

Mary helped her to a seat where she put her feet up on a tufted ottoman. Gie sighed deeply. "Scare up a drink for me, will you? You know what I want. Simeon's best bourbon, straight. Three jiggers. And a champagne as well."

Tesh-Lucianne plopped down near her. "You ought to be shot! Roguey makes our sausage. What'd you bring me this thing for?"

"To broaden your horizons," Gie said, taking her drinks from Mary and sipping, then smiling over the immediate salutary effects. "It's from a friend of mine in New York. Called Polish sausage. You'll like it. Or you'll give it back to me, since I like it."

"Mary, please show this odd duck her new dress so she can leave the premises," Tesh-Lucianne said.

"Thank you. I'll leave when I'm good and ready," Gie said, mischief rich in her tone. "I'm ready for your unveiling, Mary. Left to herself, Tesh-Lucianne'll never quit her nonsense."

Mary went to the tall chiffonier and, making the sounds of a drumroll, swung the doors open.

"As I live and breathe!" Tesh-Lucianne cried.

"What? I can hardly see to my elbow. Bring it over here," Gie commanded.

Mary laid the dress across Gie's lap and explained the details of the garment. "I made the front in natural linen. It's four hand-pleated panels from rounded neck to hem. Each panel is trimmed in a chevron pattern of slender ribbons in sunny yellow, gunboat gray, and hunter green. In the center of each panel are three buttons. But to make it easy for you to get in and out of, behind each button is a small clasp. The dress fabric is a special soft wool I got a year ago from Ireland. Feel it."

Gie felt the fabric, and cooed.

"It's called cashmere. I dyed it your favorite color, lawn green."

"It's stunning, Gie," Tesh-Lucianne breathed. "Mary even made two pockets on each side."

"Yes," Mary said, gently guiding Gie's fingers to feel them. "Inside the one on the right is a pouch for your glasses when you're not wearing them."

"Oh!" Gie glowed.

"And last but not least," Mary smiled and held up a rope belt made of the same trim around the dress panels, "this belt hooks into the fabric wherever you want, so you can make it as tight or as loose as you feel comfortable. I've also constructed a fabric circle to loop your keys so you can always find them."

Gie's eyes were a murky gray. She stared straight ahead through her thick glasses. Her moving fingers around the dress gave sight of it to her. Then she was quiet for a long moment. "Mary, do you want The House of M back?"

Mary's jaw dropped. She looked at Gie like she would a foreign object.

"Daddy A.B. and I didn't like it one whit your losing your business to Delaclaire."

"Gie?" Tesh-Lucianne sounded perplexed.

"There's not a thing we plan to do with the business here in Norfolk. Let them have it, lock, stock, and barrel. But, if you're willing, we're going to set you up in Richmond on a grander scale. It won't be The House of M. Rather, it'll be called Mary's Haute Couture."

"You don't mean it!" Mary finally exclaimed.

"What's more," Gie said, "to honor your legendary talents, you will not only set style standards, you'll be in total control. Daddy A.B. and I will be silent partners. You'll have ten percent. We'll split ninety and carry all the expenses for the first five years. By that time, you should have your business legs under you and the shop paying for itself."

Mary felt like she'd been hit with a hot rag. Could this really be? This is what she'd worked for all her life. Or was it? Before she could ask a question, Tesh-Lucianne spoke up.

"What's Daddy A.B. got to do with this?"

"Why, he and I have been doing business together too long to talk about," Gie said. "But that's another story."

Mary used her walking stick to make her way to the wingback chair across from Gie. She sat. Her head was reeling with this offer. Why now, of all times?

"No," Tesh-Lucianne said, "I want to know, and I've got the time."

"Suffice it to say, love, your daddy and I have been in bed together since way back, when I lost my parents and was working to get my own toilette business going."

"What do you mean—*in bed together?*" Tesh-Lucianne pressed. She looked to Mary, "I need a wet one."

Mary rose and went to the butler's tray while listening intently to Gie.

"You were so on your head to marry Simeon," Gie said with little warmth in her voice, "we decided to let you, but we never believed it was right. Then when you had that bunch of miscarriages, we got more worried for you."

If Mary hadn't handed Tesh-Lucianne her drink at that moment, she believed the woman might have fallen over.

"We?" Tesh-Lucianne said.

Gie went on. "Simeon has always been driven to please Daddy A.B., as well as his own father. That poor man is nothing more than the social climbing issue of mill merchants out of the south of France. America was good to Etienne

Louvestre, and both by hook and by crook he got rich. Then, by whatever notion made sense only to him, he regarded Simeon as a failure almost from birth. You know full well Simeon's been a constant disappointment to him all his life."

"That's outright horse putty!" Tesh-Lucianne exclaimed.

Gie sipped her drink and held up her hand. "No word a lie! Just look at what Simeon's up to now. He's letting Lumley, the scoundrel, lead him around like a pet monkey, jumping and doing tricks at his bidding. Simeon has spent nearly his whole life at sea. Even when the two of you got married, where was he most of the time? At sea."

"He was in the Navy," Tesh-Lucianne said defensively.

"Then Providence stepped in. He had that bad fall and hurt his leg. He said it had something to do with a bad heart. Anyway, he got an early discharge and opened the chandlery. Where? Near the sea."

"You have a point to all this?" Tesh-Lucianne said, clearly building a snit.

"I'll thank you not to rush me," Gie said, smiling like she was the one who knew the punch line of an inside joke. "What Simeon knows about being a senator you could put on the head of a pin. He's still letting somebody else make decisions for him. Simeon must actually believe that his father expects him to win and engrave the Louvestre name in the history books as a high government official."

"That's my husband you're talking about," Tesh-Lucianne said. Her voice was high and quivery. She slugged her drink and pushed to stand up, her face flush with anger. "I'll thank you to take your words off him."

"And he is my friend. That's why I can tell the truth. Face facts. Simeon's career ambitions are as nondescript and aimless as he is," Gie continued, "though, I must say now, he's going off into a ditch with Lumley. We know about that man. We had him thoroughly checked out when he and Withers got here. The man's a fraud, Tesh-Lucianne."

"Come again? Which one are you talking about? Lumley or my husband?" Fire sparked in her eyes.

"Both," Gie snorted derisively. "Simeon's going to spend a lot of money, give a lot of speeches, make a lot of pledges, and nothing'll come of the efforts. He doesn't have whatever it is that's needed to succeed in the political arena. He should stay a ship's chandler. It is, at least, a living." Gie fluttered her hands.

"Lumley's a killer, deadlier than a cobra snake. He's wrapped himself around Simeon, his next victim. That's why Daddy A.B. and I want y'all to move with me to his big house in Richmond."

Both Tesh-Lucianne and Mary swiveled their heads to stare at Gie.

"Didn't see that one coming, did you?" She smiled mockingly.

"You expect me to leave my husband? Why would I do that? I love Simeon and he loves me. Our marriage is 'til death do us part. You've gone totally 'round the bend." Tesh-Lucianne stared in confusion at her friend.

"The fact of the matter is," Gie responded casually, "Simeon's going nowhere fast. Daddy A.B. and I have had our feelers out, and from what information we've gotten back, it'll be a cold day in hell before Simeon takes any high government office, even with Daddy A.B.'s endorsement."

Tesh-Lucianne was on her feet. Her mouth opened and closed but nothing came out.

Mary's eyes followed both of them like a feather in cross winds.

"Look, Tesh-Lucianne," Gie said, smacking her lips over her drink, "Daddy A.B. and I are withdrawing our financial support from Simeon's campaign. He'll be like a pierced balloon in the sky when the full force of that comes on him."

"But why?" Tesh-Lucianne was pie-eyed.

Gie looked at her friend pathetically. She sighed and let her feeble vision trail toward the windows. "Money," she answered eventually.

"Money!"

"Everything comes down to it. We'd be foolish to continue spending good money. And, I hate to add, you're not well. Even I can see how bad off you are, and I can't see the thick veins in my own hands." She held them up. "Have you looked at yourself in the mirror recently? You're a fright. Circles under your eyes. Skin the color of parched flour. From what I hear, you can't sleep a whole night without screaming awake from another nightmare about what ...," she ran a pink tongue over her bottom lip considering how best to delicately frame her thought, "what happened but didn't happen in that alley in town."

"My health is just fine, I thank you," Tesh-Lucianne harrumphed. "What I want to know is, what has Simeon done that you would treat him like your worst enemy?"

Gie turned to Mary and held out her glass. "Refill this for me, love."

As Mary poured the drink, Gie spoke to Tesh-Lucianne. "I have nothing against Simeon. I don't think Daddy A.B. does either, any farther than the crimes of taking his little girl away from him and giving him no grandchildren to boot. It comes down to the remaining bottom line. Money."

"I still do not understand," Tesh-Lucianne said, pulling up an ottoman and sitting down in front of Gie.

"War brings change. Change brings opportunities. Opportunities, for those who have an eye for them, bring money. Money brings comfort, satisfaction, and options. We are simply being circumspect in that regard."

Tesh-Lucianne wagged her head, her expression confused. "Why would even that make me leave my husband?"

"Silly girl," Gie said. "He's baggage. Moreover, if Simeon is not going to be a senator and you won't be a senator's wife, he'll be considered an 'also-ran' among people—not a Navy man or even a chandler. How do you think his father is going to take all this? He'll stop paying for the upkeep of this house, for one."

Tesh-Lucianne looked up so fast, Mary thought the woman might crack her neck. "This house is paid for. Was paid for long ago."

"True," Gie said, "but who do you think helps subsidize the maintenance? These grounds are huge. The house is huge. You thought Simeon paid the ongoing expenses for all this?"

Tesh-Lucianne grew pale. She didn't respond. Her world was coming apart at the seams, and those seams were ripping loudly. Weakly, staring at her feet, she asked, "What about Roguey, Devereaux, and Golen?"

"What about them?" Gie said, staring at the lowering level of her drink. "Try to think clearly, my friend. They're ciphers in your ledger book. All you have to do is draw a line through them. Give them up to the war."

Mary bit her lip to hold her peace.

"The house is one thing," Tesh-Lucianne protested, "but those folks are like family. Are you suggesting I set them free?"

"Hell no!" Gie cried. "Just leave them. The war'll claim them soon enough. Daddy A.B. and I are the family you can truly count on. We're rich as moguls on our own. And, in this unprecedented time of supply, demand, and urgency, we've decided to pool our resources, so to speak. Maybe 'mine our sources' would be more accurate, since a lot of land we own together in Virginia and other states is paying off in black gold—coal. The government needs it and we have it. They are willing to pay top dollar for it." She put her fingers close to her glasses and surveyed her nails. "Daddy A.B. is so sweet. He said I also need some looking after with my failing eyesight and all. And he's just the one to do it."

"You've always bragged that you were a stand-alone article," Mary said, not willing to remain silent any longer.

"People change when times change. And a woman can say a lot of things when she's young and able," Gie chuckled. "Daddy A.B. and I've been *together* a long time. We're just going to make it legal finally, that's all, to maximize protection and consolidation of our financial holdings."

Tesh-Lucianne grabbed her head and rocked. "I don't believe this. We've been like sisters." She stopped and glared at Gie.

The older woman placidly tasted her drink a time and then said, "Don't strain yourself, dear. Never in a million years will you figure out what I'm really saying about that. I'll just give you a hint. Life is full of workable arrangements."

"I'll thank you to remember you had no arrangement when the people of Norfolk wanted to run you out of town for what you did," Tesh-Lucianne snorted.

Gie's words were measured, her smile enigmatic. "Bedding that slave? Or having his baby? I forget which."

"Daddy A.B. took you in, even when your family wanted to erase you from their Bible cover. Daddy A.B. doted on you. He encouraged you in your business. He put you in your own suite in the big house's north side, a place of honor he'd declared no one would live in after Mama." Tesh-Lucianne looked aghast at Gie. Then her fingers released her drink and it fell to the floor. Gie ignored her.

"Worst day of my life was when that baby came out of me," Gie said, her eyes intense in memory. "Though I still tingle to recall how that sire of hers made me stupid in the head for a while, I couldn't think about anything but him between my legs. You know, to this day, I don't remember his name. I wanted him so much I ached. Literally, I couldn't eat. I couldn't sleep. I would even go to his cabin on Papa's slave row and pay his wife cold hard cash to leave for a while so I could get into their bed with him. I had hoped my herbs would keep me from getting pregnant."

Her eyes blinked behind the thick glasses as she glanced at Mary and Tesh-Lucianne. "He ruined me for other men."

Tesh-Lucianne found her voice. "You've got some rough language in you."

Gie continued as if she hadn't heard. "To this day, I hate the double standard. For a man to do what I did was him sowing his wild oats. For me, a white woman, to do that—well, I might just as well have been an aberration of the Holy Word. Papa eventually stepped in. My punishment was I had to watch while my buck twisted from a tall tree as Papa slowly razored off his pleasurements."

Both Mary and Tesh-Lucianne sat in numb silence.

Gie grimaced and continued after a moment. "Nobody else knows the secret I'm going to reveal to you." She lowered her voice. "Later that night, I slipped back to where the body still hung. It was dreadful. After what Papa and his men did, it didn't look human. So I quickly collected his balls and his nasty—it was still plump in death—into a jar. I've kept them to this very day. I gaze at them often, and sometimes I touch myself as I remember how grand those made me feel. But," her voice became less misty as she focused, "all things come to an end."

For a detached moment, Mary watched Tesh-Lucianne wring her hands while moaning softly, sadly. Her own alarms went off. She sank into a chair and turned to Gie. "Meaning what?"

"Your tone sounds forward, Miss Dressmaker," Gie scolded. "But I'll answer you. I paid Sheriff Bridges and his deputy, Gates, a visit. I encouraged them to think about the many facilities the town of Norfolk could benefit from if it had possession of a certain prime waterfront property."

Mary's eyes widened in fear.

"I'm letting you know this, Mary," Gie stated, "because you have a choice to make. You can say nothing about this to Coolie, and with your silence you'll buy into a deal with me and Daddy A.B. that will gain you your fashion empire. Or you can choose her friendship, which I guarantee will net you nothing in the end. Every woman has her price. I want to know what's yours, Mary Louvestre?" Gie's opal eyes glittered maliciously in the light.

Mary watched Gie, herself whirling deep in a hostile mood. She said nothing more. At that moment, she hated the woman on the sofa and did not trust herself to open her mouth as she tried desperately to hold in the dangerous urge that blossomed in her heart.

"Daddy A.B. will be here soon," Gie announced. "He's coming to see about his best girl. So I'll give you until sunset tomorrow to give me your answer."

Mary wrapped her arms around herself and said nothing.

Gie shrugged. "I'll tell you this. Whatever you decide, soon Travelers Rest will be a cinder." Her eyes never left Mary's and her voice sounded hollow as she began to laugh. "I'd swear, this drink or my infirmity has turned me rabid. But I think I rather like it."

Mary felt a tremble that wracked her from lower spine to the top of her head. Suddenly she felt as if she were trapped inside a child's spinning top. Colors and fabrics whirled around together. The image of Tesh-Lucianne bent over heaving her innards onto the floor went out of focus. Gie, who sat tall on the divan, laughed maniacally. Mary rubbed her eyes with her fists, but the woman continued to shimmer and distort like an elastic figurine.

Mary couldn't get her breath. The room had a nauseating stench. Nothing made sense. She was sure the world now tilted on the axis of a madman or madwoman. She struggled to her feet and stumbled forward. Her heart pounded. Off balance with everything, all the air suddenly went out of her lungs like a stuck balloon. Blackness enveloped her completely.

CHAPTER 40

Around three the next morning, with the house more dark than light, Mary jolted up from a tangled sleep. She looked around and realized she was in her bedroom. She began to remember coming to, getting up on hands and knees, and struggling over to the chair at her sewing table. Dizzy, she had poured a glass of water from the pitcher on a side table. Only then did she realize Tesh-Lucianne and Gie were gone. She didn't know how long they'd let her lay there. Things were getting stranger and stranger, she thought as she stumbled to bed.

Now in the early dark, Gie's visit rushed to her mind in broken images. She didn't want to deal with her ultimatum right now. Pushing back the covers, she forced herself out of bed. There was a lot to do and little time to do it.

She slipped down the hall and into Simeon's study. Though the raccoon was gone, she still didn't take any chances. Once inside, she waited to let her eyes adjust to the darkness. She made a quiet survey of the room. Then she was at her task, quickly and deftly copying more of the ship's plans.

She remembered that catching the fat critter had been a job. He'd found a warm, cozy home and was not happy about relinquishing it. Simeon tried to shoo him out by waving his hands in its face. But he'd turned green and turned tail when the creature snarled and bared its teeth at him. Roguey's turn amounted to beating the floor with one of her pots to scare him away. But the animal had only watched her with large disinterested eyes. Finally the old gardener, Golen, was called in. He studied the situation, then threaded a long length of twine with chunks of Roguey's honey-glazed ham and biscuits slathered with apricot preserves.

"I don't see how come you got to feed the varmint like white folk," Roguey had complained to him.

Raccoons, the gardener knew, would eat mostly anything, but they did prefer meat and sweets. "He gonna follow this out the window and drag it to the brook," Golen said, "'cause you know he gotta wash it first. 'Coons don't trust food to be clean."

Mary and the others huddled at the door to the room, watching as the old man scooted slowly across the floor with a makeshift trap in hand. He laid it out, draped one end out the window, backed away, and went outside. He reappeared at the open window and began to tug the line. The creature sniffed the air. It slowly roused from the warm bed it had made of Simeon's favorite rag rug. It began to eagerly follow the food that dragged along the floor, over the window ledge and onto the porch.

As soon as it was away, Simeon bounded to the window and slammed it shut. "Well," he said triumphantly, "that's that."

Finishing all the tracing she dared do for now, Mary thought, if only it were that easy to escape.

That morning's foray was taut but easy enough. She had copied a good portion of the plans. The next day Mary hoped her efforts would go as smoothly. She'd chosen to dress now in a black outfit made on the order of men's cotton pajamas. She liked that she had an ease of movement in them.

She arrived at the study door with no trouble. But when she tried to turn the knob, it didn't move. She jiggled the handle. It failed to turn. It was locked. Why? she wondered.

As quickly as possible, she made her way to the kitchen. The house keys hung on a large ring just inside the swinging doors. A dozen keys passed through her fingers, but not one looked like the skeleton for the study. She went through the keys again and again to make sure she hadn't overlooked what she was after. Exasperated, she gave up and stealthily returned to her room.

"Simeon got back from Richmond way late las' night," Roguey told Mary a little while later as they ate breakfast before sunup. "He say he goin' back to work at the chandlery t'morrow. Wants me to be packin' his lunches with 'nough casin' his lawyer frien' turns up to eat like he likes doin."

Mary knew she needed to copy as much as possible before he left. Outside, under cover of the huge oak tree, she studied the office window. She silently examined the verandah and the window ledge. She hoped Simeon had left the window unlocked. He usually did, but she imagined the raccoon might make him resort to securing it. Still, it was her only possibility. Her instincts said the prudent thing to do was hurry.

A deep breath, and quickly she was on the verandah, the window sash in both hands, and with persistent tugging, she lifted it up. Another instant saw her hoisting herself up to the ledge and pressing herself inside. The moccasins on her feet sounded only a tiny thump as she hopped from the windowsill to the floor, but the pain in her knee lanced hotly.

Her fingers were fast as soon as she found the sheaf of ship's plans where she left off before. One square of tracing paper. Sketch. Fold. Tuck it in her bosom. Another piece of paper. Sketch. Fold. Tuck. Only one more large sheet of renderings to go. Needlessly, she fingered the stack of supply papers in the pouch she carried on her hip. It was a nervous gesture since she made sure she had plenty of pieces of the tracing paper before she left out. Wait. What was that? She cocked her ear.

She heard a key turn in the office door lock. Mary launched herself to the back of the room. There was no time to get back through the window. If whoever was coming had a lamp, it would be impossible to not see her, even in as large a room as this. Her eyes swung around desperately, seeking a place to hide. As the door began to open, she spotted a small space between two bookcases. Panic raced through her—she saw she'd left the plans open on the desk, and a small square of tracing paper lay on top. In addition, she had left the window open to make a fast exit if she had to. Her mind raced. She knew this little oversight could derail everything.

She edged out of the space and down on all fours. She crawled toward the door, mimicking the low, guttural sound of an animal. She desperately hoped that whoever was at the door would fear it to be the raccoon had returned and was now on the attack. The door slammed shut again.

Mary wanted to laugh, but lost no time. She grabbed up her tracing paper, dashed to the window, and burst through it. She fell to the verandah with a thud, came up on her knees, grabbed the walking stick she'd left leaning against the wall, and tore away. She ran, as best she could, back to the safety of the oak tree. From behind it, she peered and watched, panting, as Tesh-Lucianne emerged onto the side porch, lantern in hand, swinging it in arcs of light.

In the hush of the early morning, Mary could hear her, singing her words like blubbering from the mouth of a drunk. "Come out, come out, whoever you are. Come out, come out, wherever you are." Tesh-Lucianne hiccupped and giggled. She then wandered the length of the porch to a grouping of rattan furniture. There, she set the lantern on the wide table and burrowed into the deep pillows of a chair. She dug a bottle from a robe pocket. "O-kay," she slurred, "I'll jus' sit myself here and wait for you. I'll have just a bit more lib-er ... lib-*a*-shun, 'til you get back." She slugged back a big drink, then clasped the bottle to her chest. "Don't know what I ever did without laud-un ... laderum ..." She held up the bottle, squinting but unable to read the label. "Don't matter to me how you say it. Works for me."

Mary stood stock-still for how long she didn't know. Sun was beginning to peek through the trees when her sore muscles told her it was safe to move. Tesh-Lucianne had laid her head back and now snored in uneasy slumber. When Mary felt it was safe, she hurried across the open lawn to the steps to the kitchen door. Just before she headed up them, she realized Roguey would be up and at work. Mary hunched low and waddled like a duck along the base of the verandah on the other side of the house to avoid being seen. Holding her stick in her hand, she bent to her knees and powered upward in a jump on the count of three. Her hand caught a narrow ledge, and she pulled herself up to the verandah. Her muscles screamed from the pain, and she wanted to scream as well. Panting and sweating, she inched up to grasp the spindles of the verandah baluster. She grunted herself through them. For a moment she lay panting on the smooth white-painted wide porch. As soon as she caught her breath, she rose and pushed through the French doors into her salon.

Roguey was at the sideboard with her cart, setting out food for the day's clients. She turned and caught sight of a disheveled Mary.

Wide-eyed and still breathing hard, Mary stared back at the cook.

Roguey shook her head. "I ain't even gon' ax."

———◈———

Nearly three the following morning, the only sounds from outside Mary's bedroom windows were calls of a few water birds and a gentle soughing of wind through the tree branches. She lay awake in the tall four-poster, set up off the floor to provide warmth against winter coldness. Plump pillows cradled her head; crisp sheets and a thick, soft quilt tucked her in.

Mary was alert and apprehensive, made even more so by the knowledge that she nearly had them all—all of the vital ship's plans. "Nearly" was the meaningful word. She had to get everything. Gripping the bed covers, she pushed them back and sat up. Take heart, she chided herself as she padded across the room to the chiffonier and began to dress. In another few minutes, she pressed her ear to the door. Hearing only silence, she breathed deeply and opened the door. This was it, she said to herself. Go!

Lighted candles, their low flames under glass, sat on floor pedestals along the hallway. Shadows were gray to black. Where there was light, it was an umber glow. Her walk was quick but careful, making only the tiniest muffled sound. The moccasins fit her feet like gloves. Her pants fit slim to her body and tied at the waist; her blouse slipped over her head and did the same. Over her shoulder she carried the pouch with her blank papers and tracing pencil.

Reaching the end of her corridor, she peeked down the hallway to Simeon's office. She listened. The house seemed to breathe calm, slow breaths—nothing out of the ordinary. Mary hastened toward the office door. When she reached the handle that gleamed in the dull light, she halted abruptly, let herself be motionless. Deliberately, she focused on her breathing, calming it. Slowly, deeply—in through her nose, out through soft lips. As her eyes adjusted to the darkness, she made out pages of a book fluttering on a zephyr that seeped through the partially open window. She loosened her grip on the doorknob and lowered her shoulders that had hiked up with tension.

The humid air that now carried a hint of rain suddenly became a noose in the room, awful to anticipate its full threat. Mary became conscious of the sweat trickling down her forehead to the edge of her lips, leaving a salty taste.

With a thud, Mary's walking stick struck the edge of the desk. She was so focused on finding the roll of blueprints that had been there yesterday and mentally rehearsing a fast trace of her pencil, that it took a moment to realize the plans were gone.

The desk surface was as clean and shiny as a new brass spittoon. She stood open-mouthed, stunned. There was only the clock, ticking dutifully with its brass balls revolving, the leather writing pad, the pen resting aside a cut-glass inkwell, and the curved blotter.

"Glory!" she cursed under her breath. She looked on one side of the desk and then the other. She excavated umbrellas in a corner stand but discovered nothing behind them. Her frantic eyes sought out the glass bookcase and peered inside.

She stopped, held herself like a plinth. She cocked her head. As if from another world, she heard her name. It was being sung like a child's wispy tune.

"Ma-ary. Ma-ary."

Oh no, she thought as she forced herself to pivot in escape. In her haste, she stumbled on the edge of the thick rug but managed to right herself with the heel of one hand on the doorjamb, the other on her walking stick.

"Ma-ary."

The call was coming closer.

She had the door open now. She was out of the office in a flash, gaining momentum down the hall. Run, she told herself. But wouldn't she make noise? No matter. She tore down the thickly carpeted hall, accidentally bumped a vase, and grimaced in horror as it teetered on its perch. She grabbed it, set it right, and continued toward her quarters. But her foot tangled with her walking stick, and she went down in a forward motion. She slid, literally on her belly, to the door of her salon.

"Ma-ary." The voice was perilously close.

She hadn't moved so fast since she was a kid, well before the man busted her kneecap.

The rest was a blur. A dash into her bedroom. A toss of clothes. No evidence of minutes before.

The door to her salon breezed open. Tesh-Lucianne, still in her nightclothes, wandered in. "I see you," she crowed.

⁂

Later in the morning, Devereaux drove the carriage to Travelers Rest. Mary's nerves were as fried as crisp okra. She could see the place was bustling as usual, if not more so. People filtered in and out of the main building and drifted over the lawn and gardens and along the several outbuildings. Lively music carried out the windows of the restaurant and bar, and Mary could also detect some of the patrons singing along.

Devereaux pulled the carriage to a stop as close to the front door as the busy traffic would allow. He helped Mary out as several men called out their hellos.

She went inside, her eyes surveying the room and atmosphere. She passed a table where men were playing cards and several tables of diners who feasted on heaping mounds of seafood and baskets of corn bread. She got a glimpse of Sweets and Verona working the crowd, laughing and talking, leaning over from time to time to titillate the men and add to their enjoyment of the place. She saw a group of patrons leave a table near the bar. Before a waitress could clean up the mess they left behind, she sat down.

Theron watched her enter. He put down the cloth he used to constantly clean the counter, and he joined her. His white shirt was crisp and his black trousers were creased. His hair had been given a vigorous brushing and appeared, not long ago, to have been tended by a barber. Though his face wore the serious expression it always did, his eyes held a tenderness when they gazed on Mary. He put a short glass of amber liquid in front of her.

"Sherry," he said. "Just got a shipment through the lines. It's from somewhere 'cross the water."

Mary tasted it. "Mmm. Good. I continue to be amazed at how you manage out here. You never seem to run short on anything. Don't you know there's a war going on, and people are complaining about shortages of nearly everything?"

Theron jutted his chin, looked out at the happy crowd. "People find a way." He brought his eyes back to Mary. "Coolie still out to Stonehaven."

"Thank goodness," Mary said. "Though I have a bone to pick with her. Had a long talk with her mother yesterday. Let me just say, the woman made me choose sides. My being here tells you where I stand."

Theron looked puzzled, then shrugged. "I ain't in none of that. I know that Bear say Coolie like a colt what won't stay in the corral. He don't know how much longer he can keep her reined."

"I'm worried about that," Mary said, "especially now."

Theron scratched his chin with long fingers. "What you sayin'?"

"I've come into information there's going to be trouble out here. I don't know when, but my sense is it could be any day."

"Gates?"

Mary nodded.

Theron stopped Sweets as she passed and asked her to bring him a beer. She looked surprised but went on. Then he turned back to Mary and spoke in a low voice. "My gut don't lie. I been feelin' a disturbance comin' on too. Though, to look around, everything seems right as rain."

Mary let her eyes scan through the haze of smoke from pipes, cigars, and steaming food that floated in the air. She watched the banjo player strumming his instrument, a couple working up some sort of dancing, and the steady promenade of people in and out.

The beer was promptly delivered and Theron gulped a swallow. He made a face and pushed it away, saying, "Sometime I try but I still ain't a drinker. Look a-yonder," he said, letting his little finger direct Mary to the sight of Sweets resting her chin in the palms of her hands as she chatted up a patron at the end of the bar. "She's as fun-lovin' as a kid. This 'bout the only home she know."

As soon as the kitchen door swung open and a large black woman wearing a stained white apron gave her the signal, Sweets excused herself and disappeared into the kitchen. In another moment, she re-emerged bearing a large tray. On it was a huge fried fish with a bright-red bow around its neck. She carried it to a large table packed with rowdy men and drinks. "Happy birthday, Dagget, you ol' fool!" The men slapped their legs and cheered both ol' Dagget and the fish. Then they gleefully dug in with their fingers.

"Can't count on yo' lyin' eyes, though," Theron commented.

"This trouble with Gates," Mary said, "I believe it's going to be hell to pay."

Theron sighed profoundly. "Listen, Miss Mary, we ain't been jes' sittin' on our thumbs out here. Ever since Gates hit town, I done had me a general feelin' of bad comin'. I hope you got some distance 'twixt here and home when it come down. A'Lawd, I know it ain't gonna be pretty. This here our home and we ain't gon' lay down for nobody. If Deputy Gates want to mix in with that, well," he opened his hands, "I hope he plan to finish what he start and leave a note with somebody to tell his next of kin."

CHAPTER 41

$\mathbf{M}$ary, back in her bedroom, began planning what she'd need for her trip north—clothing, shoes, food, medicinal herbs, maps, and compass. She took a break to go out to Golen to secure a gourd. He had several to choose from, and she chose a long one. Then she set about waterproofing it. In it, she would secret the copies of the blueprints.

With an increasing sense of urgency, she had crafted, sewn, and packed into every moment she could, every effort toward getting ready. To her stash of necessities she added a short, thin bamboo pole and several quills she had treated with a strong solution. At last she remembered the gun Tesh-Lucianne had given her. She went to the chifforobe and took it out of the box, hefted it, checked the bullets, and pushed it into the side fold of her pack. Finally, she remembered a weapon of her youth Tug had made for her. Digging in the bottom of the chifforobe, she found it tied neatly in a packet. It was her slingshot and several rocks. She smiled at the memory of Tug teaching her how to use it until she had become proficient.

She gathered provisions in small net bags—pumpkin seeds, raisins, pecans, walnuts, dried apples, peppermint, cloves of garlic, salt and pepper—and packed them below a false bottom of a tapestry bag, along with a pewter plate she'd freed from the china cabinet and a small pot from the kitchen. Over those she placed two Union suits to layer for warmth. Then she added a second pair of moccasins, another pair of wool pants, and several pairs of socks. From her herb shed, she added a small hatchet. Finished packing, she pushed her bags into the chifforobe.

As a ruse to be away without being missed for a while, Mary had asked Tesh-Lucianne for permission to see a friend who lived outside Richmond. She also said she had received word that someone else she was very fond of, who lived up that way, had taken sick of a lung disease. She felt she knew how to cure the sickness. When she asked, obsequiously, for time away, Tesh-Lucianne had reluctantly agreed.

Briefly, while continuing her preparations, Mary's mind turned to Anders. The other day he had invited her to his tent at the camp bivouacked just outside of town. She had never been inside a tent before and marveled at how compact and neat his was. So like Anders to have everything in order. She sat on a low cot covered by a green wool blanket. Nearby there was a makeshift table that held his grooming items. A pair of black boots stood nearby, like shiny sentinels.

Anders saw her looking at them. "I use heated wax and a lot of elbow grease to keep them that way." He smiled. "Vanity."

"If you put a piece of fresh potato in the toes at night, your shoes will always stay soft and fresh. In case your feet are vain too. Just thought I'd add that." She smiled mischievously at him.

Anders, standing in a slice of light filtering through the tent flap, grinned.

"I like it here," Mary said as she closed her eyes and filled her nostrils with the scent of his quarters. "Smells manly. I like that too."

Then Anders stood before her, gently lifting under her arms to stand her in front of him. His eyes were lustrous, his mouth a little slack. "I am pitiful."

That was the last thing Mary expected him to say. "What?"

Anders stared into her eyes for a long moment, and said nothing. When he spoke, his voice was sad. "I am pitiful. A black man who cannot be with the woman he loves, without permission from a white man who likely will not give it.

"I hoped and I prayed and I planned. And for what?" he sighed. "Every time doubt or despair came to me in my loneliest times, I would push them away. Just hold on, I told myself, a solution is bound to present itself. But it hasn't. What's worse yet is I feel more powerless and despairing than I ever did before—and so much in love with you."

Anders wrapped his arms around her and held her tightly, as if never wanting to let go—as did she.

"Pitiful times," Mary said into his chest. "Whatever we have will not end just because the Navy will soon send you home. We have now. With any luck, we'll find each other again. Then we won't be pitiful anymore."

Did she really believe that, she silently questioned. If she continued with her plans, would it ever be possible for her to return to the South again? She couldn't let herself think about that now. She just wanted to be there with him, together was all.

As evening was softly falling, the two shadows cast on the walls of Anders's tent. Mary knew she should leave. But, at this moment, everything within her wanted to just meld into one, as much as to stay. For some reason, this evening felt different.

Anders seemed to sense her feeling combining with his own. "Mary." His voice was husky with desire as his dark eyes gazed into hers. She was quiet. He pulled her body to his and found it pliant and yielding.

For so long, Mary had kept herself in such tight control, and now, finally, she had allowed him to convince her that she really did want the "us" she and

Anders could represent: something more, something better for them both. How possible it felt right now. In his arms, she let go and no longer felt held hostage to the enduring fears of what her heart couldn't hope to have.

Anders pulled back and stared languidly into her liquid eyes, glinting with reflected soft light from the lantern in the corner of the tent. His breath came in short pants as he slowly led her to the neatly made cot.

He tilted her chin up, kissed her sweetly. She returned the kiss and let her teeth capture his moist lower lip. They moaned together. Then she put her lips on top of his and sucked. When she let go, his tongue pushed inside her mouth, curled around her teeth, and braided with hers.

The flame in the lantern twisted in a mild zephyr highlighting the strength in Anders's high cheekbones and wide forehead. She felt his shaky hands work to delicately unbutton her blouse, finally accomplishing the task of slipping it off her shoulders. He untied the fastenings on her skirt and pushed it down over her hips, looking at her appreciatively from head to toe. Her desire was becoming so intense, her legs quivered like plucked guitar strings.

Mary watched as Anders, his eyes never leaving hers, clumsily unbuttoned and removed his trousers. Mary was breathless when she felt Anders's chiseled body on top of hers. She lunged forward and kissed his chin, his neck, his shoulders, and pressed her body tightly against his groin.

Breath came sparingly and the pounding of her heart swelled in her ears as desire spread her legs. His hardness grew against her thigh and she pulled his lips down to her wanting breasts. As his mouth closed over her erect nipples, her loins bucked desperately, and there was no controlling the frantic swivel of her hips.

Anders arched over her, straining to contain himself as he hungrily checked her eyes for permission. She stroked his long hardness and guided him into her soft wetness.

"Oh," she cried, canting her hips upward. Her head whipped back and forth on the pillow, crazy in unbridled frenzy. With every one of his vital thrusts, she wanted to cry out his name; wanted to scream something, anything to confirm the joy of this coming together, but her throat constricted in the passion within, growing as strong as any act of God. He groaned. Mary felt the muscles of Anders's back, now bathed in sweat, hold for an eternity of seconds over her. His intelligent fingers found the sensitive place inside her mound. Stroking gently at first as she writhed underneath him, they pressed upward, rotating in faster and faster turns. Then with his other hand, he lifted her buttocks and she wrapped her legs around him as he thrust himself deeper inside her.

Her thighs trembled; her mind was dizzy. The feeling erupted in the core of her womb, traveled hotly downward, spreading out to the whole of her, insisting, demanding she succumb, and in one violent surge, she clung to Anders's breathing as he too released and his seed generously filled up all of her empty places.

They lay spent, entwined in each other's arms and legs. As Anders lifted his head and peered into her dazed features and smiled, an owl hooted distantly. Mary was startled at first, knowing the superstition that it foretold imminent death. Choosing to ignore it and anything else at that moment, she smiled too.

CHAPTER 42

In the late morning of the following day, the sound of an explosion shattered the air. Its force was such that the Louvestre house jolted and settled back into place with little kicks and jerks. Mary had been walking toward her desk and was thrown to the floor by the shock. When she scrambled to her feet, she saw black smoke purl into the sky from the distance, blanketing the horizon until it had the appearance of spilled ink.

From somewhere in the house, Tesh-Lucianne screamed shrilly, and on reflex, Mary rushed to the door. It would not budge. She pulled, and finally, after slamming her shoulder into it several times, the door cracked and gave way. She raced down the hall toward the staircase.

"Tesh-Lucianne!" Mary called out. "Where are you?" Again came the scream.

She peered up the stairs and the darkened doors along the wide entry. She heard snuffling and followed the sound to a corner where light was lost to the recessed bluish-gray triangle of space. There she found Tesh-Lucianne clutching her knees to her chest and rocking. The atmosphere smelled musky with her flop sweat.

Mary bent down to her and shook her arm gently. "Tesh-Lucianne, are you all right?"

Tesh-Lucianne's green eyes never glinted in the light. She did not look up. She continued to rock in silence.

Roguey appeared. Her head poked around, searching. "Mary? Y'all in here?"

"Over here," Mary said. "I think Tesh-Lucianne's in shock but I can't get her to move to see if she's hurt."

With a grunt, Roguey squatted down next to Mary. Her eyes examined Tesh-Lucianne. "Ain't no blood far's I can see jes' lookin."

"C'mon, Tesh-Lucianne," Mary said, trying to leverage her up.

Roguey angled to the other side as much as space allowed. "A sack of wet sand couldn't feel heavier when she ain't helpin' us none."

Tesh-Lucianne allowed herself to be manipulated toward the center of the elegant entry. There her eyes sought Mary's guilelessly. "Was that the Devil beatin' his wife?"

Mary gave a soft laugh. "No."

"No, ma'am. Sun's shinin' but it ain't rainin' and that wasn't thunder," Roguey said. "But the sky's smoky as all get-out. Can't hardly see nothin'. All that noise and bleatin' come from yonder at the Navy Yard."

A chill ran through Mary's soul.

Tesh-Lucianne suddenly became alert. Her eyes grew wide. "Navy Yard? Simeon's there! He's dead!"

Mary and Roguey exchanged worried glances as they laced their arms through Tesh-Lucianne's and nearly carried her to the kitchen. Mary's limp made the effort difficult. She was conscious of an ache in her limb, but she put it out of her mind. Once they got Tesh-Lucianne into one of the kitchen chairs, Mary let her eyes and hands survey the woman's body for possible injuries. She found none and sighed with relief. "Don't worry. We don't know anything for sure right now. Somebody'll get word to us soon."

For a moment, Tesh-Lucianne's mat of burnished hair hid her face as she sat folded so far over that she appeared to have caved in on herself. When a series of short booms shook the trees outside the kitchen window, Tesh-Lucianne sat bolt upright and slapped her hands over her eyes, then wailed a long keening sound. "He's dead," she uttered again in a pitiful voice. "I just know it."

Golen, rail-thin and in his dark work clothes, stepped into the kitchen doors as if a shadow emerging from the smoke. Tesh-Lucianne tensed, her eyes wild as if staring at a ghost. She bolted from the chair, her hair on end, and hugged the end of the counter. "Death!" she screamed, pointing at Golen. "I knew he'd come."

"Get us some brandy, will you?" Mary said to Roguey, trying to calm herself. Turning to Tesh-Lucianne, she spoke as soothingly as possible, "That's only old Golen. You know him. He just came to see we're safe. Look. See him now?"

Tesh-Lucianne turned around and folded herself into Mary's arms. "Simeon's dead, isn't he? I'm all alone now!"

"Roguey, the brandy," Mary ordered, more sharply this time. Then, attempting to be delicate, she said to Tesh-Lucianne, "You know Simeon. He's like a cat. He's got nine lives."

Suddenly a knocking sounded so hard on the kitchen's French doors that both Tesh-Lucianne and Mary nearly levitated. Tesh-Lucianne squealed as she saw the wind whip up the hem of a man's long black overcoat. The man was bent, framed in the middle of the glass panes. His hat was pulled down so low it was impossible to make out his features. Tesh-Lucianne stood trembling, her arms wrapped around herself. "A beast!" she cried.

"Open this door, dammit!" the man cursed.

Mary peered into the whirling gloom to sort out who it could possibly be. She freed the door, and the man brushed past her.

"Took your damned sweet time!"

Tesh-Lucianne brightened. "Daddy A.B.!" She fled into his welcoming arms. In his protection, she let loose. Tears spilled down her cheeks, and she wept like a child.

Mary watched as father and daughter clung to each other, all that each needed right then.

Tesh-Lucianne managed to quiet herself as Roguey arrived back to the kitchen with the brandy. Daddy A.B. grabbed a glass and held it to his daughter's lips. "Get me one," he ordered in a quick torrent. "Make it twice this much to start."

After a short while, everyone got settled. Roguey lit more candles. The sky was still dark though midday was coming on. In the distance toward the shipyard the sky seemed peppered by tiny black pellets, ash raining down and staining everything below. In the opposite direction, dark storm clouds still chased across the landscape like distorted objects in a bad dream.

"My man got the carriage as far as the curve of the drive out there, when we were blocked by a fallen tree. He's out there now. I haven't walked so far since I don't know when." He cast a glance around the room at the others. "But I heard that scream. I knew it was my little girl. Shows you what you can do when you have to."

Tesh-Lucianne, much calmer now, clutched at Daddy A.B.'s string tie. "Simeon's dead, Daddy."

The old man glanced at Mary, who wagged her head. He patted his daughter's hair. He could see she was not well. "Simeon's not dead. Mary's leaving soon to take him his noon meal. Anyhow, Daddy A.B.'s here. I'm gon' take you back home. Would you like that? To sleep in your old room under the quilt with the star in the center? And Cook Telma will make the potato soup you've always liked. As many bowls as that tummy of yours can hold. How'd that be?" He tickled her middle.

Tesh-Lucianne laid her head on his chest, giggled, and bobbed her chin. "Uhn-huh."

"You'll come on back home with Daddy. It's hard being all grown up. I know."

Mary had never seen Daddy A.B. display such compassion. Or was it? Her brows pleated as she tried to think through just what was happening. Mary spoke apologetically, not wanting to intrude but needing to ask, "Daddy A.B., don't you think Tesh-Lucianne just needs a little sleep? I'm sure she'll be fine after that."

The fire-eater glared at her, and when he spoke, Mary stepped back at the ferocity of his tone. "This is over. Hellfire and the war can take the rest for all I care."

Mary winced. Was he going to take Tesh-Lucianne from her home here, just whisk her away like she didn't have a husband and a place of belonging right here in this marvelous, majestic, many-columned temple near the sea? What about the rest of the household? Did they matter to him?

"Daddy A.B.," Mary started.

His head pulled up and the blackness of his eyes bore on her. His voice rasped. "Don't you ever call me that again, y'hear? I'm *Massa* Clairoux to you. Don't you ever act like I'm somethin' to you or you're somethin' to me. It's *slave* Mary, to me. Go make yourself useful, slave." His eyes inclined over to Roguey. "Both of you. Get out of my sight."

Daddy A.B. turned back to his daughter. He did not see Roguey swivel and sight him with her own fierce eyes, her jaw locked tight. He did not hear a sound flare in her throat and nostrils, which would have frightened anyone in her wake as she bore down upon him, gaining speed and thrust.

Mary blocked Roguey at the last second, clutching her at the chest and whispering, "We'll both die if you call this now. Leave it, Roguey. Hear me?"

Finally, with consummate disgust, Roguey turned away.

"Then I won't cry," Tesh-Lucianne said to him in a little girl's voice, as if nothing else had occurred in the room. "I won't cry anymore."

"No, l'il darlin'," he whispered hoarsely into her ear. "Daddy A.B. won't let you cry anymore. Not ever again."

Roguey threw a scornful look back at the pair and growled as Mary urged her out of the room.

<hr />

Within another anxious hour, a nearby neighbor, Rupert Davies, brought news about the explosion. The boiler of the CSS *Virginia* had blown while the engine was being tested. Mary and Roguey hung back in the entry, listening as Daddy A.B., at the door, accepted the news. Daddy A.B.'s driver had negotiated his rolling chair from the carriage to the main house, and Daddy A.B. was more comfortable now, though his face and voice belied it.

"How bad?" he asked.

"Don't have much detail," Mary could hear Davies say, "but word is we ain't got a prayer against the North if we don't get that engine fixed damned fast. And even that might not be soon enough."

"I'm not talking about the engine, fool!" Daddy A.B. fired back at him. "What about Simeon?"

"My apology, sir," Davies said. "No call to concern yourself on that score. Nobody on shore was hurt, although the explosion caused broken windows and minor trouble to some buildings."

Daddy A.B. grumbled to nobody in particular. "This damn war's gettin' on my damn nerves, dammit!" Rudely, he wheeled away, leaving Davies standing at the threshold, hat in hand.

Mary moved to the door. "Thank you, Mr. Davies. Are you sure that's all you know?"

"For right now," he said, and turned to leave. Then he turned back. "Maybe it's nothing. That engine's blown before. But if you've got someone on that ship that you're thinking about, you might want to pray." Davies placed his tall hat on his tumble of thick gray hair and retreated down the steps.

Mary gasped. With Roguey following, she shot back down the hallway. "I'm going over there."

Daddy A.B. and his chair practically tripped them as he wheeled out of Simeon's study, intercepting their path. "Where do you think you're goin'?" His voice was abrasive, his face red. His breathing came in short, heavy pants, pushing past the fat cigar stuck at the corner of his mouth. "You so high and mighty, you make your own decisions around here, when you come and go and where?"

Mary stopped, grasping her walking stick so tightly her fingernails nearly bit into the dense, hard wood. She stared at him.

"Daddy A.B.'s here now. Things are going to be different as I call them." He punctuated his statement with a puff of acrid smoke.

Mary continued to fix on him, no anger, no rebuff, no retaliation, just directly. Her stomach tightened, and her nerves pricked like hot needles, but she stood her ground.

Roguey's eyes darted back and forth between the two silent combatants. This was dangerous.

The old man's hoarse half-whisper crackled in the air. "You act like you don't know who I am and what I can do."

Gie's words of the day before rushed into Mary's mind: *We're going to set you up with Mary's Haute Couture. You'll be in total control. Daddy A.B. and I will be silent partners.* This man, who could not have been more clear about who he was and what he thought of her, a *silent partner*? Gie's offer was nothing but another lie they thought they could pull over a witless slave. Mary's nostrils flared with a contempt she could not hide. She said nothing, but her eyes flashed, daring him to challenge her further.

Daddy A.B. flinched when he caught Mary's expression, but he maintained his own look of rage. He snorted, then slowly wheeled back out of her path.

Mary's walking stick glinted in the light as she lunged forward along the hall.

Daddy A.B. pulled back into the shadows, mumbling under his breath, "You don't know who you're messing with." Before he slammed the study door, he shouted, "You're playing with fire, gal! I'm serious!"

Mary had had enough. Over her shoulder she loudly retorted, "You make me sick you pigheaded old fool!" A roar of her laughter followed her words.

Roguey spoke to Mary in a harsh whisper, "Now you done gone and loss yo' mind!"

Mary fumed all the way to the ferry. She'd had the forethought to ask Roguey to pack a lunch for Simeon, and seating herself and setting the basket near a railing, she was only vaguely aware of the other passengers on the ferry. It was evident many of them were worried about family, friends, and other loved ones who worked on the ship. Their voices were pitched low and full of concern. "God help us," someone murmured. A speculative drawling from someone else was passionate: "Lawd bless 'em to live and let nothin' else to happen."

Mary stared up at the sky. She must, at least for the moment, block thoughts about Anders and concentrate on finishing what she started. She had to copy the last page of the blueprints to make this risk worth taking. Simeon had said he was about to turn them over to the Navy representatives since he had completed his work detailing the renovation. If he had already done so, she was sunk. She had to know if the plans were still in his office. If so, she might be able to copy that last page.

Mary worked her approach toward the chandlery through a press of people and chaos and uproar all along the docks. Gawkers were gathered to see what they could see. Mary goosed her neck to look over them and could discern broken pilings, open crates of what she couldn't tell, and damage to portions of the walkway. Workmen were cleaning up, cajoling each other to get a move on. But mostly, eyes were drawn to the huge ironclad, black smoke still belching from it.

Mary wanted to stay and keep vigil herself until she could learn about Anders's welfare. But as people talked, many seemed to derive pleasure from declaring aloud the worst. Mary's skin crawled as she listened. She caught sight of two old men down front, jaws working their chewing tobacco, their rheumy eyes watching the rescue commotion around the *Virginia*. They were consumed with the ship's being towed in. "Engine blow in a can even that big can't be a pretty sight," one said. The other one grumbled, "Hope it was niggers down in the hole who took the hit. Sho' got scaled like a bunch of lobsters. Save good white folks that a-way."

Nausea rose in Mary as she hurried past and finally reached the bustling chandlery. As she entered, men were gathered in knots worrying with each other in the charged atmosphere of disturbance. Simeon caught sight of her and waved a hand in greeting. Mary held up the basket she was carrying and pointed to his office, then approached him instead when he beckoned to her.

Simeon handed her a key. "The office is locked. Too much commotion to leave it open. Lock the door behind you. I've another if I need to come in."

"I'm glad to see you're okay. We were worried about you. All of us, especially Tesh-Lucianne."

"I'm shook up, but dandy," Simeon said heartily. "No damage here, thank the Lord. A potential buyer for the chandlery is coming today. My days connected to the sea are numbered. I'm soon to be back on the campaign trail."

As other customers wanted Simeon's attention, Mary made her way to his office. As soon as she had flipped the lock behind her she flew to Simeon's drafting table. All she found were sea charts and various drawings. None were what she was looking for. She scanned the piles of disarray in the room and finally noticed a long bound roll of papers on the low table near the fireplace.

God let it be so, she implored as her hands untied the strings. She laid the pages out and leafed through them quickly. Bless! These were the ones. She pulled out the last page. She could see much detail that would take time to trace fully. She knew she had to hurry.

First, she set a small table by the window with Simeon's lunch. Then she went to work tracing the plans. Her fingers sketched furiously. At every sound she stopped, her nerves quivering like plucked guitar strings. But she continued, forcing herself to stay focused on the task at hand. She had to get this. Had to! She couldn't let herself fret about every nuance of sound. The doubts and worries her mind might allow would be toxic, undermine her efforts, and cause mistakes she could not afford to make. No time for do-overs. No time for corrections.

She had to hold onto the honorable sense, if not the clear determination, that what she was doing was the right thing. Bloodshed of humanity, where everybody suffered, fed upon itself, and horrors never got any better in the long run. No, she wasn't God. And bless that she couldn't wave a mighty hand to make everything right instantly. She was a woman with a pencil in her hand, producing something that might, indeed, promote change, or at least a climate for change. If nothing else, it might stop a senseless battle and make people stop, think, and—especially—hope.

She heard a noise in the hall outside—footsteps. She froze. The chandlery was still bustling with people. Banter rose outside the locked door. "I tol' you, hemp rope was better for the job, but no, you got your own head about it," she heard one man say. The second man replied, chuckling, "I'll agree if that's the only way to get you to leave me alone."

Then she heard a jangle of keys. She stared at the shadow of a man cast onto the office door's frosted glass. Was the doorknob turning? In another second, she would be discovered standing in the middle of the floor, looking guilty as sin, with a death grip on the plans.

Just a couple of more lines were left to draw. She was a firestorm of activity as she balled the traced pages into her fist and into her pouch. She was rolling up the plans when there was a jiggling of the doorknob.

Where had she put the twine that tied the ends? She spied them on a low side table. She snatched them up, and hands shaking, managed to tie the ends together again. She still held them when she heard a passerby in the hall call out to the men, "Tom! Walt! Good to see you!"

Thankfully, Tom and Walt took a moment to ask after the man's family before they turned back to the office door. She had barely set the roll back on the coffee table and made it back to Simeon's lunch setting when the door opened.

A heavyset man in a Navy uniform uttered, "What the hell?" He was glaring at Mary.

"Don't worry, Tom," the other Navy man said. "That's that famous colored woman who makes dresses. She belongs to the Louvestres. Mary, isn't it?" he asked as he smiled a bit.

"Yes, sir."

The first man looked at her with distrust. "What you doin' back in here?"

"I brought Simeon his lunch and was setting it out for him." She made her voice pleasant.

"We come for a long pack of papers," the heavyset man said. "You seen 'em?"

"I haven't had a chance to tidy up," Mary said as she glanced casually at the clutter of the office. She nodded her head toward the low table. "Maybe what you're looking for is over there by the fireplace? That's the only long packet I see. I'd be happy to look around for you."

The heavyset man lumbered over, snatched up the thick roll, and headed out. The other man put two fingers to his hat as a courtesy.

And they were gone.

Mary's knees had as much strength in them at that moment as spit in the wind. If not for her walking stick, they would have given out. Shaking, she held herself upright and willed herself to calm down.

Goodness gracious! Even though her nerves weren't worth the broken stuffings of a doll, she still stood. That was something, wasn't it? She had to believe that it was.

CHAPTER 43

The return ferry from Portsmouth was pulling into dock when Mary spotted Devereaux. He was upset and waiting anxiously for her. As soon as they moved a short distance from others who were departing, he said, "More tragic news I must give you. Things have gone from bad to worse. Travelers Rest has been torched."

"Coolie?" Mary's voice implored him.

He shook his head and shrugged helplessly. "One of The Travelers got word to me there was a blaze and much gunfire. It is a mess. As they tried to put out the fire, Gates and his bunch lay in the long grass picking them off."

Mary stopped walking and repeated, "What about Coolie?"

Devereaux laced and unlaced his fingers. He glanced away from her. "She was mad as a wet hen. She went after Gates with a gun."

Mary's fingers flew to her lips, silencing a cry. Then she hurried toward the carriage. "Get me there."

"What? It is true craziness out there. Madmen are trying to kill each other!"

Mary whipped around. "If you don't take me, I'll drive myself. What's it going to be?"

Devereaux raced the carriage as best he could through the crowded streets. As they approached Travelers Rest, they heard gunfire and saw white puffs of smoke curl above the treetops. Where the road bent into a V-shape, Mary told Devereaux to stop. She maneuvered from the carriage and started up the path toward the main building when two men broke through the corridor of trees. In the arms of one was the limp body of a woman. It was Coolie.

"Thurston Stone!" Mary cried. "Jitter!"

"It's not as bad as it looks," Thurston said. "Coolie's unconscious. Took a blow to the head after she got off a shot at Gates."

Devereaux helped Jitter carry Coolie tenderly to the carriage. Once they got her inside, Thurston said, "I'm going back. We're going to fight this out 'til we see who's standin' last. Take care of her, Miss Mary. I don't think Gates is hurt bad, maybe a flesh wound. But when he gets on his feet again, Coolie's life won't mean as much as pig slop."

"I want to get her home," Mary said impatiently.

"I'm comin' too," Jitter said, starting to enter the carriage.

"Jitter," Thurston said, "we need to go back. It's a dogfight and we've got to help The Travelers."

Mary nodded. "Go. I'll take care of her."

Reluctantly, not wanting to leave, Jitter backed away. He chewed on the inside of his jaw, then bit his bottom lip.

"Come on! Now!" Thurston urged. "We've got to go. Mary's got her."

As Mary enfolded a moaning Coolie into her arms, and Devereaux pushed the horses to their limit, Jitter hesitated a moment longer, watching. "Comin' as fast as I can!" he called, then did a quick trot, cursing his still stiff boots as he disappeared back into the smoke and woods behind Thurston.

—•—

All was bedlam at Travelers Rest. Scattering patrons and posse were indistinguishable from each other as bullets from rifles and pistols strafed errantly from both sides. Cries from the wounded rose on the wind. Gates had led a garrison of twelve men, sitting tall in the saddle, well-armed, mean, and ready to tussle.

Around the previous night's campfire, he had laid out his plan to destroy Coolie's place. Each one was given a job and accepted his orders roundly. They had waited patiently until midday, when Travelers Rest would be bustling. As they got close, Gates jumped off his horse and bellied along the riverbank, aiming to reach the inn carrying a jar of kerosene stuffed with a thick rag to set on fire and toss through the inn's big window. He actually hoped Coolie was not inside. He wanted to destroy her inn, not her.

Gates crawled as close to the inn as he dared. With the window in sight, he rose to his knees, lit the fuse, and hurled the incendiary. His aim missed shattering the window, but he was gratified as an enormous swoosh of fire spread along the porch.

Instead of sending those inside scattering like dead leaves to the wind, the men inside Travelers Rest did not panic. It seemed they were ready for the attack. Some fired out windows, others poured out shooting. Gates's men, surprised by the show of firepower, took it upon themselves to shoot without his directive. Then, when the man closest to Gates took a fist-sized hole in his thigh, he was helpless to stop them from splitting off, diving into long grass, and taking cover behind trees. Gates tore off in a run to hide in a fencing of brush during the long exchange of shots, but he nearly staggered when he rose up to call the charge. His worst nightmare appeared through the shimmering dust and bluish smoke.

"Snake! You ain't nothin' but a low-down snake!"

Gates squinted to make out more clearly the figure he thought he saw. "Coolie!" he cried. Then his ears registered a loud crack as he began to lunge forward. He looked stunned at her as his left leg went out from under him. Despite the pain that felt like a branding iron, instinct told him to roll. As he did, he grabbed a rock.

"I want a piece of you! You goin' down!" Coolie screamed as she advanced on him.

With his remaining energy, Gates hurled the rock in her direction, hoping to slow if not stop her before he collapsed in the mud.

Coolie cursed as the stone hit her in the head, and she too went down. She could hear Jitter and others calling her name as they searched for her, but when she tried to answer, the intensifying smoke set her to choking. She knew if she was to survive, she had to get to the river. Digging her fingernails into the moist grass, she dragged herself along. Sweat and blood trailing down her forehead stung her eyes. Grunting, she heaved herself forward with all she had. But earth and sky became a dizzy swirling of shapes she could no longer identify as she hurtled down the slope to the water.

Roguey was at the front gate when Devereaux drew the carriage to a stop.

"I knew from the clip-clop of the horses trouble was comin'," Roguey said, helping Mary step out. Then she saw Coolie lying on the seat. "A'Lawd!"

"She'll be okay," Mary said. "Gates whacked her on the head with a rock, but Thurston told me Coolie did him one better. She shot him."

"Oh my soul!" Roguey cried. "Is he dead?"

"No, but I'm not sure how badly he's hurt."

Roguey sucked her teeth. "This girl be banging on the jailhouse door!"

With Devereaux assisting, they soon had Coolie lying on the divan in Mary's salon.

Roguey looked at her head. "She gon' have a goose egg for sho."

Coolie came around with little pants and moans, then tried to sit up as Mary applied a cool cloth to her forehead. Coolie looked up at her. "Did I kill him?"

Mary shook her head and turned to Devereaux at the door. "I've got to get Coolie away. Will you drive us? No questions asked?"

Devereaux did not hesitate. "I, Devereaux Rainier Leodegrance de Perouse, will deliver you to safety."

"We'll be ready within the half hour."

"And so shall I."

Mary returned to Coolie's side. "How are you feeling?"

"The room's turnin' 'round on me like I'm drunk." She touched the top of her head and winced. "But I'm okay. And if Gates ain't dead, he gonna be."

"You want somethin' to drink?" Roguey asked.

"I ain't never gon' turn down good liquor," she said with a lopsided smile.

"Just a jigger," Mary said. "We'll be leaving soon."

"Leavin'?" Coolie asked, leaning her head back and closing her eyes.

"Where we goin'?"

"Away," Mary said. Suddenly, she felt woozy herself and sat down next to Coolie.

Roguey looked concerned. "Wha's the matter?"

For a moment, Mary couldn't speak. She hadn't expected it to come so soon, but here it was. Time to go. She had the plans secreted in her gourd. Maps had been studied. Travel gear was ready, although packing for two hadn't been part of her plan. Somehow time had moved too fast. The fact was she had to get Coolie to safety. Perhaps Richmond might be far enough. All Mary knew at the moment was she couldn't let Coolie stay in Norfolk. Coolie might be nonchalant about Gates and the violence he represented, but Mary wasn't.

She let her eyes roam the marvelous setting that was her salon, the place that had been both her solace and the center of her creativity. For years, she had defined herself in this room. The prospect of leaving it left her weak. Tears glistened in her eyes as she took in the long mahogany worktable, the drafting table with pullout drawers made for her by Simeon, the Chippendale desk and accessories. She smiled looking at the ever-present buffet provided by Roguey. Hers had only been to ask. She had loved it here.

Mary took Roguey's arm and ushered her over to the elegant inlaid-mahogany chiffonier. She opened the double doors and extracted a large package wrapped in a cloth and tied with twine. She handed it to the cook and smiled. "For you. But open it later."

"I ain't waitin'," Roguey said, tearing into it to see a shoulder pouch made from fine brown leather that closed with a brass hook. She ran her fingers gently across it. "I declare. You made this for me?" She glanced at a nodding Mary while examining the expert stitching with her fingers outside and inside. She touched on a packet in the bottom of the pouch. When she took it out, she saw it was wrapped in muslin.

Mary placed her body between Roguey's and Coolie's line of sight.

Roguey's eyes widened in disbelief as she opened the flannel pouch. It was full of gold coins. "No you didn't!" she exclaimed.

"Look," Mary said, "I don't know if Gates or some of his men are going to turn up here any minute looking for Coolie. We've got to go. The Louvestres think I'm leaving to tend to a sick friend up near Richmond."

Roguey clutched her packages to her chest. "If y'all ever get up Tennessee way, be sure to look me up." She patted the pouch. "Sooner than later, it's gon' be me'n Jewel Baxter and a wagon headin' west." She and Mary hugged fiercely. Then, looking her in the eye, she made a simple statement. "You always got a frien'."

Mary's eyes began to well up as she tore herself away from the cook's embrace. She extracted from the bottom of the chiffonier two large tapestry valises, her beaver medicine pouch, and a long gourd tied with ropes on each end.

"Let's get to the carriage," Mary said.

The two women hurried Coolie from the salon, down the corridors through the entry to the front door where Devereaux stood waiting. Goaded by the knowledge that Gates and his men could be bearing down upon them at this minute, they urged the younger woman along to make their escape.

"Y'all pushin' me," Coolie complained. "I'm doin' the bes' I can."

As soon as Devereaux saw them, he dashed forward to take Mary's bags and the women followed him out to the carriage. Once they were able to get Coolie settled in the back seat with a blanket around her, Mary turned to Roguey. Their look was soft on each other.

At that instant they heard the sound of hoofbeats. In alarm, Roguey and Devereaux were about to hurl Mary into the carriage when the lone rider pounded up the curved driveway, kicking up dust behind him.

"Wait!" Roguey exclaimed. "It ain't Gates."

As the rider approached, they realized he was a black youth. Breathless, he reined up and yanked off his battered hat. "I'm glad I caught you," he panted. "Well, no I ain't."

"What!" Roguey exclaimed impatiently.

"Mr. Simeon sent me, Miss Mary." Then he seemed to stall. He stared down at the ground.

"Say it or don't say it," Roguey insisted, "but do somethin'!"

"The explosion on the *Virginia*—the ship. It was bad, real bad. Lots of men got hurt. Some killed." His eyes regarded Mary sadly, and he dropped his voice almost to a whisper. "Anders was one of them."

Mary stared at him, mouth open, waiting for his next words. "And?"

"The boiler blew. He helped the other men get out, but before he could get to the hatch the steam got him." The boy gulped. "I'm sorry. Anders didn't make it. Tore him up somethin' fierce." He looked from Mary to the others, and not knowing what else to say, swung his horse around and galloped off.

Silence seemed to go on forever. Devereaux and Roguey watched Mary, not knowing what to expect or what to say. Roguey grabbed Mary's arm as much in support as in consolation.

Mary stood, just blinking. Little registered from what the young messenger had said. As though something snapped her back to reality, she asked, "What did he say? Anders is hurt? He needs me. I have to get to him. Right now."

She wrested herself away from Roguey and started into the carriage. "Take me to Anders. I have to get to him."

Devereaux didn't move. He just stared at her, not knowing how to answer.

Mary's eyes flashed in anger. "What are you waiting for? We've got to go to Anders now!"

Roguey grasped Mary's shoulders and whirled her around so they were face to face. She spoke tenderly. "You can't go to him. It's too late. He's gone."

"What do you mean? I have to go."

"Mary, he's done crossed over," Roguey said more firmly. She pulled Mary to her breast and held her for a moment.

Mary lifted her head to look into Roguey's eyes as realization hit with concussive force. Like a child, she put her hands to her ears, hoping that not hearing would keep it from being real. "No," she shouted, yanking away. But Roguey wouldn't let her go. "No, no, no," she muttered, each one softer than the last, until she was just sobbing the words into Roguey's strong shoulder.

The cook took a large cloth from her apron pocket and dabbed at Mary's eyes, allowing her to cry, but just for a moment, knowing Gates might turn the corner at any time. Then, Roguey stepped back and shook her.

"Listen chile, you prob'ly can't understand much of what I'm tellin' you right now, but three things done happened in a row. Three bad things. Daddy A.B. gon' make yo' life hell if you stay. Gates likely know Coolie with you already, and he be comin' for sho'. Now this. Anders is dead, but you can't grieve him now. You want to live, you got to go. You got to go. You hear me?"

Mary watched Roguey's lips move, but she heard no sound. She saw the old cook's rough hands clutch hers. With her legs feeling like lead, she grasped her walking stick and allowed Devereaux and Roguey to help her toward the carriage. Abruptly, she stopped. Yanking away from them, she hustled back inside the house. "Something I've got to get."

"Mary! Lawd, she done los' her min'!" Roguey said, watching Mary's retreating back, then swiveled to scan the roadway.

In another moment, Mary returned. She was pushing an envelope into her pocket.

"Git on in that ride, girl. Now!" Roguey demanded.

As Mary's feet cleared the top step, Roguey slammed the carriage door. Glancing up at Devereaux, already on the driver's bench, she shouted, "Go!"

Devereaux set the horses on a dead run.

Mary became aware of the rocking motion of the carriage and looked out into the muted light of evening. She squeezed her eyes shut as the rush of words echoed in her head: *Anders is dead.* Involuntarily she pressed her palms against her ears, heaved a dry sob, and closed her eyes. She slumped unconscious against the seat.

With tears spilling down her cheeks, Coolie took the blanket off herself and tucked it over Mary, then laid her head on her friend's lap.

⸺•⸺

When Mary woke again, early dawn peeped over the treetops in soft ribbons of rosy hues. She glanced around. She was still inside the carriage, but it had stopped. Poking her head out the window, she could make out Devereaux coming out of the trees along the road bank. Only when she tried to pull herself upright did she notice Coolie's absence. She opened the door and aimed herself out, nearly falling face forward from the pain of a throbbing headache. Swaying and feeling nauseous, she forced herself to pause and get her bearings. As she did so, the churning in her stomach lessened some, but she still put one hand on the side of the carriage for support and held tightly to her walking stick with the other. She waited until she calmed, then proceeded toward Devereaux.

"Mademoiselle," he said, "you are better?"

"Yes. A bit. Where's Coolie?"

At that instant, Coolie rounded a wide tree, resituating her clothes. "Had to take care of business," she said. She let her eyes examine Mary. "Lemme get you some water. Where's that canteen?"

"It is there," Devereaux said, pointing to the driver's seat. He helped Mary to a large rock in a small copse of trees and eased her to sit.

"Where are we?" Mary asked, taking the canteen from Coolie. She drank, feeling the soothing liquid flow down her parched throat.

"Just outside Richmond," Devereaux said.

"I slept that long?"

"Oui. About Anders, I am so sorry. It is very hard ..."

Mary flushed with unwelcome memories. She held up a hand to him. "Thank you. But not now, please."

Coolie looked from Mary to Devereaux. She clasped and unclasped her hands. She stared at the ground, then smiled at a thought. Pawing through the bag she had over her shoulder, she came up with a hairbrush. Mary accepted the grooming gesture as Coolie lifted the kufi from her head and began running the brush gently through Mary's hair.

"You want to talk?"

Mary shook her head. Talk about Anders was the last thing she wanted to do right now. If she did, she feared she would hear herself reveal how much she loved him, and the shame she felt for not telling him. He'd wanted so much to hear her say that she loved him as much as he loved her. But she had told herself she was being practical, even responsible, not to do so.

After a moment, her thoughts returned to the task at hand, to the urgency of the moment. She straightened her shoulders, stood up, and headed toward the carriage. There was a job to do that one only she could do. She hated to slip away from the memory of Anders for even a short time, but she knew to her soul her grieving would be long-lasting.

Coolie and Devereaux watched her, puzzled. As she strode along purposefully, Mary glanced back at them, still standing where she left them. "Well, are you two waiting for kingdom to come? Let's go!"

Mary looked up to a clearing blue sky. She must move on. She couldn't—she wouldn't—fail. Anders wouldn't have it.

CHAPTER 44

At a turn in the road outside Richmond, Mary asked Devereaux to curb the carriage. She got out. They had traveled nearly all day, and Devereaux thought they just wanted to stretch and take a break.

"Coolie and I will be leaving you here."

"But ... but mademoiselle," Devereaux stammered, "we are nowhere."

Mary pulled a velvet pouch from her tapestry bag and handed it to her favorite driver.

He glanced inside, and his eyes rolled open. "I do not know what is this."

"Simeon told you that he would not buy Ann-Marie, and you were not to see her again."

"Yes," Devereaux said, shaking his head. "Yet I cannot live without her."

"So now you don't have to," Mary said. "There's enough in there for you both to begin a new life."

"Mon Dieu! I have helped so many others to a new life. I never figured a way for myself and my Ann-Marie."

"What matters is what you figure to do now," Mary said as she lifted her tapestry bag from the carriage.

Devereaux was quickly there to help. "I will collect my Ann-Marie. We can do this."

"Yes," Mary said, "yes, you can."

Coolie said, "Y'all gon' run?"

"Oh, indeed!" Devereaux said jubilantly. Happiness was manifest all over him. Taking Mary's hands, he pumped them and gushed, "How can I ever thank you?"

"By never looking back," she said.

Devereaux grinned at the two women. "'Y'all gon' run?'" he mocked Coolie with a grin.

"Like rabbits," Mary said as she and Coolie picked up the bags.

Coolie smiled widely, shrugged her shoulders, and said, "Guess we is."

Within a half hour of setting out on foot, following a jog into the woods, the women came upon a small, deserted shed. Pushing their way inside through a creaking door, it provided some haven from the bitter bite of the cold wind.

"What we gon' do in here?" Coolie asked.

"Dress for the road," Mary said, opening the traveling bags.

She pulled out tops and pants for herself and Coolie. In another bag she had secreted a backpack, having constructed it after the military haversack. Provisions were inside: foodstuffs, more clothes, and a few tools that might be needed. Under it was rolled bedding, a small hatchet, and a large knife. She also had packed the gun—fully-loaded—given to her by Tesh-Lucianne, and extra bullets.

"It's as cold out here as a muskrat's toes," Coolie said, jumping up and down to warm herself. "It's a little snug, but I love my outfit."

"I didn't have time to make one just for you," Mary said while dressing. "It's my size, but we'll make do."

"What's it made of?"

"Buckskin, to be durable, lined with flannel for warmth. We have a ways to go. But just in case they're not warm enough I have a similar outfit of wool. We may have to share."

"Pants," Coolie said, preening and modeling them for Mary. "Why didn't I ever think of wearing them before? They're so cute."

"Cute doesn't matter. Don't forget the moccasins."

Coolie held them up and squealed with delight. "Knee-length and," she peered inside, "what's that?"

"Lamb's wool, to help protect against blisters and keep your feet warm too. I hope it's not much of a squeeze because the last trouble you need on the trail is hurting feet. Moccasins won't squeeze your feet like hard leathers."

Mary looked around the dismal space. The cracked and splintered shelter walls barely stood erect. They creaked and groaned in the sway of every wind. Laid out now in a circle on the dirt floor—with its perimeter of hairy dust, spider webs, and other debris—were the provisions she'd packed. They now seemed sparse. She had not planned for a companion on this journey.

So much had happened so fast, she hadn't had a chance to think further about what to do with Coolie. Spur of the moment was to get her away from Gates. It didn't seem right to ask Devereaux to take Coolie into Richmond alone, not that she would have gone with him anyway. Further, Mary had not had a chance to make any contact for Coolie there. Maybe she could coax Coolie to join one of the Underground Railroad conductors at the first station they reached, to escape north. Given what she had heard in talk from Bear and other Travelers, she had only a possible idea of where such a way station might be. As she glanced out at the lowering light of the pewter sky, she sensed they'd better get going once more.

Mary was about to take up a bag when her ears picked up a swooshing sound. She tried to dismiss it, but she knew that now she had to pay close attention to everything around her. She stood stock-still, listening intently. What was that? Wind through the fingers of a tree branch? The rustling of a dried brush rolling errantly by? The hair on her neck told her otherwise. She looked out through a crack in the wall. Movement, wasn't it, not far from the shed? What if someone were out there lurking? Fear began to set up in her gut, but she knew she could not reveal this to Coolie.

Coolie began to speak, but Mary indicated for her to shush.

"What is it?"

Mary grabbed her arm and threw her a stern look. Frightened, Coolie stopped.

Scooting closer to a ragged crack in the wall, Mary studied the landscape. She relaxed her face and narrowed her eyes, letting them rove slowly in search of anything out of place. After awhile, she stood straight again.

"Did you see somebody?" Coolie whispered, eyes wide.

"No. It was probably the wind. But we better hurry."

Coolie watched Mary expertly recheck her knife and pistol. Mary slung across her body the shoulder strap of the hollowed-out gourd containing the ship's blueprints. She looked directly at her younger friend.

"I'm not going to kid you, Coolie, this trip is not going to be easy. I have no idea what or who we'll meet along the way. When our food runs out—and it surely will soon—we'll have to forage. We've a long way to go, and honestly, I'm not always going to be sure of the right direction. But we're going. We won't be seeing towns or townspeople for a while. We need to skirt them to ensure more safety. You got this?"

"Where we goin'?" Coolie asked, ignoring her last question.

"North," Mary said. She looked up at the sky, clouds the color of gunmetal gray rolling in.

"Will that be far?"

"Not if we had good horses, great weather, a really thorough, detailed map, and good sense," Mary joked, trying to lighten the mood. She looked down at the middle finger of her left hand, at the gold ring she wore showcasing the elegant Louvestre crest. Touching it delicately for a long moment, she pulled it off, slipped it in a small pouch in her bag, and stood for a moment, fighting off rising emotion. This is it, she thought, no going back now. She smiled wanly and grasped her gold-headed walking stick. With a deep breath, she said, "Ready for adventure, young spirit?"

"Don't know about all that, but I'm ready to follow you."

⸺⸱⸻

Curious-er and curious-er, thought Gates, watching the women covertly. Gates had been sitting atop his favorite chestnut, Nomad, in the shadows of the Louvestre drive. He'd had a strong sense that Coolie would somehow get to Mary. He'd scratched his chin and let his gray eyes follow the dancing curve of a flying bird overhead as he told himself not to act precipitously. Hidden in a copse of maples near the Louvestre home, he caught a glimpse of Mary and Coolie inside the carriage, which Devereaux was forcing the horses to haul ass fine-tuned. Gates knew he was onto something. He decided to follow. This might prove interesting.

Now, from his vantage point a distance away, the deputy saw Mary and Coolie enter a shack, and after a while, exit—wearing buckskin, of all things.

"Well, well," he said to himself as he stroked the stubble on his chin. The hunter in him was tweaked. He licked his lips and smiled cannily. Whatever they're up to, he thought, this'll make for great sport. This was a game. They were on foot, and he was on his righteous steed. No contest.

After a few hours rest, the women pushed on before dawn to get a head start on the day. They trudged along, barely able to see one foot in front of the other, making a path where there was none, but soon the thin ribbon of color over the hills broadened in the gathering light. During the night, the temperature had dipped to teeth-chattering cold, but the landscape was crisp and beautiful.

"I can see my breath in front of my face," Coolie complained. "Can it get any worse than this?"

"Yes," Mary said, quickening the pace.

"How can you walk so daggone fast with your bum leg? I can hardly keep up." Coolie followed along what passed for the trail. Trying to convince herself, she said, "This trip might not be so bad. Yeah. Yeah. I can do this. Ah! Nature!"

Mary laughed but did not divert her attention from the terrain. She did not want to lead them in circles. She knew from her days in the woods that it was easy to get disoriented, especially in a steady wind. It plays tricks on the brain just as being extremely cold does. The route was proving to be more difficult than she imagined, with too many creeks, streams, and treacherous ice pockets. "So tell me again where we're headin'?" Coolie asked. Looking down, she picked her way over jagged rocks. She held her arms out like a bumbling high wire circus performer, slipping and sliding, teetering, unable to keep her balance. "Hellfire!" she cried. "What could be so dang important for us to be out here in this godforsaken place, doin' godforsaken stuff, to get to God only knows where?"

"We're on a mission."

"Ow!" Coolie exclaimed as she stubbed her toe on a rock. The heavy backpack made her turn leeward. "What kinda damn fool mission?"

"To save your life, for one."

"Yeah? Then what?"

"Then there's someplace I've got to be."

"Without me?"

"Coolie, let's just do this for now," Mary stated and walked on.

Coolie muttered to herself, peeved. When her backpack caught in a low-hanging willow tree branch, she went splat to the ground. There she sat splay-legged, gathering a genuine snit. She hadn't asked for this. She just wanted a toot to wherever Mary was going. Now she realized at first chance Mary might dump her. The heck with this! She charged up, slinging off the pack. "Look, you can take your rescue work and put it in a pipe and smoke it!" She stalked off.

Mary kept walking.

Came a rustle in the woods just ahead of her, and Coolie pulled up. Looking around, she realized Mary was nowhere near. Alarmed that a bear might have her in his sights, she turned tail. Retrieving the backpack, she hollered, "Hey! Wait!" She stumbled after Mary, who was some distance ahead. "What about rescuing me now? I coulda been a bear supper, all carved up for momma and daddy and baby bear to eat."

"Oh, I thought it was only a snake."

Coolie searched down at her feet, picking them up gingerly. "Snake? What kinda snake?"

"A big one."

"Goat turd on a tin roof on a hot summer day!" Coolie cursed.

They continued about a mile before Coolie began to drop back, plodding along at a slower pace. Mary kept leading the way, moving on, casting an eye back at her unhappy companion.

Were this a leisurely stroll, Mary would have regarded the woods as spectacular. The trees' gnarled branches etched black against a dusky-blue sky. A few low bushes were still showy with fading blossoms of rust, orange, and mustard. Autumn wildflowers carpeted the thin grasses sloping along their walk and competed with towering cattails.

Mary was happy to finally see a stand of birch. Using her hatchet, she lopped off a few small twigs and some bark. She tied them onto her bag.

As they traveled, they came upon occasional small pools from which they drank and refilled their canteens. Mary found a fallen log and made a quick meal of jerky and some dried berries she'd collected along the way. Coolie muttered that no one could live long on a diet like that, but seeing Mary's serious expression, she grew quiet and just ate.

"Sittin' on cold rocks and logs could give us the piles," Coolie whined. "Don't you know that?"

"Are you straining?"

Coolie darted a look at Mary. "When I had any time to do much 'sides squat 'tween two shoes and squeeze a little water?"

"Well then, when the call comes, you're in for a surprise and a relief."

Coolie cocked a look at Mary. "If I wasn't sure, I'd swear you been drinkin'."

Mary chuckled.

Much later, as the sky deepened into a flow of evening colors, Mary began to scan the area for a place to set up for the night. Valley areas were unacceptable because the cold that descended at night would make the temperature much colder. Hilltops were susceptible to more wind and that would keep them cold too. What she was searching for was a place on the south side of a ridge or tree grove where the sun had provided the longest-lasting heat and the ground would be warmer. She also had to find a place near fresh water.

Finally, when they were both dog-tired, she located just what she wanted: an area open enough that she wouldn't have to worry about setting things on fire when she made camp and a high rock wall at their backs to conceal them. Mary cleared leaves and debris from around an embankment, then took a wide length of cloth from her bedroll and began collecting fresh pine sprigs.

"That for the fire?" Coolie asked.

"Some of it," Mary said. "But you know pine on its own doesn't make a good fire. Most of it's for our beds. It'll not only make a good mattress that smells fresh, but also keep our weary bones off the cold ground. Get some of that brush over there, will you? We need to keep it light and airy underneath us." Coolie fetched the brush, then followed Mary's directions for collecting ferns, mosses, and other leaves for their bedding.

Mary next searched around until she found a long pole. When she could not find another on the ground, she sized it with a low-hanging tree branch and, using her hatchet, cut that one the same length as the other. After she dragged them back to camp, she went looking for a sturdy branch about the thickness of her arm to make into a ridgepole or a pole she'd set between the forks of two trees. She found what she was looking for not far away, and soon pounded them all into the ground. Leaving the east side open toward the firepit and the morning sun, she filled in the west side with sticks and brush and thatched deadwood and some large maple tree leaves to create a sloping roof. Finally, she piled a few inches of sod on top of the leaves and bark slabs to keep the wind from blowing away the leaves. When she was finished, it was tall enough for both women to stand inside and long enough for them to sleep comfortably.

"How come you know 'bout these things?" Coolie asked as she watched.

Mary paused and stretched her back. "Know about what things?"

"Survivin' out here kinda stuff. Livin' off the land like some kind of trapper or hunter or Injun or somethin'."

"Before my knee got busted, I studied the old medicine ways with Miss Effie. She taught me tracking and hunting too. My daddy, Tug, taught me more. And he trained me to fight with my stick." She indicated her walking stick nearby.

"I'll be," Coolie said. "What you don't know 'bout one 'nother."

Mary maneuvered down toward the water's edge where she used her hatchet to chop off the heads of several cattails. She next built a windbreak and reflector behind the firepit she'd established. It would send out more light and heat into the shelter.

Huddled in a blanket, Coolie sat on a boulder and watched Mary with amazement. The wind sighed around them, but where they were situated, its cold bite could not take a plug out of them.

Mary picked up the cattails she'd cut, opened the heads with her knife, and tore out the fluff of seed heads onto a bed of birchbark. She struck a couple of matches before the fluff began to smolder and flame. As the fire got going, Mary fed it with dried twigs. Coolie was instantly cheered as she stuck her feet toward it.

Mary used her hatchet again and cut a branch from a willow tree. She trimmed it to make a fishing pole. Then she extracted from her bag a ball of twine and a fishhook. She searched around and found a couple of fallen bird feathers that she made into a bobber. Under a log she found a worm to work over the barb, then went to the river and cast out. Puffy clouds had taken on a scarlet hue. Mary smiled to herself, taking a moment to wonder if clouds mated in the sky to produce such outrageous color.

Ripples circled out and a huge bass surfaced for a moment and darted back under. In another moment, Mary's line snapped taut. She worked her pole and line expertly and soon strung the big fish through its gills onto another small branch and carried it back to camp.

After scaling and gutting her catch, Mary speared it to rotisserie over the fire. In another pot Mary fed a handful of rice into roiling water. As the fish began to sizzle over the flame, she dusted it with herbs from her pack. Soon Coolie's mouth was watering at the scent.

"That's one fine fish you done put up here," Coolie said, drawing her knees up to her chest as she watched, fascinated. Mary had been lucky enough to also find some cress in the wet base of a tree. This she began to sauté with some wild onion in a little butter she had liberated from Roguey's kitchen.

"This tasty treat," Mary said of the rolled butter as she held it up for Coolie to see, "won't last us long. But for now, we dine well." She dropped another dollop into the cress, along with some salt and pepper.

Coolie ate ravenously. Mary ate too, but slowly, appreciating every taste.

"Uhn, unh, unh. Give me a little mo'?" Coolie sucked butter and herbs from her fingers. "Lawd a mercy, you done good. Oh. Oh. Yes. This is good. Oh."

"Coolie, you make eating a very sensual experience."

"Hell, food this finger-lickin', I might run naked in these woods hollering hallelujah!"

"Remember the bear," Mary chided mischievously.

"You sure know how to ruin the moment." Coolie pretended to pout as she took another bite.

Mary sighed happily.

Dessert was coffee and a couple of sweet biscuits. Finally, Coolie sat back, closing her eyes. "Them was precious vittles," she murmured, "Gawd bless me today and tomorrow."

Mary laughed out loud. Coolie, mouth open and beginning to snore, didn't move.

The stars were full out when Mary woke Coolie after driving four sticks into the ground near the fire. Coolie was incredulous when told to remove her moccasins. Mary repeated that they had to keep their footwear as dry as possible and take special care of their feet. She placed each shoe over a stake near the fire. She had heated river water in the large pot she had in her stores. "Coolie, put your little tootsies in here. I've soap to wash with."

"I just wanna lay back down," Coolie whined.

"Feet first," Mary said. After Coolie washed her feet in the hot water and dried them, Mary massaged honey-lemon balm into Coolie's skin. She handed her friend fresh socks—wool on the outside for warmth, cotton on the inside for comfort. They were red—Coolie's favorite color—and she was a kid again, thoroughly delighted.

Mary had put blankets over the pine needles and other soft gatherings of their makeshift beds. She sent Coolie into hers. And after washing and anointing her own feet, she put on fresh socks. Then she too lay down.

Somewhere close, an owl hooted. Another bird cawed and something chuffed. Mary was drifting off when she felt Coolie slide beside her.

"Don't want you gettin' scared," Coolie said, scooting close.

Mary allowed Cooley to snuggle, knowing it was calming the other woman's fears. She let her thoughts drift along on the cottony clouds of the night sky. The fire no longer blazed—she knew better than to do that—but its existence provided a modicum of safety. Animals were not likely to wander in where there was a fire. And, finally, she was warm. The day's trek had made her joints tighten and her leg ache, as she'd expected. Her mind turned to the days ahead. The way she figured, they had to do ten miles a day if they had any hope of reaching Washington before depleting their provisions.

Coolie placed an arm across Mary and began to make soft sucking noises. She remembered how Anders had done the same when he was lost in sleep. The pain of his death was still so fresh that she didn't want to recall his bed and his embrace. He'd so often reminded her how much he loved her, and that, no matter what, somehow they would be together one day. She shut her eyelids tight against a trickle of tears.

Suddenly, Mary quickened at a sound she knew did not belong. It was a soft noise, like a flatfooted shoe scudding against pliable ground. Beneath the blanket, Mary slipped her hand onto her belt loop and dislodged her knife.

Gates squinted. He felt fairly sure the women, especially Coolie, were not aware he was tracking them. Mary, though, was pretty wily. Tracking in the wilds, for him, was as natural as a fish swimming in water. He would find them and capture them. But first he'd thought he'd be patient and learn just why they were out here to begin with. Of course, any slave could try to run, but with these two that didn't add up. They were up to something. He'd wait on this a little bit. When he was ready, he would take them.

CHAPTER 45

The winds had shifted around from the north overnight, bringing cooler temperatures and leaving a thin frost by morning. Mary could see her breath.

She made hot coffee, cooked rice with dried fruit, and set out beef jerky, biscuits, and some of the precious butter to fuel them. Before they left camp, Mary drenched their fire with water, buried their trash, and swept the area with twigs and leaves— all before sunup. She wanted to put as much distance as possible between them and the disturbing sound she had heard the night before last.

Coolie tried gamely to keep pace with Mary but constantly muttered about the rugged terrain, snakes, being hungry or cold, the weight of her pack. "This ain't no fun no mo," Coolie called out to Mary, who was well ahead of her on the trail.

Their route led to a wooded valley with a burbling stream edged by thick, drying rhododendron patches before plunging into dense woods. Eventually, they faced a big rise of rock and vegetation almost lethal in appearance. Going up was the only option. Soon they were breathing hard. The sun was shining, but the cold was unyielding.

"I'm 'fraid to pee or poop," Coolie complained. "Might freeze goin' down."

"Then where would you be?" Mary asked. "Stuck."

"I'd have a long brown thing hanging between my legs," Coolie said. "Hmm. A long brown thing."

"If you don't stop," Mary laughed.

"It might have some uses." Coolie said, "You know, pokin' around."

"Girl ..."

"The thing might stretch from now to forever. Ain't that a thought? Mos' men don't know what to do with what they got. In and out, hump-a, hump-a.

And you s'posed to go all to pieces for the joy of the thing pokin' inside you. Ain't nothin' there to make the cheese mo' bindin', if you get my meanin'. Clabber my stomach just thinkin' about it."

Mary stopped and marched back to Coolie and got nose to nose with her. "Jack in the bush," she said, no humor in her at all.

"Sorry, I'll quit," Coolie said. "I'm just shootin' off at the mouth."

Mary walked back to where she had shucked her load, picked it up again, and headed out.

Coolie, trying to soothe herself, pulled a harmonica from a pocket and began to play softly. Mary stopped again, turned back, snatched the instrument from her, and stalked on ahead. Coolie was outdone. She set up muttering and complaining once more. Her legs were getting tired, she said. She knew she'd be sore in the morning, she complained. The backpack hurt her shoulders. Her feet hurt too. When were they going to stop and rest, get something to eat? "I'm hungry. Is the whole trip gonna be like this?" She irritably slapped her backpack to the ground with a thud.

Mary stopped and waited, looking as cool and collected as if they were not marching to Kingdom Come. Coolie, who looked the total opposite, finally caught up.

"My plan is to travel as far as we can before nightfall." Mary explained that the information she had gleaned earlier from The Travelers was that there should be a clearing not too far distant. "I know you're getting tired and hungry, but can you hold out for a little longer?"

Coolie reluctantly bobbed her head.

"Watch your footing. You don't want to trip and fall."

Coolie marched on behind Mary, trying to make a game of placing her footsteps into Mary's. She adored the woman. That was the only reason she was doing this crazy stunt. She lived a town life and couldn't think of anything she liked less than this. She believed in comfort. That was what she'd built Travelers Rest for. Before that redneck, peckerwood, no-nothin', ferret-faced, pasty-skinned cracker of a scoundrel had burnt it down! Oooh! If she could just get her hands around his stupid neck. She snorted angrily at the thought of Gates.

Coolie pulled out a corncob pipe and tobacco from a pocket. Nothing like Virginia tobacco to lift her spirits, she thought, trying to put memories out of her mind. Feeling calmer at the thought of its enjoyment, she packed the bowl, lit it with a match, and puffed. The tobacco was smooth, its smoke relaxing, like stretching out on warm turf. How satisfying. She smoked as she trudged after Mary, who carefully picked a way through the thick vegetation. Finally, after hours of walking in silence, Mary called to her, "We'll camp here."

As Coolie trudged closer, she suddenly saw Mary's knife flash with a vicious blow. A searing screech, then utter silence, sent horror through Coolie. Mary reached down and held up something for Coolie to see. A four-legged thing that looked like a big rat, with its head partially cut off, its yellow teeth shining, dripped blood into a pool on the ground.

"What is that thing?" Coolie asked, turning up her nose.

"Possum."

"I ain't never see'd a possum look like that," Coolie countered.

"Don't you worry about it. When it's cooked, you'll love it. Soup'll be up shortly."

She glanced at the creature and at Mary skeptically. The wind blew and Coolie hugged herself against the chill as she sat down on a rock.

Mary deftly skinned and gutted the creature, washed her knife and stuck it back into the loop on her belt. She looked over at Coolie. "You could get up off your apathy and help. Go gather wood for fire."

"A-pen-thy," Coolie repeated awkwardly, feeling the sounds across her tongue. "What's that?"

"Your lazy tail! I'm tired too," Mary said with growing annoyance.

"Listen to you. How come you ain't said nothin' 'fore you walk all over my back with sharp claws?"

"I assumed you'd pitch in."

Coolie looked forlornly at her sore feet. "Assumin' ain't tellin'. I'm s'posed to read yo' min'? When you think I became a gypsy with a crystal ball that I can look into the future or yo' min'—busy as it 'pears to be—to tell the first thing about what we need out here at any time anyways? Before you string me on the hangman's tree, least ways give me a clue first."

Mary stopped, looked up at Coolie, and began to laugh. Coolie's hair had gone wild in the wind. Leaves stuck to it like some ill-fitting crown. Dirt smudged her cheeks. Mary could only imagine she looked just as ridiculous, and the thought doubled her over with laughter. When the laughing began to subside, she wiped tears from her eyes and looked up at Coolie again.

The puzzled woman snorted. "What's so funny?"

Another roar of laughter hit Mary even harder, and she had to hold her gut. The more she tried to stop, the more she couldn't. Finally she panted, trying to catch her breath, and cried, "Whoo! I needed that." Then, still chortling, Mary set back to work. Coolie just shook her head.

In a short time, the two were sitting on blankets by the fire, having a fine dinner of roast possum, baked wild yam slices, and cattail soup.

Coolie stretched her bare feet close to the fire.

"I wouldn't scoot much closer to that blaze if I were you. Be kind to your feet."

"Be kind to my feet. Be kind to my feet," Coolie sang. She picked up two thick twigs and drummed a catchy march on the ground. She bobbed her head and rocked her shoulders in rhythm with the beat. "Be kind to my feet. Coolie, be kind to yo' feet. You need yo' feet. You got to love yo' feet. Gotta wash 'em up, gotta rub 'em down, gotta be kind, be kind, be kind to yo' feet."

Mary observed her as one might when assessing the need to dash and run.

Later, as Coolie cleaned up their makeshift dishes with sand and seawater and bussed the camp area, Mary put together mattresses of branches, twigs, and mosses she'd collected earlier. She was pleased that she could manage springy bedding instead of having to sleep on bare ground instead. They were settled into their beds, close to the fire's warmth. Sleep was coming on when a night bird shrieked.

Coolie's eyes shot open. "What was that?"

"Nothing."

"When do nothin' sound like that?"

"Go to sleep. Tomorrow will be here sooner than you expect."

The screech blared again, and Coolie wormed a little closer to Mary. "I ain't scared," she declared. "I ain't a-scared of nothin' ridin' nor walkin'. Sho'ly!" She darted a look all around to make sure there was nothing riding or walking.

Golden early-morning light too soon shimmered through a thin mist. Mary checked the campsite to make sure they had collected all their gear and that the fire had been buried. She stopped, looked out at the breathtaking sight, breathed in deeply, and exhaled.

Coolie watched her and did the same. She coughed. "My Gawd, what is that?"

"Fresh air," Mary answered as she set off, her walking stick taking charge.

"Lawd, glory on the half shell!" Coolie exclaimed, following after her.

"Where in the world do you get those quaint sayings?"

Coolie looked blank. "What?"

———•——

Mary wondered if it had sunk in to her friend yet what had actually happened, what they had done. They had left their homeplace. There would be no going back. The younger woman could imagine all she wanted that this was a swing into footloose adventure—a joke, nothing so dire as facing a new future fraught with danger and building a new life, wherever that might be. She had said nothing, and since whatever Coolie thought was usually quickly on her tongue, Mary surmised that to her this was just fantasy. It would come to her, and likely soon. She wondered if saying nothing was doing Coolie a disservice or even if she should have brought her along at all. Yet, what else could have been done?

As she and Coolie pressed on, Mary became aware that the wind kicking up was colder. She pulled her wrap closer around her and glanced over to see Coolie doing the same thing. She felt a flutter on her cheeks. She looked up to see fat snowflakes filtering down.

"This don't make no kinda sense," Coolie said.

Mary turned to her. "What?"

"How can the sun be shinin' and snow fallin' at the same time? Ain't that a clever God?"

"I'd say."

"Well," Coolie said, thinking it over. "Maybe God's confused. I know if I was God and had to do all He got to do every minute of every single day, I'd be confused."

"Coolie," Mary said, "you're a treasure trove of truly worthless but wonderful thoughts."

"Yes." Coolie bobbed her head, then jumped to a new subject. "What we gon' do if we meet somebody on the trail?"

"That depends."

"Yeah," Coolie pondered. "Tonight when we make camp, I'm gon' make me slingshot."

"You know how to use one?"

"I can pick the ink off a beer label at fifty feet."

"Now that's a worthwhile skill," Mary quipped.

"Yeah," Coolie agreed.

The damp soil, becoming muddy under the light snowfall, made for slow going, but at least their footing was clearer than in the underbrush of the dark forest. Mary was glad she had spent time waterproofing the moccasins. Even so, she could feel some dampness seeping in through the tight threads at the soles. No matter. She would make sure, when they stopped for lunch, to dry their boots by the fire, wash and anoint their feet with oils, and put on fresh socks. She prayed this was the worst of their worries.

When she reached the crest of a hill and glanced back, she was startled. She squinted over the trees. Even in the breezy air and gathering fog she was sure of what she saw. Smoke curled up. Campfire smoke. She was concerned for two reasons: One, whoever was behind them was either a bad camper, or two, a bad man who didn't care that the fire might be seen. Or was someone after them? Taunting them?

"Hey." Coolie's eyes turned on her. "Hey? What's going on?"

"Maybe nothing. Maybe something," was all Mary said.

"That's helpful information," Coolie said, being snide.

"Come on. Let's act like we've got someplace to go."

After another hour, Coolie called, "I'm hungry."

"Don't you have any other feelings? That one's getting old."

"To who?" countered Coolie. "Even a fool know he gotta eat."

"There are some dried berries in your pack. Eat them for now," Mary said. She felt fretful. "We've got to keep moving."

"You been actin' strange. What you ain't tellin' me?"

"It's nothing."

"Oooh! Oooh!" Coolie said, singing. "Mary tole a bad one and to one of her own kind. Quick, you got to make it right or your hair gon' fall out. And I don't mean the ones on yo' head."

Mary chuckled. "Coolie Parts, you've got to get hold of yourself. Discipline. Persistence. And quiet. Come on, now."

Ahead, they saw a young colored boy carrying a pail of water. He was singing. They waited until he passed through the brush. Not too far away, Mary spotted a shoddy barn set amongst a thicket of pines. Once inside, they crouched behind a pile of barrels. They were so close to each other that Mary could feel the nervous fear of Coolie and see the wetness of her bottom lip as it trembled. As their breathing quieted, Mary began to hear other sounds— muffled grunts and shuffles.

Holding up her hand to indicate Coolie should stay put, Mary picked her way back toward the sounds. She peeked over a stand of hay to see two youngsters enjoying themselves in a naked way. Apparently, they were not aware of her, so she sneaked back to Coolie, who looked at her questioningly. Mary shook her head.

"Excuse me," came a voice from behind them. They pivoted to stare into the vicious end of a shotgun trained on them by a half-naked, barefooted, young blonde fellow. "Who in hell are y'all niggers and what you doin' here in Pa's barn?"

Mary looked directly at him. "Where is here?"

"Who is it?" piped a young girl's voice.

"Stay back, Lee-Ann. It's a couple of women nigras." The boy's gun wavered but he held his eyes steady on Mary and Coolie. "Y'all tryin' to run or somethin'?"

"We've got business." Mary continued her direct look, which unsettled him.

"In this here barn?"

"We only stopped to rest," Mary said, gaining calm. "We've been on our journey for a couple of days and we're tired."

"Yeah?" The young man seemed interested.

The young girl called out in a singsongy voice, "Junior. Jun-ior." It was an invitation. He glanced behind him, then back at Mary and Coolie. "Well," he said to them, "if I was wantin' to get out of here right quick-like, I'd get myself down to the creek. They's a couple of boats. If I knew what was good for me, I'd get in one and take it across to Sawyer's Pass or down to Runion, which would get me a good distance away from here."

"Jun-ior."

"Look," he said, hopping from one foot to the other, the gun pointing south now. "I gotta go. I got business too."

"How come you helpin' us?" Coolie said, eyeing him suspiciously.

The boy grinned sheepishly and opened his hands. "Hey, we both tryin' to get lucky, ain't we?"

Pulse pounding, Mary and Coolie scurried through the heavy trees in a half-crouch. They made their way across a ranging field bereft of livestock, down an embankment where footing was slick, to a rickety dock. Two shabby canoes were tied up—one large, one small. Chill winds burned Mary's eyes, and she rubbed them, then darted a look back over where they had come.

"You think that boy set somebody after us?" Coolie said, breathing hard.

"Likely. He's not going to let it be said he helped some coloreds steal a boat now, would he?"

Mary decided to take the smaller one, figuring she could maneuver it more quickly and easily in the water. She fought with the retaining rope that was cinched by a thick fraying knot holding the canoe in dock. Though she knew well how to break anchor, she struggled because her hands were like ice and the aged rope splintered with each yank. In the marsh, fog swirled up in tall tendrils. With one more strong pull, she felt the rope give way.

"Finally!" Mary exclaimed as the boat rocked free. Blowing hard now, her breath was small, visible puffs in the air. She tossed her bags inside, patted the gourd strapped across her body to be sure it was still in place, then turned to urge Coolie to get in with her own pack.

Coolie resisted. She stood, staring. "I been livin' my whole life near a riverbank but ..."

"Come on," Mary insisted.

Coolie didn't move.

"But what?" Mary was growing impatient.

"But I never learned to swim," Coolie grumped. "I ain't gittin' in that thing."

"Coolie," Mary said in even tones as she climbed in and took up an oar, "I'm going to count to three. If you're not in here then I'm leaving without you."

Coolie looked around bleakly, then back at the boat where Mary had placed the oar in the water.

"One ..."

"Can you swim?"

"I'm a fish," Mary said.

Coolie's expression was dubious.

"Two ..."

A disturbing sound crashed behind them.

Mary cast an anxious glance at Coolie, who still stood wringing her hands, fretting, and muttering to herself.

"Get in the boat, Coolie. This is it. Three ..."

Another loud noise, and Coolie held her nose and jumped into the boat. Mary dug the oar deep into the current and pushed off.

Coolie's hands grabbed the rim, and she slowly opened her eyes to peek back into the thicket where a loud ruckus was mounting. A horse whinnied.

"You know how to drive one of these things?"

"The boat, you mean? Of course," Mary said. "And you don't drive it, you steer it."

Coolie's eyes never left the woods behind them. Movement swayed in the bushes. "I'd say you better get on with it then."

Mary glanced up to see a horse clopping out from the tall pines, followed by a man in a wagon. It was a man who looked a century old, as did his horse, hauling cords of firewood. She dug the oar into the water as hard as she could to propel them into the fog, not turning back to see that the commotion was not the threat she had imagined.

Not knowing what they might encounter, Mary rowed into the opal-colored fog hovering over the water. It seemed to swallow them whole within minutes. It was soupy, but the boat cooperated under Mary's hand as she regained old skills. Once free from the shore's muddy sludge, the boat began to move smartly.

Coolie continued surveillance, letting her eyes rake along the shoreline for sight of anyone who might be pursuing them. Soon, in the cottony mystery of the fog, it was impossible to tell if sounds on the water were close or far away.

They canoed what Mary guessed was a couple of miles as she kept their course parallel to the shore. Her aim was to put as much distance as possible between them and whoever might be pursuing. Rosy sunlight glazed the water in dancing ribbons and was lowering on the dusky horizon when Mary knew she had to rest. But they had no anchor. When she spied a large rock coming near, she unloosed a parse of rope from her belt and positioned herself, wide-legged for balance, to hook it.

"Hey!" Coolie cried, surprised. But before she could say more, Mary had circled the rope overhead and lassoed the craggy top of the rock. Pulling hand over hand, she hauled the canoe toward it. When the boat harbored at its side, she was able to secure it tightly, where it bobbed gently.

Coolie narrowed her eyes at Mary. "Tell me again, why am I doin' this?"

Mary's face, though ruined by fatigue, brightened at her irrepressible companion.

"I got to wee-wee," Coolie said. "All this ain't good for my nerves."

Mary laughed softly, then went silent when she saw a faint light arcing on shore. She heard a click—she knew she did. It was definitely a click. In an instant she'd launched herself onto Coolie and crushed them both to the bottom of the boat to conceal their position.

"Ooomph!" muffled Coolie through Mary's shoulder.

"Somebody's out there," Mary whispered urgently into her ear.

They both lay quiet and still. Mary's ears picked up the muffled sounds of more movement on shore. To her horror, gunfire rained at them in pops and screams. Mary's hand flew to cover Coolie's mouth.

After a time, the gunfire ceased. The air reeked of gunpowder. She slowly lifted off Coolie and peeked, wide-eyed, over the side of the boat toward shore. It was almost evening and shapes and forms blurred into a dark background. She hoped that the shooter was having a hard time seeing them too. After moments of quiet passed, she reached her arm up and quickly severed the rope from the rock with her knife. Pop, pop, pop! More blasts of peppering gunfire bombarded them. She fell back and rolled toward the side. Staying as low as possible, she grabbed the oar and pushed it into the water, coursing them on a zigzag path as the current carried them downstream. When she thought it was safe, she steered toward shore, where the boat eventually scudded onto a muddy bank.

"Come on," she yelled to Coolie as she grabbed up bags.

This time, Mary didn't have to ask twice. Coolie nearly bowled her over following suit.

CHAPTER 46

Mary set a fast pace for about an hour until it was too dark to see where they were going. They were freezing and hungry but grateful to have escaped. As they hurried, she kept search for a place to camp.

"Damn, how'm I gonna see that in the dark?" Coolie threw her a disdainful look, disappearing into the thicket to pee.

"Let me hear you out there," Mary said.

"Hear me what? Pee on a rock so you can find me?"

"Never mind. Just hurry."

While Mary waited, she spotted a depression in a small bluff that looked like the entrance to a cave or animal den. Just under its lip was a circle of rocks on the ground. Was that a cooking fire? When Coolie returned, hiking up her pants, Mary said, "You stay with the gear. I'll go check it out."

Coolie was not at all happy about Mary leaving her. She inched as close to the clearing as she could, watching Mary disappear into the cave. In seconds, she raced outside again. A white man, with the look of Christ's disciple or a lunatic, was chasing her with an upraised club. Coolie, alarmed, ran to help. She yanked the disciple's robe, causing him to trip over a log. He rolled and looked up at her, blinking.

"Now what did you go and do that for?" he said, scratching his head absently.

Coolie glared at him. "You were trying to kill my friend."

"Oh," he replied thoughtfully, "yes, that."

Both women, astonished and breathing hard, stared at him. Coolie picked up his club, ready to pounce if he made a wrong move.

"Help me up, girl," he said casually, addressing Coolie, holding out a limp hand. When she did not move, he cleared his throat and repeated his request.

Coolie reluctantly reached out and helped him up. The face that loomed in the growing moonlight was that of a sallow man with hoary hair, intense blue eyes, and a body that would be described, in the most charitable sense, as lean beneath the tattered brown robes that covered him.

"I'm Clemmus Darwin. This is my home." He stuck out his hand to shake.

Mary, stupefied, started to say something, but his head jerked around. "No. Introductions later. It's dangerous out here. We best get inside."

The cave extended back about twenty feet into a bunker of dark-red clay walls. The roof, if you could call it that, was slats of wood propped with hand-hewn post about a foot thick. It was really just a shaft in the earth that was mostly hand dug. It could have started as a den for bears that was expanded, almost like adding rooms onto a one-room shack. Candles threw off a dim hue. It was dry, but musty.

"I'm Mary Louvestre. This is Coolie Parts."

"How do you do?" Clemmus bobbed his head in acknowledgement. "Much I'm proud to show you." He was as delighted as a child at a party. "Over here, as you can see, is my hearth fire. I spend most of my time before it, especially when it's so cold." Indicating a box bed built up off the ground a little to the rear, he went on, "My sleeping quarters. I've managed to barter with trappers for fur covers. Just beyond is my workplace. I concoct ointments and salves. As you can see, my stores are full right now."

Wood posts marked the entrance like supports in a doorway. In one was a hodgepodge of various sized planks and smooth stones. Slats of a boat were used for a makeshift desk. There were shelves stacked with books.

"All the comforts ..." Mary said.

Clemmus led them into another entrance. They ducked their heads so as not to bump them on the support beam. Inside was a gurgling sound and the splash of water dripping.

"Thirsty?" he asked, grinning. "Running water, fresh as the night air."

"Well, I'll be," Coolie huffed.

"Oh, you must think I'm a terrible host. Pardon my manners. You must be hungry. I have food."

In a short while they sat comfortably on fur pallets around a well-nourished fire, chatting like old friends while finishing the last of fish, bread, soup, and wine.

"Miss Mary, I thank you for such a delicious meal," Clemmus said.

"You provided the wine," she said.

"Indeed," he nodded. "And I don't know the last time I had such lovely dinner companions."

"Then you can do the dishes," Mary laughed.

Long curving fingernails scratched through his riotous white hair. "That's a deal."

"So, Clemmy," Coolie said, leaning back against a stack of wood and patting her full stomach, "what're you doin' livin' out here all by yo' self? Searchin' for God?"

His liquid blue-gray eyes stared at her directly. "Actually, yes," he said finally.

Mary chuckled. Coolie shook her head.

"You're judging me wrongly. I am half-Pamunkey Indian, half-white. Several years ago, my parents and younger brother were killed as our covered wagon rolled westward. My Indian father had it in his head he didn't want to be owned by somebody else. He said he'd take his chances on getting us to land where deer ran free, game was plentiful, and he could sit outside of an evening and smoke, fart, and drink whatever he damn well pleased. Wasn't Indians that attacked us, it was white men. Robbed us of about everything we had. Somehow I was spared."

"How long have you been out here?" Mary asked.

"Fifteen, twenty years. Could be longer. I tend to lose track."

"Why do you have to search out here among wild animals and," Coolie glanced around, "mouse droppings."

"I've nowhere else to be and, after all, the hermit monks live like I do. Took to the province of silence and sacrifice," he explained.

Clemmus leaned toward the fire's warmth, his face glowing. He took out a pipe and filled it. "I'll tell you something. Most people think living in these woods is solitary. I used to think that too. But the truth is, there's so much coming and going, especially lately, that sometimes I want to put up a sign saying 'Gone Fishing.'"

The women laughed.

"I mean it," he continued, lighting his pipe. "You've got your hunters and trappers. You've got roaming Indians. You've got parties of runaways. They could be colored, or these days, boys who thought they wanted to be soldiers and now just want to get back home. You've got religious mystics like me trying to talk with God and a host of other odd sorts." He glanced at them. "What group would you ladies fit into?"

Mary said, "None of the aforementioned. We're just travelers."

"Travelers going where, if I might ask?"

"North," Mary replied, casting a look at Coolie.

"You sure picked a ripe time of year to be going north. Every squirrel I know has burrowed in with his hoards and nuts and won't be seen again until spring. Maybe you should stay here until then."

Mary sighed. "That's a tempting offer, but we can't."

"She's got something that can't wait," Coolie said, lighting up her own pipe. "But don't ask me what it is. She dummies up on that subject."

"Can you stay a few days?" Clemmus asked. "I'd love the company and I'll use that time to help build you provisions you're going to need if you follow through on this ill-timed idea to go north right now."

"Let me sleep on it," Mary said.

"There's more danger in the woods besides the heavy snow coming. Thieves, marauders, and slave catchers are but a few. And don't think you'll get welcome from the Negroes who have been living out here either. They're more suspicious than anybody. If they don't shoot first they'll turn you away because they fear you're bringing trouble. You really should think long and hard about leaving out. Two women alone, it's just not safe."

After a couple of moments of silence, Clemmus opened his hands as if dismissing the issue. Then he said, "I'll be back." The women exchanged glances at hearing him root around. Soon he returned with apples and paw paws and dried cranberries. He handed them around. "Dessert. Wish I had sugar for the coffee."

Mary dug into her bag, and like a magician, produced a pouch. "And so."

Clemmus grinned in delight. He set a pot on the fire and in no time the cave smelled of fresh brewed coffee. Just before it boiled, he tossed in the sugar, some brown powder, and a spice.

"Umm," Mary said, tasting it, "what's your secret?"

"A little chocolate and spicy red pepper."

"Clemmy, this is divine," Coolie cooed. "You sure you didn't put somethin' else in it? I'm feelin' kinda mellow."

He smiled crookedly. "Another secret. Trust me, you'll sleep like a baby and wake up rested. Now for your bedding." He stood again and crossed to the wall opposite Mary and Coolie. With a crook-ended pole he pulled down two long canvas packs that lowered from a ceiling attachment. He yanked on a cord. In an instant they fell down into large hammocks. He turned back to his guests and made a low sweeping bow.

Coolie giggled at his performance. "You're just full of surprises."

"You will sleep very comfortably here. Now, I gather covers for you."

By now Coolie's eyes were at half-mast and she lowered herself into the hammock.

"See," Clemmus said, "you're already asleep."

Next morning, the women woke to delicious smells of roasting meat. When Mary finally managed to extricate herself from the hammock she joined Clemmus at the fire.

"Before dawn I went out to check my traps and found two fat cottontails," he said, cradling hot coffee in his hands. He turned the rabbit carcasses on a spit above the fire. "We'll have one for breakfast and the other I'll pack for you in some herbs since you insist on leaving. You might get a couple days' worth of meals out of it."

"I don't know how to thank you," Mary said.

Clemmus eyed her. "There is one way."

Mary looked at him cautiously.

"You can let me copy your walking stick for others I'll pattern after it. The craftsmanship is superb. The wood is ebony, isn't it?

"It is," Mary said proudly. "One of many I have. Had. This one is my particular dear friend. I can do almost anything with it, from hooking a tree branch to fighting off a predator."

"You, fighting?" Clemmus laughed at the thought. He shook his head. "I've noticed you rubbing your leg."

"Let me gift you a soothing ointment to take away your aches and pains ... Food's almost ready."

Coolie and Mary used the spring to freshen up. The water was cold and sobering. Clemmus was setting a croker sack of provisions for them at the entrance when they emerged. Then he squatted near the fire, looking distracted. "I'm worried for you," he said. "When I was just out, I got a bad feeling that terrible weather's coming sooner than I expected."

"I have the same feeling," Mary said, starting to pack up her gear. "We best get on. I can't tell you how important it is that we do."

"Even with that man after you?" Clemmus said.

Mary stopped still. She swung around. "What man?"

"The one tracking you. He's a righteous bad one, he is."

"How do you know that?"

"From a distance, I spotted smoke off a ways, so I climbed to a high ridge to see better. Looked like he was breaking camp. I watched a while longer and I could make out that he was coming this way, purposeful like a hunter would do. I don't recognize his signs so he's not one from around here. And another thing," Clemmus paused, showing agitation, "he's got a rifle. He used it this morning. I watched when he brought down a duck with one shot. That bird didn't have time to make out a will. Guess he was breakfast."

"Where is the man?" Mary asked. "How far away?"

Clemmus pulled at his ragged beard and scratched, thinking. "Half a day away, I imagine."

Coolie grinned. "If he's who I think he is, I slowed him up. I put a bullet hole in his leg."

Clemmus's eyebrows shot up at that revelation. "Y'all runaways?"

"In a manner of speaking," Mary said.

"What manner is that?" Clemmus asked.

"Coolie's free. I would be considered the escaped slave."

Clemmus's smile faded, and he stared into the fire. "A lone man out here like he is tells me he's a tracker. I trade with quite a few of them and have never seen this fellow before. Unusual, this time of year, for someone to be traveling by himself."

"What makes you think he's alone?" Mary asked, concerned.

"I stayed on the ridge for a while, watching his movements. I didn't see anybody with him. Funny thing though ..." He stalled, looking at the fire.

"Glory's comin', Clemmy! What?" Coolie urged.

He looked up, licked his lips, and said softly, "I saw him take up his gun, turn to his horse, and fire. The poor thing went down. The man didn't bury him, just left him there. Sinful."

"Sin an' a shame!" Coolie sputtered. "The devil's in him and the truth give him a country mile! Rat bastard."

Mary looked disgusted.

"I saw him take up his pack. He's coming. And if he is a slave catcher or bounty hunter, I don't believe he's aiming to take you two back. At least not upright." He looked worriedly into their faces as the fire glowed amber about them.

"If I'm right in my guess," Coolie said, "he's one Deputy Elam Gates out of Norfolk, where we're from. That sick bastard. He probably wants my hide for what I done to him and a piece of Mary's for helping me get away."

Clemmus was no longer just fretting over them, he felt protective. "If you stay, we could hide. I know places he couldn't find you in three blue moons. But, if you're out there somewhere, I don't know how you can outrun him. You ready for that?"

"I'm ready for whatever he puts out," exclaimed Coolie. "I got a big rock in my pack with his name on it."

Clemmus clucked at her. "You are David to his Goliath. A rock against a rifle doesn't sound like very good odds, but from what I've seen of your spunk, I'd take a chance on you." He laughed.

Mary exchanged looks with Coolie.

"He must be mad as a wet hen," Mary said, "to follow us this far in this weather with what must be a painful wound."

They sat quietly for a moment. The fire crackled loudly as they basked in its warmth.

Clemmus made breakfast of hoecakes, roast rabbit, and hot coffee. They ate quickly, their mood solemn. Afterward, Clemmus pointed to a couple of pouches he'd put near their packs.

"I dressed and trussed that other rabbit so you'll be able to carry it fine. You also have some smoked jerky that'll make a good soup with the herbs I've added." He looked at Mary. "Also, I put in a pouch some of my herb ointment that will help soothe your leg."

"Clemmy, you're a good man," Coolie said, smiling at him.

He looked abashed.

"Why don't you get the hell outta here and go be with people?" Coolie asked. "You can help 'em with your ointments and salves and the sturdy, stylish walking sticks you're gonna make. That's where God is. That's where you can hear His voice, out among the people you're helpin', doing what you love. Don't that make sense?"

"You're too beautiful to be so wise," he said to Coolie. "Maybe I could write about my life out here and tell about the herbs I've found to help people."

"How could you go wrong?" Coolie asked sincerely. "Then, maybe, you could teach others how to help people in the same way."

Clemmus stared down at the ground for a long time. When he looked up, tears were in his eyes. "You can spend hours lying on your back in the depths of a silent cave, far away from anybody you know, pleading with God to talk to you. Then along come two women who talk to you louder than God has. And suddenly you realize that, through them, God has talked and been found."

Glowing, he rose and pumped their hands, grinning. "I know what I'm to do. Now, here's what I want you to do." He drew them a map in the dirt. "When you reach this area, veer inland about five miles. You will come to Livingstone Bridge. It is the home of Loyal Livingstone. He's a good man who believes everyone deserves to be free. He'll help you more. Between here and there though," he looked at them soberly, "are many dangers."

"Like what?" Coolie asked.

He shrugged. "Who knows? The forest changes every day."

Soon, standing at the entrance, they said their goodbyes. Coolie brightened as if she'd had an insight. "Clemmy, why don't you come with us? Our trip would be lots more fun and interestin' with you along."

"I have my own destiny, dear one," he said. "I go away from you, but never believe that I don't have you in my heart. Go with God."

Mary touched his face with her fingers. "You are blessed, Clemmus Darwin, this very day."

His tears fell along her hand. Then he looked up. "Wait. I've something else for you." He hurried to the back of the cave and returned with a jar of chocolate. "Be sweet. Be lethal when you have to. Stay dangerous all the time. I will hold your names close to my heart in my daily prayers."

"As will we you," Mary said.

CHAPTER 47

After a couple of hours, Mary and Coolie emerged from a deep canopy of trees. The sky was gray and ominous.

"We're in for rain and lots of it," Mary said. No sooner than her words were uttered, fat drops poured like from a gushing pump. Some were slush, just on the verge of snowflakes. Soon, Mary and Coolie were soaked to their skin, and cold beyond that.

Coolie's teeth were chattering. "Ain't we gon' stop?"

"Stop?" Mary said, exasperated. "Stop where? These bare trees can't give us cover. There's no place where we can hide. We have to keep going."

Reading Mary's expression, Coolie knew not to argue.

The rain didn't relent the entire day. The trees of the landscape blurred from gray to coal-black silhouettes as temperatures dipped and the wind gained speed. Coolie seemed to be swaying on her feet from fatigue but recovered some after eating dried fruit Mary provided. Mary spotted a cliff overhang where they could make camp. Coolie threw herself on the ground in a shivering heap and curled up in a ball.

Mary dropped her things nearby. "I'll be back," she said.

In the forest, Mary collected the driest wood she could find and made a fire. When she went back to Coolie, she saw she had vomited. She cleaned her face and took off her moccasins and socks and put them on stakes near the fire to dry. From her pack she pulled out clean, thick socks for Coolie's feet and pulled her close to the fire.

"I'm scared," Coolie said, hunched over. "Not about Gates. I just don't want to let you down."

Mary scooted closer to her. "There's no way you could do that."

"I don't feel good." Coolie held her middle.

"As soon as you get warm you'll be fine." Mary tried to sound convincing.

"No, I won't. I got something comin' on. I can feel it."

"You rest. I'll get us something to eat. You'll feel better then."

Coolie allowed Mary to lay her by the fire. Peering at Coolie's face, with dark circles under her eyes and her breathing phlegmy, Mary was worried. She soothed Coolie's brow with tender fingertips and watched as the younger woman's eyes drooped.

"We'll stay here for the night, Coolie. Maybe the rain will let up by dawn. We've got a good ways to go yet. Try to stay strong." She touched Coolie's forehead with the back of her hand and was surprised to feel the heat of it. She got up and retrieved her backpack. "I'm going to make a willow bark tea."

Mary made the drink and pulled together a thick layer of pine needles and forest debris to make a mattress to keep them off the ground. Over that she put Coolie's rain gear. She helped Coolie lie down, and she was asleep almost instantly. Mary had no interest in eating at all. She lay down and was soon gone too.

At dawn, Mary could see Coolie's condition had passed from poor to troublesome. Sleet tormented the ground, and Coolie shivered so badly she could hardly sit up. Her eyes looked rheumy, and her lips were chapped.

In the gray light, storm swirled around them in ghostly specters. Mary poked the coals, added more twigs and branches, and soon had a healthy fire where she made a soup of tubers she had found. She also pulled out some of the jerky Clemmus had given them and soaked it in the soup as well. When she could begin to make out distinct forms about them—trees, leaves, sodden though they were—she shook Coolie to wake her.

Coolie did not rouse.

"Hey, sleepyhead," Mary said, making her voice pleasant, "rise and shine. I've got hot soup."

When she shook Coolie again, the sounds she heard were from someone delirious, as if talking from a dream. Mary felt Coolie's forehead again. It was warm, yet Coolie shivered. This was not good. She knew she had to do something.

She removed the blankets from around Coolie and then stripped her naked. Within seconds, Mary undressed herself and placed Coolie back on the pine straw bedding, laying her on one side of their heaviest blanket. Mary wrapped her arms around the younger woman, drawing her into her own warmth. Quick as she could, she made a cocoon of the blanket about them. Coolie stirred as she felt Mary's closeness, and she pressed nearer. Her eyes remained closed as she moaned. Mary held her tightly and cooed soft, comforting sounds as one would to soothe a sick child.

"Sleep now," Mary gentled her. "Rest."

Mary laid with Coolie as she slept for the next several hours. The seesaw of shivering and sweating had subsided.

When Coolie stirred, Mary got dressed and hurried to a nearby creek and soon had more willow bark boiling. She bathed Coolie with some of the liquid. The rest she fed to her in sips. She worried that Coolie would move at a snail's pace when she moved at all. Yet Mary knew they had to get on—Gates had to be getting dangerously close. He might even be in a position to observe them both right now.

———

Assessing Coolie's condition, Mary suggested they remain in camp a while longer to give Coolie more time to recover.

"I ain't stayin' put," Coolie insisted, shakily standing up. "We goin'. A blind man could see you got fret in yo' face."

They managed to go a distance of a few miles, walking a path that became more rolling and flanked by fulsome patches of dry rhododendron. Mary figured they could travel as long as she gave Coolie frequent rest breaks and some food.

"What, no dessert?" Coolie said teasingly, after one of their food breaks.

"For you I have this," Mary said, holding up a small pouch. "Chocolate, compliments of Clemmus."

Mary was pleased that Coolie was becoming her old self with her steady complaints—her feet hurt, the pack was too heavy, she was tired, when were they going to eat again, and where in hell were they anyway? The more they walked, the louder were Coolie's reports. Finally, Mary stopped, turned back, and walked up to her on the trail.

"You've got to be quiet," Mary told her again. "Quiet as you can."

"Why? Nobody out here but two crazy women and bears and raccoons and beavers, all of us cold and with no more dessert."

"And don't forget Deputy Gates." Mary gave her a playful slap on the shoulder.

Mary mentally referred to Clemmus's directions to their next way-stop and felt they were on course. Again, pulling out Anders's compass, she checked their direction. Yes, they were going right. When everything about their persons and everything they had was either soggy or damp with the continuing rain, Mary calculated that maybe they made ten miles. She decided they needed to make camp early, get in from the elements, and rest. She spied what looked like a natural alcove under an overhang that would keep off the rain. She indicated to Coolie to hold back while she slowly ventured inside. After rooting out a couple of river rats, she found it to be immensely inhabitable. She told Coolie to get their gear out of the rain and went in search of firewood. Soon, she had a roaring fire going, soup cooking, and Coolie telling stories of some of her more colorful patrons at Travelers Rest. Then Coolie became reflective.

"You and Anders. Y'all was tryin' to be together?"

Mary ate her soup.

"Was y'all gon' try to run away? Leave the South, leave Norfolk? Leave Coolie?"

Mary smiled sadly. "We hadn't planned that far yet."

Coolie looked not only beautiful but content, if just for this moment, highlighted in the golden glow of the campfire. Her brow pleated. "How was you gonna work that out?"

Mary gave a quiet laugh. "I didn't have a notion."

"You think you gon' miss anything else, you being a famous fashion designer and all?"

"I miss everything," Mary said with a deep sigh. "Especially what I had hoped for."

Coolie cocked her head in question.

"Never mind," Mary said.

"You know that Lumley come out to my place tellin' me Simeon gon' try and shut me down. He say as a new senator he gonna make an example out of me how he gon' clean up Norfolk. Say my Travelers Rest was a den of thieves and scoundrels and liars the likes of low character as to taint the whole town and undermine its high integrity." Coolie sighed. "Hope I said that the way he done."

Mary stirred the fire with a long stick.

"Simeon been knowin' me my whole life. No way was I gonna believe he would do that." She glanced at Mary, who seemed lost in thought and was saying nothing. "I knowed Gates took my blue cross. Wish I'd killed that pond scum."

Mary looked up. "Gates did not take your cross."

"No?" Coolie's voice was incredulous.

Mary shook her head. "Lumley did."

"I'll be damned. How you know that?"

"I have my ways," Mary said. "But what I'm saying is true."

"What a conniving no-count. Let me tell you 'bout him." Coolie spoke loudly, then caught herself. She lowered her voice to a theatrical whisper. "Thing is, Lumley kept a whore out at my place. Name was Justine. She was Negro but she got skin color like me and black hair down to her butt like the tail of a bay horse. Pretty as ... well, anything you love. Before Lumley fully partnered up with Withers, he sat around my bar and restaurant eatin', bein' with Justine, and drinkin'—lots of drinkin'. That's when he'd talk out of his head like, sayin', 'I'm somebody. Y'all just don't know it yet.' Justine never laughed at him when he say that. Lumley act like he needed that from her. Like he'd have paid a million dollars just to get her to do that for him."

Mary nodded.

"When he was get-down, slobberin' drunk, he'd go on and on 'bout his mother, Miss Ginny Kay. Lord he loved that woman, worshipped her like somebody do a saint. But when he commence to talkin' about his daddy, I thought sure he was gon' bring the house down. He pure hated that man. Said he'd-a killed him and if he'd had a chance, he'd dig him up and do it again. The man told him every day, from when he was a little boy, that he was pig shit with maggots for a brain. Wasn't never gonna be anything but. Said his father would spit on the floor and grind his shoe into it. 'That's you,' he told Lumley," Coolie said.

"Then Withers started coming in. Something in me say he wasn't like Lumley, but they took up together like folk do when they been knowin' each other or knowin' they kin or got some connection time back. I commenced to learnin' 'bout the likes of them in fits and starts. They cooked up that whole cockamamie story 'bout them being lawyers and all since way back when. Curious, though. Withers would ask me, from time to time, if I knew of any blacks who might be needin' a little help. Took me a while to believe he was on the up and up. Then I told him about some. He asked me a few questions and next thing I knew, they got to safety somewhere up North. Wasn't nothing to tell me Lumley was in on that at all."

Mary was quiet, letting Coolie deliver her story how she wanted.

"Lumley'd been hearin' stories 'bout Simeon, his rich family and connections, Tesh-Lucianne and all she got. Then when he got wind Simeon was part of the engineer group to make a better ship for the South and being approached by major players for some high political office, Lumley got his idea, his plan. After several drinks one night, Lumley turn to Justine but speak loud enough for everybody to hear. 'Goin' get me a fish on the line', he said. Lumley wangled his way into Simeon, just as he done others before. That old con, he knew just how to play Simeon. Guess they still playin', whilst we out here in all this cold tryin' to get north for only you know why."

Mary stared off.

"If Simeon don't win no high position in the government, what then?"

"If that happens," Mary said, "if Simeon's spirit is not broken, he can go back to his chandlery. That is, if Lumley leaves him a cent to his name. And Lumley? He'll go off to find something new to feed off. That's what parasites do."

"Things always level out. So that fool stole my cross? I shit on his soul!"

After camp was settled and Coolie was asleep, Mary took her pack, her hatchet, and disappeared into the night.

Next day, when she and Coolie had proceeded a short way, they heard a thud, a sputtering, and a groan in the background.

"What was that?" Coolie asked, wide-eyed.

"Just some things leveling out," Mary said, continuing to press along.

"Shit in a heart attack!" he yelled out involuntarily, massaging his shin. Gates had seen the danger and somersaulted over it, but still managed to bang his knee into a long-hanging branch of an oak. "Dammit on a stick!" He yanked his pant leg up. When he saw he was not badly hurt, he smiled smugly.

Had Gates not been the expert hunter he was, his life would have been worth nothing. A thin tripwire would have sent slivers, covered in God knew what, into his skin. Spying it at the last minute, he threw himself over it in a mess of hands and arms and legs. He had to admit a new respect for his quarry, Mary. He stood completely still for a long time, letting his eyes search every detail of where he was. Finally, he saw the next danger—a small tree branch, bent unnaturally, that did not move in the wind. He smiled. Well I'll be damned!

Gates slowly backed his steps until he saw how he could skirt what was likely a deathtrap. He used his large knife to cut a new path. It would take more than a clever nigger woman to outsmart him. Ahead, he spied a few branches that had fallen to the base of a pine tree. Good. Providence was still with him. Since this trip had come up on him unexpectedly, he did not have proper clothes to be out in this cold, so keeping warm was paramount. As he began stacking firewood, he saw something. Light glinted off a small tin. Could it be some chew? Somebody coming through here another time might have dropped it. A little bit of it placed between his lower lip and gum on the right side would hit the spot. He imagined the taste of it. What could be more perfect than some chew, a swig of whiskey, and a cozy fire? Lord knew he needed a little comfort now that he was on foot.

For all the years he had been riding his horse, Nomad had been surefooted. He supposed he hadn't thought that the horse had gotten old on him when Nomad stepped into that rut on the trail and was trapped. "Whoa, Nomad!" he cried and pulled on the reins. But the horse's eyes were wild and he reared up, practically yanking his foreleg from its socket. Gates heart ached when he heard the horse scream. He looked down at the dangling appendage and just shook his head. There was nothing he or anyone else could do to save Nomad. He took up his rifle and did what he knew he had to do.

Sleet pounded down and the ground was too hard for him to even think of burying him. The most he could do was cover Nomad under rocks to deter the scavengers that would come soon enough. He couldn't protect him any further. Gates wiped his eyes, picked up his saddlebags, and moved on out. Nomad was dear and he would grieve, but it would not stop his pursuit of Mary and Coolie. As for Coolie, she never knew how much her rebuff affected him.

Gates shook his head. So much for that! He couldn't handle such thoughts right now. Other things were more pressing. He turned his thoughts back to the tobacco tin. Slowly, his hand fingered through the twigs surrounding it, then stopped. Wait a minute, he thought, wasn't this just a bit too convenient? No, he'd better let that tin alone. It was booby-trapped in some way for sure. Instead, he'd just gather firewood and tuck in for the night. He sniggered arrogantly. It would be a cold day in hell when an old nigger who sewed for a living got the best of him in the woods.

CHAPTER 48

Mary began to grow frantic. She had thought they would have reached the home of Loyal Livingstone by now. The path Clemmus sent them on seemed simple and direct. Yet she and Coolie were still wandering in the grim, fierce weather—haggard and injured.

The thick skies promised only more storm.

She drew her scarf tighter about her head and over her face so that she was looking out through the netting of its fabric. Still, her eyes were scratchy from tiredness and the constant watchfulness. She blew on her hands. Would she ever be warm again? If she could only find another cave where they could set up camp, but the landscape revealed nothing but mounds of white mass. Never had she been much of a religious person—not the moaning for heaven, oh Lord help me Bible-clenching type—but she did believe in a creator that set everything into motion, maybe with a plan. She wasn't sure if what she'd call God was a presence that looked down on the humans he'd made with any regard. Just in case he might be listening and so inclined to help them, she sent up a plea.

Her brow darkened as she looked at the horizon in the pinched light. She thought she heard something out of the way. She turned her head and stepped down awkwardly onto a slippery patch of ground. Her ankle twisted and sharp pain lanced up her leg. She was trying to be so careful. What had she stepped on? Bending down to rub her ankle, she spotted a spike of color. She dug into the snow and unearthed the ragged body of a child's doll. Was it left by a child fleeing with her family from the war? For days, survival and so many other things had consumed her that the war and its aspects had been little in her mind. Since they had not traveled close to battle, she had the luxury of not imagining what might be going on in this conflict. But the shock of seeing the battered and distorted face of this doll drove it home to her again. This was why she was out here. She had a role in this war, one she hoped would make for a better someday.

She took another step forward and went down. Her foot plunged deep into snow and water, up to her sorry knee. Panting hard from shock and the effort to extricate herself, she cried out inwardly, please God, if you're out there, help us. Now!

Temperatures continued to plummet and the wind, the harsh first cousin to cold, cut into their clothes and skin like a scalpel. Her whole life, Mary had never known a Virginia winter to be so extreme. Monotony and fear consumed Mary. Desperation would be next. Swaddled in blankets, Mary and Coolie stayed close to their campfire. They faced another freezing night and were running low on food. Mary had taken their moccasins and socks and perched them on poles by the fire to dry. She gave dry socks to Coolie, and after an ointment of lemon verbena on her own feet, slipped into a clean pair. The weather was so devilish that even slathering on the mixture of calendula ointment and lanolin couldn't keep their skin from cracking. Mary had not known what it was to feel so scoured raw. Even her lips cracked to bleeding. Jocularity between her and Coolie quelled. They sat quietly, too exhausted to even quibble.

The next day proceeded with the sameness of the day before. The cold maintained its frigidness. The snow was unrelenting. They nursed their injuries, and much to their dismay, found no food. Mary constantly searched for the markers and turns Clemmus told her about and was frustrated to see nothing but unending white. From the distance they'd traveled, she was sure they should be near the round of pine trees and towering maples he said marked the turn to the road to Livingstone's house. Yet, squinting into the distance, elements of the landscape were barely distinguishable, smoothed over by a carpet of thick snow. How she yearned for something different to break the boredom.

Mary had thought earlier in the day that she heard a stirring on the same trail they had traveled. Mary climbed onto a brow of rock to survey. Nothing showed itself, but she remained suspicious. That night, as Coolie slept near their fire, Mary disappeared into the woods. On cat feet she moved purposefully, all senses out, backtracking until she found what she thought she might—Deputy Elam Gates.

She could see his small fire in a circle of stones. He'd gathered pine branches, which rested clumsily against a tree for a little shelter. The wind rippled through the branches. A log on the fire crackled and popped, sending sparkles of light into the night sky as he slept.

Gates had removed his boots and rolled them loosely as a makeshift headrest. From the bottle turned on its side, he'd also enjoyed a little liquid pleasure in the form of rotgut whiskey. Mary's nostrils confirmed that. Probably that was what had put him out so completely.

She scooted ever closer and continued to survey cautiously. His rifle perched near his head. She peered down at a dirty frying pan. Looked like dinner had been fish, and from the crumbs, a biscuit. If she had not been aiming for absolute quiet, she might have clucked in disgust at the messy quarters. But then, he was a mess of a man in her estimation.

She stayed still as a church mouse until she heard his deep snores. Then she insinuated herself near where he lay. She could kill him as he slept—after all the trouble he'd caused her and, especially, Coolie. She could keep him from bothering either of them again. And then he wouldn't be able to stop her from her real purpose—getting to Washington with the precious papers. The world wouldn't be so bad off without him.

She'd never killed anyone. Could there be any other way? She knew Gates would hound them forever. He'd never stop chasing them. Men like Gates, once they got the bit in their teeth, never let go.

There was no alternative. Ever so quietly, she stepped over to where he lay and twisted open the top of the small jar she carried. God forgive me, she silently beseeched.

———◆———

The snow soared down in fat flakes the size of quarters. Wind blew strong out of the north and bent and whipped the trees etched against the sky. Gates was cold and stunned by a headache that made him see stars. He had lost sight of the women but that didn't matter. He would find them, he was certain. The problem was he felt feverish and sick to his stomach. As he walked along, he felt something crawling on his leg, the same leg where he'd taken Coolie's bullet. He swatted at it. Whatever it was seemed attached to his skin. He slapped at it again. When it fell to the ground, he bent to examine it.

Damn that nigger, he thought. It had to have been Mary, but how she'd managed to find or keep it was beyond him. Spiders of this sort only lived in warm, moist places. From the markings on it, he could tell it was the dreaded black widow. He threw down his bag and yanked the matches from it. Shit! Shit! Shit! He only had a few left. As he struck one, the wind lifted the flame right off the stick. Hands shaking in his urgency, he struck another. He needed to cauterize the wound, but being out in the open wind wasn't helping one bit. This time the flame held. When he applied it to the bite, it sizzled on his skin and went out. Desperately, he rolled his eyes toward the heavens.

Angry and frustrated now, he picked up his bags and threw them toward a short length of scrub below. Tumbling after them, he rose up on his elbows and huddled close around another match. He struggled to keep it aflame in the curled cup of his hands. Soon as he got a steady flame, he slowly angled it down toward his leg. In another moment, fire overrode the cold and tore open nerves in his body. Still, he held it to the bite, watching the skin bubble like frying fat. Panting from pain, he threw the match into the snow.

He had to calm himself, he thought. If he didn't, the poison might just as well wrap itself around the innards of his heart and kill him quick. He spotted his pack, grabbed it, and retrieved the jar of moonshine he'd stashed in the side pocket. He poured a little on the angry burned mass and swore. He took a long swig for himself. Sweating like the temperature was a hundred, he leaned back against the bushes. He knew he needed help soon or he was a goner. Though he might not succumb to the venom, he was ill-equipped to deal with the complications that would likely come up.

Furious, he looked down at the blistering wound. It hurt like hell. Suddenly, so did his stomach. He rolled and retched into the innocent snow. As he washed his face with clean snow, the other end of him abruptly swelled and insisted on release. Struggling to get out of his trousers, he made a mess of them and himself. It wasn't easy trying to clean his backside and pants with the cold snow. When he shrugged into his pants again, the wetness chilled him. Damn those women, damn himself, damn Coolie Parts! Damn her to hell.

Why was it all of his life he'd fallen for the wrong one? Why couldn't he just stick to his resolve—poke 'em when he had the urge, leave 'em when he didn't? Much as he didn't want to, his heart got involved. He hated Coolie Parts. But he loved Coolie Parts. Hell, he'd known that well and good soon as he laid eyes on her. But he had to play his part as lawman so's folks would respect him. That nigger wench—she never gave him any play at all. It made him feel somewhat better that she didn't give a mind to that simpering Jitter Conroy either. But, by damn, her heart belonged to that consarn seamstress! Hellfire! Ain't no accountin' for that. Weren't right.

The stinging bite on his leg recalled him to the present. The area was a bluish-purple now. His mouth tasted gall, his butt hurt, and he was forced to wear wet pants. How much worse could it get?

He could die. He retracted his lips back from his teeth to approximate a smile. Well, if he was going down, he'd see to it that those wenches did too. Awkwardly, with difficulty, he hauled himself up. Pulling his wet pants from his backside, he limped disgustedly on.

After a while, Gates climbed to the top of a ridge, trying to get his bearings. He could see where several streams merged into one and fed fiercely into the horizon. Too much danger there. This had to have occurred to Mary as well, he thought. Their trek must have turned inward, where he could see the landscape became denser, thicker, and gauging distance, became more confusing. Over another ridge it was possible to see a ragged settlement through the trees. But the snow and wind were mind-dulling, and guessing how far from here to there would only be a distortion for sure. The wind slapped his face. If only the cold would dull the pain in his leg.

To the extent that he could think clearly at all, he reasoned he had two choices. He could leave the trail and try to reach one of the settlements for help, or stay on the path after them and risk his life. The poison was already coursing through his body. Soon sweats and swelling would set in if he didn't get an antidote.

As he was trying to decide what to do, he caught sight of two figures far ahead—at least, he thought that's what he saw. He'd find them and fix them. Fix them good.

CHAPTER 49

M ary didn't worry about Gates any more. No doubt the spider's venom had coursed hotly through his veins and—by now, in this weather—he was pushing up daisies. Clemmus had described a turn in the road where trees scalloped the path. Who but he would suggest that was a way to find anything in an entire area full of scalloped passageways? The ground was spongy and boggy, with a high number of thin but deceitful runoff runnels to cross. Looking down at her frayed moccasins, she could only shake her head. She had done her best constructing them, but they were no match for the elements' constant tearing at the seams. Little by little, they were being destroyed by trundling steadily forward through the muck.

Mary's eyes were thoughtful, as if weighing every increment of their travel. Yet from time to time they welled up with tears as she became overwhelmed at the enormity of their task. No—*her* task. Coolie didn't ask for this. She didn't steal plans to take to Washington. This was all her own idea. She'd only brought Coolie along to save her from Gates.

Well, maybe at least she had done that right. Coolie was safe—that is, if they didn't perish out in this bitter cold. If and when they found the Livingstone place, maybe she could get Coolie settled and go on ahead. If the couple was as trustworthy as Clemmus said, Coolie would be all right. That would allow her to make up time and get to Washington before too much else slowed her down. She'd hate to leave Coolie, but her quest to get the plans to the Secretary of the Navy still burned inside her. Going it alone would be faster and safer all around.

"We're not going to find any decent food where we are," Mary said. "We'll move closer to the coast. By following it, we won't be so lost. And we'll have the added benefit of following the beach to provide us a bonnet of protection that way."

As they inched along, she observed that the foliage grew more dense, and the area was replete with small tributaries that made their trek muddier and more treacherous with slimy slickness underfoot.

Oh, for a bath, she mused. That would be wonderful about now. She could imagine herself somewhere warm, in a huge tin tub, steaming water billowing up, soaking her clean; someplace where she could clean and dry her clothes and leisurely eat good food. She had spent so many grubby days on the trail where it was too frigid or too unsafe to do anything other than take care of her feet. She was tired of being grubby.

Mary heard Coolie behind her. That brought her out of her imaginings and back to grim reality. Coolie sighed heavily, mumbled to herself in complaint about the cold, and stumbled and cursed. Because of that young rebel, a deaf man would have a hard time not locating them, Mary thought.

High-pitched howls sounded, and Mary wondered if the wild dogs might be pursuing them. Two tired women were easy prey for a pack of hungry beasts. She felt beleaguered but frightened enough to press an advantage against being eaten alive. They needed safe shelter. But where?

Mary squeezed her eyelids and opened them again, trying to clear her blurry vision. She thought she saw something. She repeated the procedure, squeezing her eyes tight and opening them again. A glistening gold shimmered in two short squares. The sun's beckoning glow navigated up the corridor of maple, poplars, and scrub pines that they followed, and illuminated the valley below. Were her eyes playing a trick? Mary stopped, stooped, and squinted.

Windows! Vaguely she could make out what she thought was a house—no, more like a cabin, surrounded by an embrace of tall trees near deeper woods. No other houses were in view. The house seemed isolated. Was there a town nearby?

Mary glanced back at Coolie, who was treading valiantly but drifting under exhaustion and the weight of her pack. "Coolie, I think I see something!"

"What?" she snapped. "Paradise and a drink?"

"Close to it. I think we've found the Livingstone's. But I'm not entirely sure." Mary struck out at a trot, but prudence made her slow down. The punishing winds could be betraying her vision. Easy, she told herself, take it easy. You know better than to rush into anything. Be aware.

She cautiously led the way down a muddy lane. As they got closer to the house, Mary could make out a clutch of crude outbuildings around it. The stream just behind the cabin moved unhurriedly, choked with ice floes and smelling of water-borne odors. It was edged by giant ferns and moss. Frost and ice crystals clung to the vegetation.

Mary knew she and Coolie were the picture of war orphans as they made their way closer to the cabin. Their clothes snagged on poplar branches whose limbs were stiff as the arms of corpses reaching out to them. Less a footpath than a trampled trail led them down a slope toward the cabin. Alongside a rickety dock, a crude raft made of logs and rope was tied up. It bumped and bobbed in the water, making hollow sounds like those heard through a glass.

"I want you to be very quiet," Mary instructed Coolie. "We don't know that this is the place or if it's safe."

She edged them along the trees to see better. Nothing moved, not a person, not a farm animal. No pungent smoke curled up into the air from a fireplace. Yet there were the two windows lit up with a golden glow. She peered closer. She could see no one.

"You stay put. I'm going to check it out," Mary said.

"You always sayin' that. I don't see how come we can't both check it out," Coolie despaired.

Mary huffed. She shook her head and motioned for Coolie to stay where she was. She would approach the house alone in case there was trouble. Coolie looked alarmed but hung back into the shadow edge of the trees.

Squatting in a silly looking duck walk, Mary silently inched toward the house. Slowly angling her way up two rickety wooden stairs, she gained the wide plank porch that hosted a couple of sturdy grapevine rockers dusted with snow. Skirting them without a sound, she flattened against the outside wall and took a second to calm her shakes. She shivered from the cold. The day's light stole tentative fingers into the thick stew of fog; not even a gull mewed on the water.

Hearing nothing, she decided to risk poking her head around and venture a look through the window. She could make out austere furnishings, only the barest of necessities—a polished plain deal table with four ladderback chairs around it in the center of the modest room, two parlor chairs in the corner by a side table stacked with books, and a cooking area surrounding a wide hearth and stone fireplace. Nearby, lying askew, was a cornhusk doll donned in a bright blue-and-white gingham dress.

The floorboard creaked under Mary's foot and the door yanked open. Backlit from the room's lamp glow, a huge figure loomed in the darkness like the most frightening emissary of death. "Hyeah!" barked a deep voice.

Mary turned tail, lurched off the porch, missed a step, stumbled, righted herself, and ran off pushing past the searing pain in her leg.

The man—the goliath—was right behind her. His footfalls thundered fast after her. "Hey!" he called.

Mary did not stop. She reached the dark forest and beat inside it. She did not see Coolie but didn't dare risk calling out to her. She scurried inside a cone of vegetation, slipping in wet slurry under her feet. Terror rifled through her as she realized the man was close upon her. She could hear the sound of his breathing.

His voice was low, husky. "You don't have to be afraid."

Mary skidded to a halt. She turned and came face to face with a white man as big as her fears. His long gray hair was bushy in the backlight of the fog, his features unclear. She snatched her knife from its sheath, gripping it tightly in her hand.

"I'm Loyal Livingstone," he said. "You don't have to be afraid. You're among friends."

———•———

Inside the tidy cabin, Livingstone introduced them to his wife. Stella was a stout woman with a square face and straight hair the color of brass tinged with gray. Short, barely reaching the height of her husband's chest, her piercing blue eyes assessed her new company with a no-nonsense expression as she silently extended a firm handshake to both Mary and Coolie. She gave the impression that she had worked hard her whole life, had taken the bitter with the sweet, and had seen no little pain, but was stoic about it all. The upturn of her chin said, "I either like you or I don't." She simply stated, "I'll make a meal." As Mary watched Stella hustle to the fireplace and stoke the embers, she took that to mean they'd been welcomed and that was that.

While Stella worked at the hearth, Mary, Coolie, and Livingstone sat at the table drinking hot coffee. His was a wise face, Mary thought, a kindly face. His intense lavender-colored eyes were set among deep, weathered seams and his substantial nose was punctuated on either side by red cheeks. His face had the look of a rag rug, homely but pleasant. He had an easy smile, and though sitting still with his legs outstretched and crossed at the ankles, his bearing evinced lots of pep and good humor.

"I don't mind telling you," he said, his big hands spreading outward, "you scared me to death."

"You the one to talk," Coolie said, still glaring at him. "How'd you know who we be? How'd you know we were comin'?"

He chuckled as Stella silently placed dishes of bread, cheese, preserves, and smoked meats before them. "Ah, let's just say word flows fast when it pours through the drinking gourd. Now eat. You can rest after, and then we'll talk more." He gestured to the divan. "One of you can sleep there. It's lumpy but comfortable. The other is my daughter's bed. She's visiting a friend near here."

"Thank you for your hospitality," Mary said. "Clemmus told us you'd help, but we don't want to bring trouble to you and your family. You see, I believe there may be a man hunting us. I thought I put him down, but lately, I'm not so sure."

Coolie gasped. She stared at Mary, her eyes wide. "Gates? Still? No, it couldn't be. Even he couldn't be that big a fool. Could he?"

As Mary sipped her coffee and filled her hungry stomach, she told Livingstone the story of Deputy Elam Gates. Upon hearing, he stood, strode to the windows, and released the hooks on the heavy tapestry draperies, making the room go dim.

CHAPTER 50

Sweating profusely despite the cold, Gates staggered on, his clothes clammy and smelling worse than stale swill. He dragged one limping boot after the other, drawing narrow gutters behind him. He was freezing, practically crawling along, but he was determined. Death would not catch him, not in this godforsaken place. The wounds, where he had been shot in the leg and from the spider bite, burned like he was being torched from the inside. He moaned. Half-crazed with fever, his stomach chose this time to send vomit in long arcs across the snow. After that, he dry retched, but the awful gnawing pain in his gut was the same.

"Okay," he said aloud to himself. "We can do this. Let's count. One, two, three for every step. Then again—one, two, three. Three is doable. We can do anything in three's."

He had been using all of his hunting instincts to stay on the heels of the women, if for nothing else than maybe they'd inadvertently lead him to help. But he was so tuckered out. He just wanted to lie down, but he knew that would be the kiss of death. He knew he'd never get up again.

The wind playfully kicked up snow faces that scared him and then hooted through the trees. He had always told himself that nothing could ever get to him. But he now knew he lied.

He pressed a hand to his temple. How could one man's head ache like this and he still be alive? It pounded like the thrum of hammers men used to lay ties for the railroad. His eyes betrayed him. Or was it his mind? He could've sworn he saw a tree to lean against, but when he reached toward where he thought it was, his arms connected with nothing but air. A time or two, he was sure he heard voices—somebody talking about his daddy, that old pisser. Thinking about that piece of rank shit, he laughed derisively.

Daddy. What a joke! He guffawed, forgetting himself in the wind's lull. Then he stopped as bile rose in his throat. He liked to think of somebody called daddy as being a strong man of character who took care of his own, someone who counted for something, not what he had got for a daddy. Cervil. Wasn't that a high-falutin' name for the dumb peckerwood cracker who wouldn't know it if you plopped down a paper and showed it to him? He couldn't read nohow. Liked to tag hisself 'Wolf' on account of him being so ferocious in barroom fights, street fights, fights anywhere—mostly brought on by his own crass mouth. Gates knew his father was less ferocious than flat-out stupid, dry grass between his ears and a coward to boot.

The sick bastard! Some fighter he was—somebody would whup up on him, he'd come home and whup up on Mama or his son. Gates never worried about taking the old man's punches when they landed upside his head, but it tore his heart and punctured his soul when the hoodlum commenced to smacking his mother around.

Gates reached a small clearing, and he decided, despite the wretched wind, to try to make a fire just to get warm for a few moments. It helped to give himself specific tasks to do, to keep his brain from going to mush. He'd have to gather dry twigs and wood. That was number one. After a few moments of searching, he found a few lengths of poplar but hadn't the strength to carry them. He used his coat as a carry and dragged the wood even though his legs stung like a mass of bees was in his pants. That was number two. Number three, he had to make a circle of stones around the fire—now to find those.

He stumbled into a rim of thickets and was about to put his hand down for a rock when he heard a low growl that curdled his blood. Easing up, he peered into the steely-gray eyes of six feral dogs that had him in their sights. Should he run? But how could he with his bum leg? And to run would probably cause the wolves to attack. He was so confused at what to do that he laughed aloud at his predicament. Then he showed his teeth. They showed theirs. Their growls were still menacing. He thought, hell, if I'm gonna die, I don't have to know about it. He pulled his flask from his pouch and chugged down a slug of the biting liquid.

"See friends, just get yourself lit up, and nothin' means nothin'." He addressed a sinister-looking, four-footed audience that had slowly begun to circle him.

He slid his hand into his pouch and pulled out some beef jerky. "Shit," he said, "I hope you're happy. That was going to be my dinner." Breaking it into bits and tossing it in their direction, he eased away in the snow and tried to figure a way to get completely free. The dogs, half-starved with ribs showing, their muzzles glittering with ice, watched him with bland expressions.

The wind whined and swells of snow dust rose and fell around them. "Look," he said to the troupe following him, "I've paid my tribute, now let me pass, will you? Pack of tick-infested brush, the lot of you." But he smiled and piloted along, his eyes prospecting for that turn in the road that might lead him to safety.

The pack of furry fellows followed at a distance.

God, did he have to pee just now. If he pissed on himself, that might speed up the process of freezing. A heart-thudding sound tore into the air. "Jesus!" cried Gates and soaked the front of his pants. He trekked on, trying to follow what he believed was the path that Mary and Coolie took. Those damn niggers! Did they really hope to escape from him? He'd see to them, but first Deputy Elam Gates needed some medicine, some rest, and something fit to put in his stomach. Nothing to do but keep plodding. He pleated his brow trying to remember what he had been thinking about before his visitors interrupted him. Oh, right. Daddy. The sot!

Gates grinned at the sky of unbroken gray as he pondered his earliest recollections of his mother, Clotely. She was a sweet, ginger-haired woman, bird-thin, who looked at him like all of God's special glory resided in his spindly body. To the frail toddler who spent most of his early days on a quilt pallet near her in their cabin, she was his whole world. She didn't have any schooling at all, but she would often lay on the quilt next to him and tell him of the dreams she had for him. They were beautiful, colorful dreams that told her the little boy would grow up to be educated and rich and high-falutin' amongst other whites. Her innocent eyes would peer so deeply and unblinking into his adoring ones that they seared into him, their power was so strong. When he cried, she'd stroke his blond locks and say sweetly, "Hush now, precious. Time'll show you just how good you is."

Through his adolescence, he didn't mind the mean and cruel business his father regularly did to him—abandoning him deep in the woods and taunting him not to come home until he had food for the table. He turned out to be a natural hunter—which served him in good stead now—and could almost bag game at will. What Gates continued to long for, especially as he got older, was time on the quilt with his mother before Daddy got home from out doing whatever.

He marveled, remembering his mother as more intoxicating than any liquor he drank and how her reassuring presence overrode the abuse his father heaped on him. He was happy to bring home his catch of the day, which mostly consisted of rabbit, squirrel, or a line of trout. Sometimes in spring and summer, he'd string wild daisies together and present them to her as a garland for her hair. She'd put it on and dance around, laughing.

Gates ran a wet tongue across his cracked bottom lip and his eyes trailed across the expanse. He was no longer walking—he was pitching and stumbling. He hauled his flask from a hip pocket and drank the last of the mash. It burned going down, but in another minute he felt almost giddy, light as a feather. That was the lift he needed. That and his anger would keep him going.

He now knew he was on the right track. He didn't have to see the women, he could read the signs of their travel. Bless Coolie. She was the sloppiest of them, to his good. Killing her would satisfy him. After he'd had his way with her. This was the one favor his daddy gave him. He made his son a killer.

As he leaned into the wind, Gates was still taken up with memories as if glancing into a gypsy's crystal ball. Looking back, he should have seen what was coming. Along with the time he spent on the quilt holding and cuddling his mother, his father's behavior had grown more bizarre.

When it all came to a head, as he recalled it now, he guessed his father had a full hand in it. Gates had come home that afternoon from hunting with a large, heavy pack on his back. He'd helped Clotely skin the animals and hang their furs on the drying rack. Then, after she got the meat in a stew pot with vegetables for dinner, she joined him on the quilt. For a time, they watched the fire in their dinky fireplace, fascinated by the shapes, sizes, and colors of the flames. Once again, while holding him in her arms, she reminded him how special he was—that she knew it from his birth. "Yo' place is among high white mens," she told him that day. "You ain't no commoner. You's a prince who jes' don't know it yet." He had stared into her glowing eyes, felt as totally consumed as if by a whirling cyclone, succumbing to its heady power. "Yes, ma'am," he'd murmured.

Then for reasons he did not understand, he put his lips to her earlobe. She murmured for him to stop, but he could no more have stopped himself than a man perched on a high ledge in the determined act of jumping.

When they kissed, her tongue explored the inside of his mouth. His whole body became a fathomless pillar of fire. This was what love was. Had to be, he told himself as his young loins exploded into an experience nothing short of bliss.

Clotely's mouth moved along his chest and over his nipples. "My baby," she murmured as she continued her course down his body.

Nothing would ever be more sweet or anguishing or satisfying, he recalled, as his member swelled at the aperture of this divine mystery. Her hand found his trousers and in another minute he was inside heaven. Oh God, let this be right with you, he prayed as she murmured his name repeatedly, swelling his heart so big it might burst and shatter into a thousand pieces.

Why did his daddy pick just that time to walk into the cabin? He yelled at Clotely that she was nothing, would always be nothing! He then hawked phlegm from his throat and spat it on the floor in front of his son. "That's what you are!"

Clotely had jumped at his rage and pulled herself away from her son while fixing her clothes. "Nasty boy," she screamed, turning on Gates. "What you tryin' to do to me? I'm yo' mama! Touchin' me like that. You are doomed to hell!"

Gates relived his mind-numbing horror at her words.

"Cervil," she had lashed, "how you been raisin' this chile?"

"Look at you!" Daddy screamed. "I no sooner find out you been diddling some colored wench, but I come home and fin' you doin' the same to yo' own mama! I'm gon' kill y'all both!" He charged at Gates.

Gates had raced to the door to get away. That's when he heard the last thing his mother would ever say to him.

"I gave you everything I got, and you do that with a nigger? You ruined! You ain't special at all. You ain't nothin' mo' than dog turd if'n you been stickin' it up some colored girl's hole then tryin' to poke me." She sank to her knees, then gathered what strength she had left and hurled her last words at him. "You … sorry ass … son of a bitch!"

Gates had raced into the woods, just to get hold of himself. When he returned to the cabin, his mother lay dead on the floor in a pool of blood. His daddy was swaying drunk on a chair.

"She was a whore," the old man slurred insolently. "And you is a prick. You gon' get same as her." Grimly, Gates remembered that the old man had nerve to try to come at him with the knife he'd used to take his mother's life. It hadn't been difficult to get it away and slit the old man's throat. He sighed heavily at the dark memory.

Coolie Parts was also going to pay for it all. All the women who had rejected him—white and black. She should pay double because she was half-white. That seemed reasonable. And that kufi-wearing fashion nigger Mary would pay too. She had everything he had ever wanted—acceptance from whites, praise, accolades, money, prestige, and power.

He thought back to Coolie. How could a woman as beautiful as she was love Mary best and make no bones about telling anyone how she felt? He had to admit his hankering for her was not just to bed her down, though that was a swell thought, but somehow to love her. He guessed he knew that from when he'd first seen her sashaying her spunky self around Travelers Rest. He knew he'd given her grief from time to time, but all he wanted was her attention—any way he could get it. Then, before he knew it, she had become an obsession for him. He couldn't get her out of his head day or night. He wanted her. She would be his prize.

But he hated her too. Now how could he figure that? The very image of her in his mind now made him furious. He couldn't help that he liked colored girls, always had. Something about their dark skin, their thick, sensuous lips and wide round hips, and how they gave it up so passionately in the sack.

———•+•———

"I don't want you to worry," Livingstone said to Mary and Coolie, setting a rifle against the doorjamb. "You can be sure from the time you entered these premises, eyes and guns were trained on you."

"Who is you," Coolie said, "Cullen Baker?"

Loyal's large brow frowned. "No. Killing wantonly is not our way. But we've dealt with troublesome sorts before."

Feeling a little relieved, Mary said, "Most of what we've got on and what we're carrying is damp or wet. We need to dry them, and us."

"We have clothes that will fit both of you," Livingstone said. He chuckled. "They're dresses though."

"I can do with a dress," Coolie said brightly. "Feels like I ain't had one on in a coon's age."

Turning the talk to her major reason for even being there, Mary offhandedly asked, "What do you hear of the war?"

"We hear that the South is outnumbered by Lincoln's forces and they're steadily making their way deeper into Southern territory. Many whites from near the northern Virginia border who turn up here left everything in the dark of night and fled for their lives. News from them is anyone who had a pig, a cow, or a horse lost everything—their homes and farms confiscated for military use."

"Loyal, you mean the South's losin' already?" Coolie said.

"I wouldn't say that. The boys have real heart, but they're still trying to become a solid fighting force under keen military leadership. From what I hear, that's beginning to happen. Southern forces are hampered by lack of communication. They use telegraph when they can, but in these little out of the way places, they're on their own. The Union forces are setting up telegraph lines everywhere they go for their leaders to stay in contact."

"Any fighting around here?" Mary asked.

"Not yet. But I fear it won't be much longer," Livingstone said. "Sometimes we can hear the boom of cannon, though it's hard to tell exactly where the sound is coming from."

"I expect we might run into some of it the way we goin," Coolie speculated.

"If north is your direction, I'd expect so. But I'll put together directions for you that might allow you to skirt that kind of danger," Livingstone told them.

"We're mighty grateful to you," Mary said.

"Obliged," Coolie added.

"Well, on to more immediate things. How're your shoes?" he asked. "If they need repair, you've come to the right place. I'm sixth in a long line of cobblers."

"My shoes need some fixin'. I'd sho'ly be obliged if you'd do somethin' to keep the wet out," Coolie said as she looked around. "Why y'all stayin' way out in no man's land where they ain't nobody but y'all?"

"You think we're alone?" Livingstone asked, smiling whimsically. "Let me tell you, just because you don't see something doesn't mean it doesn't exist. Many people live out here, some in cabins back in the woods, others occupy buried shelters, others manage underground. Many more are in covert hiding places creatively concealed so no one could detect them even close up. We're Quakers. Pacifists. We do not believe in slavery, and abhor slapping chains on another human being because of the color of his skin."

He went to the fireplace, and with a poker, stirred the embers. "The fact is, if you passed through here a month from now you would find no one. We've been here a while and rarely had trouble. Now, certain townsfolk are growing more vocal against our ways and beliefs. If that were all, we'd stay. Since it has finally settled in that we will not fight in their war, and they've come to realize the depth of our peaceful political and social views, they are becoming more aggressive at our presence."

Livingstone looked over at Mary and Coolie. "That is both bad and good. We don't like being persecuted or rousted off our land. But that's the price we're willing to pay for remaining true to what we believe. One day they'll ride out here to give us trouble only to find nothing to trouble. We'll have been long gone."

"And what's the good?" Mary asked.

"We'll be joining others like ourselves in a place called Iowa. Do you know of it?"

Both Mary and Coolie shook their heads.

"There, our people have bought many acres and created a village that is self-contained. If ever you get out that way and want to start anew, I'll guarantee we'll do everything to help you."

"How do you live, make money?" Coolie asked.

"We work our farms and sell in town," Livingstone said. "Most of us have some profession and sell specific products. I make and sell shoes. My wife makes quilts and my daughter, Lee-Ann, she's only ten, has learned to make preserves and we sell that too. But out here, we all share. No one goes without."

Much later, Coolie slumped. Eyes half-closed, she murmured, "I'm fadin'."

Livingstone bestowed upon her a kindly twinkle from his eyes. "My manners. Come on. We'll get you tucked in."

From outside came a loud thump. Alarm sharpened in Mary's eyes as Livingstone swept her from her chair onto the floor. Coolie slapped a hand over her own mouth as Stella dragged her down. Livingstone shot to his feet, snuffed out the lantern, grabbed up his rifle, and slid to the window. Slowly, he angled back a corner of the curtain and looked out. "Lawd a mercy! There's a man out there, facedown in the snow."

Mary and Coolie looked at each other in horror and cried in unison, "Gates!"

Mary yanked Coolie to her feet, helped grab up their possessions, and quickly followed Stella to a far corner of the kitchen where she lifted a rag rug. Livingstone pulled on a thick rope and a door rose up. "Get them down there, where they'll be safe," he instructed his wife. "I'll handle things up here."

Despite her fear, Mary turned to him. "I think I should stay and help you."

"Go!" he ordered.

Mary scurried after Stella and Coolie, descending into a well of impenetrable darkness. Stella lit the wick on a kerosene lantern, and light flushed into the sparse room. While Stella set up a blaze in the small fireplace, Coolie couldn't believe her eyes. Mary was climbing back up the staircase.

"Je-sus bless me in the night!" Coolie cried softly. "Mary, what you doin'?"

Mary put her hands up to shush Coolie, who kept softly pleading with her to come back down and hide. Mary ignored the pleas and ever so quietly slid the floor lid up a notch to peek into the room above. She was puzzled. How had Gates survived the spider bite under such circumstances?

"This is one for the books," Livingstone said, peering out the door.

"What?" Mary whispered.

"A man facedown in the snow." He paused. "And imagine a whole posse of dogs lined up behind him."

Mary couldn't imagine. She watched and waited until Livingstone kicked the door open and half-dragged Elam Gates to the narrow divan that sat under the window. Mary's throat constricted as she saw him again. She thought he'd be dead by now, hoped so anyway. Yet, like a bad penny, he kept turning up.

Though his appearance was as pallid as parchment, Gates was still the enemy. The hairy growth along his jaw and chin said he hadn't shaved in several days. His breathing was shallow if at all. Could he be dead now, she wondered? But at that instant, he coughed and tried to sit up, his long blond hair stringy and dirty, his clothes in tatters. His body reeked of offal.

"Ho, now friend, I got you," Livingstone said.

Gates cried out when the big man eased him back down. He grabbed Livingstone's shirt and mustered, "Spider bite ... my leg." Then he fainted again.

Mary watched as her host pulled Gates's trouser leg up and gasped. From her vantage point, she too could see the angry, open sore. She quietly raised the trap door and moved closer to examine it. The bite was now a large irregular area, a bluish sinking patch with ragged edges surrounded by infected blisters. His entire leg was purple with bruises.

"He's got a fever too," Livingstone said, feeling Gates's forehead. "Dastardly or not, he's a human being so I've got to do all I can to help him. I've some willow bark on the shelf back there. Can you make some tea?"

"Yes," Mary said, feeling sorry that she had caused such pain to another person—even Deputy Elam Gates.

At that moment, the front door pounded open. "You all right?" queried a man holding out his pistol.

"This poor soul won't be aiming to hurt anybody, at least for a few days," Livingstone said. He turned to Mary. "This is Peter Udall, one of my neighbors."

Mary nodded her head silently. She was ill at ease and didn't know what to say. She was a runaway slave, and Livingstone was introducing her in a tone like she might have been his cousin.

Peter lowered his gun. "You don't have to feel funny around me, ma'am," he chuckled. "I'm not the sheriff and frankly don't like the sonovagun much neither."

"Thank you," Mary said. As she went in search of the willow bark, she heard Livingstone say to Peter, "Guess you best get Doc Latham over here. This fellow is low, sick beyond what I know to do to help him much."

"I'll let the rest of the men know the devil's afoot but they can go back home," Peter said. "I'll try to catch the doc before he takes off rabbit hunting." Then he was gone.

Not long after, Mary brought a cup of the steaming tea to Livingstone, who had drawn his rocker near where Gates slept. Livingstone nodded thanks. "Mary, go back downstairs and get some sleep. Everything up here is taken care of. I've got to rouse this fellow enough to get a few sips down him."

She stepped behind the deputy in case he woke up. Staring at Gates, she said, "He doesn't look evil, does he?"

"My friend, it's been my difficult discovery that evil often looks better than anyone else in the crowd."

Once below ground again, Mary suddenly felt exhausted. After cleaning herself in the basins of fresh water Stella provided, she used the balm that Clemmus gave her to assuage the pain in her leg, massaging it in until she felt some relief. The last of her tasks was tending to her feet, and Lord did that lemon verbena lotion almost make her swoon. She worked it all along her toes, between them, massaging it into her heels. Then she put on fresh socks, the nightgown Stella had laid on her cot, and folded herself under the blankets.

"So how do I look?"

Mary was closing her eyes for sleep when Coolie spoke. Much as she didn't want to, she batted awake again. "Coolie, you're as pretty as ever."

The exotic beauty pranced across the plank floor in a yellow-and-green print cotton, cinched at her tiny waist, with her hair now combed in a jaunty upswing to the side. Her face was good-natured and her smile gleamed brightly. She was obviously feeling better.

"Oh, aren't you the one, like the model at the fashion show," Mary said.

"Really?"

"Coolie, there's not another woman in the room on par with you."

Coolie laughed and swatted air at her. "Oh, you."

Coolie was as feisty as a junkyard dog, Mary reflected, and she was a most fetching woman. Her wavy maple-brown hair cascaded to her shoulders in tendrils that were kissed by the sun, and her heart-shaped face was the color of butter biscuits right out of the oven.

"What you feelin' 'bout Gates upstairs?" Coolie pulled the hem of the dress between her legs and sat on the cot across from Mary.

"Sorry."

"Sorry?"

"I meant to kill him, not cause him grief."

Coolie goosed her neck at Mary. "You the one put that hurtin' on Gates?"

Mary looked down. "Guilty."

Coolie hooted and slapped her thigh. "You a warhorse, ain't you? Ol' folks say you gotta watch out for them quiet ones." Coolie's eyes were eager. "How you done it?"

Mary didn't answer. Though Coolie was obviously wide awake and wanted to talk, even about Gates, Mary didn't feel good talking about how she tried to kill the man, regardless of how he'd hunted them. Maybe he wasn't trying to kill them, just wanted to take them back to Norfolk. No, she didn't believe that. Deep in her soul she knew if Gates caught them and had his way, she and Coolie would never see Norfolk—or anywhere else—again.

"Go to sleep Coolie, and let me get some rest." She pulled the covers over herself and turned her back to Coolie.

She couldn't get to sleep right away. She was thinking about how she'd tell Coolie that she had to go on alone, that there was something really important she had to get done. She didn't like the idea of having to endure more cold and more snow, but she knew she had to get back on the route to Washington. She didn't like the idea of being out in the wild all by herself, but for both their sakes, Coolie would have to stay with the Livingstones.

CHAPTER 51

U nder the wan light of a low oil lantern, Mary and Coolie were startled awake by the whispered utterings of Loyal Livingstone, who was kneeling at Mary's bedside. "Men in town're coming to see who the sick stranger is. We need to get you out of here."

He continued, "Stella put together some clothes and provisions for you. I contacted a friend at the wharf who'll take you on his boat to the next stop. That will buy you some time."

"What about Gates?" Mary asked.

"Doc said he'll recover, but he'll likely be down three or four days. We'll keep him here as long as we can. He's tough though, already fighting to get up. Come on. We've got to hurry before he wakes again. And the ferryman won't wait."

Mary gathered up bags, and on second thought she put her ring and Anders's letter into the secure tin she wore in the hussy sack around her neck. Then she strapped the gourd over her body and stopped. "Livingstone, could Coolie stay here with you and your family?"

Coolie audibly gasped. She looked stricken.

"Well," he hesitated, "we maybe could place her with one of the other families until Gates is far away. He couldn't find her, I assure you."

"No you ain't," Coolie stated, hands on hips. "I know you ain't fixin' to leave me, figurin' on Gates or nobody else. Is that why you wouldn't talk to me las' night?"

"Coolie," Mary said patiently, "I want you to have the opportunity for a new life."

"What I done done with you don't count?" Coolie was growing belligerent.

"Look, I don't want to argue with you. We don't know what's going to happen with me. I'm running from the law and into ... I don't know what. I just know I have to do what I've got to do."

"I ain't got nobody but you," Coolie begged tearfully. "Please don't leave me here. I know I been complainin' but I promise I won't no mo'. I'll be quiet and walk like you and do whatever you say. Jus' don't leave me. I love you. I promise I'll be good."

Livingstone stood anxiously at the bottom of the steps, watching the women.

"I love you, is what you ain't figured out," Coolie whispered, "even if you don't love me back."

"Of course I do," Mary said. "I just don't want any harm to come to you."

"You leavin' me won't do me no harm?" Coolie's face was wet with tears.

Mary was exasperated and conflicted. She had known it would be hard, but not this painful. Damn you Coolie Parts, she thought, why can't you make this easier?

"I'm goin'," Coolie said, getting her gumption back. "Ahead of you or followin' you, I'm goin'. Shame on you if you don't like the looks of my behind."

Mary opened her hands to Livingstone, who laughed as Coolie stomped ahead of him and wiggled her bottom when she reached the top of the stairs. He quipped to Mary, "You better be glad it's love she feels for you."

Mary had to laugh with him.

Livingstone hid the women in the back of his wagon and was powering through the darkness and driving snow when a thundering herd of six riders appeared like tricks of the wind before them, scaring the horses and sending the wagon skittering to the side of the road.

Fear was so great that Mary felt detached from herself. This is it, she thought, these men are going to wrench us from our hiding place of hay, shackle us and then drag us down the main street of town behind a horse at a fast clip, forcing any Negroes in the vicinity to view the spectacle as an object lesson. Coolie, as she had promised, lay still and quiet.

"Mr. Livingstone," came a deep, commanding voice with the tenor of a young man. "Hold your horses! I can see you're in a great hurry, and it's my sorry duty to hinder you, but you know me and my men are under orders to patrol this district." The voice was countrified but with charm.

"Hull Patterson?" the women heard Livingstone say. "Portia's boy? In all this snow it's hard to tell. But didn't I make a new pair of boots for you and your mother not long ago?"

Livingstone knew Miss Portia to be a churchly woman, stern and unforgiving in her ways but definitely a help to the helpless. He was squinting through the snowflakes at a man in his mid-twenties, with jug ears outstanding under a black ten-gallon hat his head had not grown into yet.

"You did that, sir," the younger voice admitted. "No finer pair crafted for humble feet for either of us in this county."

"Thank you. Then you know I'm an honest man on my way to do honest work. Important work, certainly so to be out on a morning like this." There was no wheedle or petition in his voice. He simply made statements, then waited.

"Sir," Hull replied, "can I trust you on the word of a gentleman and respected leader in your church that what you're doing—driving lickety-split out here—is the work of a good citizen, and you are not taking me for a perfect fool?"

Livingstone did not hesitate. "On all counts."

Mary heard a horse sidle near where she lay.

Livingstone watched Hull pull a pouch of tobacco from his inside coat pocket and take his time measuring the right amount for a good chew. He put it inside his bottom lip and then said, "I'm skimming my eyes over your load back here. I don't want to coax none of these covers up, because between me, you, and the gatepost, the weather's not getting any better by the minute. So, without detailing to me what all you are carrying, can I also understand that you are not concealing contraband of any sort?" He lowered his head in supplication.

"You may," Livingstone confirmed.

Hull drew close to Livingstone, hunched over the pommel of his saddle, and displayed a wide set of stained teeth. He smiled fixedly, and they locked eyes for a long moment. "Then you can pass."

"Thank you," Livingstone said, and slapped the reins.

Hull spoke as the wagon began to move. "If you're trying to make the ferry, it runs in twenty minutes. Sorry to tell you, but you're about thirty minutes out."

Livingstone drove the horses as fast as he safely could through the trees, bumping over deep ruts in the road, in and out of scudding patches of fog. Wind lashed his face and keened through the trees. His eyes smarted as he stared dead ahead. Finally, when he believed their escape was clear, he turned to the packs of hay and lumpy burlap bags stowed in the wagon bed. "Y'all all right under there?"

"I'll give you two guesses," Coolie snipped.

He smiled. Coolie was—well, Coolie.

"I got to stretch my legs out," she complained in a loud whisper. "I'm gittin' me a cramp."

"Shh-h-h!" Mary cautioned.

"Shut up? Me?"

"Coolie!"

"Okay. I'm shuttin' up, though them bullies back there put me off. And bumpin' on the planks. Think I'm gettin' me a blister on my butt too."

"I swear, you're still not housebroken," Mary snapped.

Still charging along, Livingstone cackled in laughter at the women's words.

At the wharf, he jumped from the wagon and ran to the dock. Several boats and ferries were scattered about, but none of them were his friend's jaunty skiff. His shoulders sagged. As he helped the women out of the wagon, he gave them the sad news. "We were too late."

"Dang! Dang! Dang!" cried Coolie, stomping around in a fitful circle.

"Wait here," he said, "I'll see if I can find you other passage."

Mary and Coolie waited on a landing that sloped down to the water. Tobacco hogsheads and cotton bales were loaded there, as well as barrels and crates of other goods. Carts and wagons stood nearby, being piled high by draymen; the side roads converging were alive with eager travelers, their bundles, bags, and accompanying crates of chickens and small livestock stacked around.

"Will you look at that," Coolie said with disgust, pointing at two fat, grunting pigs trying to bury themselves in a shallow mudhole.

Before Mary could answer, Livingstone returned. He shook his head. "No captain's willing to take on two coloreds. The authorities are constantly checking on them and if they get caught, there goes their livelihood. They're just not willing to risk it."

"No matter," Mary said, "we have our own means of transportation."

"Naw," Coolie said, drawing back in attitude. "You don't mean ..."

Mary lifted up one foot and then the other, and nodded.

"With all these boats here?" Coolie goosed her neck back and forth to define her stand. "I ain't even ..."

"The way I see it," Mary explained, "you have two choices. I intend to go."

Coolie harrumphed and turned away, acting wounded.

Livingstone quickly gave Mary information about another safe house and the latest information on avoiding military skirmishes on their way farther north. "You're definitely going to be getting near soldier country, so watch out."

Mary called her thanks and let her walking stick lead on.

Coolie watched for a moment, then bumped her backpack into place and caught up to her.

Mary glanced over her shoulder and kept to her pace.

Coolie grumped offhandedly, "Ten to one you woulda missed me inside a day. I didn't want that on my conscience."

CHAPTER 52

Her whole body ached constantly now. Mary and Coolie tramped all that day in wind and snow blowing off the river. As fortune had it, they discovered a narrow fishing shanty that stood precariously at the edge of a clutch of maple and pine trees near the water. They put up there for the night. Coolie slept fitfully on a bed of pine boughs. Too restless herself to sleep, Mary hunched near the small fire she'd made outside. She tried for a little comfort and to settle her mind enough to think.

She hadn't been sure how long the journey to Washington would take, but she felt it should be closer than it seemed right now. She had to catch herself up from feeling sad, from feeling that she might fail. She longed for the encouragement and comfort Anders had always given her. He hadn't come to mind often lately—when he did, she made a point of blocking those painful memories. But tonight the comfort of his strong embrace was exactly what she needed to thwart rising despair. My dearest Anders, I do miss you.

Why is it, she wondered, that you miss things and people most when they're no longer around? She even missed the comical conversations she and Tesh-Lucianne used to share, of how well Mary's designs were going and how much the people in town and away thought of them and of her.

She reached into the pouch hanging from her neck and pulled out her ring. Looking at the carnelian stone surrounded by gold and the Louvestre crest in the center, she knew Tesh-Lucianne and Simeon would always have a place in her heart, even though she never expected to see them again. They, of all people, wouldn't understand what she was trying to do or why. Heck, she thought, sometimes she didn't understand what she was trying to do or why. Enough, she reminded herself. This was getting maudlin. Time passes through even the darkest hour. Tomorrow she'd be good again.

She pulled her blanket tighter about her shoulders, and at that instant, spied Coolie's small pack lying open. She could see the corncob pipe inside. Mary laughed to herself. She had never tried smoking. Lots of people seemed to like it and said it relaxed them. She reached over for it. Packing the bowl with tobacco, she lit a twig in the fire and put it to the tobacco, puffing as she had seen Coolie do. As the smoke filled her lungs, she coughed and whacked a fist against her chest. But after a few more tries, she managed to get the hang of drawing the smoke in easily. She sat back and enjoyed the euphoria she felt and the rich aroma filling her nostrils. Her muscles relaxed by degrees as she sat puffing, watching the night, and thinking.

She was worried about Gates as much as she was worried about anything. He was proving to be a diehard enemy. Livingstone said Gates would be down at least three days, but she wondered about that. So far he had shown himself to be pretty hardy and certainly dedicated to his task, which appeared to be the undoing of herself and Coolie. She sucked in the smoke, held it, then let it out in little clouds. Why he was so adamant, she couldn't figure. It was like they had killed somebody. She nearly choked on a laugh at that—she *had* tried to kill him. The wind gusted and twirled more falling snowflakes. The only way to beat Gates, she figured, was to think like him.

So I will, she thought. That would mean I wouldn't lie on a sickbed any longer than I had to. I'd believe that the women had gone either on their own or with assistance. I'd say Livingstone helped them, but to where? Not the waterways. They were being patrolled vigilantly, and I'd bet no one would chance taking the women on board. Railroad was out. They weren't near a major city, and even if they were, the two would be conspicuous. Wagon? If Livingstone had taken them by wagon, he hadn't gone too far from his home place. Dutiful family man that he was, he wouldn't leave his loved ones to fend for themselves. No, a man like that would make sure he was on guard by the door to ensure nothing happened to them.

As she continued inside Gates's head, she dismissed that the women would be on horseback. Those animals were too dear for anyone to part with. That meant they were on foot again, clearly headed north, and wouldn't be that far ahead of him. Just how long would it take, calculating generously, to catch up to them? Mary could just imagine Gates sitting up in bed considering the ugly reality she was envisioning.

One of the first things her father had taught her was to parry. "Sense where your opponent is going to strike," he'd told her, "then make sure you're not there. Deceive his senses of you. Come at him when he's sure you're either wounded or incapable of doing him harm."

Her mind filled with images of Gates coming for them. Experienced hunter that he was, he'd press up river searching for footprints, broken branches in the lowering trees, and their own human spoor, some of which simply couldn't be hidden. He'd hide behind a tall oak, listen quietly, all the while watching for movement and anything out of place. His hobble would slow him but never stop him. Gates with a gimpy leg too, Mary thought. How ironic!

"Coolie, I want you to be a big girl tonight," Mary told her on their third night out in the wilds after leaving the Livingstones.

"And what you gon' be doin'?" Coolie was roasting a sock on a pole over the fire.

Mary started to correct her efforts to dry the footwear but decided it was more trouble than she wanted to deal with now. "I'm going out. I don't know how long, but don't you worry. I'll be back."

Coolie watched Mary ankle holster her knife, check the bullets in her pistol, and stuff it into her belt at the small of her back. Mary slid her hatchet into the loop of her belt and looked Coolie in the eye. "Gates is somewhere near. I'm going to see if we can come to an understanding."

In the late hours of the night, Mary crept forward with the cold pricking her skin and the deep snow slowing her up. Danger was close. She knew it, could feel it, had felt it for days pressing in on them. Nearby, waves rose high, crashed and broke onto the beach in fingers of foam that reached into the short scrubs. With every moment that passed, her tension rose.

Mary had become fully aware of their pursuer. He seemed to no longer care about being stealthy and wily. His movements were not subterfuge. His grunts and small exclamations disclosed his whereabouts not that distant behind them. That he'd made such gain on them could mean one thing—he was no longer a pursuer but a killer who didn't much care if he died, so long as she and Coolie did.

Mary had left Coolie hiding within the jagged crevice of a boulder near their camp. No way could anyone detect she was there if Coolie stayed still and silent. For herself, the way ahead through the trees wasn't very clear, but her mission was to draw Gates's attention. Meeting an enemy one-on-one was best.

She skimmed the back side of a large pine tree and halted, looking up at dark clouds streaking ominously over the tall ridge. She slowed her breathing until she was completely still, and made no sound. She let her eyes play across the land. Finding him would be no trouble at all. Gates wasn't the only one good at tracking.

This had been an area of sure expertise for the old medicine woman on the Clairoux farm who taught Mary. She had been ten or eleven—somewhere around her fourth year of study with the exacting tyrant, Miss Effie. The old woman's ways were hard. Mary thought sometimes that codger laid it on her simply because she could. By this time, Mary had learned so much about plants and herbs and their various treatments that she thought she couldn't stuff much more information into her head. At first, Mary wondered how she could memorize all of the greens, herbs, and twigs they collected since Miss Effie wouldn't let her mark anything down. Everything had to be set to memory.

"Walkin' 'round markin' things down make white folks nervous," Miss Effie said, pursing her lips. "Lord knows, they got enough trouble on they minds jus' bein' white."

Then one morning, Miss Effie said they were going into the woods. They reached a thicket that Mary found scary. The trees so bent their tops together that only pinpricks of light landed on a sliver of tree trunk, a leaf, or a spot on the ground. As they worked, Miss Effie informed Mary that what she had learned was enough for her to take wherever she traveled, to help herself and others.

"I done teached you 'bout everything I know. Las' thing was how to track somebody or some thing. You think you 'members how to do that?" The woman laughed.

The old woman's cackle caused Mary to swing around from where she was collecting. There was no sign of Miss Effie. Mary's first thought was that it was the worst time for a test like this. Rain hadn't come for weeks so the ground was hard-packed. A herd of cattle could've run over the terrain, and it wouldn't show a sign. Or would it? Mary put her hand to her chin, thinking. Yes, she did remember. She remembered both then and now.

First light was still far off when she found Gates's camp. Her eyes surveyed the hillside where he had put down. She detected no signs of other people. He was sitting on a large rock cooking a meal that, if her nose told her right, consisted of boiled jerky, biscuits, and coffee. He looked up, canting his head in thought. Mary hung back in a tree's deep shadow. She watched Gates walk to a canvas pouch hanging from a low tree branch. He pulled out a bottle and grinned. Licking his lips, he poured a liberal amount into his hot coffee. Then, starting to replace the flask in the pouch, he had second thoughts and swigged a long one. He grinned again. Two more stiff drinks followed.

Mary didn't have to guess what was in the container. She let her gaze sweep around, then focused on him in particular. She watched him slump down against a tree stump by the fire and wave the bottle back and forth in time with a ditty he sang:

> Gonna take my time,
> They ain't worryin' me,
> Gonna take my time,
> Drop 'em when I'm ready,
> Those two fine nigra ladies from Norfolk.
> Hey, ho! Hey, ho! This I know!
> Their hearts they owe to each other.
> But their souls belong to me, oh!

He laughed.

Mary squeezed her lips against the disgust she felt rising. After a while, she saw his head sink down onto his chest and the cup totter out of his hand, leaking its liquid onto the ground.

"Hey, ho! This I know. Uh-oh. Got to squeeze the weasel," Gates muttered in half-drunken tones. He hiccupped and tried to stand, but his legs proved too unsteady. He awkwardly angled himself up against the stump to relieve himself. When he finished, he deposited himself into his previous repose.

Mary squirmed deeper into the natural bend of some shrubbery and shivered against the numbing wind. She gingerly touched her leg. It was an agony that she wasn't able to tend it like she usually did, with hot and cold compresses and camphor rubs. Nothing to do about that now, so put it out of your mind, she told herself. Just waiting—waiting still was the way of the hunter. Training with both Tug and Miss Effie, she had learned to sit or stand without moving a muscle, without blinking, or swatting an annoying fly, for however long it took, then take her prey so quietly it did not cause a stir.

She peered through the dense trees at the dying fire and the face of Elam Gates. He certainly wasn't a bad-looking sort, almost handsome, she had to admit. His disheveled blond hair was long and curly and his unscrubbed face sported several days' stubble, but these only added to his sordid attractiveness. She didn't kid herself though. He was no sweet cherub in the arms of blessed sleep. Deputy Elam Gates was, in many ways, the most dangerous man she knew.

Mary had taken the gun from her pack but she didn't believe she'd fire on Gates, reprobate that he was. She inhaled and watched his chest rise and fall in the rhythm of sleep, but she knew he was crafty. He might be asleep or he might not. What was the expression, "Every closed eye ain't sleep and every goodbye ain't gone"? If he had gotten the scent of her he was only playing possum, waiting to deliver fate to her on a platter. Her fingers felt along her belt. She did have her hatchet. She could send it through the air to give him a permanent part in his hair.

Was that movement from him? Be alert, she told herself. As she continued to study him, she detected nothing overt. Wait a minute—did his foot twitch? Her awareness heightened. He wasn't asleep. She swallowed hard. Her throat and mouth were as dry as dirt clods. Beads of sweat popped across her forehead. She knew she couldn't squat here all night. Her plan had been to try to talk some sense into him, but after observing him for a while, nothing indicated that was a reasonable idea. Now she was glad she'd planned a contingency.

Mary had almost decided to return to her own camp when a shadow seemed to loom near her. Then a bullet slammed into the tree where she had been hiding, tearing off splinters. She pressed deeper to the ground and scooted back into the cover of thick brush.

Gates was rushing her, waving his pistol as he ran.

"Goddamn! Goddamn!" he shrieked. "Fool! Tryin' to slip up on me! You ain't the onliest one got the smarts out here." His footfalls thudded toward her. He crashed through brush certain she could not escape quickly. He turned around near the tree where Mary had been crouching. "Come out. Come out, wherever you are," he sang mockingly.

Mary's heart raced, but she did not respond. She held her breath, watching as he backed near her.

"Ma-ary," he continued in singsong. "I know it's you. Come on out. I won't hurt you."

He turned around, holding his gun high. "We can talk. We don't have to play cat and mouse with each other, now do we?"

He took one more step, and Mary yanked on a vine. It coiled around Gates's legs, then a branch tilted and he swung up hanging bound feet up, head down, yelling, "What the hell?" His pistol flew out of his hand.

Keeping herself concealed, she crept from behind him and swiftly tied a blindfold over his eyes. He went to howling. "I'll get you, nigger bitch! I'll do so much damage to you, your own mother won't know you!" His yelling died into muffled exclamations when she grabbed his head by the hair and shoved a filthy rag into his mouth. Swinging and violently fighting against the rope that held him, Mary had to dodge his frantic lashing before she managed to manacle his hands with lengths of rope.

She didn't have the heart to try again to kill him. Not like this. If she'd been attacked, that would have been a different thing again. This would put him out of commission for a while, maybe a long while, she thought. The night was blistering cold and she couldn't leave him that way entirely. Still silent, she quickly set up a fire nearby to keep him warm.

Trussed him up like a pig for the pit, she thought as she blended back into the woods and made for her camp. Without the aid of her walking stick, she did not see a deep trough and stepped down hard in it. When she came out of it, the wind gusted and a tree bough delivered a sound whack to her head. She staggered. Lord! Was this her punishment for what she had just done to Gates?

Wind whistled through the skeletons of trees. New snow had fallen, hiding the tracks she'd made before. She had been walking a long time. Why was it taking her so long to reach camp? Had she made a wrong turn? She couldn't keep her thoughts clear. Coolie—got to get back to Coolie. It's so cold, so cold. She knew she was stumbling like a drunk, and couldn't do a thing about it.

The woods, she thought, a wo-n-n-derful place, just a wo-n-n-derful place. She grabbed her head and fell to her knees, pitching a slide into a high snowbank.

—————•+•—————

Coolie had waited by the campfire for what she believed was way too long. She thought she'd better go out and see if she could spot Mary, but Mary had told her to stay put. She put a hand up to shield her eyes from the elements. Low-hanging tree branches, thick undergrowth, and vines obscured any sight of her. She stopped as she heard a sound. It might be a bear. Or was it Gates? What should she do? Then, with no more thought, she acted.

Coolie ran, jumping over logs and thick vines with the look of smooth snakes, through thorny overgrowth she knew was so sharp it would slice her to death if she fell into it. She ran on, for how long she didn't know. The wind howled in her ears. Her heart throbbed in heavy percussion. Another sound brought her up. She whirled, fists up, ready to take on any opponent. No one came to fight. But there in a thick snowbank, Mary lay motionless.

At the sight, Coolie thought she might go out of her mind. Not Mary. Oh no, not her Mary. She bent down and called her name. Nothing. She shook Mary's shoulders. No response. Coolie saw that Mary's complexion had gone ashen and her lips were pale.

Trying to pull her upright, Coolie sobbed, "Mary! Mary! Is you dead? Please don't be dead." She shook her vigorously yet again. "Come on, come on! Wake up. You can't leave me out here. You know I don't know my way to the nearest outhouse, much less where we're s'posed to be headed."

Tugging her gloves off, she wet two fingers in her mouth, then placed them under Mary's nose. She felt some warmth. Mary's breath was thin and raspy, but at least she was breathing.

Coolie tried to lift Mary. The woman was solid like a granite boulder! She tried to drag her. If she could just get her back to camp, maybe she could think of something to help. She got in front of Mary, grabbed her arms high above her head, and yanked and tugged, yanked and tugged. Within a half hour with the wind kicking and screaming, Coolie had successfully dragged Mary a few feet.

She cast around for something to help her. She saw one long stick and not too far away was another. Now, what was it her trapper friend had told her about this? Racking her brain, she retrieved the poles. Now what? She pounded her forehead. "Tell me, tell me," she shouted to no one, trying to remember. It came to her. She needed to link the two poles together, put Mary on them, and drag her back to camp. Now, all she needed was a rope.

The woods were unforgiving when it came to relinquishing anything resembling rope. Coolie searched all around, aware that Mary's breathing was growing ever more shallow, and the snow was coming down heavily, quilting the ground. Those flakes might just as well have weighed that of a horse's hoof and been sharpened by a sword master, Coolie thought in anger.

She looked around trees, under rocks and logs, but found nothing that would help her. She was about ready to scream when she spied rope in an open pocket of Mary's satchel. It must have fallen open when she was dragging Mary because she hadn't seen it before. Well, no matter, she saw it now. With a few minutes work, Coolie had made a half-decent litter. An hour later, when she found her way back to camp, bless God, the fire was low but still going.

She immediately threw twigs on the fire to build it up, then laid a blanket next to it. Rolling Mary off the litter, she bundled her up with another blanket. Attempts to get her to drink some water got her nowhere. Then a light went on in her head. She'd do what Mary always did to soothe her. From the packed bags she retrieved a jar of lanolin and a hairbrush.

Coolie rubbed balm into her palms and massaged it into Mary for what seemed like ages, taking out from the blanket an arm, then a leg, and so on. Then Coolie drew Mary's head onto her lap. She brushed Mary's lovely hair and prayed and sang every hymn she could remember. Yet Mary remained still and cold.

Frustrated, she threw her head back and yelled to the heavens, "Help me God! Or are you too busy up there?"

She sang the last hymn her poor ragged memory yielded up.

Blessed be the tie that binds
Our hearts in Christian love;
The fellowship of kindred minds
Is like to that above.
Amen.

Coolie fell across Mary, hugging and rocking, holding on for dear life. She sensed she was losing her. Desperate, she straddled Mary's listless body. She screamed, "No you don't! You ain't goin' nowhere without me, and I ain't goin'!" Filled with anger as well as terror, she began to slap Mary's cheeks again and again, harder and harder. "Come back to me. Come on back!"

Coolie lowered her head and gave way to sobs of despair. Around her, the night was as still as if the world and all of its parts had stopped.

Suddenly, Mary sucked in a deep draught of air and coughed.

At first Coolie stared at her in disbelief, then broke into a wide grin. "Yes!" she cheered and waved her hands in the air.

Mary lifted her head and looked into Coolie's wet eyes. She murmured, "What's got you in such a lather?"

"You," Coolie whooped, jumped up and danced. "You. You. You!"

CHAPTER 53

The weather turned bad and stayed bad for days. Thunder continued to grumble and rain clattered down. Mary constantly searched for food as they walked. Just when they seemed to run out, the Great Man Above seemed to provide. During a downpour, Mary spied trout in a watery cavern of tree roots. She was sure they were the biggest of their kind she'd ever seen. Now, how to catch those tricky buggers? She'd have to be sly.

Glancing around, she puzzled what to do. She might hate herself in a little while for doing this because of the cold and steady rain, but she took off her wrap to make a dredge. Most times, she knew, the fish would simply swim over or around something coming at them like that. But, since they were back in the corner of the stream, her plan was simple. She'd move fast, scoop them up, and throw them to shore. These fish were crafty, she thought, but this time of the year, with the water cooled, they were lethargic. They were probably sizing her up all the while she was doing the same to them.

Before she got into action, she spotted a large scallop shell and retrieved it. A light went on in her head. In deft movements, she pushed each end of the wrap under heavy stones on each side of the waterway and pressed it beneath the surface. This would serve as her blind. She began to pound on the ground to frighten the fish out of their cover. When they swam out, she used all of her might and a shell to scoop them up, throwing them into the air to fall on the ground behind her. Food—real food!

She laughed in excitement as she looked at four big fish flopping and floundering about her. They ate two that night and cooked the others to bring with them for the next day's journey.

Coolie added a surprise to the meal.

"Where'd you get that?"

"Our host. He had a lot. He'll never miss it." She took a sip of moonshine and sighed, "Ahh!" As she passed it to Mary, she said, "Here. Do you good and he'p you too. You're a wonder, Mary Louvestre."

"And you're a little thief." Mary giggled.

"Always good to keep check on who you truly is."

In silence, they let the brew and the crackling fire soothe them for a time.

"You ever give any min' to what we left back in Norfolk?" Coolie asked.

"I do."

"I do too," Coolie said, dragging on the bottle. "I loved Travelers Rest. I loved the people who worked with me—Theron, Verona, Sweets's own crazy self. The men who came through were my friends and family. They counted on me. And I just left them to save my sorry ass."

"You know that's not true," Mary cautioned. "Gates was on you like the underside of a toad. If you hadn't left, no telling what might have happened."

Coolie made a rude sound with her lips. "Gates! Put up my place to snuff! You know that peckerwood didn't hit town no time 'fore he had a mess of trouble stirred up."

"I hate that neither he nor Bridges never did anything to make right what happened with Pluck," Mary said, shaking her head. "But then, what could I really expect?"

"Bear told me that it was scary, all the stuff the Travelers found out Gates was up to about and around. I mean, how could this happen just so? This rebel cuss arrives in Norfolk claimin' to be a long-lost cousin of Sheriff Bridges. Sheriff's mother, Miz Clara-Jean, got snowed by him, took him in regardless the awful things everybody'd heard, and made him deputy with power of life and death over coloreds. Don't make no sense to me."

"As far as I can tell, Gates became Bridges's executioner."

"Yeah, Bridges is a self-proclaimed mama's boy—with a gun he daren't use. If Miz Clara-Jean say, 'You ain't goin' out and arrest nobody today,' the gallute jes' get on back into bed, I s'pose. The man closin' in on forty and his mama won't let him marry. Say they ain't been nobody good enough. You know, the glass get mighty clouded when I try to see the clear of that bunch."

Mary nodded.

Coolie swigged and eyed Mary. "You thinkin' more 'bout Anders?"

"All the time."

"Why can't you lie? I don't want to hear that." Coolie smiled crookedly. "If you loved him so much, how come you didn't jes' run off together? It wasn't that you couldn't. Y'all both had ways."

"He wanted to. I was the one who held back. I thought about it and thought about it until my brain was sore, but I couldn't imagine how we could make a life together. I was stupid and small. Probably, I didn't want to give up what I believed was the good life, for all that amounted to."

"What the Louvestres did to you wasn't right."

"What's right in the world of whites?" Mary sounded angry. "Who can figure?"

Coolie snorted. "What Negroes got? Work. Family, if they let us. Though I can't say much about my own. A mother who didn't want nothin' to do with me, a father I never knew." She stared wistfully at the fire. "Onliest thing I kept for me really, when you go deep down, was love. I tried to throw some of it to the white woman who birthed me, but it didn't stick. I took it back from her, but I'm holdin' it still." She eyed Mary, who seemed lost in thought. "What you thinkin'?"

"That I was a forest-for-the-trees kind of person. Everything I came to know told me that if I just worked hard, gave it my all, and trusted, that my future would be different, more secure than most Negroes. I was ambitious, I admit it. I have a talent, and I wanted to set the world on fire with it. But it was all a dream that somebody could shake me out of, and it faded in the light of day."

"You still a magician with fashion. When we get to where we goin' you can start again, on your own this time, maybe."

"Maybe."

"Look, like you tell me, you got yourself. It be up to you what you do with it."

Mary looked at her friend and smiled. "Why, Coolie Parts, do I detect wisdom under that wild mane of yours?"

<hr />

When Gates came to, upside down and hogtied like he was, he went from mad to furious, to out-for-hellfire vengeance whatever the cost. The problem now was, how to get free?

He struggled against the ropes. The nigger seamstress knew very well how to make expert knots. He spent frustrating minutes trying to rip them loose with his teeth, but the effort was useless. For the life of him, he couldn't figure how she had concocted the trap without him hearing a sound. Fact was, she had. Maybe he had to give the devil his due and admit that if she was smart enough to end him up this way, without a sign his eagle eye could detect, she was every bit as good as he was. And he, Elam Gates, was by far the best there was at what he did. People paid good money for his services.

Take Simeon Louvestre for instance. He had paid him, under the table, a whopping sum to make sure Mary was guarded from any and all sorts of trouble. With so much money on the table around deals to take over her company and make it something even bigger and better, Simeon didn't want anything to go wrong.

Simeon knew Mary had bought his lie—hook, line, and sinker. He was trying to do all he could to assure her that she was going to head her own company because he needed the image the company could bring with Delaclaire at the lead. *The man who clothes everyone*—it would be a wonderful slogan for his political campaign. He had needed Mary to pull off a fabulous fashion show, for the clothes as well as the publicity. Then he had to move her out of the way. Gates remembered, word for word, what Simeon had said: "Coloreds are so stupid, they'd believe anything a nice white person told them."

Simeon worried that when Mary learned the truth she might suddenly feign not being able to create or cause customers to become disgruntled and threaten the cash flow. He couldn't have that. His bank accounts were already low and that might make him bankrupt. No way could he endure that social disaster—or recriminations from his father or Daddy A.B. Worse yet, she might get so mad she'd chuck it all and run. He needed her. She *was* The House of M; he just couldn't let her know or rely on it. Moreover, Simeon needed cash. He was being squeezed on both sides by people who had their own agendas against him—Daddy A.B. and Gie on one side and Lumley on the other.

Gates looked forward to telling Mary every whit and hum of this. Then, just before his fingers squeezed the last breath from her throat, he would reveal Lumley's plan.

Lumley thought if she met a violent end, the story of the benevolent, rich white man who nurtured the special talent of a nigra slave would raise Simeon up in the estimation of others on either side of the race issue. When he ultimately acknowledged she did not have the savvy to take it to the next level, he'd had the good sense to take back his investment, bringing in smarter, white talent, and turn it in to an enterprise better serving his people of the South. Why, such a man could surely go far in whatever were his ambitions.

Gates's goal was to get the hundred dollars Lumley offered for taking out Mary. Then, in an unexpected turn of events, she and Coolie had dashed out together into no man's land. He'd sported around with them since, doing his smoke signals and noises to spook them. That Mary was a clever girl. He had to give her that. But it was time to give her something else.

Gates had exhausted every other way he could think to get out of the ropes. After taking a hesitating breath, he stretched and stuck his wrists into the smoldering fire. He didn't want to but knew no other way to escape. His nostrils sucked up the scent of his own burning flesh. In seconds, the pain registered in his brain. His inchoate screams began low, grew louder, ultimately sending seabirds screeching high in the wind. When the fire burned through and his hands were loose, he was able to extricate the knife he kept on his inner right leg and cut free.

He fell like a ragdoll to the ground, cracking his head into the fire's embers before rolling away. By the time he had cut the ties from his legs, he had raised not only raw red welts but another level of madness and cruelty for one Mary Louvestre.

Excruciating pain seared his whole body. But he was alive. His mind was as blurry as the bowl of clouds that swirled dizzyingly overhead. Between the frigid and the pain, he no longer cared about anything. He had one objective and one only. He took the extra pistol from his saddlebag, shrugged on his duster, threw a blanket around his shoulders, and limped into the corridors of night. With every step he took and every lancing pain, he created new and imaginative ways to make those two women truly pay.

———•—•———

Mary set them a fast, zigzagging pace, doing all she could to confuse a trail if Gates managed to follow. She knew that somehow he would. Their footprints in the snow were as good as spoken language, telling him where they were, so she pressed along where bruised shrubs set up rough turf along a valley area. Leading them past a tall falling cataract, she hurried them near where it crashed on the rocks, geysering up plumes of water.

With her leg aching her almost to tears, Mary climbed the brow of a high hill to peer over the way they had come. The woods looked impenetrable and little stirred. Tender wind webbed trees, shrubs, and snow altogether over the vast land below. Fog filigreed in gauzy shapes through the low shrubs and the byways they traveled along. A briny smell filled her nostrils with the scent of fish and seaweed.

Suddenly, Mary's head flew up. The shot exploded blindingly, rattling the bushes just beyond her. As soon as she realized she was still upright and breathing, she chased down the rise toward Coolie, who had let out an ear-splitting shriek. While running to her, Mary saw another bullet bark off the tip of Coolie's ear. Coolie grabbed it, her mouth open in shock. Mary tackled her to the ground as she screamed, holding the ear that was oozing blood. Coolie cast her a desperate look. Keep panic at bay, Mary told herself.

Gates, she thought. The man was not human! After all he'd endured, to be still coming!

Mary's back pressed against a maple's trunk. She waited, thinking, needing to assess the threat. Following a hunch, she popped up and hurled rocks high to gauge his direction. Immediately, bullets seared the air above her head. Aiming to sow as much confusion as possible, she hunched low, and still breathing hard, darted from tree stand to tree stand toward where she thought he was. Moving by blind instinct, she used her slingshot to volley a barrage of pea-sized missiles into the shadowed area where she guessed he was hiding. He shrieked when the hot pepper-coated seedpods rained down on him. They were meant to burn like hell, Mary thought, and apparently they did.

Satisfied she'd hit her mark, she forced herself to be patient. She silently made her way back to Coolie. She knew the chance for them to get away would come moments later, when Gates would be in the throes of dry heaves caused by the herbs that had intensified after contact with his skin. She could hear him swearing between deep-throated coughs. Then in another instant, the two women stared at the frightening incubus that was the Deputy of Norfolk, emerging out of the fog and running in their direction, wild-eyed, drooling, and firing his pistol at them but missing because he was unable to gauge anything at all.

Mary motioned to Coolie to stay down. She ran in the open toward the riverbank, leading Gates away from Coolie. He was right on her heels, moving slower because of his hobbled leg. Hoping to find some way across the raging waters of the falls, she searched desperately but found none. She glanced over her shoulder. He was right behind her, then surprisingly, he detoured.

Frantically, she looked around, wondering where he'd gone. She noticed a thick log bumping along in the stream. How could that help her? Think, think, she told herself. With her gimpy leg, how could she possibly maneuver a spinning log in fast current to get to the far side?

Coolie's scream tore the air once more. Everything else went out of Mary's head. Mary raced back to where Coolie had been. There, Gates hovered over her, slobbering and looking crazed. With knife held high, he had Coolie cornered and was about to slice her head right down the middle.

"Ha-yah!" Mary called. "Ha-yah!" She was dashing as fast as her legs would carry her toward Gates, swinging her walking stick.

He glanced around at her, laughing with the sound of a hyena, and fired his gun in her direction. The bullet lodged into a nearby stripling. He aimed at her again as Mary jerked to the right. The gun clicked under his finger, out of bullets. Exasperated, he threw it at her as she came at him.

She managed to strike a harsh blow to his head with her walking stick, then dashed back the way she'd come and waded into the river. Enraged, Gates slammed Coolie against a tree trunk where she lay trying to get her breath as he took off after Mary. Half-crazed from the new assault to his skin, he screamed again and again, less human than a crazed force in action.

She was deep in the icy water, planning to sink below the log and float to where he couldn't locate her. But she was too late. In a sick instant she realized the crazy man was plowing into the freezing currents of the river after her. Mary thought she heard Coolie moan, but she wasn't sure.

"Daa ... Jesus!" Gates yelled, realizing his dilemma in the treacherous torrent. He hollered. "Mary Louvestre, I gotta tell you something before you die out there."

The freezing water boiled around her as she treaded erratic waves and kept her eyes trained on Gates. "Tell it then," she hollered back.

Gates grinned, struggling against the onrushing waters. "I'm gonna kill you, and I'm takin' your scalp back to Lumley for the hundred dollars bounty he promised. Then Lumley and Simeon can dance on your grave. How do you like that?"

Mary was stunned. The chaos of both her emotions and the water currents were becoming noose-like around her. Urgent to get free, she worried that Gates might still find a way to come up on her again. What to do?

She fumbled forward, awkwardly. She was able to size up that Gates had stumbled far out into the water. He had been so caught up in his ranting that he had not realized just how far from shore he was.

Frenziedly, he struggled back, his arms thrashing like pinwheels, but his legs felt like anvils. The injured one assisted him not at all. He screamed in terror. The restless current rolled and thrashed over rocks and boulders, frothing and spraying a curtain that nearly blinded him. Deep, raging crosscurrents grabbed at his legs as he kicked and fought and swirled about in their hungry surges. She saw him terror-stricken, his fingers tearing uselessly at the braids of water.

"Gates," Mary shouted. "Don't fight. Relax or you'll drown!"

Mary stared at his face. For a brief moment he gazed back at her, and she saw panic weave a brocade of emotions across his face. Against her better judgment, she started fighting toward him. Maybe she could save him. But then a massive wave slapped his upper body and a primitive yowl emanated from his throat.

For whatever reason, he stopped fighting and forced himself upright, bobbing in the water. An eerie calm settled over him. Neither the cold nor the fuming waters seemed to bother him. Setting his chin in resolve, he lifted a large curved knife overhead. Light glinted off it as he aimed, and she knew his aim was deadly. She had nowhere to go. She knew she was like a deer in the glare of the sun, completely at his mercy. Of that, she was sure he would gladly offer her none. Oh, God, was this the end? Time came in inconceivable bursts. Mary's blood ran cold, and she braced herself for the pain.

Water streamed off his fingers and Gates's malevolent smile was on her as he drew back to hurl the knife. Then their ears thundered with the impact of sounds like a volley of cannon fire over the water. Gates screamed an animal howl of protest.

Mary could not believe her eyes—Gates's hand disappeared in a burst of blood. The expression on his face became a rictus of pain, or was it anger? The next bullet spun him like a child's top as blood feathered ever-widening streaks in the shifting waves. She waited, panting, her heart in her throat.

Gates's words came as mean as the man himself. "Mary, you were a fool! Coolie Parts, nobody loves you, bitch!" His macabre laughter rose up insanely, but it froze in his throat. His eyes widened when he heard the low rumble of something growing louder in approach. Then he saw it. A huge, rough log the size of a nightmare crashed along the watery passage, barreling straight at him. Helpless to get out of the way, it tore into him, splitting his skull like a melon, his eyes in total incomprehension of the inevitable as his body, arms splayed like a cross, sank into the bridling funnel that claimed everything, including his hat, to the depths of a watery coffin.

Who fired the shots? She looked out over the water to shore but could only make out vague forms. Coolie had no gun. Was there a new enemy? She could hear Coolie yelling frantically.

Using the log as a float, Mary kicked through the tortuous waters toward the shore. Her foot felt a solid, rocky underwater ledge, but she miscalculated and misstepped. The log slipped from her fingers. Grabbing for it, it turned in the water, throwing her completely off balance. She groped for something to hold onto but only plunged back into the depths of icy waters.

"Mary! Mary! Mary!" Coolie's cries rent the air like sweeps of a scythe that blazed across a tired earth.

Panic seized Mary as the water wrenched away from her that one thing that had made her feel safe in the world—her walking stick. Then the gourd with the important papers inside was lifted off her shoulders by the current and carried away. She reached for it, touched it, missed—and then she just drifted, her thoughts muddled.

Mary found the water oddly soothing as she sank. This was cold water, wasn't it? Then why did she feel such warmth and comfort that she just wanted to rest? She'd be fine. Just drift, let go. She didn't even need to breathe, simply submit to the greater force and float away. In her head she could see Washington. She was walking down Main Street. Crowds of people lined the sidewalks as she strode along. *Glory, glory, hallelujah! Since I laid my burden down.* She was triumphant. *Glory, glory, hallelujah! Since I laid my burden down.* Her journey would soon be finished. *I feel better, so much better, Since I laid my burden down. I feel better, so much better, Since I laid my burden down.* Coolie was there too. Beautiful Coolie. She would manage to be just fine. Just fine. Just fi...

Then blackness.

CHAPTER 54

Mary mumbled as consciousness pressed in through a murky haze. She had been half-waking, half-dreaming, drowning, beaching, sucking air in her nightmares until, in the gray light when the trees around her were beginning to take a discernible form, she pushed to full wakefulness. She struggled to sit up. Her tongue felt fat and she was so thirsty. Slowly, she opened her eyes to see a man standing over her. He held a cup out to her in both hands. Odd, she thought, she couldn't tell if he was young or old. He seemed to be ageless, or was it that her vision still hadn't cleared? She squinted. Was his skin yellowish? No, it couldn't be, she corrected herself as she tried to pull herself up. The effort was too ambitious for her condition.

"My head," Mary said in a hoarse voice. She held her palms to the side of her face and tried to stop the world from revolving.

He set the cup on the ground and helped her up against the trunk of a tall oak. "Drink," he said, pointing to two abused silver stirrup cups he'd placed beside her. "Sip water, then tea. Yeh. Both help. Feel better."

"Tea? What kind of tea?" Mary asked.

"Cricket make good tea," he said with an easy smile. "You like. Yeh."

"Coolie! My God, Coolie!" Mary cried after sipping the water. In a flash she recalled Coolie falling to the beach.

"What is Coolie?" he said. "I Cricket. Yeh. Cricket."

"My friend." Mary tried to rise, but Cricket's fingers pressed into her shoulder and pushed her back down. Mary looked at him in panic.

He pointed to a form lying in a bed of blankets. Coolie's face and halo of hair were highlighted by the golds and reds of the close campfire.

"Shh! Shh!" He folded his hands together and laid his head on them. "Need rest, sleep. Yeh. Like you."

Mary was fighting to come around. "Cricket? What kind of name is that?" She pressed fingertips to her temples. "Am I awake or dreaming?"

"Yes," said the young man, whose smooth face was round as a plate, kindly avuncular features drawn upon it.

She pulled her blanket closer around her and realized she felt the wool with all her skin. "I'm naked under here!"

He cocked his head at her.

She lifted the blanket a little. "No clothes!"

"Yeh. Yeh." He bobbed his head, smiling.

"You rescued me?"

"Res-coo?" His tongue tried out the syllables. "Res-coo."

"You saved my life," Mary said, clutching the blanket close to her chin.

"Yeh. Cricket save. And other man." He handed her the cup of brown liquid. "Drink."

Mary's brow furrowed as she tried to take in all he was saying. What other man? Information was leeching into her mind, slowly. Her field of vision expanded over the campsite. She realized someone else was there, picking up around camp, dragging his right foot, and casting surreptitious looks at her back over his shoulder. He was a burly man who had the look of a dastardly slave catcher she'd once seen. His lopsided features and long gray beard struck her as sinister. She instantly disliked him. "Who's that?" she asked, indicating with her chin.

"Too many questions," Cricket said. "His name Jubal. Yeh, Jubal Stull. Trapper. Hurt foot in accident." He pointed to the tea. "Drink tea now. Yeh. You tired. Sleep. Get well."

A drawing of people Mary had seen in a magazine once came to mind. "Are you a Chinese? I've never seen a Chinaman before."

"Yeh. See one now, yeh. Cricket speak good English, yeh?" He squatted beside her, his eyes examining her face.

"Lord," Mary groaned to herself, "and even with a Southern accent."

"Yeh." He pushed the cup toward her again and bobbed his head encouragingly.

She sipped the hot tea. "Yech."

"Me Cricket. What you?"

"Mary. My name is Mary."

"Mary, yeh, yeh. Me Cricket." He pointed to himself.

"I got that part. What happened out there?"

"White men fight each other. North. South," Cricket explained. He made gun cracks with his lips and pantomimed men falling on the ground.

"I don't mean on the battlefield. What happened to me in the water?"

Cricket's luminous dark eyes glistened, and Mary could see firelight playing, not so much in them but on them, like a screen. "Man shoot at you. He miss you. Hit friend. I shoot him. Man dead." Cricket spoke casually. He indicated Coolie with his head as he put two hands over his left side. "Your friend hurt here."

Suddenly, Mary thought she couldn't breathe or swallow. She started to crawl to Coolie, but movement caused dry retching to seize her.

"Calm," Cricket helped resume her seat. "Other friend get more wood for fire. Res-coo too."

"What? What other friend?" Mary asked with growing alarm.

"He come back soon, yeh." He smiled.

At that moment, a man entered the clearing wearing a sailor's peacoat and watch cap with a fur covering. As he peeled back his hat, Mary pressed her fingers to her lips and muffled a cry. "Jitter? Jitter Conroy?" Then she laughed incredulously.

"Miss Mary, glad to see St. Peter didn't call your name," he said, dumping his haul of wood on the ground.

"What're you doing here?"

"I been followin' behind y'all since you left Norfolk." Jitter flopped down next to her. "Saw you leavin' out of a shed near Richmond with funny clothes on. Thought maybe you was headed on some adventure, and I didn't want to be left out. I was just about to call to you when I saw Gates hidin' behind a tree watchin' you. I figured he was up to no good, so I stayed back, trackin' y'all all the time. Then when that low piece of trash tried to kill you, I put a bead on him and shot. Chinaman over here shot too, though I didn't know it at the time."

"Yeh," Cricket said.

"One of us hit him high, the other one low," Jitter said. "Gates won't be botherin' y'all or nobody else no more."

"Coolie?" Mary said. "How bad is she?"

He glanced at the sleeping woman. "Chinaman say he used to be a doctor in his country 'fore he come over here runnin' from other Chinamen who wanted to kill him over there. He gave her some tea and she's been out since."

"How bad?" Mary repeated.

"Bad enough."

"We're going to have to get her back to Livingstone's," Mary said. "He and his wife are the Quakers who helped us a few days back. I'm sure Coolie can stay with them until she heals. Then they'll help get her back to Norfolk."

"No'm," Jitter said. "We ain't goin' back to Norfolk. Can't go back. Ain't nothin' for either one of us there."

"I thought you joined the Army. Your father got you an officer's position."

"Yeah, but not no more. That wasn't for me. Pa said he didn't want a boy who wouldn't stay and fight for his country, 'stead had to run after the funky skirts of some fast-tail nigger girl who was born a no-count and wouldn't never be anything but." Jitter grinned mischievously. "That's what he said in so many words. But I did tell him that her skirts ain't the least bit funky. I say, 'Pa, she ain't none of that. And, what's more, I love her.' That's when he commenced to spewin' and sputterin' and grabbed his gun. I had to take off runnin' on my horse and hoof out like greased lightnin', 'cause that old man is a crack shot. He called after me, 'You ain't no son of mine! Good riddance to bad rubbish!' He'd pulled his hat off and waggled a finger through a bullet hole at the crown."

"He did all that?" Mary said.

"Said he'd see I got hung." Jitter looked over at Coolie. "Ain't that somethin'?"

"Yes," Mary said thoughtfully.

Cricket beamed at her. "Yeh. Yeh."

"If you say yeh one more time I'm going to scream," Mary said to his agreeable face. "No more yeh. Okay?"

"You—O-kay," Cricket said, smiling. He bowed and poured her more tea, which she deliberately ignored.

"You makin' sounds like you ain't goin' back to Livingstone's with us," Jitter said.

"I've got to go on."

"Rest. Need rest now," Cricket said. He put his hands together and lay his head on them. "You wake. Then eat. I have food."

Mary sighed and watched him go to his cooking pots to stir one and then another.

Cricket looked at her and sighed too.

Mary glanced around at her things. "The gourd! Where's my gourd?" she said in a panic.

Cricket and Jitter stared at her and each other, perplexed.

Mary grabbed the blanket and wrapped it around her while struggling to her feet. She was wobbly and Cricket quickly was there for her to lean on. She broke free. "Where are my clothes?" she demanded.

"Where do you think you're goin'?" Jitter asked.

Mary's eyes were wide. "To get my gourd," she huffed. "I want my clothes."

Cricket pointed toward her buckskin top and pants, hanging on drying poles near the fire.

Heedless of the fact that three men were there, she dropped the blanket and began to throw her clothes on.

"Dang, Miss Mary," Jitter murmured. "I don't mean nothin' by it, but you mighty pretty."

"Give me some privacy please, boys."

Hunching over each other and giggling like school kids, Jitter and Cricket turned their backs around. Jubal simply left camp.

Mary jammed one leg into her trousers, danced a bit for balance, then pushed the other leg inside. She shrugged into her jacket. "Where did you find me, Cricket?" she asked. "The gourd might still be around there somewhere."

Cricket pointed back in the distance where the temperamental riverbank shot up with poplars, tall sedge, cypress hacked by harsh elements, laurel, and long-limbed willow. In the spring and summery freshness those slopes would be home to a host of slithering snakes, turtles, bluegill, bass, grouper, oysters, and nesting birds. All of God's bugs and creatures would bear witness as honeysuckle bloomed, wildflowers spread like a carpet, and berries grew big as a man's hopeful heart. Today, as Mary looked out, the landscape was barren and forbidding, the unending white of snow broken only by gnarled trees and sparse green patches of rhododendron. Old folks who knew the ways had told that watching crows could tell more about danger than could be seen. But even crows knew to keep out of this miserable weather, she thought. She sighed, glimpsing the water that, like jagged teeth, had frozen long spikes of ice about the overhang where they had made camp.

"You stay here and take care of Coolie," Mary said to Jitter. "I'll be back before too long."

"Maybe you ought to have this," he said, holding out his gun.

"To shoot what, another Gates?" As Mary stood, she let out a small squeal. The pain in her leg was formidable. She swallowed hard and squeezed her eyes shut for a moment. Then she straightened up and looked at Jitter. "Watch over her."

"You know I will. Coolie will be fine. Y'all watch out for bears."

"Mary," Cricket called, catching up to her. "I go. I help. I help you."

She looked at him clumsily, slinging his rifle strap over his body. He hustled alongside, holding a long pole out to her. It wasn't her walking stick, but a staff would serve. "Right," she said, accepting it. "Well, come on then."

Mary led the way through the gusty, swirling wind and forced herself down the riverbank. Her eyes scoured terrain for any sign of the gourd. She had to get it back. The whole journey depended on it.

Willows extended massive arms covered with snow. Mary had an eerie feeling, like being in a dream, moving in slow motion. Mud was caked in places and slippery in others, and snow was piled over the earth like a cloak. She sidestepped left and back to the right as she searched up and down.

Finally, she caught sight of the gourd. The long strap had snagged on a jagged rock. It was hanging on, but barely, in the racing river water.

How could she get it? she wondered. And could she get it before it was swept away? Mulling the situation, she thought to use her new staff to knock it loose and send it to where she might grab it.

Suddenly, Cricket was up to his chin in the torrential assault. "Simple," he told her. "I hold you. You get it."

Mary saw how hard he was fighting the whitewater right alongside her. "Hold on to my waist," she said.

"Hurry."

She extended herself out over the roiling waters and aimed her staff in the direction of the hanging gourd. It lifted and turned in the swirls, teasing her. Water surged and churned. She wanted out of there as quickly as she could. No telling when another log like the one that took out Gates might tear down the chute.

Three times she tried to snag the gourd. Three times she got only a gagging mouthful of water for her trouble.

"Sweep stick," Cricket instructed. "Hook."

Icy water slapped their faces, making it hard for Mary to keep fixed on the gourd. It appeared to be losing purchase from the rocks that held it where it was.

She sprawled on the water, letting it gurgle underneath her, and used her feet like fins. She got near enough to the gourd to lift the strap just before whitewater surged up as if intent on snatching it from her possession.

Another bolt of water shot up. She would have lost the gourd, and the water would have won if Cricket had not stayed so valiant. Cold stiffened her in raw pain as she grabbed the gourd. Something in the water hit her hand, and it hurt like hell. Her hand was so frozen, she thought it might shatter. She would have cried out but for fear of swallowing more water than she could drink. Again, the gourd nearly slipped through her fingers, yet Cricket never let her go. Finally it was safe in her grasp. She clutched the gourd to her chest, and Cricket clutched her as they fought their way back to shore.

Back at the blazing campfire, Mary fell exhausted into her blankets. Glancing to see Coolie still sleeping peacefully, she cradled the gourd against her body as she knocked back into a righteous sleep herself.

Jubal lay under his blanket, studying on Mary and that gourd she wouldn't let out of her sight. She'd risked her life to go back and get it. She had it on a strap draped across her body. Must be something valuable inside. Something really important—money, jewels? Maybe she stole something from some white folks. So what would it matter if he stole from her?

He needed money. His partner, Stanley the Stupid, hadn't set one of their traps right, and when he went back to check on them, they were empty. He was enraged. He picked up a rock and bashed the man's head in right then and there, but not before Stanley got a chance to shove him. Jubal knew he was in trouble as soon as he went off balance. He'd screamed in pain as a metal clamp pierced his ankle. The sharp claws of the bear trap ate into his flesh and wouldn't let go, regardless of how he struggled. The more he tried to pry it open, the tighter it gripped. He was a strong man but couldn't do a thing against a trap meant to capture a three-or four-hundred-pound animal. A full day went by as he'd passed in and out of consciousness. He was delirious and cried out every time he moved. The bleeding had stopped, but he was nearly out of his mind in pain, moaning, when the Chinaman, Cricket, found him.

Jubal quickly manufactured a story about how his friend attacked him, and he had stepped into the trap while defending himself. For a slant-eye, Jubal thought that Cricket fellow was crafty. He'd quickly set up ropes and pulleys to release the inner coil. When it did, a scream tore from Jubal's throat that cost him consciousness again. Then Cricket, as stupid and trusting as Stanley had been, dragged him back to his camp and took care of him. All the while Jubal was recovering, he was figuring to rob Cricket of his supplies and any money he carried, killing him if necessary.

Better now after a week's tending, Jubal meant to move on. Why not right now? With that Jitter fellow and the two nigra women, they'd draw too much attention. Dark night still held them in its grip. Everyone was asleep. He figured this was as good a time as any to steal that gourd. He licked his lips in anticipation. If she put up a fight, all the better. He hadn't been in a good brawl for a month. It was time for one, woman or not. Kept a man on his toes.

Jubal eased from under his sleeping blanket and slithered belly down across the little camp circle toward Mary. His knife was about to cut the gourd strap when he stopped. Behind him, he heard a pistol hammer being cocked.

"Another move and you'll be pushin' up daisies."

He turned and saw Jitter holding his gun on him. Jubal stretched his lips back in a smile. "I ain't meanin' nothin'."

"Damn right you ain't. Get on 'way from her."

"Hol' on, jus' hol' on." Jubal raised his arms placatingly. "Put that gun down 'fore you hurt somebody."

"I ain't aimin' to hurt you," Jitter growled. "You move anywhere but away and I'll kill you."

Mary, roused by the disturbance, sat up in alarm. "Jitter? What's going on?" Now Cricket joined them.

"He was gonna ... mess ... with you," Coolie said, standing on wobbly legs. "I saw."

Jubal's lips retracted in a wider false grin that showed no more than four brown teeth in his mouth. He held his arms in the air. "I wouldn't do nothin' like that. I thought I saw somethin' over here. A snake or somethin'. I come to check."

"No snakes in winter," Cricket said. His eyes were angry.

Jubal saw he was cornered, with no way out. He brushed his hands together, one, two, three. "So what's it gonna be? You gonna shoot or 'llow me to go back to my warm bed?"

"Ooo," cried Coolie. She swayed, and Jitter raced to grab her before she collapsed to the ground.

Jubal sprang up, dashed for his pack, and spun around to run. Before he could, he collided with Cricket's lightning strike of both hands against his ribs. A sudden kick attacked Jubal's midsection, and he fell like a broken tree branch. Knees to his chest, he rolled on the ground, moaning.

"You bad man," Cricket exclaimed. "You lie. I help you and you do this?"

Jubal panted, heaving. "Hey, worl's full of 'em."

Cricket slowly approached him. His face was fury. Jubal panicked and surged up, trying to grab Cricket's feet, but the Chinaman was too fast to be snared. Jubal fell against the wall of the overhang and foundered on his back, looking up in horror. The rest of the group watched entranced as, from overhead, an icicle as big as a man's leg broke off and made a swift, lethal descent into his heart.

—————

Dawn brightened along the horizon in ribbons of cheery colors. That and a blazing fire lifted everyone's spirits, as did the delicious aromas from fresh fish sizzling on a spit and the scents from Cricket's cooking pots, where he was intent at the moment.

"Why you come out here?" Coolie asked Jitter, who was pouring coffee and passing it around.

"By the way, thanks for this," Mary said gratefully, lifting her cup.

Jitter nodded acknowledgement. Then he stared at Coolie for a moment before he spoke. "You really need to ask?"

A sudden thought caused Mary concern. "Are you a deserter?"

"In a manner of speaking. I'm not plannin' on going back to the Army nohow, so it don't matter."

"Why? What you gon' do?" Coolie asked. She pressed her hand to the bandage on her side and then pulled the blanket closer around her.

Jitter glanced at Mary, then down at the fire, then nervously back at Coolie. He licked his tongue over his lips and rubbed his palms along his thighs. Before he lost his nerve, he blurted, "I mean to ask you to marry me."

Coolie slapped her hand to her chest and guffawed. "That's funny. Really funny."

Embarrassed now, Jitter dug a finger against the side sole of a boot. That was not the response he was looking for.

Coolie measured him and grew serious. "Truth is, you know I got me a hankerin' for Miss Mary here."

"Who on God's green earth don't know that?" Jitter said. "If there is a poor, ignorant sap out there I'll write 'im a letter."

Cricket watched from his vantage point as Coolie harrumphed and folded her arms over her chest. Mary appeared utterly puzzled.

"I don't see why the three of us can't make a new life together—up North."

"Jitter, I don't love you," Coolie stated flatly.

"Yes'm. I know that. But I love you enough for both of us. I'm thinkin', if you give me half a chance, I might grow on you some. Sorta. A little." He made a funny face. "I'm a hard worker. I wash up real good, and I wouldn't like nothin' better'n takin' care of you."

Mary looked at Jitter and smiled. "Jitter, I'm going to Washington. Alone. I have important business to attend to there."

"Yes'm," Jitter said, "and I aim to help get you there."

"You under the misunderstandin' that black and white can live better together there?" Coolie asked, smirking.

"We got to live somewhere, and Washington would have its problems too with the likes of us. But, what I do know is money levels everything out. And I got me some. Been savin' for a while, plus what I emancipated from Daddy's cashbox before I skedaddled outta there." He chuckled as he turned out the pockets of his jacket, pants, and carryall. The women stared at the growing pile of bills and gold coins. "Guess Jubal was planning to rob the wrong person, eh? Plus, I got me a trust I can cash in soon's I get me a lawyer."

"A'Lawd!" Coolie exclaimed.

"Ain't none of it Confederate. I'm supposin' that'll buy a lot of respect, wherever we go."

"How much you got?" Coolie asked.

"Enough to give us a fresh start."

"How much is that?" Coolie said.

"Do you know the word *rich*?" Jitter lowered himself to one knee. "Coolie, please, will you marry me?"

"What we gon' do with him?" Coolie asked, ignoring his repeated proposal. "You best put that money somewhere for safekeepin'. I ain't studyin' you right now."

Jitter's face showed what he felt inside—dejected and rejected.

Coolie softened. "Lemme think on it. Okay?"

Jitter stood up and smiled down at her. "Seriously?"

"Now leave me alone, man," she said as Cricket put food in front of her. "Can't you see I got me somethin' to do here?" She stabbed a fork into the fish and chomped down on it. She turned her head back and forth. "Mmm, mmm, mmm. We talkin' manna from heaven!"

"Yeh," Cricket said, then glanced at Mary. "Ready?"

"More than ready."

As the three of them ate, Coolie glanced over at Jubal's body beneath a blanket. "Can't we do somethin' with him?"

"Jubal?" Jitter said between bites. "He ain't botherin' nobody."

"Can't leave him like that," Coolie said. "He was pig shit, but we got to do somethin'."

"Ground too hard for bury," Cricket said.

"I'll wrap him," Jitter said, "but foxes or wild dogs gon' make him dinner soon as we're gone."

"Reckon so," Coolie said. "That be the way of things."

The wind lifted a sudden howl. "It's tunin' up out there," Jitter said. "We gon' need more wood to keep warm. I best be seein' to that." He put his hat on and went into the frosty day.

Coolie chuckled softly while staring at the fire. "What a crazy fool notion Jitter got." She glanced up at Mary, who did not respond.

After a long moment, Mary said, "I want you to accept his proposal."

"What?"

Mary nodded. "Yes. You need somebody where you're going. The world can be a hard place for a woman alone."

She stopped, checked herself. Where had she heard that sentiment before? She might believe that for some women, but Coolie Parts was something else again. Coolie would survive. She might grate on some folk because she was so direct and her mouth hadn't yet learned to hold back some. But she would not only survive, she'd be all right. Still, she could use somebody to balance her and soften her quick temper, as well as give her some security. Jitter could be that somebody.

"Whether you stay in the South or go further north, you're going to be in a whole other place than what you've always known. You won't have your bar, or your reputation, or the care of people who know you or who your mother is." She watched Coolie begin to pout. "Building a new life is hard. Having a man to help you might not be a bad idea. Even if he is white."

"Where you gon' be?"

"That I don't know. First things first. I keep telling you I have to get to Washington. After that, I don't know what will happen to me. So please, let Jitter take you back to Livingstone's. You need time to heal."

Coolie squawked, "Without you?"

"Don't worry. It's all going to work out. Trust me," Mary reassured her softly.

Later that night, as they were falling asleep, Coolie whispered to Mary, "Y'all ever wanted to have a baby? I mean, you and Anders, maybe?"

Mary took so long to answer that Coolie thought she might have been asleep. "I don't know. Besides, I'm too old for that now. And Anders is gone."

Coolie sighed. "Didn't you ever think about it?"

"I never met anyone I even thought about having a baby with, until Anders," Mary said. "But the hen was out of the coop by then."

The fire cast off a warm glow, and shadows danced along the stone wall in its light.

"Can I get in on this conversation?" Jitter said. "I might have some input."

"How?" Coolie said. "We talkin' babies. What men got to do with that?"

"You don't know?"

They all laughed and enjoyed the feeling of fellowship, fleeting though it was now.

"I help," Cricket stated, breaking the warm silence that followed. "I go Washington with you. I good man. I help."

"A Chinaman with a Southern accent. Where do you come from?" Coolie asked,

"Tennessee. I left my people to work the railroad. Hard, hard work. But white men not want me. Black men not sure about me. Winter come. Now I go home to family. Family is good."

"Yes," Mary agreed, "family is good."

Later, as the men cleaned camp to leave out, Coolie watched Mary prepare for travel. She checked for just what she needed and stuffed some personal items into the backpack Coolie had been hauling. Then she pulled a pair of long johns over the pair she already had on. She put on a pair of thick wool socks and pushed her feet into the moccasins she had repadded with two layers of lamb's wool. Then she put on a heavy sweater, her buckskin pants, and another sweater. Jitter had given her his watch cap with the fur. She tugged it down over her thick auburn mane, caught up into a knot at her neck. Lastly, she checked the foodstuffs Cricket offered and her dwindling supply of medicinal herbs and ointments. Digging into her hussy sack, she looked wistfully at her ring with the Louvestre crest and felt for Anders's letter to Guillaume. It too was still there, intact.

"I hate you goin." Coolie's voice was low.

"Coolie, you and I are family. Sisters. I don't want any more harm to come to you because of me. Go with Jitter. He's a decent man. He loves you with all his heart. You see that now. You'll not be allowed to marry in the legal sense but your bond together can be a strong one. Let yourself do that, because there can be no life with me like that."

She tried to meet Coolie's eyes, but they were downcast.

"I want you to look at me, Coolie. If you can't do it right away, I'll wait."

Coolie's face agitated in emotions she could hardly control, but in tiny stages she raised her face to look Mary in the eye.

"Good. Now I want you to hear me say something. I do love you, like family. Anders's death killed something inside me. Hard as it is for me to accept, I know I missed my turn at long true love and that was with him. You've been blessed with a real chance to have that." She clutched Coolie's hands and choked back tears. "Take it. You owe it to yourself, and to Jitter. I know how it feels to be loved by a man the way he loves you. Don't be like me. Love him in the time you have together. Life is short. Way too short." She shook her head, then chuckled. "Go be a pain in the ass to Jitter. I'm hitting the trail."

CHAPTER 55

Hard travel had scored deep into her bones. Misery was no longer applicable. Tired was too soft a term. Mind-weary was too subtle. Mary was happy to finally find a dense copse of trees that provided her shelter from the wind and snow. Expert now, she set up camp, moving numbly by rote.

Suddenly, something drew her up, an unexpected sound coming off the water. Peering into the heavy fog, Mary spotted a dark man poling a simple raft-like structure with a shack. Crude craft though it was, she had to admit a flatboat was a cheap way to travel and even live on the water if need be. Nothing speedy about it though, as such boats had trouble going against the currents with only a long pole in the hands of a strong man to keep it proceeding.

She cocked her ear. Did she hear singing? Who could that possibly be? Standing stock-still, she monitored the boat's movement and the sounds.

Wind carried lilting strains, all right. But the rhythm of the words was peculiar. It sounded very much like the way Devereaux sang a mixture of French and English. She pondered—a colored man, in a boat, in the fog, on the water, singing? Angry waves rushed to shore in a crash and hiss, but his song was sunny and gay. She bent and strained her eyes to get a glimpse of its source. Not until the winds momentarily lifted a curtain of cloudy fog strands could she see clearly. She sucked in a breath and hastened through the tall weeds and sea debris to the shore.

Cheered, she wondered if maybe this boatman might take her up river, get her closer to her destination. A respite from walking filled her with hope. The cold and ever-present damp was a misery. She'd looked forward to the challenge of being back on her journey, but the cruel elements had so tamed her enthusiasm that she'd be glad to even hitch a ride on the back of a turtle. Waving her arms wildly to draw the man's attention, she cried, "Hey! Hey! Help!"

He had been aiming the prow toward shore, but when he saw a colored woman waving a vicious-looking staff in his direction, he stopped poling backward and studied her for a moment.

"Help what?" The soupy fog brought up his rolling baritone.

"Me. Who else do you see out here?"

"Wait a minute, let me count." He pushed the boat to shore, jumped off, and tied up. Sizing up her good looks, he beamed a smile as he approached.

Mary tsk-tsked to herself as she noted his quick once-over of her. "Is your boat big enough for another passenger? I'm going north and could use a lift."

"Oui, about the passenger. No, about going north."

"Are you French?"

"Partly. That makes my humble vessel international." He continued to exude good cheer.

"Can I try to convince you to help me out? Even just a little bit?"

He gave her a rubbery smile. "My terms are negotiable, madame."

"It's mademoiselle," she corrected.

His eyebrows lifted. "Intriguing."

"Then let's start with a warm fire. I've one going back over in here," she said as she nodded toward the beach shrubs and walked in that direction.

He rubbed his hands together. "Cold out here. Could use me some warmth about now. Working on the water can be hard on a man's back and shoulders." He noted her directness and straight back despite the tired slackness he'd initially seen on her face and the limp. She did not turn around or answer him. He was pleased that she did not appear afraid. He smiled appreciatively as he watched her walk ahead of him.

As Mary maneuvered up the sandy slope, through sea grape and thick vines to more solid ground, she was very aware of the man. She wasn't about to let anything or anyone too near before they'd been assessed, and was taking his measure. She saw he was impressive, with the worthy look of a lord. He was built high and muscular, around six feet five and full-bodied. Fortyish, maybe. Skin the color of polished walnut, with large doe-shaped eyes that were a shade of brandy, as best she could tell in the shifting light. There were rugged creases on his big open face. His well-defined jaw and luscious lips were set off by long bushy hair cascading in a dark mass to his shoulders. Overall, she thought, he was quite handsome.

Now bounding alongside her, he carried himself with a swaggering authority, radiating a crackling energy that exuded a devil-may-care attitude. She snorted disdainfully to herself as she edged through the sinuous branches of the tree bank, lusty wind crowding in after her. Some sort of rogue, no doubt. A gambler, with that outlaw look. What might be his price for a ride north? Time would tell.

Flopping down by the blaze, his face was genial and his voice musical when he announced, "I'm Carthorne Bittibay, once a slave captured from Haiti, now adventurer and businessman." His teeth glinted in a crooked smile as he gave her a direct look. "And you, mademoiselle, are ...?"

Mary settled herself down on a blanket opposite him. "I am Mary Louvestre."

When she was no further forthcoming, he asked, "Is there more?"

She shrugged noncommittally. "You hungry? I was going to make something to eat."

"What you got?" His eyes and lips lit up.

For some reason she felt irked by his easy way with her. How dare he be so familiar when they'd only met. "I can make cattail root soup. I've some dried in my bag and herbs to tasty it up. There's a freshwater stream nearby. I might be able to rustle up some fish."

"That's all?"

She pinched her lips. "I am not a general store."

"Wait," he said, jumping to his feet. "I'll be right back."

Mary pretended to busy herself, adding more twigs and cracked boughs to the fire, but it didn't escape her that he glided away with the magnetism of a lion filled with self-confidence and the very pleasure of moving. Over his considerable frame he wore a black dress coat that reached to his knees, a collarless blue striped shirt tucked into black pants, and a black hat with wide brim—all of which had seen better days. Oddly, she noted, he also wore gorgeous black Balmoral boots that ran to his knee. Who did he have to kill to get those, she wondered. But the man did have style, she had to admit—real panache.

In moments, he returned holding up two small nets of oysters. "Hauled them in not long ago. Got some potatoes I traded a man for and," he patted his pocket, "tobacco."

Mary pointed to a pot already simmering on the fire. "Then, with my herbs, we'll have a fine oyster stew."

"We've got supper."

As Bittibay shucked the oysters and Mary set everything to cooking, he asked, "So, you goin' nawth?"

His voice was as soft as a cloud, Mary thought, low with sounds of the South and a cadence that might have come from his home, Haiti. "I didn't say."

"That's why I'm asking." He pushed his ragged hat back on his head, enjoying that she was obviously pretending to be piqued with him.

She felt self-conscious under his appreciative scrutiny, and her answer to that was irritation. What was it about him? Her heart caught as she realized he reminded her of Anders, not so much in looks as in manner. They both had that ease. Like now. Bittibay lay languidly by the fire, not seeming to have a care in the world and as if entertaining a guest at his table. And though she kept up a mask of hard exterior, he was somehow promoting those same feelings in her.

He waved his hand to get her attention. "I was asking what causes you to be wandering the wilderness alone?"

"Something I have to do."

"Uhn-huh," he responded as he threw a twig into the fire and watched it spark.

"You? How come a colored man such as yourself is out here on these rough waters in a boat all by his lonesome?"

"Running whiskey from Kentucky all up and down these parts."

"Isn't that dangerous? How can you, Mr. Carthorne Bittibay, get around when most white folks can't with this war going on?"

He looked over the red-gold dancing flames at her. "Who you know don't like whiskey? Who you know don't want to make friends with somebody who got some?" He stared at her, grinned ever wider, and flashed his eyebrows up and down. "Huh? Huh?"

The man was funny too, Mary thought, and she had to laugh at his antics.

"Started as a hire-out," he said. "My owner, Turin Blassingame, said he'd make more money the way I trade. People like me. For years I went out with a full load, come back empty with money stuffed in my sack. He'd give me a little something, not much, but I didn't care. I loved being out plying my trade. I went new places. I met interesting people. Like yourself."

"Something happen?" She was trying to dismiss a growing personal interest in him.

His face grew sober. "The war—when it came upon us, Master Blassingame suddenly was in a fit that I was going to run off with his money. Said he didn't want me out on my own anymore where he couldn't keep track of me and my doings. Seemed like overnight the man turned mean as a hurt wolf."

Mary let silence hang a moment, then asked, "You have a family?"

"*Had* me a family," Bittibay said sharply. "Blassingame took my woman to his bed—forced her, whilst I was out selling for him. Claimed if she didn't, when I come in again, he was going sell me south to a cotton plantation. I walked into our tiny shack and sniffed a rusty smell. In a second, I knew it was blood. Elise had opened her veins with a jagged piece of tin. My chile was inside her when she did it. Friends told me later she said I deserved better than a wife turned whore by a white man."

Mary couldn't speak, she was so moved. Tears filled her eyes as she watched the pain in his.

"I stormed into his house," Bittibay continued, transported back to the moment of discovering his wife. "I planted my feet in his parlor and say, 'Sir, how come you do that?' You know what he said?"

She shook her head.

His own welling eyes turned to Mary. "He laughed. Like I had told him a joke. Said that big-butt gal wasn't nothin' to him but a bedwarmer when he wanted one. Just wanted to remind me he was boss. Then and there I could've killed him. But I didn't. I packed what little I had, took his boat and some of the money he had stashed under the cooling house floorboards, and I've been out here on the water ever since. That's who *I* am, Miss Mary." His voice had built up heat, and his fierce eyes were full of portent.

"I'm sorry," she said, knowing there was nothing else she could say to this abused man. She began cleaning up after their meal.

Bittibay saw the sorrow his words had conjured in Mary. "Don't do that now," he appealed to her. "Let's just sit a minute. I'll help you with that a little later."

"Really?"

"Women's work, men's work, it's just work far's I'm concerned. If we share the job, it gets done faster. And, with my particular skills, done so much better."

"Oh!" she laughed. "Such arrogance!"

"You're quick, Miss Mary. No flies on you!" Bittibay's eyebrows again danced comically.

For some reason, for the first time in weeks, Mary felt elegant despite her tattered clothing. She watched him pull out a large pipe and stuff it with tobacco. He lit it with a twig from the fire, and a billow of rich-smelling smoke wafted over to her. She closed her eyes and savored the aroma.

"Here," she heard him say.

She opened her eyes to see he was handing her the pipe.

"Go on." He made encouraging backhand motions.

Hesitating only a moment, she took pipe in hand and puffed. The smoke filled her lungs and head with immeasurable pleasure. She handed it out to him, but he motioned for her to keep it. After a little while, she said, "I don't believe I've tasted tobacco like this before. It's nice. Very nice."

"Blend of my own. I know it from my homeland."

"Haiti?"

"Uhn-huh," he said in mellow tones. "It's way over the waters. An island." Bittibay reached into his coat and pulled out a large flask of whiskey.

"I'm beginning to believe we're a Commonwealth of drunks," Mary said, eyeing the flask. "I haven't met a soul so far on this trip who wasn't carrying."

"Then it's been your luck to meet the right people." Holding the whiskey up in invitation, he said, "Some of my best. So, how long have you been on this trip all by yourself?"

"Much too long, that's for sure. I started out from Norfolk—that's where I'm from—a good while back. It seems like an eternity. I'm alone because I have to be, leastways for this part."

"Somebody after you?"

"Not anymore. Not that I know of."

"I'm not trying to pry. Not too hard, anyway." He smiled at her. "But surely you can understand why I might wonder?"

"Yes, I understand."

She stared into the fire and he stared at her for a while. "Unh-huh! Now that we got that clear ..."

They chuckled together.

"You are obviously one helluva woman. I can't rightly imagine what you've been through getting this far. That'd be admirable for a man on a horse, much less a woman on foot. Wish we had more time for me to know you, Miss Mary."

Relaxing and riding on the spirit of tobacco ecstasy, she observed his long fingers pull two turtle shells from his pack. Into each he poured a long stream of clear liquid. He lifted a shell to her lips and she took a sip. It burned down her throat and spread out, soothing every kink and ache in her body. My God, she thought, it was magic—he was magic. She had to check herself.

"Are you a voodoo man?" she asked suspiciously. "Are you working roots on me?"

"Nothing of the sort," he said. "I just thought we could do with a moment when we shut out the world and all of our concerns."

"I'm not concerned about anything," Mary said, losing some of her flint.

"Exactly." He smiled and opened his hands as if he'd answered a mystery.

He leaned back on a propped up elbow. "Take another, then chase it with a sip of that hot tea you made."

Mary did so and instantly felt her shoulders relax. "Mr. Carthorne ..."

"Call me Bittibay. Please."

She cleared her throat. "Bittibay, I'm trying to get to Washington as quickly as I can. I've important business there. Can you take me in your boat?"

"Nope," Bittibay said summarily, "though I'd sure like to. I got a full load of whiskey and a buyer waiting on it in Richmond. The South's a thirsty place right now."

Mary stared forlornly into middle space.

Bittibay fished in his jacket pocket. "Here," he said. "You're not far from where you want to go. This'll keep ya from gettin' lost. In case you don't have one. Weather this time of year can send you in circles otherwise." He held a compass out to Mary.

"Thank you. That's very kind. I lost mine a ways back in the river." She felt sad that he wouldn't help her. In rebuff, she wished he would go.

Bittibay chuckled, divining her thoughts. "Look, I'm not some hardhearted man leaving you out here to fend for yourself like I couldn't care less. You're almost there, and you're not out here all by yourself."

"What do you mean?" Mary felt a flash of worry.

"These woods are alive not only with trees and mutts, but all sorts of people live in here. Escaped slaves, for one. Whole camps of them, though they're not likely to let you see them. Suspicious lot, they are. But that's how they survive. Bands of Indians too. Mostly they're kind to coloreds. Some even have colored wives. Singly, these folks'll help you any way they can. The ones to watch out for are white trappers. Traded with them once or twice, my whiskey for their furs— raccoon, fox, and bear. Lately made myself a good deal—a keg of Louisville's finest for these beautiful riding boots. But they're a bad lot when it comes to women. Act like nobody half-schooled 'em."

He downed another whiskey swig and wiped his mouth with the back of his hand. "I helped a white girl get away from them not long ago. Name was Arvelle-Rossa Eva Marie Scott. Imagine. A name like that on a sprig like her. She said her mama gave her that name, a proper-sounding name, being they were dirt poor, and she didn't have the way of something else better.

"One day when I come up on her, Arvelle-Rossa was wandering barefoot along shore, hardly no clothes, blood caked on her face like somebody hit her hard, lots of times. She told me men had kidnapped her by a creek near her family's cabin and had their way with her for months. They kept her in a place the likes of a stand-up coffin, taking her out to use her and sometimes to give her something to eat. One day she realized the lock had not closed completely on the chain across her prison. She worked it open. Then she lit out, running as far and as fast as she could. She begged my help. I tucked her in a whiskey cask whenever we came up on people. 'Til we hit North Carolina. That's where she said she had people. For all she'd been through, she was nice. She smiled a lot and cleaned up around the boat, skinned fish when I caught them, did all she could to repay me. Then she asked if I wanted to bed down with her, but I didn't. I told her I thought maybe she'd seen enough of that to last her a while."

"You're a good man," Mary said, convinced that was true.

"That's one thing I'm surely not," Bittibay pronounced. "Any man try to get 'twixt me an' my cargo or me and my boat, I'll torment their souls and those of their unborn children." He pulled back his coat and revealed a gun the size of Virginia. "Since my wife died two years ago, I haven't had a woman I couldn't buy and leave when I got good an' ready. Haven't wanted any ties. Just want to live until I don't. Maybe I'll get me a dog for company. Name him Shadrach like the one came out of the fiery furnace." He smiled at her, then his eyes closed.

Moonlight frothed and filtered through the hoary trees and overgrown bushes, giving them cover. Firelight pushed back against the darkness and cold and illumined the refuge their campsite afforded. Mary let Bittibay slumber as her mind cast back to Anders. How alike the two men were and yet how different. They both had easy ways and generous laughter. They both had dreams of independence for themselves, home, and family. Anders's turn of phrase was more poetic than Bittibay's, but he was just as fierce about what he wanted. Both had a way of making a woman feel safe and secure and appreciated. Both, behind their irrepressible ways, were tough and iron-willed.

"Tie up with me, Mary."

She was startled to look into Bittibay's eyes, open and warm.

"Why would I want to do that? I've known you two hours."

"I know you. Though you're strong and determined, a lovely woman like yourself could use a man looking after you."

"So, you're applying for the job? Thought you wanted a dog."

He chuckled as he sat up, still not taking his eyes off her. He opened his fingers appealingly. "In my beautiful homeland, black people fought for freedom a long time ago and won. We own our own lives there, our homes, families, businesses, churches. What few whites come on the island are traders who sail off with the tide. Lots of opportunities there. I'm smart, and I know how to make a good deal. No trouble trading in whiskey and, in no time, we'd be set up."

"You figured all this out when?"

His laugh was like the sound of a drumroll. "Look, it came to me." He slapped his hands together. "Just like that. Pay attention now, 'cause I'm selling. I can make a good living and I promise you won't go for want. I'd bet any woman who would strike out by herself walking to Washington could do about anything she wanted there. And I'd help you."

"What if I didn't like you?"

He made an incredulous face. "Im-possee-bley!" he exclaimed with a French flourish. "Anyway, it's a big island. You go where you want, do what you want. If that's not with me, I'd be sad." He pouted.

She chuckled to hide her mind's desire to say yes, to put down her burden of commitment and run off with this handsome man who said he would do right by her.

"There, that's it. Smile. Feel happy. What I'm saying is, you'll have choices, more choices than you've probably ever had."

"Hmm. You assume too much."

"Probably. But we could do it. Me, you, and—the dog, Shadrach."

Why now, Mary thought, when I'm so close. How had it happened? Over the course of a meal, a smoke, and a drink, Bittibay had managed to worm himself into her thoughts and desires. What he proposed was seductive, as was he. Her heart, she thought, had been sealed up, and now she felt it wedge open a bit by this stranger from a strange land. Life was funny. Reflecting on herself, she realized she wasn't so used up that, at the right time, she could have given Bittibay a twirl, charmer that he was. This was a mean twist of fate.

"You're a temptation, Bittibay." She sighed. "But I can't. Maybe I could catch up with you later."

"Soon as I drop my load in Richmond, I'm heading home. And home is Haiti." Now it was Bittibay's turn to look sad.

<hr/>

When she woke the next morning, Bittibay was gone. Not a sign of him anywhere save for a brown bottle of whiskey and piece of paper staked near where she lay. She picked it up and read: *If you ever need me—or maybe decide you want a fresh start with me on a beautiful island—contact Tangeray Jones, barrel-maker on First Street, Washington.*

Mary walked out into a clear morning through the border of twisted vegetation to the water. Pale sunlight dappled the frosty hills. Soft hues patinaed the blurry horizon. Cold wind skittered through tree branches and across the slow purling sea. She smiled and waved at the disappearing figure of Carthorne Bittibay, now on his way. Aloud she said, "Haiti-man! You take the cake!"

Mary doused the fire, buried her trash, gathered her belongings, picked up her staff, and walked on.

CHAPTER 56

$\mathbf{M}$ary's next days on the trail differed little from all those that had gone before. Rainstorms plagued her, drenching her cold to the bone. Violent snowfall assaulted her as she fought her way along, seeking shelter amongst thin trees, in dugouts, caves, under overhangs—one had nearly crushed her under its burden of snow. How she hadn't become sick she didn't know. Winds razored through her clothes and moccasins, which she tried to repair nightly and failed as too much damage had been done.

She tried to keep a steady pace, but things happened. She accidentally stepped into a puddle hiding hard rocks that sent bolts of excruciating pain through her leg and into an exploding headache the likes of which she had never known. She was without anything to assuage her pain—no herbs, no ointments, no balm. She had used up the last. The best she could do at the end of each day was make a decent fire and scrunch up to it for warmth.

Her leg was an agony that never started or stopped. It was simply a statement of her being, forcing her to drag it along like she would a separate appendage. At times, the pain that lanced through her caused her to collapse. She gave way to the tears as she rubbed her knee and ankle vigorously until she could force herself to press forward again. Fatigue had become a manifest entity within her, and blistered feet slowed her steps. Feeling the urgent need to not only get Virginia plans into the right hands but to rest for a long, long time, she pushed on.

A few days after leaving Bittibay, wind-driven snow practically blinded her. Hearing a muffled shot, she squatted and duck walked into shrub to hide. She was sure she had been spotted, as she'd been walking right out in the open, not even trying to disguise herself at all. Her fatigue and pain had caused her not to care. And, since she'd seen no one for days, she'd grown lazy in her reconnaissance, feeling there was no one else out in what looked like an abandoned land anyway.

"Hoya!" a man's voice called out. "Hey!"

Mary stayed low and quiet. Angry winds howled, surrounding her in icy spheres. Trying as she may, she couldn't discern where the voice came from.

"I see you over there," the voice said.

Mary heard footsteps scrunch and crack the hard ground cover. He was making way toward her.

"Look," he said, "I don't want to shoot, but I will. I don't mean nobody no harm. I'm just tryin' to get home."

Mary took a deep breath, and against her own better judgment, slowly rose up to see what must have been the most pitiful looking Confederate soldier ever was. Young, white, and small built, the clothes he had on looked like he'd found them in a scavenger hunt. His basic uniform was Confederate gray, but on his head was a Union cap. Over his shoulders was a blue blanket and a torn haversack. His boots surely had belonged to a man three times his size.

"You're what's protecting the Confederacy?" Mary asked incredulously of the emerging vision.

"What you talkin' about? I cain't even protect me," his voice squawked. "Goldurnit! Will y'all please come on out from there so's I can see what I'm dealin' with? I'm 'bout to freeze my butt off out here, but I got to make certain you ain't the enemy."

Silence.

"What if I do?" she said finally.

"A woman?" He sounded wary. "Who's with you?"

"I'm alone."

"How come?"

"I'm not the enemy." Mary paused, then asked, "You hungry?"

"I'm so hungry I could eat my shoe leather or take a bite of you."

Mary stood up fully. "What's your name?"

"David," he said. "David Zachariah Makheadne. Hey, there's maybe a place over there where we can be 'til the worst of this blows over." His indication demonstrated that he had no gloves and his pink hands were severely blistered. He trudged off but stopped when he realized she was not following. "Hey, I can either shoot you, take your stuff and go over there, or we can go over there together. You choose."

"I have food. If we can get dry, I can make us some soup."

David's face slowly blossomed into a wide grin showing several missing teeth, top and bottom. "Whoo-ee, you talkin' my language!"

Eventually, insisting themselves through the turbulent winds and wet, they found a small indenture, not a cave so much as a curved space protected on three sides by rock and trees. David collected wood and hauled water from a nearby creek, and soon Mary had hot soup cooking, using root vegetables she found and herbs from her bag.

David sat with his back against the rock wall, his scrawny elbows on his knobby knees, staring at the cooking pot. Tied to her belt, Mary had the turtle shell bowls Bittibay had left behind. She filled one and handed it to David, who smiled gratefully. She nodded at him and filled another for herself.

Once their feet and legs were warmed by the decent fire, and they had eaten, David asked, "What you doin' out here?"

Mary pondered a moment, then decided not to answer him. "I would ask you the same."

"You could," he agreed. "And I'll tell you again. I'm goin' home."

"I'm beginning to wonder if there's anybody actually fighting this war. Everyone I've met has been trying to leave it."

"Yeah, well, I'm here to tell you they's plenty a good ol' boys fightin' for God and country—patriots all. But lots of us are sick of the fightin' and camp life. More dysentery passed around than the plate on Sunday," he said with disgust. "And forget about outhouses. There's so much shit in the woods, come spring every goddamn flower and weed there is gonna bloom. Then they's the bad food. That stuff they call hardtack is so full of weevils that, when you pour water on it, the little buggers float to the top ready to make new ones. Made me sick to look at 'em. And you want to know the worst?"

Mary shook her head that she didn't.

"The military doctors," he went on. "I know they's overworked and don't have much morphine to give, but seem like all they do is cut. From hangnail to busted leg, they gon' lop it spang off. There be piles and piles of arms and legs and goodness knows what-all else. See, my job was to clean up the hospital and operating area. It was so bad." He shook his head despairingly. "I'm twenty years old and I don't think I'll ever sleep without nightmares of what I done already witnessed in this war."

He went silent. Mary watched emptiness overtake his gaze, as if his soul were disappearing.

"Me and my three brothers were stupid when we got the call to sign up to fight," he finally continued. "Country life can be pretty boring. So we thought, hellfire, this is our chance to see some of this country. We thought we'd get nice uniforms we could prance around in, have a good time boozing it up with the guys in camp, have a hoot with a few women, and shoot us some Yankees. Then go home to tell stories and lies to our kids about what it meant to fight for the good ol' South. Yessirree! That's what we thought. Well, the real story was gruesome." He hung his head to his chest, his head full of vivid battlefield vignettes.

"More soup?" Mary asked, trying to break the spell. She held out her hand for his bowl.

He nodded, then bluntly demanded, "You runnin'?"

"No."

"What then?" He gave her the bowl and watched with avid eyes as she refilled it.

"Business."

He belly laughed. "Lord-y! A colored woman on the trail headin' north. On *business*. And you ain't runnin'? Right."

"No, I am not running."

He made a rude sound through his lips.

"If you didn't want the answer, why'd you ask?"

He waved a dismissive hand. "You a feisty one. I ain't messin' with you. It's your business. I ain't in it. Got enough to handle my own self, tryin' to keep from freezin' my johnson and killing off the family line.

"A few months ago I got my first letter from Ma telling me Pa was down with the grippe and getting worse, couldn't I come home for just a little while and help her out on our tiny, little farm? I went to my sergeant, told him what the deal was, and he 'bout cussed me out. Said to put that out of my mind. I was a soldier now in this blankety-blank Army, with blankety-blank responsibilities. I told him I was a son first and foremost. Next thing I knew, he swept his leg and knocked my feet out from under me. Got in my face spittin' globs, looking madder 'n a wet hen, and told me to get my pasty ass back to my tent. For a while after that, I fretted but kept to my clean-up, though the battle picture was gettin' worse every day. Sick soldiers. Dead soldiers. Bloody body parts. Puke and pine with not a headstone to honor who they was and what they done."

He ate more before he spoke again.

"Passel of women trailed along with us, helpin' out here and there. Some of them would burn pine knots, when they could find them, to cover up the awful stench that got into our clothes. Seemed like the stink wormed right up into our own skin. Well, by that time the second letter came from Ma sayin' Pa had died, that the bank was claimin' what little piece of land we scrabbled for, and she was set off alone. I went crazy when the sarge told me I still couldn't go home. Said, 'Got to keep sharp, young man. That's the key word—man. You got to stand up. You got a job to do, 'long with keeping the nigras in check.'" He glanced at Mary. "No offense."

"None taken," she said quietly.

"I swear to the livin' Lord, I mean that too. No offense. It was a nig ... colored man what saved my sorry behind when fightin' got hot." He pulled on his ear and showed where half of the appendage was gone. "See this? Bullet scorched my hair and took off all but this, it come so close. I went down. A Yankee hauled over a rise, with his rifle trained on me. I just shut my eyes, knowin' I was goin' to meet my maker. But Riley, old retainer to our Captain Jack, out of Stone Mountain, he appeared out of the smoke and ran right at the man with nothin' but a wood club. Beat hell and tarnation out of that soldier boy and carried me back to camp, where I prayed the rest of my ear wouldn't be sliced off and tossed into the pile."

Mary was silent.

David lifted his youthful face and said softly, "Did you know colored men are fightin' for both the North and the South? I don't mean soldiers in the proper sense, though many of them want to be. Army officials don't hold with that. But they're out there on the front, diggin' trenches, workin' every job possible in camp, and when able, they grab a gun and mix it up with the best we got."

"What happened with Riley?"

David finished his soup, set his bowl next to him, and patted his concave belly. "Ol' Riley," he smiled, remembering. "Well, when I woke up in the hospital, I had this bandage on my head. Riley come in to see me, said, 'To them that have ears, let them hear.' I said, 'What'd you say?' We 'bout fell out laughing. Ol' Riley, he got killed though."

Mary continued to listen.

"Wasn't even no Yankee that done it neither," David said. "We had this pisspot from Kentucky, Sergeant Cavendish Toole. Called hisself a ladies' man. The women trailers come around to do laundry, this and that. Sweetest one in the world, Miss Addie, did for us mostly. Nice girl with short auburn curls. Kinda scrubbed-looking in her homespun clothes. Couldn't of been more'n sixteen. Wanted to become a missionary and help people, she said. One day, Toole decided he wanted her to do more in his tent than wash his shirts and underwear, if you get me?"

Mary nodded that she got him.

"She let out one scream and Riley lowered the boom on Toole. Knocked him in the head and put him down. Riley was helpin' Miss Addie out of Toole's tent when the sergeant snatched up his pistol and in two pops took out Riley's knees. Then he used the butt of that thing to wipe off every feature of Riley's face. I was mortified! I wasn't fightin' for that bullcrap! That was it for me. Come daybreak, I was gone. I'm still gone and gonna be more gone by tomorrow."

"Where are you from?" Mary eventually asked.

"South Carolina," David said. "Little nowhere corner of ground, but we got roots there. You?"

"I'm from Norfolk."

"Y'all ain't had no fightin' there yet?"

"No. Not before I left."

"Won't be long. Folks silly to think this war gon' be over anytime soon. I been out there on the front line. The North is strong and they outnumber us time and again with lots more shot than we got. They believe they right just as much as we do. I tell you, I don't hold with no Yankees, but they got fire in their eyes and they comin'. Won't stop 'til they done run down the entire South if they can."

"The South's in a bad way?"

"No'm, ain't sayin' that. We fightin' 'em tooth and nail, but it won't be over tomorrow and it's gon' be bloody every inch of the way."

"Where are your two brothers?"

"Gone." He stated the fact so flatly there was no cause to ask more.

They stared at each other, two odd dinner companions who would never meet again

"If you don't fight, won't they send somebody after you as a deserter?"

David shrugged. "Won't find me. I'll take Ma and disappear so far into the backcountry, they'll find elves and a pot of gold at the end of the rainbow before they get a whiff of us."

Mary laughed.

David belched. "Wish I had me something to wash this down with."

"Not to worry," Mary said. Digging into her bag, she withdrew a small flask. "Compliments of a fellow traveler named Bittibay, from a place over the waters called Haiti."

Mary saw Bittibay in her mind's eye, on his boat, grinning his white teeth, tipping his hat, bidding her fond farewell, and laughing big like he did. With all the troubles of this trip for me, Mary thought, he's one of the good memories.

And now young David would be another. When she heard nothing for a long spell, she looked up to see David had fallen fast asleep.

They parted the next morning. It had been a tough couple of days since she'd bid him farewell. She had wished him well trying to get back home, then took up the next leg of her journey. As she endured the blistering cold and snow, several times she had to hide from troops, Confederate and Union, that passed by. Brave boys, Mary thought, but how long will they have to go on killing each other over freedom? Most of them looked so tired. Some, with bloody uniforms torn and muddy, appeared to have taken ferocious hits in battle. Many had drawn faces, appearing hungry and greatly in need of both food and rest. Behind them, others carried wounded on stretchers and in wagons. Sadly, following them was the cart hauling the casualties, blankets pulled up over their faces until they could be properly buried. Yet there they were tramping on in faith, and following orders to another battlefront to capture the hopes of their homeland.

One evening, after she'd made camp and was searching for edible greens or roots, she pulled up to see a soldier holding one hand up as if to wave. She didn't wave back. In the fading light, she could make out that he was maybe forty, his wavy brown hair flecked with gray. His blue eyes seemed to be staring at something over her shoulder and with her heart thudding she turned to see. There was nothing.

"Sir?" Mary called softly.

The man didn't move.

Mary edged closer. "Sir?"

When she got near she saw he was dead, frozen stiff. His face and hands were blue. Snow lay on his shoulders, drifting down the front of his coat, its military buttons still gleaming. She inched closer to him, standing knee deep in a snow-filled hole. Blood was spattered around his thighs from bullet wounds. Further inspection revealed two more bullet holes in his chest. Tentatively, she reached her fingers out to sweep the snow off his remains and say a little prayer for him.

She stopped, wondering if another soldier lurked nearby. He might think she was trying to steal something from the dead. He might put a bullet in her back. Cautiously, she glanced around and listened. Nothing. She spotted a small pine branch, retrieved it, and gently whisked the snow off the man's thin face. Was he someone's father or brother, she wondered, who would never return to those at home who longed to see him again? How—why—did he come to an end such as this?

Mary snapped a pine branch in two and tied the pieces in the form of a tiny cross with a length of rope from her belt. She planted it in front of the dead man. Then she noticed something in the snow and bent to pick it up. It was his hat. She brushed it and set it gently on his head. Touching two fingers to her heart in homage, she placed them over his. Then she clasped her hands together in benediction. She hoped her gesture eased this soldier's transition, that even in his death he knew that someone had touched him and cared.

Next day on the trail, she encountered less snowfall but winds that she could have sworn had razors embedded in them. She was wrapped up, but every exposed portion of her body felt cut hundreds of times by icy sharpness.

From the directions given her, she realized this, finally, was the road out of Virginia, and she urged herself on against the blowing snow. Suddenly, the ground thundered under Mary's feet. She realized that, somewhere close, cannons were firing. She did not want to get caught in the middle of a battle. She tried to hustle a little faster, but the trail was rugged and pitted with ice. Using her staff to avoid pitfalls was constant, her eyes searching not only ahead but surveying around her so as not to be caught off guard by anything or anyone. She swung her head to the side to turn from the wind and missed a hole that clenched her staff, twisting her off balance. She clung to the pole to brace herself, but the staff splintered and she was felled like a tree, slamming down to the ground on her battered leg. After a few minutes of self-examination, she determined that she was bruised but all right—nothing appeared to be broken. Looking down at the ruined staff that had helped her so far, she nodded in thanks, rose up, and went on.

God am I exhausted, she thought. But she was heading in, she was getting nearer. This was the leg toward Washington, and she was walking it, dragging her throbbing leg, and carrying her gourd.

True luck came when she reached the Potomac River, although it didn't seem that way immediately. Gloomily looking out over its dense banks and wide rolling expanse, she could see no way to cross. She wandered along, fighting hopelessness. She couldn't get this far and no farther, she thought. She simply couldn't. Snow pelted her face as she stumbled along the slope trying to figure a way. Lifting her leg to maneuver over a bush, her gourd strap caught on tangled branches, and she was again thrown off balance. Her leg went out from under her, twisting her foot in a thick ground vine, and she careened downward until a large rock blocked the rest of her fall. She lay there trying out different parts of her body to see if she had broken anything. Slowly, her head woozy, she crawled on hands and knees to where she could hoist herself up. When she did, her leg was seared by pain. She looked down and saw that her buckskin pants had been sliced through, and blood trickled from a cut to her knee. She threw her head back, wanting to yell and curse, more from exasperation than from the pain. She pulled a rag from her bag to use as a bandage.

She rested and waited for the throbbing in her leg to subside. After a moment in the silence, she heard voices. Now, she was relieved she had not cried out.

Muffling small grunts and staying carefully hidden, Mary limped cautiously down the hill. She knew she had to get close enough to see whether the voices might be friend or foe. At water's edge, she saw a small group of people. They stood with bags and belongings on what looked like a makeshift dock. There, a barrel-chested white man barked orders to get on board if they were getting. "On board" was a log raft enclosed only by ropes strung around its sides. A few who were already loaded stood holding on to the ropes.

A ferry, she thought. Think. What must she do to get on? Think!

Quickly, she took the fur cap off her head and unpinned her hair, letting it fall to her shoulders. Acting as if she had a right to join the other passengers, she boldly advanced upon them and spoke. "What is the cost of passage?"

The man's dark eyes probed her. "What?"

"What's the charge?"

Completely taken aback by her and her manner, he ran a calloused red hand over his buzzed brown hair. "How much is it worth to you?"

"Two cents."

"Didn't cost us nothing," a young boy from the raft shouted.

"Two cents," Mary repeated.

"You a nigra?"

"Do I look like one?"

"I can't hardly tell."

She took two cents out of a small pouch and held it out to the man. Then, to seal the deal, she dug out the last of the whiskey Bittibay had given her.

Upon seeing that, his toothless grin was blinding in the light. "Why, ma'am, let me help you up here," he said with clumsy graciousness.

Bittibay was right, she thought, a lot of thirsty people out here.

Hours passed on the water before signs of Washington came into Mary's view. Around the outer edges of town, military encampments sprawled. When the ferry landed, many people milled about, which made it easy for Mary to blend into the flow of traffic. After a time she reached sidewalks. The sights were almost overwhelming—buggies with spry horses, and people entering cheery shops where bells tinkled greetings, and restaurants with big windows that showed diners gathered around white-clothed tables. Occasionally, when a door opened, she caught a whiff of food cooking. Glorious! And so many people were out! They didn't even seem to mind cold weather like this. The atmosphere was anything but dreary. It held a feeling of merriment. She felt invigorated, her own excitement growing. Then it hit her—it was coming into Christmastime, and the town was dressed up.

After asking several people for directions, she approached an imposing structure. The guard standing by the door eyed the tattered, filthy woman suspiciously. "You want to see who?" he demanded of Mary.

CHAPTER 57

"Miss Louvestre, that was quite a story." Secretary of the Navy Gideon Welles leaned back in his chair, appraising Mary with fresh estimations. "If these papers are true, the Union owes you a debt of gratitude. Your feat for a woman alone shames me. Had I been in your position, I wonder what I would've done."

She carefully extracted the small pieces of paper from the gourd, arranged them together like pieces of a puzzle on his large desk, and deciphered her code on each piece. There, in all of its glory, was the ironclad, the CSS *Virginia*, once the *Merrimac*. Welles remained quiet in front of the papers for a long time. He studied intently the secret inner quarters of the Southern fighter before him. Then, turning to her with a stunned expression, he said, "Miss Mary, this is truly incredible. This document will ensure us a better chance at victory."

"I hope so." Mary sagged into a chair.

Welles noticed. "You must be more tired than I ever could imagine. Let's get you downstairs and on your way."

"If I could beg a favor?"

"Certainly," Welles said.

"I have a letter here. A friend of mine wanted it posted if anything happened to him." She extracted it from the leather hussy sack she wore around her neck.

"And did something happen?" Welles's face conveyed his concern.

"Yes."

"It would be my honor, this very day." Welles took the envelope and slipped it into his jacket pocket. He reached into his wallet and peeled off some bills. "I doubt you had planned where to stay once reaching the city."

"I know no one here," she admitted. "I hadn't thought that far."

"Allow me the liberty to see you have comfortable accommodations. Will that be acceptable?" He extended the money to her. "I will see to other compensation for you—officially that is—but for now, please accept this to help you through a few days."

Mary was surprised. "I had no idea." She started again. "You don't have to—"

Secretary Welles stopped her with a raised palm, his warm smile set between his large mutton chop sideburns. "Ah, but I do. Now, I'll have my assistant take you to a boarding house. The owner, Miss Leontyne Nair, is a friend. She'll provide you with a hot bath, a change of clothes, and good food for starters. How does that sound?"

Mary sighed tiredly and smiled. "That would be wonderful. I'm all grime."

He reached out his hand to shake hers, and Mary laughed as he pumped it with excessive vigor. "Even in grime you are stunning, Miss Mary."

She scoffed, then pretended to preen. "Here we are showing the latest in road travel—featuring scruff, filth, and decorative ragged tatters."

"Which, on you, are still quite fetching." His eyes twinkled as he ushered her to the door. "If you need anything before we talk again, just let Miss Nair know, and it will be taken care of. I'll meet with you again in the next few days. My assistant will call on you later about our next appointment, at your convenience of course."

"Next appointment? Your kindness, it ... it overwhelms me," Mary stammered. "I never expected such generosity."

"It is my experienced observation that people of great nobility often are unaware of who they are and the impact they have." Bowing slightly, he bid her goodbye.

Standing outside the office building as Mr. Welles's carriage arrived for her, Mary felt too tired to cry, yet she was filled with a palpable relief. She wasn't sure what to think about all that had just happened. It began to sink in that her mission had been accomplished. She had succeeded.

The driver helped settle Mary into her seat and drove down the busy streets of Washington, an amazing city at Christmastime that was showy and glittery through her coach window. As to questions of what else to do now, she put those aside. It was enough to be here, safe, having survived.

Soon, she stood in a lavish second-story apartment of the boarding house, with a luxurious four-poster bed and a sitting room. Wide, lace-curtained windows showed an expansive view overlooking the lights of the city. Two white-jacketed servants brought in a massive tin tub. When they poured in gallons and gallons of hot water, steam and bubbles billowed up in a fragrant haze. Leontyne Nair swept in behind them toting a small tray with a tall drink, two fat crab cakes, a bowl of oysters with sauce, and bread for dipping.

"Miss Nair, I can't think what to do first," Mary said to the white woman who appeared to be about her same age.

Tall, with a style and flair that simply took over a room in a homey way, Miss Nair said, "I can help with that." She pulled up next to the tub a small table with a white doily in the center. On it went the tray with food and drink. Opening her hand invitingly, she said, "In with you now. Oh, and I'm putting this bell right here too, so when you want more hot water, just ring. One of the ladies will be in to heat you up again. There's a robe for you on the parlor chair.

And help yourself to any of the clothes in the highboy and chiffonier. Whenever you're ready for dinner, just come on down. If you decide to nap first, please do."

"Thank you, Miss Nair," Mary said softly. "I'm overwhelmed."

"Well, get your overwhelmed self into that water while it's hot. Gideon ... Secretary Welles has directed me to do everything possible to see to your swift recovery. You are to remain here under my care for as long as it takes. His note informed me a doctor will be by to see about you later tonight. He is very concerned about your leg."

"I never expected any of this," Mary said.

"When Secretary Welles likes someone as he does you, which is rare, he is exceedingly gracious."

Mary shed her clothes and stepped into the water. "Oh my God. I may never get out. Miss Nair, this is paradise." She settled up to her chin in the suds and smiled tiredly but happily.

"Call me Leontyne, will you?"

"Okay," Mary chuckled too. "Leontyne and Mary. L and M, just like the alphabet."

Leontyne settled on a chair and continued. "Secretary Welles has provided money. I am to take you shopping for whatever you need while you recuperate. I am instructed to acquaint you with the city, show you the sights so to speak. Which I will not mind at all, believe me. We will dine at nice places and there are certain people I will introduce you to at Gideon's behest."

Mary drew an arm out of the soothing warmth, patted her hand on a tea towel on the table, and broke off a morsel of the tantalizing food. "Why? Why is he doing all this for an old black woman?"

"Clearly, he has seen something in you. You'll know soon enough what his agenda is. For now, Mary, your job is to let yourself be indulged. Is that so hard?"

"Only thing harder is asking for more of these wonderful crab cakes."

"My grandmother's recipe. More will be on the way in an instant." She smiled at Mary as she rose to leave. "You know, there are some people I like right away. You're one of them. I'm glad you'll be staying with me. I think we're going to become fast friends."

After the click of the closing door faded, Mary settled back in the restorative waters that smelled of lavender and lay her head against the rim of the tub. God bless Welles and bless Leontyne, she thought. She sank deeper into the water's heat and let flashes of the last leg of her long journey slip through her tired mind. It was going to take time, she told herself, to get used to the fact that her work—at least, this work—was done.

It was all right to remember now, lying in a hot bath compliments of Secretary Welles and his friend, Leontyne Nair. She had given up her elegant salon. She had left behind the only family she had—the Louvestres, Tug, and Miss Effie, Coolie ... and Anders. Maybe she could've stayed in Norfolk and worked everything to her advantage. But for how long? Who knew? Who could chance to predict anything anymore? She was so tired. She didn't want to think beyond her tub and its fragrant water. Soon, she drifted off to sleep in the water.

When she woke, she rang for more hot water and sank further down in the bath. She wiggled her toes. She could actually feel her left foot again. Her knee, though still throbbing, was manageable. She thought that when she got out and before she cooled down, she'd rub it with liberal amounts of camphor and lanolin, for their healing effects.

After more time in the tub's soothing warmth, she dried herself. She wrapped a robe's thick comfort around her body and looked out at the spectacular view of the city as she toweled her wet hair. Ah, Anders, she thought, why couldn't you be here with me? Why couldn't we be here together? I was such a fool.

Fresh tears burned in her eyes when, suddenly, she thought she heard laughter. She went to the door and cocked an ear. The hallway was quiet. Was it someone next door? Planting herself next to the wall, she heard no evidence of residency. Was she going batty? She heard the sound again and had to smile, realizing it was a memory, a potent memory. It was the giant sound of water cascading and burbling over rocks into a gentle, warm pool. It was Anders's laughter, and it was Bittibay's. She could see them. Their dark faces shining, arms open in welcome for her. She shook her head to clear the vision. What a notion.

Sipping her drink, an adage yielded up in her head: "... lest you entertain angels unaware." Putting her drink down on the table, she silently thanked Anders and Bittibay—for their invitation, for their welcome back to the world.

CHAPTER 58

M ary had been at the boarding house several months and Welles had been as good as his word. They had met several times to discuss her life and experiences. He couldn't seem to get enough of her stories or their growing fellowship. A government commendation for her had come through for what she had done to help the Union, and he had seen to it that she was generously compensated. His question on their most recent meeting, however, threw her.

Welles made certain their appointment was set for the end of the day. His assistant had brought in a platter of sliced duck and venison, boiled potatoes and greens, and a stout port as accompaniment. After they dined, Welles pushed his plate away and looked at her. "Mary, I want you to work for us."

"Excuse me?"

"There's much to be done during this war and afterward," Welles said. "Obviously, you're intelligent and resourceful. You'll be handsomely paid."

"Doing what?" Her eyes widened in surprise.

"What you do," he said. "Find things out. You'll be sponsored into the South and other areas from time to time, and you'll filter around with your eyes and ears open, then report back to me. When specific information is needed, I will let you know."

"Sir, I am too worn out for that kind of thing," Mary hedged.

His eyes were bright. "Will you think about it?"

She hesitated, then agreed. "I will think about it, that's all I promise. You must remember, I'm still Negro, and in the eyes of most Southerners, a slave. For that alone, my life would be in peril. If there was even a suspicion regarding my real ... business. Well, there could be a tree with my name on it and a bonfire at my feet."

He stroked his chin, pondering. "How about this? Your background is

Mediterranean heritage and you are a woman of independent means traveling to find a location for your new business."

"And that is?"

"Textiles. I understand you know them. I can arrange documents verifying your identity, and the department will provide what finances you require." He smiled, then snapped his fingers. "And I have just the person to assist you! He'll travel with you, ostensibly to assist you in your business opportunity, but specifically to protect you. His name is James Aubrey-Hamilton—full of bonhomie, good with people, a great business head on his shoulders. Good Southerner. You'll like him. Folks'll trust him, especially when he vouches for your substantial assets."

"Interesting."

"You cannot venture out as Mary Louvestre, of course. Too dangerous. So your cover will be as a Miss Victoria Silk." He looked pleased with himself.

"Oh, you're good," Mary said with a wry smile to hide her slight discomfort.

"That's why I have this job," he said as he lifted his goblet high. "A toast to continued alliance."

A knock at the door interrupted them. A younger man entered. "Excuse me, sir."

"What is it, Stevens?" Welles asked brusquely.

"An urgent message from the White House, sir. Your immediate reply is requested."

Mary began to rise, but Welles motioned for her to stay. "Wait, please. I'll just be a minute."

As Welles conversed in low tones with his assistant, Mary's mind took in what he was asking of her. It was overwhelming, too much to absorb or immediately respond to. She looked down at the Louvestre crest on the ring she wore—so many memories, so many promises broken. Her mind ranged back over all the people she wanted to help, all the people who had helped her succeed on this journey, all the people she would never see or might never find again. Anders. Tug. Roguey. Dear dramatic Devereaux. Beautiful, brash, delightful Coolie.

Mary knew she needed time to study on Welles's offer. Victoria Silk. She liked the sound of Victoria—victorious, which she was. And she was like silk too—so much stronger than appearance belied. But oh, she felt so washed out, so worn. The only thing she knew right then was that she alone would control her life, her future. She would determine what she would do. And if she were to have a new name, it would be of her choice, not one chosen for her.

Welles returned to his chair. "So? Have you had time to think?"

"I am honored, sir. I cannot give you my answer now. But if I was to accept— *if*, then such a woman of means would need a name befitting her status, it would be a name such as Veronica Marie Evangeline Anders du Moiré."

"Ho!" Welles threw his head back in laughter. "Yes, yes that is the name of a woman of means."

As he ushered Mary to the door, Welles told her again how ecstatic he was to have the ship's plans she had brought him. He shared that he had been working with John Ericsson, designer of the *Monitor*, to modify the Northern ironclad for battle in Hampton Roads against the *Merrimac*.

"If we don't take her down, we'll at least manage to damage that beast," Welles exclaimed. "Now, next time we meet I want you to give me your decision, Miss Veronica Marie Evangeline Anders du Moiré."

——

When Mary went to the dining room for breakfast a few mornings later, Leontyne asked, "Have you read the daily yet?"

Seating herself with the other lodgers at the table, Mary answered that she had not.

"There's going to be dancing in the street," Leontyne said. "We stopped the monster and still have a chokehold on the South."

Lively talk around the table was of the great naval battle between the two ironclads. The North counted on holding the blockade and the South aimed to break it. Without the goods and services ships brought to Southern harbors, the South would continue to wilt. Fever was high on both sides. Though she'd been keeping up with regular accounts of the war, Mary listened silently but intently to the conversations. When she finished her meal, she excused herself with the *Daily National Intelligencer* and went back to her room.

Settling into her parlor chair, she sipped coffee while she read the journalist's account of the entanglement.

Naval Disaster in Hampton Roads

We learn that on Saturday last the Confederate iron-plated steamer Merrimac came out of her harbor and attacked two vessels of our blockading squadron in Hampton Roads. The Cumberland sloop-of-war, twenty-four guns, (sailing ship), commanded by Capt. Marston, was run down by the heavy armored steamer and sunk. The frigate Congress, carrying fifty guns, (sailing ship), was next run down and captured. The United States steamer Minnesota, in endeavoring to go to the relief of her companions, got aground. The Merrimac, without doing further damage, returned to her harbor at Portsmouth.

This work of destruction was effected, as we learn, in the afternoon of Saturday last, about three o'clock. Several hours later the United States iron-plated steamer Monitor, commanded by Lieut. Worden, arrived in Hampton Roads, where it is to be hoped that her presence will at least prevent a repetition of such disasters.

While we were deceiving ourselves with the idea that the rebel steamer Merrimac was a failure, she has come out of her lair, run down our sloop-of-war Cumberland, captured and destroyed the sailing frigate Congress, and driven the steam frigate Minnesota aground. This was on Saturday.

Yesterday, however, the tables were turned. The Ericsson iron-clad battery "Monitor" arrived at Hampton Roads on Saturday night, and yesterday morning went up to the protection of the Minnesota. On the approach of the Merrimac, supported as on Saturday by two other steamers, she was engaged by the Monitor in a desperate close contest, which lasted four hours, and at its close the Merrimac was driven back to Norfolk.

The particulars of this affair are furnished by telegraph. The arrival of the Monitor on Saturday night was truly providential; and it is a fortunate coincidence that the telegraph was yesterday completed to Fortress Monroe, so that the news of Sunday's victory comes to mitigate the mortification over Saturday's disaster ....

CHAPTER 59

Winds were picking up on the dying rays of a busy day while Mary angled a display into one of her large windows. A zephyr whisked up a piece of newspaper and playfully whirled it around, hitting the sign suspended from two chains that read "BUTTONS: Fashion Salon." The bell over the front doors tinkled, and Mary looked up from her work. She saw two figures in hooded cloaks, one tall, one short.

The voice from the short one said, "If you ain't a sight for two good eyes."

Slowly, Mary stood up. Her voice wasn't there the first time she called on it. She cleared her throat. Only with the second attempt did she breathe, "Coolie."

The short one pulled off her hood and smiled mischievously, "In the flesh."

Mary swept across the room and drew Coolie into a tight embrace.

Jitter, a shy smile on his face, pushed back the hood of his cloak and watched the two women.

"What are you doing here?" Mary finally exclaimed through tears of joy.

"Coolie kept saying we had to find you," Jitter answered. "I kept asking her how we'd do that, but you know Coolie when she's of a mind. She set to packing. That was two days ago when we left Baltimore."

"We rode the colored car even though Jitter said we could ride the white cars and I could act like his servant." She chuckled. "Me act like a servant? They'd have thrown us out of there before we made it a mile."

Mary couldn't stop laughing.

"I was so worried about you," Coolie said, looking moon-eyed at Mary. "The terrible storms, snow, and rain. Others said it was one of the coldest, hardest winters in their knowin'. It was cold as a dead rat when we was out there. I was scared you was lost, snowbound somewhere, freezin' and dyin' like ash, with your clothes all tore up and not hardly a sole on your moccasins and—"

"I get the picture," Mary said.

"I was all prepared to come to Washington, find your remains if possible, and speak softly over your grave about what a fine person you were and how the world would be a lesser place because you weren't in it no more. I would tell that women around the country would mourn your passin' and especially what you did with your design so women wouldn't have to wear corsets no more." Coolie paused a minute. "But I knew you wasn't—weren't—dead. If you was, somehow I would've knowed when it happened."

"I'm so glad to see you two," Mary said as she looked at each of them. "But why now?"

Jitter grinned at Coolie and said, "Go ahead, tell it."

Mary smiled again and moved to the coffee service to pour each of them a cup. "You're learning."

"I could do with something that's got more punch than coffee," Coolie said.

Mary interrupted her and started to rise. "I've got a small bar over here."

"I think it best I don't this early in the day." Coolie grabbed Mary's hand and pressed it to her stomach. "Got to do all I can to take care of myself."

Mary's fingers flew to her mouth and she sat down with a thud. Shock registered on her face.

"Didn't take you too long to get it," Coolie said with a roar of laughter. "I had me two strong reasons to find you. You know I'm too old to be tryin' to carry a chile. I figure, if it's tryin' to get here that hard to choose my womb to carry it in, this baby's definitely got somethin' important to say. He special."

"Coolie made me give up the sweet place where we were livin' in Baltimore, pack up everythin', and come here to Washington," Jitter said. "If we found you dead, that was one thing. But alive, well, we'd make you own up to your responsibilities to this young'un. He belongs to all of us."

"How do you know it's a he?" Mary said.

Coolie patted her belly with the gentle rise in it. "I know. And it ain't 'cause girl babies s'posed to ride high on your stomach and boy babies low. Or is it the other way around?"

"You said there were two reasons to find me."

A troubled look crossed Coolie's eyes. "The Travelers're in trouble. Ain't had nothin' but problems since we lef'. A couple got through the passage and stopped in Baltimore on their way to Canada. One on the line told them where to find us. They told us that many of the families out in Stonehaven had been livin' in terror that they were goin' to be killed in the night, especially after ..." Coolie's voice trailed off as she cut her eyes downward.

"After what?"

"They killed Bear first. Then Thurston Stone," Coolie said.

Horror filled Mary's face.

"Some put it out that Thurston was a Yankee spy all along," Coolie said. "That was supposed to be the real reason he had been helpin' black folks."

Jitter added, "Rumor told it that his mission was to get blacks to thinkin' they were as good as whites and deserved the same opportunities in this world. He was to subvert their thinkin' that their sole purpose in life was to serve whites now and forevermore." Jitter shook his head sadly. "They hacked up

Thurston's body. Delivered parts of it to blacks and parts to the whites around who supported what he'd been doin'."

Silence hung for a moment as Mary took in so much news—the joy of Coolie's baby, the shock of Thurston's and Bear's murders.

Coolie finally spoke again. "News from our new Quaker friends is that we've got to get the rest of them folk out of there, out of Virginia," Coolie said, "if any of them gon' survive."

"Get them to where?" Mary asked.

"We was hopin' you might know that," Coolie said.

"A walking journey from Norfolk to Washington does not make me a world traveler." Then Mary brightened. "But I might know someone who could help you."

Coolie looked to Mary, then Jitter. "You goin' to go back with us?" she asked.

"No." Mary leaned forward to clasp Coolie's hands in hers. "I accomplished what it was I had to do. I'm beginning to get accustomed to a new life here, where I feel safe and have a chance to succeed. You'll do just fine without me. It's dangerous down there. I don't have to tell you that. So you be careful."

Coolie looked sad. "But I thought if we could just find you, we'd all be together again and go help our friends."

"I'm so glad that you found me. Jitter, promise you'll take care of Miss Spunky here and the baby, regardless of what happens in this war."

"You know I will, Miss Mary."

"Please come, Mary," Coolie begged. "I need you."

"And you'll always know where to find me," Mary said reassuringly.

"That don't mean you can't go with us." Coolie was now crying and pleading.

Mary shook her head as she smiled and gripped Coolie's hands. What she couldn't tell them had much to do with Secretary Welles's offer. She hadn't yet made up her mind. Frankly, she wasn't sure she wanted to give up her new life. And Lord knew she certainly didn't need any more urgency pressing upon her. But then—a gleam shined in her eyes—then again, maybe ...

"See me on down the road, you two."

ACKNOWLEDGMENTS

My thanks for aid in this work are numerous. Paula Stahel, my mentor and collaborator, who single-handedly reached into the material, extracted its potential, and declared: This is it! Her skill pulled the many aspects of the work together cohesively and lifted it to its highest possibilities.

To Joe Coccaro, my editor at Köehler Books, I truly bow to your insights and creativity. A friend of mine who is a famous sculptor said you don't carve out a design; rather you see the raw material and release the form. That was what Joe did, and I thank him.

Endless gratitude goes to Arsenia Walker, the muse on my shoulder, who encouraged this manuscript the past few years. She pushed, prompted, insisted, and sat with me, poring over scene after scene, line by line, questioning, challenging, using the Socratic Method to extract from me my very best.

The unsung heroes of this work are the many librarians around the country who provided expert research and guidance.

There were several readers whose sharp eyes and minds helped provide greater clarity, especially Paul Clancy and Hunt Lewis.

This project took more than ten years, on and off, to complete. Hence there are many others, too numerous to mention, to whom I offer appreciation. Of special mention is honored professor at The Ohio State University, a truly singular man, Dr. Edward Q. Moulton.

And last, but certainly not least, I thank Alex Haley, with whom I partnered in writing *Roots* about a third of the way into that project. During our marriage, we grew into a master-apprentice relationship as I honed my craft and developed an undying love for writing. I especially learned persistence. He often told me that the difference between success and failure many times lies in hanging in there when you just don't know.

Bless!